ALSO BY ANDREW LEWIS CONN

P

HOGARTH
London / New York

O,
AFRICA!

**ANDREW
LEWIS
CONN**

A Novel

Copyright © 2014 by Andrew Lewis Conn

Published in the United States by Hogarth,
an imprint of the Crown Publishing Group,
a division of Random House LLC,
a Penguin Random House Company, New York.
www.crownpublishing.com

HOGARTH is a trademark of the Random House Group Limited,
and the H colophon is a trademark of Random House LLC.

Library of Congress Cataloging-in-Publication Data
Conn, Andrew Lewis.
    O, Africa! : a novel / Andrew Lewis Conn.—First edition.
        pages cm.
    1. Twins—Fiction. 2. Motion picture authorship—History—
20th century—Fiction. 3. Motion picture industry—History—
20th century—Fiction. 4. Africa—History—Fiction. I. Title.
PS3603.O542O23   2014
813'.6—dc23   2013028712

ISBN 978-0-8041-3828-4
eBook ISBN 978-0-8041-3829-1

Printed in the United States of America

Book design by Barbara Sturman
Jacket design by Elena Giavaldi
Jacket illustration by Ben Wiseman

10 9 8 7 6 5 4 3 2 1

First Edition

To Jennifer Conn,

my Micah and Izzy, this time around

Whenever there's too much technology,

people return to primitive feats.

—DON DELILLO, *Great Jones Street*

Contents

PART I

THE OLD
WORLD

1

ARCADIA

L ouder than words.

"Action," his brother says in a whisper, followed by a knock on the piano crate. Then again, this time louder, "Action," trailed by a tapping on the trunk: one, two, three. "C'mon, kid, we're ready!"

It was hot inside the Bechstein box, and Izzy, with his claustrophobia and nerves, wasn't doing well. Wedged in a contortionist's pose, the cameraman's limbs wrapped round the Bell & Howell—one glove on the hand crank as controlled as a butler winding a clock after putting out the last light, the other jamming a tripod leg into a corner of the crate with the force of a fisherman spearing a swordfish. As he peered through the lens turret poking out of the hole that'd been cut from the side of the box, it occurred to Izzy—Isidor Grand, the more sober, reflective, and retiring of the twins—that his position pressed inside the dark black box was not dissimilar to the workings of the human eye, with its iris, cornea, pupil, and lens functioning in concord, gathering images, bringing them into focus, inscribing scenes on the black retinal wall, and propelling them back out into the world for the purpose of inspection, investigation, joy.

Apart from the heat, which was stifling, and the dark, which was terrifying, Izzy enjoyed remaining hidden, preferring to concede the center of attention to Micah—his red-haired brother with his rooster raucousness, Cheshire teeth, and Barnum whiffs of sawdust and hucksterism—Micah, the movie director, who enjoyed nothing more than racing around a set, distressed sandwich in one hand, megaphone in the other, carrying on five conversations at once, giddy from the fumes coming off his own moxie, lack of sleep, and professional charm. This was no set, however. This was Coney Island. At the beginning of summer. On a Sunday.

For the location shooting of *Quicktime*, the brothers' twelfth feature, every precaution had been taken to mask the production's twin crowd generators: the movie camera itself and the film's comedic star, Henry Till. Izzy had instructed his crew that only natural light would be used for street scenes, and he had taken care to hide the camera at every opportunity. Till, meanwhile, was instructed not to place his trademark black horn-rimmed glasses on his talc-white face until Micah provided a cue that they were ready to do a take.

Filming had gone disastrously so far. It took all day to nail a quick bit of business at Broadway and Forty-Third Street in which the comedian accidentally blows into a whistle, bringing traffic to a halt. The second day's tracking shot of Till strolling with his girl down Fifth Avenue in the Twenties (camera nestled in a baby carriage) was busted up when a loaded paddy wagon rolled into shooting range and wouldn't clear out. A simple series of establishing shots on day three was called off on account of an Olympian midday thunderstorm. Now in serious danger of falling behind schedule after just a half week's work, the company retreated to the Brooklyn Armory on Fifteenth Street and Eighth Avenue, where they worked on a rear-projection chase sequence.

A modest man but a world-class perfectionist, Till hated the artificial look of process shots and generally avoided them, even in the thrill comedies that had made him famous. But they had no choice; they couldn't risk tying up midtown traffic for entire days for the picture's finale. Instead Till sat atop a wooden crate, gripping flying reins and rocking to and fro while stock footage projected behind him. Add a bit of camera undercranking and the audience would be treated to an eighty-mile-per-hour drive through Manhattan's man-made canyons.

Never would a chase be more fitting. The story of New York's last horse-drawn carriage and a family's resistance against being bought out by a railway monopoly, *Quicktime* would honor the values of the past while serving as an ode to the accelerated pace of modern life. About this, Micah, Izzy, and Till agreed: *Quicktime* was no comedy. A celebration of propulsion, a précis on beginnings and endpoints, the picture would exist as a catalog of vectors, a continuous riot of locomotion. And as if in tribute to the Grand brothers' undertaking, on the very day the company invaded Coney Island, Miss Amelia Earhart had taken to the skies from Newfoundland, the first woman to fly across the Atlantic Ocean. It occurred to Micah and Izzy as filming commenced against this backdrop of the pilot's conquering of space and distance that they and the rather handsome aviatrix were in pursuit of the same lofty goal.

The location setting was not unfamiliar to Oscar Spiro, the company's first assistant director, ace electrician, focus puller, and indispensable jack-of-all-trades. A hate-filled, volatile-tempered dwarf, Spiro despised Coney Island and its seminal importance in his biography. Spiro's parents, Count Milo and Mercy Midge, had been headliners in Midget City, the amusement park's half-scale re-creation of some lost fifteenth-century Mitteleuropean city populated by three hundred stunted performers. Situated in this carnival dwarf ghetto were dollhouse-scaled homes and stamp-size shops, a miniature Athenian-style city hall, and a Yiddish theater that featured the world's finest diminutive Hebraic thespians. There was even a fearsome pint-size police department that patrolled the place on foot, responding to threat and insult through dispensation of their own outsize sense of midget justice.

"The sulfurous pit of my degraded youth," Spiro groaned when Micah originally proposed shooting there, recalling with a chill his childhood memories of elephants and camels plodding through the streets, the perpetual sound of roller coasters' prehistoric groans, the beer-and-sausage smells of the immigrant poor. "Why must I return?"

With his China doll's hands, Spiro could rack focus in tight corners that others couldn't reach; with his tiny frame, he could pitch the camera in places fellow operators wouldn't contemplate; with his eagerness to swing the newer, lightweight, handheld models around like dance partners, he could set the fixed film frame aspin. And so the Grand brothers' films gained notoriety for their wild camera setups, resplendent comic violence, and champagne-bottle explosiveness. Theirs was a jaunty American comedic expressionism, worlds away from the proscenium-bound, diorama-style filmmaking of just twenty years before or the pomp and polish of the medium's leading figure.

"Yes, well, of course Chaplin is a genius," Micah said during a deli debriefing after seeing *The Gold Rush*. "The trouble is, he keeps reminding you of it."

"He does lay it on a bit thick," Izzy agreed, slathering mustard on a corned-beef sandwich. "The orphans and blind girls and wretched poor . . ."

"I'll take my comedy without the side of schmaltz, thanks," said Micah, gouging a corner out of a pastrami on rye. "The plight of the common man, the universal struggle, and all that bunk! You really want to help people, make them laugh for an hour and a half, forget their troubles. Besides, takes a lot of salt making millions parading around in a pair of torn trousers."

"I agree," Izzy said. "Besides, there's something vulgar about the man. Now, Keaton on the other hand."

"Yes, I know. . . ."

Izzy found Buster Keaton's stoicism unbearably moving. Mystical, even; an expression of philosophy. Keaton's ramrod bearing and T-square mouth suggested something fundamental about the pain of comedy, its seriousness, ironclad systems of retribution that attended defying the laws of gravity. And the Great Stone Face got Izzy thinking about history in weird ways, too, as if something of the Founding Fathers, the carnage of the Civil War, the trenches and mustard gas of the Great War, had etched its way into Keaton's unsmiling demeanor. In Keaton's haunted, handsome face—still as a daguerreotype—Izzy found a figure as archetypal and solemn as Lincoln.

The star of *Quicktime* was an altogether different creature. If Henry Till displayed neither the precision-instrument bearing of Keaton nor the poetic lyricism of Chaplin, neither could he be counted as one of the goons and grotesques supporting the comic pantheon's second tier, baby beasts like Fatty Arbuckle and Harry Langdon. The secret of Till's appeal was his very ordinariness. He could appear equally convincing as a department-store clerk or a college freshman, a policeman or a cab-driver, a bachelor or a boyfriend. Till's "glasses" character, introduced in 1920, was a new kind of silent-film figure: not maudlin nor eccentric nor outsize, but a bright go-getter on the make, a smiling, athletic young man in a white suit who looked like he'd just quit divinity school to hustle encyclopedias door-to-door. Till had bounce. The most conventional, least palpably perverse of the great film comedians, slender, inconspicuously handsome, with grasshopper legs and a strong square jaw, Till was cinema's first true everyman.

The work was not without risk. In August 1919, Till nearly killed himself while taking a publicity photo on the set of *Jumping Beans* when a smoke bomb accidentally exploded in his hand. Till's thumb and fore-finger, and half the palm of his right hand, were blown off, and he was temporarily blinded, with second-degree burns covering much of his face. Six months later Till returned, wearing a white prosthetic specially designed by Sam Goldwyn (who had once worked for a glove company), which included a false thumb and an artificially built-out palm. He taught himself to play sports and sign autographs with his left hand and continued to perform his own stunts (including the famous hanging-from-the-clock-hands climax of *Without a Net!*). Within a month of his return, Till married his frequent co-star Emily Davies, started a brood, and became the most dedicated of family men, keeping a giant Christmas tree on year-round display in his Los Angeles compound. One of the best-paid actors in Hollywood, who earned more from savvy real-estate investments than he did in pictures, Till wore his mammoth paychecks as casually as a pair of slippers. Conservative with money, faithful to his wife, a churchgoer and a teetotaler, a man of eminently gentle midwestern courtesy, Henry Till stood on this summer day outside a Luna Park concession stall, shuffling around unrecognized in a seersucker suit, awaiting the arrival of a co-star who was in every conceivable way his opposite.

They were waiting on Babe Ruth. Ever since the ballplayer had named Till his favorite film star ("Kid moves like an outfielder"), it had become Micah's mission to secure Ruth for a cameo in Imperial Pictures' next production. *Quicktime* wouldn't be the first motion picture the athlete had appeared in. Ruth had already played imaginary versions of himself in a couple of lousy pieces of public-relations legerdemain that attempted to portray the hard-drinking, hard-living ballplayer—who as a child was turned over by saloon-owning parents to a Baltimore orphanage—as an aw-shucks country boy complete with a saintly widowed mother, pig-tailed kid sister, and a mutt named Herman.

But this would be different: For *Quicktime* the boys had asked Ruth simply to appear for a few minutes as himself, part of the tapestry of New York life they hoped to capture in the film. When word came down from Ruth's camp that the Great Bambino would be happy to partici-pate and that he'd be available for a few hours before game time on the production's final day of location filming, Sunday, June 17, 1928, Till's stable of regular gag men fell into a tizzy. *Quicktime* had no script. There were never any scripts. "We have islands we need to get to," Shecky Sug-arman said of the team's working method. That is, they'd work toward agreed-upon plot points, linking together a succession of complex jokes, setups, and payoffs, fleshing out the set pieces and bits of physical busi-ness as they went along.

Once the terms had been agreed upon, the ballplayer's public-relations man asked that an emissary from the production meet Ruth's car on Surf Avenue to escort him past the fairground's crescent-mooned entrance and into the heart of Luna Park, to the candy-striped conces-sion booth where shooting would take place. Owing to the Babe's love of kids, this important assignment was entrusted to Billy Conklin, the production company's freckled seventeen-year-old best boy, who was himself, like the ballplayer he idolized, an orphan.

"Where do you need me?" asks Ruth.

Nattily dressed in a three-piece houndstooth suit, droopy-lidded and snub-nosed, more boxer than ballplayer, on this day the Sultan of

Swat is suffering from razor burn and a bad hangover, rendering his cheeks pinker and more porcine than usual. Six feet two inches tall, 235 pounds, with a forty-eight-inch waist, Ruth looks like half a ready-made comedy duo when placed beside the skinny string-bean actor.

"Christ Almighty," Micah whispers to his knife-size assistant as Spiro takes a light-meter reading. "It's like Jack and the Beanstalk."

"I suppose that makes me the magic seed?"

"No, magic seed's what you spilled last night."

"Your idea to shoot this thing in Coney?" Ruth asks Micah in a voice that's rich and warm and vaguely southern as a gaggle of children stare agog at their hero.

"Yeah."

"Some day!"

"Indeed . . . ," says Micah, studying the convex planes of the ball-player's face. "So, Mr. Ruth, we've worked out some business we'd like to have you try here, what our scriptwriters call a 'substitution gag,' involving a misunderstanding at a ball-toss game."

"What's your name again?"

"Micah, Micah Grand. I'm the picture's director."

"Well, let's not make a study of it, Doc. Let's just shoot the damn thing and see how she lays."

"Indeed!"

Working out the mechanics of the scene, Ruth proves himself to be a natural, expertly blocking himself in relation to the camera, flattering himself with the best angles and shadows, and affording himself pride of place in all his shared frames with Till. The ballplayer shows a trusting, natural rapport with the child extras that Billy had wrangled for the day from Manhattan's Society for the Relief of Half-Orphan & Destitute Children, and he works hard to put at ease the picture's leading lady, Mildred Mack, making a show of shielding her between takes from the glassy midday sun spray. ("My only regret, doll," he tells the button-shy, teacup-quiet four-foot-eleven pixie, "is it's clear skies all the way. Else I'd have a chance to lay my jacket over a puddle for ya.")

And it is Ruth who suggests the scene's comic highlight: the kicker to the topper. Babe's idea is to get into a pointing contest with Till outside the game booth, culminating in the ballplayer poking a finger through the actor's eyeglass frames, revealing them to be without lenses.

"Okay, so you do that," says Till, riffing off Ruth's suggestion, pantomiming. "Then I'll come crashing down on your foot, like this."

"Just watch the gams, kid," Ruth jokes. "They're all a lady's got."

"Good, good, good," Micah chimes in. "And then Babe"—already on a first-name basis—"lets out a howl and throws *another* baseball, knocking over the bottles in the adjacent booth."

"Right." Sugarman nods, part of the huddle, jotting down continuity notes on his trusty clipboard. "And Alvy here hands another doll to Mildred."

"All right, boys," Micah says, clapping his hands, "let's not wait for the paint to dry!"

Izzy, still entombed in the crate but having grown accustomed to its musty accommodations, begins rolling. Around the park, word has begun to spread that the ballplayer and the comic actor are filming a movie together, and large crowds start to gather. The midway is already packed with people on this summer day, but proportions begin tipping in their direction, iron filings pulled by a magnet. Jostling to get a better look, the spectators start blocking and knocking into the piano crate, obscuring shots and ruining takes. Soon it becomes pointless to keep the camera hidden any longer.

"Out of the box, Itz," Micah says, kicking a heel against the crate, calling his brother by his least-favored nickname, embarrassing him.

The coffin lid pops open, and out climbs Izzy. Squinting in the acid sunlight, visibly damp and ashen, hands wrapped around the tripod's harpoon legs, film spools and cores clinging to him like barnacles, Izzy appears an aquatic creature out of a Jules Verne story. Once the camera is revealed to the crowd, however, a funny thing happens: People instinctively begin backing away, opening a clear path for Izzy and offering the crew a wide berth. A private perimeter magically inscribes itself around the proceedings—a self-described arena of light and space that limns its own boundaries and carries the promise of something extraordinary held within. And though the film being made is a silent one, as soon as the mechanical apparatus makes its presence felt, the crowd instantly falls quiet.

If this is some form of occultism, it finds its proper high priest in Micah. The change that overtakes him during filming is always the same and always startling. His face tightens like a patty on a hot skillet, and a fearsome concentration knits itself upon his brow. It is not that boyishness abandons him in these moments—rather, he gains the prodigious concentration of an inquisitive boy given a new toy that he immediately sets about disassembling. Watching Micah stride around a set, megaphone in hand, cap perched at an impetuous angle, making himself instant master of whatever situation he's placed himself in, Izzy likens his brother to a young, fair-haired Alexander. Micah is bold, he is brave, he is possessed of an almost wounding beauty. He is everything Izzy wishes to be. The same womb, at the same time, and yet here a creature so unfamiliar, so alien: Izzy an orbiting moon to Micah's sun.

"Thank you all for coming," Micah says, playing to the gallery, beaming like an idol in the sunshine, grasping his yellow megaphone like a circus ringmaster, like all good directors an excellent actor himself, in fine control of his voice. "The name of the picture is *Quicktime*, and you'll be able to see it in theaters in four or five months. My name is Micah Grand, moviemaker. Now let's hear it for your heroes: Babe Ruth and Henry Till!" And up goes the applause. Then, huddling with the actors, "You're doing fine, Babe, just fine. Now all we need is a close-up of you after Alvy hands the doll over to Mildred."

"A close-up?" jokes Ruth. "Of this mug? I was under the impression you wanted to sell some tickets."

Micah shrugs, shoulders hitched, palms flipped. Shorthanding it, Izzy brings the camera a few feet nearer. Peering through the viewfinder, the cameraman makes instant calibrations, converting the living spectacle to chiaroscuro dailies they'd be reviewing a few days from now. And there in the theater of Izzy's visual imagination, the ballplayer's face appears: stamped in black and white, as flat and familiar as a penny, his ranginess and terrestrial radiance captured indelibly, like an insect caught in amber. The day's filming finds Ruth, off to a hot start this season, in high spirits. Moreover, Micah and the Babe have taken an immediate liking to each other, two well-paid professionals rewarded for play, a couple of overfed cunt hounds who enjoy nothing more than bantering male camaraderie, good food and drink, hot knishes, and all the other attendant privileges money and talent bring. Izzy, on the other hand, is terrified of the ballplayer: his strongman's torso and too-skinny legs, his barbarian's mitts and satanic left-handedness, his huge slab face and auto-grille smile, his broad flat nose and Asian-lidded eyes, his outsize human footprint and monstrous physical ease. For most of the day's filming, Izzy keeps his eye fixed to the viewfinder—a buffer between himself and this brute life force.

"You the one taking pictures?" Ruth asks when it's over, the sequence securely in the can, equipment packed away, the company having called it quits for the day.

"Yes," Izzy says, keeping pocketed red, nail-bitten hands. "Micah and I are brothers."

"Kid's like a pilot light. He never goes out."

"Huh," appreciating the description. "You were really good out there, Mr. Ruth. Thank you for a fine day's work."

"It's like ball playing, kid. Can't call this work."

Had the Grand boys not gone to the pictures on April 1, 1915, instead of becoming filmmakers, they might have entered one of the respectable professions—law, medicine, accounting, manufacturing—and remained lifelong movie lovers instead of taking their chances as young men on an untested and disreputable industry. The clincher wasn't Chaplin or Keaton, Arbuckle or Langdon. It wasn't *A Trip to the Moon* or *The Great Train Robbery* or *Caligari* that did it. No, the singular work that opened the boys up to the possibilities of the art—that convinced them that moviemaking could be (indeed *was*) the indisputably great art form of their burgeoning century—was D. W. Griffith's *Birth of a Nation*.

They had read about the picture for months and months, and after their father had received the tickets by post, the boys kept the talismans pinned to their shared bedroom wall. They were alone among their friends in being allowed to see the film at all and sensed how privileged they were to get to go rather than spend another Saturday evening in temple. Though their bar mitzvah was already two years behind them, the twins suspected that this picture might be the vessel that transported them to manhood, that the country wasn't the only thing waiting to be born.

Just a generation before, entire swaths of family on both sides had been wiped out in the frigid potato fields of Russia and Poland, yet here they were with an anglicized name, living on the perimeter of Ocean Parkway in the Midwood section of Brooklyn in a good-size family house with a Greek-columned porch. Here they were with a father who had traded in his rabbinical beard and heavy black suit for a waxed mustache, a bowler hat, and tweeds. Here was Dr. Julius Grand—a professionally trained pediatrician, good with a violin—who through conspicuous application of New World manners and dress was attempting to hoist the family into the mushrooming century, having himself left behind the flaming cups and leeches and old wives' tales for antibiotics and vaccinations and X-rays. Here, with their *Birth of a Nation* tickets tacked to the wall like frogs on a specimen tray, the prospect of an authentic churchgoing experience, a quintessential American day spent dreaming in the dark, imbibing miracles. Here, something more than the promise of pleasure: the unspoken oath movies made of a never-ending present, of the possibility of unencumbered self-invention.

"Don't do it, Micah!" Izzy pleaded with his brother in the alley behind their temple the afternoon of their bar mitzvah, as Micah carefully unshrouded from a paper napkin like the Passover *afikoman* a sandwich of ham and mustard on crusty white bread. "Please don't do it!"

"Why not?" asked the swine eater. "Tastes good."

"Micah!" Izzy scolded his brother, who had had the audacity to memorize phonetically his portion of the haftarah while Izzy had labored for hours learning Hebrew with a chorus of davening, cigar-stinking cantors. "All of our relatives are inside."

"This isn't Eve and the apple in the Garden of Eden we're talking about, Izzy. It's a snack from Paulie's down the street. The world won't stop spinning if you take a bite."

"I won't do it, Micah! Not today of all days!"

"Okay, Itz." Tearing from the sandwich hunks of phosphorescent meat, Micah leered at his brother like a demon out of Hieronymus Bosch. "More for me, then."

"You're hateful," Izzy sputtered, shaking his clenched fists, at once appalled by and attracted to Micah's heroic rejection, the ruthless casting off of assumption and expectation to which Izzy himself was incapable of committing.

They shared a room. They had slept together, dreamed together; for years eaten, bathed, and crapped together. There were oceanic depths of closeness there. Yet Micah—not even one full day into his teens—had the temerity to be not afraid. To be not a good boy. To have the integrity to be bad, the audacity to be *against*. Micah, who cheated off his brother's exams. Micah, who abandoned Izzy's hands to pedagogic ruler smackings and neighborhood beatings. Micah, the effortlessly popular playground wise guy who deigned to allow Izzy to fill his schoolyard shadow. Micah, who had conquered puberty without embarrassment over either vocal cracking or sprouting red carpets of hair. Micah, who had just finished wiping his mouth with the stringy ends of his prayer shawl and had now gone fishing in his pants for his privates.

"Micah, what are you doing?"

"What does it look like?"

"Stop that please."

"Gotta do it, Itz." Slapping away at the thing.

"Why?!"

"Because it feels good!"

"It's our *bar mitzvah*, Micah! Why do you need to ruin everything?"

"What exactly am I ruining?"

"But what about *them*!"

"Who?"

"Abraham and Isaac and David and Noah and all those guys in heaven."

"I hate to break it to you, Itz, but no one's watching."

"What about Mom and Dad? Don't you love them?"

"Course I love Mom and Dad." Beating it harder now, leaning for support with one hand against the temple's brick wall. "But that's got nothing to do with it, Itz. . . . Twenty-five, twenty-six, twenty-seven . . . *Argh!* . . . Now wish your brother mazel tov."

Two years later, a second bar mitzvah. At three hours *The Birth of a Nation* was the longest movie they'd seen, at two dollars a ticket an extravagant outing; the boys dressed in better than their synagogue suits. After it was over, Micah stared straight ahead, remaining stock-still in his seat at Times Square's Liberty Theatre until the lights came up, the curtain came down, and the present came flooding back to claim him. Izzy, meanwhile, had pulled from his jacket pocket a small spiral notebook and had begun rapidly sketching from memory various shots from the film. He had always been interested in optics—the boys' father kept a collection of kaleidoscopes, spectroscopes, prisms, magnifying glasses, and magic lanterns that he'd obsessed over—and he was determined to unearth how the thing was done, how Griffith had pieced together the bricks and columns of this magnificent temple of light.

At home Izzy worked away converting his crude pencil sketches into a series of thumb-governed animated flip books, while Micah mimicked the manners of an antebellum southern gentleman, affecting a light, lilting accent, wandering the hallways in long, languorous strides, taking extravagant puffs from a hollow honeycomb pipe. While one son slept in a southerner's straw hat, moonily dreaming of plantation days—thinking about the characters' relationships with one another, imagining entire story arcs and counterlives that preceded and ran in parallel to the main action—the other had taped construction-paper drawings all over the walls of their shared bedroom—sketches that, in the way they recalled the film's framing, lighting, and shot selection, were as impressive as a symphony played from memory by a musical savant.

Though their father had sent away for the tickets and, with his interest in optics and photochemistry, was himself in thrall to the picture, its power over the boys left him feeling uneasy. Julius Grand's eyes had been ruined by the time he'd turned twenty from studiously reading all night by candlelight. Yet here in the figure of his son Micah, with his ease and fluency, was an exemplar of the adopted nation's addiction to speed, surface, and sensation. The usual patrimonial competition was heightened for having as its backdrop a new country with shifting modes that challenged a father's mastery. Here in Micah was a boy who announced with every American step that he would not do his homework, would not study the Talmud, would not eat his peas or bring a sweater. Here was a boy who Julius Grand feared was destined not to commit to any serious endeavor, not to pursue a sober profession, not to enjoy the satisfactions of living a thoughtful life. Dr. Grand's hopes, then, rested with Izzy. Only Izzy wasn't easy and was swayed by his twin's influence as surely as a girl twirled around a ballroom floor by a nimble dancer.

"Don't worry about the mess," their father said, trying to appease the boys' mother. "It's good they're so enthusiastic about something. The pictures are just a fad. They'll be great men someday."

"What do you think of my drawings, Dad?" Micah pleaded as Izzy grumbled something about being the rightful creator of the charcoals. "There's stuff that didn't even make it into the movie."

"Wonderful! Like Mozart once wrote to his father when he was a child," said Dr. Grand. "'*Komponiert ist schon alles—aber geschrieben noch nicht.*' Everything is already composed but not yet written down."

"Except the movies are even better than music," Micah said. "They're bigger."

Attuned to his sons' sensitivities and eager to truly know his rival even if it meant loosening his grip on his sons, Julius bought the three of them tickets to the next week's show. And the one after that. And the one after that.

"It's magic," Micah explained after their umpteenth viewing, removing a coin from his brother's ear once they were safely beyond the theater's spell.

"No it's not," Izzy protested from a face drained of color and already too old for its age. "I think I have some sense of how he did it."

"Just because you can explain it, that doesn't mean it didn't happen to you," Micah answered, insouciantly pulling a chain of knotted colored handkerchiefs from his brother's lapel pocket. "Magic, plain and simple."

Micah had seen yellowing newspaper photographs of Lincoln and the battle dead and was familiar, too, with Mathew Brady's work, but this was something else entirely, a frontal assault on the senses too great to be rationalized away. Armies marching over the plains. Georgia in flames. The killing of a king.

The president's assassination occurred halfway through the picture. As lugubrious, long-limbed Lincoln took his seat in the balcony box of Ford's Theatre, Izzy began decoding with ruthless detachment the visual techniques Griffith was using to squeeze suspense from a historic fact, the outcome of which was unalterable, as settled-upon as Bible stories. He's making us part of it, Izzy thought, nodding along in rapturous agreement with Griffith's directorial choices, the naturalistic restraint he demanded of his actors, his shot selection, the gathering storm of his editing rhythms. When, on-screen, Lincoln's bodyguard abandoned his post outside the president's box to get a better look at the play, a gentleman four or five rows in front of the Grand family let rip a plaintive cry. "Hang him!" shouted another voice from the balcony, and soon the theater was filled with gasping patrons, women in Sunday finery exiting the rows, turning away from the spectacle and quickly moving up the theater aisle, hands covering their eyes. It was unbearable, this living parade of imagery unspooling around them: an insert shot of Booth cocking the pistol, the schoolboy's chalk-eraser clap of gunpowder, Lincoln slumped forward in his chair, the assassin's Tarzan swing down the bunting onto the stage, Booth's mad cry of *"Sic semper tyrannis!,"* the chairscape howling in grief at the sight of the slain president, a bearded, sacrificial figure.

Then intermission. For all the magnificence of the first half of the picture—the porch-breeze poignancy of the Stoneman family drama, the savage authority of the battle scenes, the majestic shock of the president's assassination—the second half, focusing on Reconstruction, was a circus of unabashed bigotry. There was a lecherous mulatto villain named Lynch. There were scenes of newly elected officials in South Carolina's state House of Representatives, slobbering Negroes drinking jugs of alcohol and waving chicken legs, propping bare feet up on their desks. There was virginal Mae Marsh, pursued through a forest by a rapacious black soldier, throwing herself from a cliff rather than allow herself to be violated. There was the advent of the Ku Klux Klan, "a veritable empire of the South," riding to the rescue to redeem the nation. History written with lightning indeed.

"Well, you have to remember, Griffith is a southerner," said their mother once they'd returned home from the theater that first night and the boys had recalibrated their heartbeats. This was a worthy attempt at cultural contextualization from a woman who could not mask her astonishment each time she opened a can of tinned soup.

"I read that an organization called the National Association for the Advancement of Colored People is protesting the film's opening," explained Dr. Grand, always instructing, but gently. "The picture may well not play in certain cities."

"I don't care," Micah said as Izzy madly scribbled away in his notepad, teasing apart the rules of cinematic grammar. "That was the greatest picture I've ever seen, and today is the best day of my entire life."

Years later, walking through the restaurant of the Knickerbocker Hotel in Hollywood, the Grand brothers spotted Griffith—a drunk, dissolute figure hunched over an untouched turkey dinner, now a contract director for hire, doing uncredited patch-up jobs on other people's pictures.

"Should we go talk to him?" Izzy asked.

"What, buy him a drink?" Micah responded. "He looks pretty well stocked in that department."

"No, it's just . . . it's because of him."

"No it's not," said Micah, the great man's table already receding behind them. "That'd be like congratulating Columbus for discovering

America—it was all lying in wait. Besides, have you seen *Birth* recently? It's a goddamned abomination. Our greatest picture, and it's a bunch of bunk."

A finger points across the sky. FOLLOW THE CROWD TO NATHAN'S instructs the red-and-yellow billboard. Observing the imperative, the gang goes forth, with each step growing in number: fans, onlookers, hangers-on, autograph hounds, and the celebrity-mad filling in chinks between crew members.

"You're not Babe Ruth," protests a youngster perhaps five or six years old, tugging at the great man's sleeve.

"What gave it away, kid?"

"Where's your bat?"

"Good point." Tousling the boy's hair.

Leading the parade, marching through walls of customers that extend from hot-dog grilling stations all the way to the curb, Micah feels light, buoyant, made of seafoam stuff. As the company converges on the corner of Surf and Stillwell avenues—greeted with handshakes from the formally dressed, fantastically named Nathan Handwerker himself—the crowd continues to multiply through its own tumbling force. Kids in swimming trunks lean over the sides of the boardwalk to get a better look, parents hold their children out of hotel- and tenement-room windows, faces jerk from opened car doors, everyone desperate for a glimpse of their heroes. As word makes its way through the park and onto the beach that the ballplayer and the movie star are here, umbrellas are folded up, mothers and fathers begin clearing from the water, and an audible, uniform wave rises out of the surf. From the tops of roller coasters—CYCLONE in ten-foot-high letters ringed with electric lights—centipede arms wave in unison cheers: "The Babe is here! Bambino is at Nathan's!"

"Anything you like, gentlemen," says Handwerker, whose very person is as long and lean as one of his sausages—an Old World tradition transformed by speed and packaging into American amusement. "It is our pleasure."

"Thanks," Micah answers, announcing himself as the man in charge while the crew plops equipment crates down around them, a Bedouin tribe settling in for the night. "We'll have two for me, two for Mr. Ruth, a couple dozen for the rest of the crew, and lemonades all around."

"Just two?" asks Ruth.

"Why?" Micah says, sensing a dare. "How many d'you normally eat?"

"Well, I only get around here once every couple of years or so now." Screwing his brow to avoid the apricot glare, turning his features even more iconic. "But when I do, I generally eat ten, twelve at a go."

"Garçon!" Micah snaps, stepping past Handwerker and laying his palms on the counter. "We'll have six dozen red hots, billed to Imperial Pictures. That's I-M-P . . ."

The parameters of the contest are established in no time. After debating the merits of speed versus quantity, it's settled: Whoever can eat the most hot dogs in fifteen minutes will be declared the winner. If Babe eats the most, the ballplayer will leave the day's shoot with a pair of Till's famous horn-rims. If Micah, masticating for the home team, proves victorious, the company will be presented with the bat with which Babe had hit his record-setting sixtieth homer the season before. Till, a vegetarian, takes the role of officiator, keeping time with a pocketwatch lifted from the pages of *Alice in Wonderland*.

"You know how hot dogs were invented, right?" Micah asks Ruth as they await the stacks of food.

"No, tell me," says Babe, loosening his trouser belt a few notches as Handwerker approaches with two trays loaded with crackling weenies the approximate length and color of dynamite sticks.

"Well, the Earl of Frankfurter was an inveterate gambler, you see. And one night at the betting tables, he began getting hungry . . ."

"Listen to this wise-apple." Ruth grins. "Say, how'd a fella like you get into the picture business anyway?"

"It was the biggest whorehouse I could find."

"Stick with me, kid, I'll show you some others."

"Gentlemen," Till intones in a voice as flat as the midwest prairie, "on your marks . . . Get set . . . Go!"

A massacre ensues. At the two-minute mark, Babe is onto his sixth hot dog while Micah is still negotiating his third. At the eight-minute mark, the ballplayer, looking pink and pampered as a newborn, is chomping on his eighteenth while the director, after scouring the heavens for signs of Providence, returns his gaze to his sixth wiener.

Through it all, Micah times his gastric eruptions so the cataclysms are drowned out by the roar that goes up whenever Babe finishes another dog. Ruth, who belches magnificently and farts at will, displays no such sense of decorum.

"Pass me another," Ruth says, hot-dog ends bulging out of squeezed fists.

"Get your own," gasps Micah, who busies himself arranging log-cabin style the two dozen dogs left on his eating stand. Then, gagging to the officiator, "We eat bun, too?"

"If it's to be any kind of contest," answers Till, "I'd say so, yes."

"Twenty, Babe, twenty! You can do it!" cries a cat-eyed boy. Ruth acknowledges the waif's encouragement with simultaneous triumphal blasts, douses his indigestion with waves of lemonade, then rounds the bases: twenty-one, twenty-two, twenty-three, twenty-four.

"And . . . time!" announces Till, delivering Micah from greater gastric doom and declaring Babe Ruth the world's first hot-dog-eating-competition champion.

"You're still eating?" Izzy asks his brother after penetrating the crowd to find Micah staring longingly at his tenth dog.

"I'm still hungry," Micah protests, wiping at a swath of mustard with his tie and letting loose a silent fart his brother instantly recognizes for its fried-liver-and-onion smell.

"Good God, Micah," Izzy says, marveling at the crop circle of crumbs and napkins and sudsy cups ringing the contestants' feet. "How do you do it?"

"Courage." Micah hiccups. "An interesting concept, one worth investigating." At a quarter to five, the sun has just begun its sink. A lemon drop, a lollipop, it dissolves over everything within reach on its long descent: the cross-weave of elevated trains, the ragtag collection of rides and carnival attractions crowned by the park's giant windup toy, then the boardwalk, the beach, the surf.... In the distance a familiar twinkling tune:

> *Meet me tonight in Dreamland,*
> *Under the silvery moon.*
> *Meet me tonight in Dreamland,*
> *Where love's sweet roses bloom.*

"So listen," Micah says through a stuffed mouth, sending spitballs of meat and bread flying toward his brother. "The big man's here."

"It's amazing we got him," Izzy answers, referring to the ballplayer. "He's a natural, too."

"No, not Ruth. I mean Marblestone," Micah says, referring to Arthur Marblestone, the 350-pound founder and president of Imperial Pictures, who—equal parts Falstaff and Shylock—presided over a motley empire of nickelodeons, camera crews, gag men, actors, and bit players.

"He's here? Where?" Izzy asks, a band of perspiration pinpricking his hairline. "The Wonder Wheel," Micah says, pointing heavenward. "His Eminence has been surveying the action from on high all day. Miss Belletti called long-distance the other night. He's concerned about overages, wants to make sure the production's on track. I didn't want to worry you."

"You make a career out of worrying me."

"Look, listen, if it didn't sound so ominous, I'd say I'm needed uptown immediately after things wind down here," Micah rambles, reflecting upon the fact that clever liars give details but the cleverest do not.

"Micah, please don't ask what you're going to ask me."

"You know the shyster can't stand me anyway." Putting an arm around his brother's shoulders and imperceptibly steering the pair of them in the direction of the park's giant aerial carousel. "Go. Talk to him. Tell him how well things are going. Here, bring him this." Placing a half-eaten, vaguely wet hot dog in his brother's hand. "A peace pipe!"

Whenever Micah found himself on a roll during a shoot—the chemistry of the participants locking into place like covalently bonded molecules—or received a compliment, or came into possession of a good hand after a run of bum luck at the poker table, his biological response was always the same. He immediately had to urinate. So, after thanking Ruth, accepting a pair of complimentary Yankee tickets, and exchanging his telephone number for that of the ballplayer's private suite at the Ansonia Hotel, Micah goes trolling around the park looking for a place to take a leak.

Heat and sunshine hopping on his face, Micah takes in the passing parade of women with parasols and men in derbies, brownies, and bowler hats; brilliantined barkers and sailors on shore leave; cigarette girls and cotton-candy kids; the entire ready-made collage of movement, light, and faces. Near the Tumble Bug, a young colored boy of perhaps ten or twelve has set up a shoeshine operation. Dressed in filthy overalls, the youth looks to be enjoying himself plenty, after finishing each shine spinning around on one knee atop a piece of corrugated cardboard, bringing himself to a halt, snapping his little rag at the client's dress shoes, and, with an outstretched palm, giving his sales pitch:

> *Just twenty cents a shine,*
> *Come rain or come shine.*
> *Not a quarter, nickel, or dime,*
> *Just twenty cents a shine!*

Marveling at the perfection of his features—the bright eyes set in an ovoid face, the lean, agile frame and black wool padded tight—Micah thinks the boy must be a symbol of something, but what? Then he checks himself. People aren't abstractions, unless they're celebrities like

Ruth or Till. Better to simply admire the smiling ten-year-old's performance and appreciate the boy for choosing a profession that allows him
to spit on his employers (!), Micah thinks as he watches him work up a
gob of saliva for his next customer.

Micah held the belief that it wasn't eyes that were windows onto
the soul but a man's hardworking shoes. In which case, what this boy
must have *seen*! Micah and his brother hadn't been allowed to go to
the pictures until they were ten, weren't allowed to visit Coney Island
until their haftarah studies were safely behind them, yet look at this kid,
already selling, hustling, sizing people up, alert as a crow. Wonder what
it's like for him waking up and looking in the mirror. All that black.
Black hair, black eyes, in a black face. Wonder what he makes of things.
Wonder if he'll be shining shoes ten years from now. Twenty? Smiling,
the boy spits on another customer's shoes.

Micah thought about black people a lot. How they lived in secret,
out in the open. How they were pulling and shaping the country, creating an entire shadow culture like an undertow sculpting the shoreline. How each encounter with a colored person almost always marked
a silent occasion of curiosity, bafflement, and shame. But these feelings
were only inklings, campfire embers. Micah didn't have the language,
the politics, or the will to explore them. And, professionally, he had
indulged in the worst of it, too, shooting a two-reeler a couple of years
before called *Scaredy Spooks*, a fright comedy with blacked-up actors, tar-
faced servants, knee-clattering darkies, and a chorus of slow-moving
pickaninnies. Micah had been forbidden from using colored actors,
instead casting tall, aquiline-nosed Avery Parkinson in the role of the
head butler, his face all but immobilized under a half inch of greasepaint
and burned cork.

"For what?" roared Marblestone when the filmmaker insisted on
employing performers from the Chitlin' Circuit for their next picture.
"To play the busboy? Let me call Paul Robeson, see if he's available."

"Look, Arthur, I'm not trying to cause a stir. I'm just looking after
the integrity of the thing," Micah shot back. "Every time the audience

see someone in blackface, it throws them out of the picture. Now, there's a very talented actor named Dooley I'd like you to see. . . ."

Loath as Micah was to admit it, Marblestone had a point: The very sight of coloreds on-screen was a cue for guffaws, a black performer's very presence in a picture meant to be taken as the negation of the hero. Micah did not see things this way. Colored people exerted a fascination over him. Their faces looked more interesting than others, better keepers of secrets, wizened and wizardly, all-seeing and ancient-seeming. Even kids' faces. Like this shoeshine boy. Could be ten. Or forty.

As a moviemaker who enjoyed some notoriety, Micah had been privy to various universes, and New York's shadow city was one of them: unforgettable nights spent exploring Jungle Alley—the string of clubs and speakeasies running along 133rd Street between Lenox Avenue and Seventh—hours lost in private poker dens past Columbia University's verdant campus, where, across green felt, he'd been introduced to Mr. Waldo, a man whose totemic silences would have reduced Marblestone to a puddle.

That first night of card playing, Micah had witnessed Mr. Waldo, sitting in a shimmering red suit, relieve a man of his ring finger by way of a cigar cutter after he'd caught him cheating. Later that same night, Micah learned that Mr. Waldo had taken in three orphan boys as his own and marveled as, at just after 2:00 A.M., his proud host introduced the youngest of the bunch, hectoring him for receiving a C on a spelling test. "How you gonna be a person in the world," asked Mr. Waldo's creased and pitted face, sending the offending exam around the table for all to inspect, "if you can't spell 'intolerance'?"

There is wonder there, Micah thinks as he leaves the shoeshine boy to go about his business—spinning, laughing, snapping, happy—and moves from the brightness of one of Luna Park's promenades to the shadows of a back alley. As he strays farther from the safety of the crew, some primitive ticking in Micah's reptile brain, some atavistic pulsing on his skin, signal him that he is being followed. Keeping one hand in his jacket pocket fastened around an exposure meter the approximate weight and size of a pistol, Micah feels his heart skip like a flat stone across the surface of a pond. Creditors, bookies, bootleggers, mistresses, sharks, sharpies—he owed lots of things to lots of people. How tragic, how comic, how appropriate to be discovered dead in the gutter with his putz in his hand.

Turning around, Micah breathes a sigh of relief. If there is a gun to be used in this scene, it's a water pistol, which she fires from her hip on cue, hitting him with marksmanlike skill just above his navel. Rose Letty is so light-skinned that Micah hadn't known she was colored when he first spotted her in Imperial's New York office. All he had known about her at the time was that she was the most exotically pretty and self-possessed of the women in the costume department. There was a regal quality to her remoteness, an aristocratic dignity in her inability to mask disdain. While the other girls went out to lunch together or gabbed about weekend plans or pored over the latest issue of *Movie Star News,* Rose inhabited a kind of pyramidal silence. There was something Cleopatra-like about the girl with the thicket of dark hair piled high atop her head like forestry gracing a mountain peak, the bee-stung lacquered lips and unblinking, kohl-eyed stare.

Better, her sense of mystery was deepened, then redeemed, by her laugh: a great big gong of a thing trailed by ice-cream-truck giggles. Micah had first heard it, had first been treated to it, had first been sucker-punched and knocked flat by it one day when Marblestone's secretary was unable to make the trip east and Rose had been assigned to attend to the men in the projection room. She entered with a tray of refreshments just as the dailies reached the climax from *Hopping Mad!,* a seven-reeler about a city boy who inherits a farm overrun by rabbits. Till was on-screen battling a bunny puppet wielding a blazing ember when up in flames went the comic's suit, out of Rose burst a balloon of laughter, and down went the tray of milk and sugar and saucers.

"Who's that?" Micah asked after she'd done clearing away the mess.

"Rose," Izzy answered through a deflated éclair, marking his brother's avidity. "Works in the costume department."

"Make sure she attends the dailies from now on, will you?"

Micah had a wife and two young boys—Margaret, Benjamin, and David—comfortably installed in a stately Fifth Avenue apartment filled with all the modern conveniences, decorative tchotchkes, framed photographs, and every other outward sign of familial solidity and content. The residence served as a kind of domestic North Star from which Micah could set a moral compass that had long since been blown leagues off course. He had become so inveterate a liar that he would grow offended when caught in the flawed stitching of one of his own mistruths, the deceptions, fabrications, and half-truths having become the very warp and woof that held the marriage together.

"Yes, I've been known to shoot a few larks in my time, but it's a *hobby*," he explained to Izzy—poor, pitiable, virginal Izzy—after his brother had spotted him ensconced with a starlet in a corner booth at the Brown Derby, arms buried in thigh beneath the table. "I encourage my wife's hobbies—needlepoint, badminton, the monitoring of Ben's chronic diarrhea—and hope she would encourage mine. Margaret knew when she married me I'm a man whose eyes have a lot of lashes. So yes, I've split a few rails in my day, I've snapped a few twigs. But it's harmless, Itz. *Harmless!*

"Besides, everyone knows the movies are all about sex. In very real ways, we owe our professional livelihood to the continued investigation of my hobby."

It wasn't the animal act itself that excited him so much as the relational shift it rendered, its planar rearrangement of perspective. The electron leap from the world of propriety to the world of sex as dramatic as the moment when a radio, sitting fat and lonely atop a mantel, is turned on, a fully animating presence flowering the room with voices and music. Off to on. Potential to kinetic. Need met by answer. Rising. Sinking. A physical exertion not unlike swimming. Swimming into a person. So she had come to him later that afternoon in the back of the screening room on West Forty-Seventh Street, with her dark mouth and thick hair and saddle of freckles across her nose, something tensile and resistant about her that excited Micah more than the willing, frothy pliancy of the other girls he'd bedded.

Slowly, Micah unbuttons his trouser fly and flaps the organ out. In the benday light of the alleyway, it looks pitiable, as pink and vulnerable as a hatchling, forever questioning him with its dumb, open mouth. The entire thing was a ridiculous proposition: the comic implement men carry between their legs, the placement of these rubbery few inches, holding the possibility of ruin. To Rose, Micah's manhood resembled a deflated balloon, a sad-looking thing one finds discarded on a table at a child's birthday party.

"Go on," she says, her six-year-old face in her smile as her lover scans the scene for an appropriate spot to relieve himself, settling on a stack of rotting kindling. "It was a good day, Micah. You earned it."

Izzy approaches with trepidation the giant red-and-yellow construction. A 150-foot-tall colossus that dominates for miles the Coney Island skyline, the Wonder Wheel looks in Izzy's imagination like an enormous clockwork gear from the camera's innards. Apart from its prodigious height, the ride is unique in design, with stationary Ferris-wheel cars suspended from its outer frame and bolted into place alternating with suspended carriages that freely swing back and forth over curved interior tracks. Hence the man costumed in a black cap and red-and-white-striped gondolier's shirt who asks ticket holders, "Still or swing?" like a server at the carving table inquiring if you'd prefer juice or gravy. Izzy doesn't have time to answer, however, for in the next moment the mogul descends, wedged into the front seat of one of the ride's undulating compartments.

"Get in, Itz," Arthur Marblestone intones, extending his carnival cane and hooking Izzy into the cab, affectionately but not without suggestive force, a mother bear swatting her cub.

From toes to crown: Marblestone's delicate feet are squeezed into a tiny pair of spats, his folds of flesh draped not in anything one could realistically call a suit but a bifurcated tent adorned with meaningless buttons, pockets, and epaulets. Huge, gnarled fingers grip the bars of the cage—fingers that had known potato peelers, broom handles, steins of beer, the pussies of prostitutes, the contents of babies' diapers, awls, axes, and vises, piano keys, strips of celluloid, movie projectors, fountain pens, checkbooks, and bricks of cash. A corona of dandruff ringed his sweating shoulders, and atop his head—a Rodin bust of a thing with a nose that could only be described as heroic—sat an enormous, crooked, vaguely sinister panama hat. Under it, only slightly obscured in shadow, an unforgettable face, a face that recounted the immensity of the immigrant project, a face that held Thoreauvian composure mixed with Rasputin-like dementia, a face marked by the unblinking eyes of an archer that could, the next moment, thicken with clouds of rheumy blindness. Simply, Marblestone possessed the most prodigious physical presence of anyone Izzy had ever met—movie stars and ballplayers included—and it made sense that the man should take up space. Marblestone was both Ahab and whale—he was the whale after *swallowing* Ahab—and his incredible bulk caused the carnival ride to quake wildly.

"I didn't know you were coming east, Mr. Marblestone," Izzy fumbles, cramming himself into the front seat beside the boss, attempting to look relaxed as he is forced to rest an elbow on the man's extraordinary girth, recognizing about Marblestone an animal smell redolent of the circus tent and the abattoir.

"This is because," the mogul says, lifting an oyster from the shimmering heap of shellfish piled high on a greasy plate resting on his lap, "your brother is a disreputable, thieving liar and a world-class son of a bitch who cannot be trusted to relay even a simple message."

The carriage rocks as it rises. One-third the way up its charted course, the cab dips and then speeds forward with a terrifying rumble, sliding along curved tracks, swinging out over the wheel's outer frame, the force of the forward motion convincing the camerman that the pair of them are about to be catapulted into the Atlantic.

"Well, despite reports of delays, today has been a rousing success," Izzy says, handing Marblestone the hot dog Micah had given him as the carriage regains its equilibrium and continues skyward, nearly grazing concession-stand rooftops as the squeaking bolts of the mechanism voice their distress. "Not only did we finish the day ahead of schedule, but Mr. Ruth proved himself wholly cooperative and, in fact, something of a natural."

The cab rises higher. As heights were near the top of Izzy's list of phobias, he screws up his courage and looks Marblestone in the face, promising to keep his eyes locked on the man so long as they remain aloft.

"Look who you're talking to, Izzy. Are you suggesting I need to slink into town under cover of night to check up on one of my own productions?" Chewing now. "Are you suggesting that Arthur Marblestone— whom no less of an authority than *Moving Picture World* referred to as, quote, 'One of the motion pictures' pioneers and great entrepreneurs,' end quote—needs to hear these things from a little *pischer* of a cameraman? Not to worry, boychick, I have informers, supplicants, underlings for that sort of thing. I know *Quicktime* is behind schedule. But, much as I disapprove of your brother, he's a talented shooter. He'll bring the picture in. No, I'm here on other business."

From their great height, the trifecta of coasters—the Thunderbolt, the Tornado, the Cyclone—resemble dinosaur fossils, skeletal frames of beasts that once ruled the earth before collapsing to the sand. The famous seaside resort had been razed over and over again since its founding, entire worlds erected and destroyed—consumed by terrible blazes that felled the Elephant Colossus and reduced Dreamland's tower to a shaft of flame. Rising, rising higher still, swinging, this wonderland, this palace of amusements, this arcadia haunted with ghosts and mummies and sarcophagi, seemed to Izzy a necropolis.

"The sea air is good for me," Marblestone says once they reach the top, inhaling and expanding his torso like a hot-air balloon. "Izzy, look here." Lifting a massive arm, stretching and pulling taut the fabric of his straw-colored suit like the sail of a ship bound for the New World. "Down there, on Surf Avenue, I ran my first nickelodeon theater twenty-five years ago. Played a different one-reeler every day. . . . Then, from that one little stand, I opened the Lyric, the Majestic, the Jewel, the Bijou Dream—places you've never heard of, all over town. Twenty years before *that*, Coney Island was the very first thing I saw when we entered

New York Harbor," he recounts. "All of which is to say I don't *need* a reason for a visit, Izzy. This place is as much home to me as anywhere."

And here the man begins to weep. Thick, gelatinous tears stream over the filthy steamship pores, pocked cheeks, and Gibraltar-like nose, are swept up in the bristles fanning out from the nostrils like a broom, and retire themselves in a dustbin of mustache. Getting caught in the downpour of Marblestone's emotional weather system was nothing new to Izzy. Marblestone would let loose the waterworks at the sight of puppies, flowers, Katzenjammer Kids, little old ladies crossing the street, the cut of a really fine suit, and prepackaged loaves of bread. He was known during screen tests to explode into wet at the sight of a beautiful girl. ("That face!" Marblestone would proclaim in wonderment, Adam encountering a fawn in the Garden of Eden. "Can you believe such a *punim*!?")

"Pass me a napkin, Itz," the mogul commands, hocking phlegm and gathering sobs in cartoon balloons.

At the ride's pinnacle, Marblestone reaches for Izzy's hands—wrapping his fists around Izzy's pianist's fingers—gripping them for support as powerful wails rack his gargantuan frame, causing the cab to rock to and fro. Izzy could not help but love the man. Even while terrified of Marblestone—the power he held over the brothers, his mass and mood swings, his expansiveness and vulgarity, his bullying compassion and Old Testament wrathfulness—Izzy admired the reins the man held over his own nervous system. Synapse to thought to action—the smashed monster's fist on the table, the room-shaking fits of belly laughter, the hot, coruscating tears—emotional formation and deployment occurred faster and more honestly in Marblestone than in smaller, lesser men. Marblestone was nothing if not a prime human specimen. He *oozed* humanity. And it was this—the saltiness of Marblestone's sweaty, flawed humanity yoked to an intuitive sense of story that flowed from him as freely as water pouring off a man at a *schvitz*—that qualified him as a supreme arbiter of audience taste.

Born in 1873 in Liozna, Belarus, taking for his birthday July Fourth (and adopting his marmoreal name as a monument to himself) after emigrating to the United States in the centennial year of 1900, following a hodgepodge history of employment, Marblestone found himself working in the kineograph department of the Edison Manufacturing Company. There, as part of a plant that manufactured batteries, X-ray machines, and dental equipment, he came to see how motion pictures in America were an industrial story, similar to railroads or oil or the garment industry.

But it was more than economics that took Marblestone from butter-and-egg man to scrap metal, from fairground operator to nickelodeon-arcade proprietor, more than dollars and cents that marked his strange but inevitable trajectory from immigrant to merchant to image weaver. It was a moral imperative, a sense of public responsibility for this foreigner's son to stamp his particular brand of pathos on the American character.

For what were motion pictures—this dream parade of stunningly lit faces—other than a personal rebuke to a century's worth of terror and poverty and totalitarianism?

"I received a fan letter the other day from a farmer in Kansas explaining that since the three-reelers came in, he *dreams* of movies," Marblestone once exalted, sitting bare-chested on his throne chair in an office decorated in ancient-Egyptian fashion with lions, scarabs, owls, and dismembered feet. "Ladies and gentlemen, we have launched the most incredible campaign in history. We have invaded people's *dreams!*"

Izzy breathes a sigh of relief as the carriage begins cruising back to earth. "Stay put, sonny boy," Marblestone says, clamping a hand on the cameraman's wriggling knee as the gondolier sends them skybound for another orbit.

"Just out of curiosity, Mr. Marblestone," Izzy ventures, bracing himself for a second flight, "how long have you been on this thing?"

"I don't know, couple hours."

"Didn't you want to meet Ruth?"

"I appreciate that the man is a national hero, but after you've crossed the Atlantic in a coffin ship, these are child's games. Clam?"

"No thank you."

"I understand. It's one of the adult *C* flavors a person has to grow into, like coffee, caviar, and cocksucking."

At this last word, Izzy flinches as if stung by an electric eel. With Marblestone's hand resting on the cameraman's knee, the memory of Izzy's maiden voyage on the Wonder Wheel comes sailing back to him. Thirteen, just a month after the disaster of the brothers' joint bar mitzvah, Izzy and his best childhood friend, Marvin, had finally been allowed to spend a day exploring the wonderland on their own. What a day they had! Shoot-the-Chutes and the Tunnel of Love, the Rocky Road to Dublin and the Oriental Scenic Railway, the Dragon's Gorge and the Buzzard's Roost, the Scrambler and the Frolic, Steeplechase horses and then the capper, the topper, the kicker, surmounting the height of heights, rotating around the great clock face of sky on the superbly named Wonder Wheel. It was just as they reached the ride's apex that Marvin rested a hand on Izzy's kneecap. And kept it there. Under Marvin's furtive, persistent fingertips, beneath his thin-wale corduroys, Izzy's leg remained still, the limb in springtime possession of the secret language of bodies. Secret knowledge, too, was locked in Izzy's eyes as they rose to meet those of his friend before flicking away to look out onto the seascape. Terrifying sensations. Unknowable, indecipherable. A secret told to himself, kept to himself. It was immediately after this outing—and the exquisite, agonizing invention of nocturnal emissions—that Marvin began ignoring him. Until weeks later in the schoolyard, in front of the other boys, Marvin suddenly demanded to know of Izzy why his helpless hands went flopping "like that." To the delight of the crowd that had formed around them, Marvin grabbed Izzy's arm and held it behind his back like a chicken wing as his friend pleaded with him to let go. Then Marvin pried loose Izzy's fingers from their fist and pulled the first two back until they snapped. A good clear sound, clean and declarative, like biting a carrot or breaking dried branches over a campfire. That night Izzy's father did not ask what had occurred as he set the small bones in silence. A month later Marvin's family up and moved west.

"When my friends and I were young, we dreamed of becoming poets," Marblestone says in a solemn voice stashed behind the loud, gruff one. "Instead we became accountants and department-store owners and movie producers. Just like you and your brother: You're the artist, he's the bookkeeper."

"You came all the way from California to tell us that, Mr. Marblestone?"

"No, I came all the way from California to let you know that when all this fades"—sweeping a hand across the seascape—"the pictures will still be there. That's the distinction. You keeping up on the talkies?"

"Yes, of course. We caught *Lights of New York* the other night at the Rialto."

"And?"

"Well, synchronization's amazing, but visually they're terrible."

"It's a gimmick. It'll pass. Besides, actors talk already. Their *faces* speak, their *eyes* are mouths."

"Yeah, Hal told me about how they had to keep the camera locked down in a glass booth to muffle the noise and spent half the time figuring out ways to hide the microphone—actors talking to flower arrangements, leaning into piano housing, that sort of thing."

"Theater conversion costs a fortune, too." Marblestone nods. "Exhibitors are still skeptical, taking a wait-and-see approach. Even so, we're in trouble. Serious trouble."

"Mr. Marblestone, I assure you today's shoot—"

"Forget about *Quicktime*, that's the least of my worries. I'm being squeezed, Izzy. Like a testicle in a bar fight I'm being squeezed!"

"By whom?"

"Creditors, auditors, exhibitors ... You're a smart boy, you know what a bank note is? We're overextended, Izzy. Your Till pictures have been the only thing keeping us afloat these past few years. Every other picture—*Tit for Tat, The Eggroll Adventures of Chow Mein Charlie, Shooting in the Dark with Uncle Johnson*—has gone bust."

"I've talked to you before about those titles ..."

"Forget the titles, Izzy! *Quicktime* could be the biggest picture of the year, it wouldn't matter. I've got to turn things around or it's back to the junk business for me."

"That's why you came to New York? To see Abernathy?"

"In part, yes. Look, I've seen the talkies, and I'm against them. We didn't work thirty years making movies into something new only to turn them back into stage plays. Sound's a fad—it'll play itself out. Leave the voices to radio; I'm willing to stake my legacy on that belief. No, for Imperial to survive, we have to go in the opposite direction. If sound pictures lock the camera down, Imperial needs to liberate it from the lot, like we did here, today, in Coney Island."

"Huh."

"You know Wallace over at Poseidon Pictures? Last time I saw him he mentioned how they'd loaned out three minutes of underwater footage from *The Call of Pirate Booty* to Robertson-Cole Pictures for *South Sea Love*. Far as I can tell, no one else is doing this. Now, here's my plan. We're going to create a vault of imagery, stock footage of the great sights of the world—the Pantheon, ancient Roman ruins, the Great Wall of China, the Eiffel Tower, the Belgian Congo—that we'll license out to other studios to use in their pictures and get paid five, six times over. If it works, it'll relieve our debt within a year. I've got prospective buyers all lined up—the Technicolor Corporation needs footage for *Cleopatra*, Numa Pictures needs insert shots for the *Tarzan* serials—the list goes on and on."

"I'm not certain I follow." Swallowing a spoonful of bile as they lift higher.

"I need you and your brother to take a trip."

"You want to take us off pictures?"

"No, the contrary, Isidor. I want your stuff stamped across all the studios' product. You'll bring Till, too. Henry's still under a two-picture contract, so you can shoot your next one while you're over there as insurance to help underwrite the trip."

"Over *where*, Mr. Marblestone?"

"You and your brother are going to have the privilege of making the first films in Africa."

"Africa? With all due respect, Mr. Marblestone, this *amusement ride* is proving difficult for me."

"Nonsense, Izzy. I have faith in your powers of resolve. That's why I've chosen you and your brother for this assignment—to make like Magellan with a movie camera. *Bubbeleh*, I've got it all lined up. The world will be our backdrop, this I promise."

From the Wonder Wheel's high, bright peak, Izzy forces himself to look out onto the vibrating horizon, the blue-and-white Scotch-plaid sky beyond. Great fingers of the Atlantic feathered out in green and gold filaments beyond the shore, merchant coins of the sea, spangles of the New World. Could it be done? Could it be captured, all of it, the pieces of the world gathered up and put back in Pandora's box? Turning again to the boss, the cameraman surveys Marblestone from head to toe, magnificent clay sculpted by force of will. Then Izzy leans forward, surrenders his vision to the foggy reflection of himself swimming in the man's polished shoes, inhales deeply, and delivers across the boss's feet a colorful plume of vomit.

2

HIDDEN CITIES

ONE

As Micah trawls between sleep and wakefulness, belly to back, legs bent spoonwise, his halfway-limp *schmegegge* still inside her, somewhere in the world the sun turns up its lampshade. Here in her bedroom, against the day, he's able to make out some markers: the too-short vase of lilies by the window, a collection of secondhand hats sprouting on the wall like midnight mushrooms, stacks of broken-spined books and outdated periodicals fanned out atop a wobbly wooden desk, lime-green Coca-Cola bottles lining the floor like bowling pins, just enough latent luminescence to connect the constellation of moles across her back. Even when he isn't here, this secret room uptown, the honest half of his life. "It's nice getting touched," she'd said once, revealing the simple secret of the great game, "in places that don't often get touched."

That first night he barely made it: New Year's streamers bolting across the room just as she'd managed to free it from his trousers. Trying again, that first time everything had gone wrong. They'd worked together like two machines laboring on opposing assembly lines, all the parts oiled and in good running order, but each with its own private function. "Slow down, honey," Rose advised gently when it was over, wiping his clotted belly with a washcloth. "It's better that way." Going for it again, Micah imagined he was Rudolph Valentino in *The Sheik*, all long strides. Now the opposite happened, the lovers reaching for each other across vast syrupy distances, speaking by way of semaphore. (The only thing worse than a quick, greedy lay being a long, lackluster one.) Rallying for a third attempt following a stamina-boosting peanut-butter-and-jelly sandwich, Micah hoped to impress with his knowledge of curious poses from worlds animal and Hindu. She finally made it, shuddering, a fish arcing out of water. "That's all I got," he said, exquisitely chafed and panting, attending to a pulled hamstring on his left leg. "That's okay, honey," she said, "we'll try the rest another time." *(The rest?!)*

A work in progress, then, that first night. Though their bodies pressed together as close as muscle and bone sinew would allow, they hadn't really slept together at all, had never really shared a charted course. Rather, each remained fixated on an idea of the other: Rose had made it with a movie director; Micah had just dipped into his first black berry. What had he expected? Did he think it would look different? Feel different? Smell different? Even during the act, he caught himself, as he was prone to do, recasting the incident in two-inch-tall movie-magazine type (A GRAND OLD TIME: DIRECTOR CONTRIBUTES TO COLORED CAUSE). Then, later, buttoning himself up in the half-light scumble, revising the late-edition headline to arrive closer to the truth (OCCASION RISEN TO: MOVIEMAKER LEARNS A THING, TWO).

A world-class pussy bandit, Micah had experienced marriage as a seven-year montage of chorus singers and starlets, secretaries and schoolteachers, cigarette girls and cocktail waitresses, all of them happily hopping into his lap, a pinwheeling collage of legs waving from taxicab windows, lewd acts performed in commissary bathrooms and the back of darkened screening rooms, the entire apparatus of movie-making at times seeming less about money and craftsmanship than a riot of unrestrained coupling. At one Hollywood dinner party Micah attended with Margaret, he excused himself between courses to bed each of the women at the table in turn, returning to his seat for palette-cleansing shots of sorbet. And this kind of ass-happy behavior wasn't frowned upon either: Each year Marblestone threw a Christmas Eve orgy that would have made Caligula blush.

"I noticed you the first time I saw you," she told him just before he left that night.

"Because I'm running the show?"

"No, because you're such a big boy."

"A big-boy?" he asked, investing the hyphenate with all its Mae West suggestiveness.

"No," she corrected him. "A big *boy*."

"So I've been found out."

"Sure have. You know what else? You fuck like a black man."

"Jeez, miss. And here I thought you were saving yourself for your wedding day."

"Well, you know what they say about black men . . . ," she said, gripping his shrinking, modest-size member.

"Don't—"

"They don't pay for anything."

When she laughed—selecting a snorting exhalation from her policeman's lineup of chortles, giggles, chuckles, hiccups, belly laughs, and guffaws—he knew that the pleasure she took in finding him more overgrown child than movie big shot was meant as a supreme compliment. With the others, Micah had been aroused not by the specific girls themselves so much as by the intensity of their interest in him, but things felt different with Rose. It wasn't the need for uptown adventure or the exoticism of her blackness, it was that they met together on this childlike plane. She appreciated his card tricks and magic acts, took a connoisseur's interest in the water pistol and the whoopee cushion, delighted in the mysteries of yo-yo suspension and wall-shadow puppetry, could wind her way around a dirty limerick with the best of them. And she appreciated, too, that fucking, the very best of it, is child's play.

Then came the difficulty of what to do about the affair, how public to make it. Limit their time together to visits to Harlem, that second metropolis, or brazenly spirit the girl around town? Mainly they spent their time together hidden away in the little one-bedroom apartment Rose shared with her half brother, Early, on West 140th Street, the two of them holed up in the postage-stamp-size bedroom, her brother coming in late at night and depositing himself on the couch like a sack of coal.

"I swear, that boy better watch out, land himself in some serious business," Rose said with a sigh one night when they were woken by Early's clattering around the living room at 3:00 A.M. Wanting to help but careful not to intervene with too strong a hand, Micah suggested hiring Early for odd jobs on the set: running errands, ferrying around extras, delivering cans of film to the lab, that sort of thing. Mainly he hoped to yoke Early to Billy Conklin, the sweet-faced, apple-bright go-getter and unofficial crew mascot, who might serve as a good influence. Anyway, it was no trouble throwing the kid a couple of bucks every once in a while, and he might learn a trade and make himself eligible for a union card in the process. Purplish black, Early was several shades darker than Rose, so they'd agreed to keep quiet their family relation-ship around the crew. That was fine by Early: Nobody needed to know he was taking handouts from the man giving the business end to his sis-ter. This suited Rose, too. If she wasn't making a conscious effort to pass for white, she was in no hurry to tell the world she was colored either.

"It's a book about passing," Rose said of the copy of Nella Larsen's *Quicksand* that Micah picked up from her bedside table.

"Seems an awful lot of effort, pretending you're something you're not."

"What, like you're doing right now? Besides, that first day in the projection room, didn't you wonder if I was black?"

"I wondered about a lot of things," Micah said. "Thought I'd get you home, wonder about you some more."

The fact that with her hair carefully teased and plaited, the right makeup, and some consideration given to the color clothes she wore, under certain circumstances Rose *could* pass for white only complicated the relationship.

"You poor dumb schmuck," chastised Marblestone, who generally took pleasure in his star director's tales of conquest. "You don't take a mistress for the dream of nookie but the dream of freedom. That's the only thing worth the running around for—the momentary spell of lib-erty that work and family and money and all the other terrible obliga-tions can't provide. Trust me, Micah, get in too deep with this *schvartze* of yours, you'll never be free."

Marblestone had a point. It was one thing for Rose to lay the powder on a little thick and let people think what they would in the white world, another altogether to announce herself Caucasian in the black one. No, Rose never set foot in Harlem's restricted clubs with Micah or anyone else, opting instead to work just a few blocks away as a coat checker and cigarette girl at the Honeypot, which favored a looser admission policy.

Rose wasn't devoid of politics, however. She held subscriptions to *FIRE!!*, *Negro World*, and *Opportunity*. She chose to patronize Foster Photoplay Company theaters rather than ascend segregated balconies to "nigger heaven." She had attended a few Saturday-afternoon meetings of the Universal Negro Improvement Association at Liberty Hall on 138th Street. She even held buried deep in a dresser drawer worthless stock from Marcus Garvey's Black Star Line Steamship Corporation, two five-dollar mimeographed certificates with engravings of the three junkyard boats the activist promised would return American blacks to their native homeland.

"You've got a lot of neat knickknacks around here," Micah said, moving on to the next curiosity on her bookshelf, dresser, and night table with the lazy disinterest of a schoolboy on a museum outing. She questioned daily whether she was like that to him: an exotic trinket, a travel souvenir, a toy on a shelf, an animal to pet at the zoo. She wondered if the feelings she had for the movie director could be described as good. Whether what they felt for each other could be labeled with that benevolent word or was instead something base and mean. If their fucking was good enough, emphatic enough, tough enough to provide cover and compensation for every other omission and deficiency. She wondered about his life with his wife and boys, what a world voided of exclusion, a daily existence of fluency and access, must be like. She tried imagining his wedding day, how he looked in top hat and tails, elegant as Duke Ellington, and whether he even acknowledged the theatrically deferential colored waiters who'd cleared the plates. She often hated him, and hated herself for wanting him.

Leaving Rose to infant sleep, Micah rises from the damp bed, pulls on a pair of crumpled boxers, and heads into the next room. There, lying on the couch, splayed out like a piece of fish on a newspaper, is Early. Normally, with all the engines firing, Micah feels irresistible, but here, now, in the gelid light, he feels as ugly and vulnerable as a freshly plucked chicken, all pink and goose-pimpled, his torso vaguely pear-shaped, his chest carpeted in what most closely resembles red pencil-eraser shavings, his cheeks packed with remnants of baby fat. He admits to himself that the sleeping teenage boy—clothed in work boots and mud-crusted dungarees, a sleeveless white T-shirt exposing arms that are just beginning to suggest lineaments of adult musculature—is possessed of greater, more natural physical authority than he is.

Micah had expected Early in Coney Island at noon to assist Billy with some grip work—hauling equipment, laying sandbags, and steadying the dolly during complicated tracking shots—but the boy didn't show until after the shoot was done. His absence was no big loss—the two of them didn't have any kind of formal arrangement—but Micah was disappointed that the kid hadn't been there to see him in all his peacock glory with Babe Ruth instead of here, a fat, freckled, forlorn man standing half naked in his sister's living room.

"Hey, Mr. Grand." Early yawns, outstretched limbs more alert than the sleepy face.

"You and Billy drop the reels off okay?"

"Yes, sir," he answers, leaving Micah to determine whether or not he is being mocked. "Dailies will be ready on Thursday."

Receiving the news, Micah walks over to the closet door, reaches into a jacket pocket, removes his money clip, peels a bill from the stack, and hands it over. The moment is charged. The wad of paper seems to Micah somehow slimmer than when he arrived, and, looking at the boy, he wonders if it is tacitly permissible for Early to have skimmed a dollar or two.

"How you doing, Early?" Rose, rubbing sleep from her eyes, in a bathrobe that exposes more cleavage than intended.

"Fine."

"One word?" Not looking at him. "Is that all a girl gets from you these days? No, let's try that again: *How're you doing, Early?*"

"Fine, just like I said." Counting them off. "That's five."

"Why don't you talk to your sister, Early?"

"Stay free of it, Em."

"Well, he could at least *try* being civil."

"Mr. Belly Button here with no shirt on is going to teach me lessons in *civility?* This ain't no movie lot, Mr. Grand."

"Don't talk to Em that way." Working with metronomic precision a distressed fingernail, not making eye contact with her brother.

"I'll go get my shirt." Exiting the room, freckles across his back like ice-cream-cone sprinkles.

"Lookit, I appreciate what Mr. Grand is trying to do for me, I do, but it'd be nice to come home some nights and not feel like I'm living in a henhouse."

"Were that description true," Rose says, flicking cracker crumbs off her thigh, "what would that make me?"

"You said it, sis."

"Now, you listen here and listen good." Turning on him with marble eyes and Medusa tendrils. "You don't have to like what I do, and you don't have to approve who I do it with, 'cause you're not the one doing it."

"Why does it have to be him, though? That's what I don't get."

"Oh, honey." Softening now, almost singing. "I don't do things 'cause I *have* to," she says, kissing her brother on the forehead. "What I do"— kissing his right cheek—"I do"—then the left—"because I *like* to."

Micah always felt better once his shirttails were tucked into his pants, his suspenders were strung tight, he had on a good pair of shoes, and all the accoutrements of his adult-impostor costume were in place. He emerged from Rose's bedroom, that fifteen-by-twenty-foot paradise, respectably dressed once more, belly flab corseted, freckles covered, confidence restored. He was relieved to see that the kid had quit the flat and pleased, too, to recognize a song, Ma Rainey's "Misery Blues," lazily playing on the phonograph, filling the room with molasses, whiskey sours, and amber light:

IIIIIII've got the blues,
Dooooooown in my shoes.
I've got thooooose
Miiiiiiiisery blues.

Before Rose, Micah's exposure to colored music had been limited mostly to coon songs, cakewalking, jubilees, and other forms of minstrelsy. She had deepened his appreciation of ragtime's joyous syncopated rat-a-tat, and then, advancing his education, introduced him to the blues and jazz singers that were just beginning to gain airtime on the radio. Music whistling like a kettle, water and electricity spraying the air, with deeper bowel movements of bass rumbling below. Sure, he'd heard black chanteuses croon torch songs before, had enjoyed Cab Calloway performing "Minnie the Moocher" at the Cotton Club, encouraging white audiences to scat along in nonsensical call-and-response, but this was musical universes removed from the familiar: neither the fizzing fun stuff of Rodgers & Hart, Hammerstein & Kern, and the Gershwin brothers nor the pink-champagne puns of Cole Porter. This music was love and sex distilled as grain alcohol—a blinding, terrifying force that glued the universe together and could just as easily set it flying apart. The absoluteness of the songs, the actuality of them! This music, so rich in history and suffering and personhood, was the valve through which the steam heat of things despairing and profound and necessary was being safely passed into the culture.

"Up on the roof having a cigarette," Rose says, explaining her brother's whereabouts, continuing to paint her toenails. "Probably setting off firecrackers." Above them, muffled by ten or twelve stories of brick and wood and concrete, comes Early's response: the whistle and pop of a bottle rocket.

"What time do you have to be at the club?"

"Ten."

"What time is it now?"

"Twenty to."

"Y'know, in movie time, twenty minutes is a veritable eternity."

Thinking how nice it would be to clean his clock and clear his head before heading to the late-night card game at Mr. Waldo's Paradise Club, a backwater southern juke joint lifted whole and dropped like a penny onto an urban street.

"This ain't no movie, Mr. Grand," Rose chides, pulling from her bathrobe the plastic water pistol, taking aim, and firing—*bull's-eye!*— right at his crotch. There was time. Here, in the palace of melting clocks, the place where the plates stopped spinning, there'd be time enough. Here, uptown, there was always enough time.

TWO

When Izzy came buzzing off the final day of a successful shoot, tradition dictated that he meet for drinks with Howard Rubin Mansfield, a Broadway-theater publicist, Great White Way raconteur, and all-round New York muckety-muck. Perhaps four inches shorter and ten years older than Izzy, Howard was in possession of a bald white pate botanically wreathed with brown hair; a snow-upon-topiary effect that, combined with his wit and general good cheer, allowed the man to bring Christmas with him wherever he went. Rather than experiencing embarrassment over his sheared crown, Howard flaunted it, reiterating its gleaming ivory circle in mother-of-pearl cuff links, Coke-bottle glasses, and bright polka-dot ties.

Though they had early on dispensed with the detailed biographical stencil work, though they saw each other for drinks only three or four times a year, though their relationship therefore occupied a zone somewhere between acquaintanceship and close friendship, Izzy felt a deep affinity with Howard, whom he felt he knew better than most of the important figures in his life. The cameraman always left their encounters feeling buoyed, better, a smarter, livelier, more interesting person, and looked forward to their meetings like a boy anticipating the first winter snow.

"I like the flicks just fine, Isidor, but for acting—*real* thespian work—one must look to the stage," Howard says, slurping his martini, flower freckles alight. "Besides, the romance in your comedy pictures never really *plays*, have you ever noticed that? The women are never memorable. You saw *The General*?" Howard asks rhetorically of Keaton's wonderwork of locomotives and the Civil War. "Buster was in love, all right, but with the *train*. Chaplin, Keaton, even your own Henry Till, they're all great but solitary figures. Why do you think that is? Are laughs such an aphrodisiac killer?"

"No, Howard, I disagree," Izzy says, confirming to himself that if he is easily, inherently Izzy, Howard is no Howie. "There's romance in the films, all right. It's just not visible on the screen—it's between them and the audience."

"Well, we disagree all the time, you and I."

"No we don't."

"Yes we do. Take you, for example—*don't mind if I do, ha-ha*—and the question of theater versus films. I know you can't *stand* legitimate theater, that you consider it all hopelessly antiquated and dull compared to your brutish popular art."

"Well, if I never again see the underside of Barrymore's chin, I'll count myself lucky."

"That's only because you don't appreciate the theater's rules and traditions, so you discount one in favor of the other. Whereas *I*—in my infinite sagaciousness and wisdom—prefer both plays *and* motion pictures."

"Huh."

"And this preference, I hope you will appreciate, is not a matter of morality but one of taste."

The martinis were immense. Izzy, not usually a drinker, consciously resists the alcohol's rising effect as it sloshes over him, overcompensating by making himself purposefully rigid, straightening his posture until he is as militarily aligned as a West Point cadet, hands pressed flat on the table, displaying fingers for days.

"Two martinis, please," Howard taxi-hails the bartender. "And for my friend here—*ha-ha*—another?"

"No, I'll have a Tom Collins instead."

"Ooooooh, I bet you'd like a Tom Collins," the bartender coos, sidling up to them.

"Yes, please," Izzy says, registering the hint of Cleopatra tincture around the server's eyelashes, the eyebrows improbably sleek and well groomed.

"Okay, honey."

This, too, Izzy finds disarming, having not been called by that term of endearment since his mother's death. It hadn't occurred to him that anything was amiss when Howard suggested they meet here, at a downtown place called Bacchus rather than one of their usual Broadway haunts. Izzy hadn't considered anything suspect when they first entered and he espied the glossy poster of Michelangelo's *David* in all his naked, ill-proportioned splendor. Nor did he really take note until now of the lighting in this poorly illumined room, more shrouded, clandestine-seeming than in other bars he had frequented, the darkness concealing rather than cradling the mysteries of romance.

But now Izzy takes it all in, and all is full of shame. A uniformed man at a corner table loosens and removes his prosthetic arm and places it across the table, a line drawn in the sand, the first acknowledgment in the shedding of secret selves. A policeman, his face half swallowed in mustache, is chatted up by a man in a derby who holds an elaborately carved horn cane. A beautiful slip of a blonde in a short red dress who couldn't possibly, but must, be a man, grazes the backs of patrons' necks as she glides by. There are married men, too, square, boxy-shaped fellows in gray and black business suits and stiff hats, gold loops glinting around their wedding-ring fingers offering the protection of magic totems, rendering acts invisible. A border collie patrols the place, and even the dog is somehow effeminate, taunting them all by seeming to walk *en pointe*.

"You know what I just noticed?"

Howard pops a drunken olive into his mouth. "What's that?"

"There are no women in this bar. Only men."

"Well, you're an observant one, Isidor."

Queer. Fruit. Twist. Fag. Pansy. Bent. Fairy. Sissy. Invert. Disturbed. Degenerate. In the life. Three-letter man. Winking, jeering, lascivious, effeminate men, Lady So-and-So of Such-and-Such. Ever since

Prohibition came in, the fairy resorts on the Bowery and in the Tenderloin had been targeted by Comstock's Society for the Suppression of Vice, which made a practice of regularly raiding the places, bashing heads, and bringing patrons up on charges of lewd behavior and disorderly conduct. (After a magazine called *The Little Review* serialized passages from it, the society also managed to have banned a book by a lunatic Irishman about a Jew wandering around Dublin, thus protecting the populace from the dangers of literary modernism.)

Being here was no good. Hollywood, for all its surface flagrant permissiveness, was in reality a very conservative place. The two things that could bring ruin there—sexual scandal and financial collapse—entwined like a pair of folded hands in a casket. Just look what they did to poor Fatty. Yet here Izzy was, with Imperial facing financial collapse, sitting enjoying a drink in this terrifying hole.

"What is this place, Howard?"

"Just a bar I know."

Izzy tries to get his breathing under control, to maintain a neutral tone. "Well, I'm not about to ask if you come here often."

"Just people relaxing, Isidor, getting to know one another, trying to have a good time. If you're uncomfortable here, we can find some other place."

"No, I'm fine."

And, in truth, Izzy *is* fine, the anthropological curiosity welling up inside him having extinguished any glow of betrayal. Removing himself by degrees, Izzy is able to appreciate the wit of the bar's name—Bacchus—its classicism, its frisson of historic credibility, its economy in yoking perversity to antiquity. His eyes adjust to the dimness, and he recognizes that if the illumination of the room is indeed poor, the place is lit up like a castle from within, made resplendent with desire.

"Meet my boyfriend!" Henry Till's four-year-old son, Tom, had announced to the crew during a visit to the star's compound, tugging Izzy along by the hand. Lost inside Till's palatial residence, Izzy had stumbled upon Tom in the games room—the boy busy kissing his own reflection in a mirror—and felt an immediate kinship with the peculiar little Narcissus. Now the jig was finally up: the risk of rank exposure at the hands of an amoral child. "Izzy is my boyfriend!"

"Your *friend*," his mother corrected. "Not boyfriend."

"No, Izzy's my *boy*friend," the child insisted. "I'm going to marry him when I grow up!"

"Hey," laughed Till, "wouldn't that be something!"

"Ha-ha!" Izzy ejaculated between clenched teeth, goose-stepping away from the incriminating scene. "Quite a precocious one you've got there, Henry! Quite . . . the . . . charming . . . young . . . lad."

Was Izzy's hot human need so obvious that it was evident even to a child? Was his foulness that apparent? After everything Izzy had done, the lifelong project of negation, his monkish emptying out of desire? On the occasions when Izzy pleasured himself—a practice he engaged in with a kind of grinding, ritual obligation, sensations dense and dull as pound cake—if someone had ever bothered to ask, he would be hard-pressed to explain over what exactly he was laboring. Recalling grade-school grammar lessons, were he forced to sentence-diagram the occasion, Izzy would be a lonesome subject in search of an object. It was a biological procedure rather than a spiritual one. When it was over, wiping himself clean, Izzy was always amazed and humbled by the trials to which he had subjected himself for a result that was, on the evidence, a warm dollop of mother-of-pearl.

"So, *Izzy*," Howard prods, "you know the one about the fellow who goes to the doctor and says, 'It hurts when I go like this'?"

"Yeah. 'So don't go like this.'"

"Right. But what if the patient says, 'Doc, it hurts *others* when I go like this'? What does the doctor say then? If he's any good, he says, 'Well, I'm not treating other patients, I'm treating *you*. And you're fine. Now, open wide and say "Ah." ' "

Izzy longed for Howard to reach out, he prayed for him to remain still. Just sitting here, close to it, swimming in suggestion, simply this triumphant acknowledgment of need was eros enough to sustain him for years. To bask in it. To baste in it. Disappearing into dark, masculine darkness. In the corner a hand drifts under a table. A shoulder begins rising, falling. Elsewhere, disappearances into alleys and men's-room stalls. The sordidness of it excites him. The sordidness of it repulses him. If Howard's touch arrives, Izzy's life, his true life, may be forced to begin. Then it comes. A hand, rising out of velveteen black, brushes his knee. And stays there. His arm. Marvin's arm.

"So, ha-ha, I was thinking," Howard says. "I make a mean Tom Collins, a much better-proportioned drink than they do here, actually, and it occurs to me also that you've never seen my apartment."

"No, I haven't."

"Well, it's got a rather spectacular view, really something to see, if I do say so myself."

"Sounds lovely."

"So I thought I might ask you back there for a drink, ha-ha, because, all kidding aside, I think I'll die if you don't touch me."

And out of the material of this dark room stretches before him the possibility of a city of bachelors. A city within a city. A city in waiting. A city within reach.

"No, Howard," Izzy says at last, removing his hand. "No, honey. No."

THREE

Micah loved playing cards. There was the weirdly physical aspect of it, a kind of athletic ramping up while settling back in one's seat. There were sensations of scent and taste, smells of cigar smoke, too-strong aftershave, green felt, fake leather, and spilled whiskey thickening the room, competing musical lines sawing away in an olfactory orchestra. There was the theatrical nature of it, the spinning of situations truthful and fictive, improvisatory fumes blasting away at full brightness. There was the narrative function of card games, how the best poker nights became lessons in storytelling, minor characters and subplots falling away, dramatic scaffolding revealing itself as empires were engineered and erased over single evenings. There was the oracular element, occult pleasures involved in testing one's affinity with those fifty-two resistant slips, a local symptom of the general need to command mastery over the inanimate and indifferent. For all these reasons, Micah put card playing on a continuum with film shoots and fucking: heightened arenas in which one confronted the limits of skill, chance, imagination, and faith. One never knew how the thing would turn out.

If Micah loved playing cards, he especially enjoyed games up in Harlem, where the card table served as the great equalizer. In these settings his colored acquaintances—actors, old-timers, and gangland associates—were relaxed, shrewd, noble. There was Mr. Waldo, leather-glove-faced at fifty, maybe sixty; there was the offhand, dismissive way he had of tossing chips into the pot like dirty plates in a cafeteria line; there was the way he'd shoot his shirtsleeves to show off expensive cuff links hanging one inch past the jacket; there was his low, tobacco-stricken voice, a physical thing you might find at the bottom of a well, like a moss-covered rock or a broken bottle. There was the gangster's young lieutenant, Ellsworth Raymond Johnson, about Early's age, pin thin, with fast, slashing eyes; a timeless, unlined face; the liquid hand movements of a deep-sea diver; and, planted prominently atop his forehead, a knotted carbuncle for which he'd earned the nickname "Bumpy."

Granted the occasional uptown invitation by James G. Wintz, a popular colored stage actor, Micah joined these Harlem games whenever he could and lost money to these princely black men liberally, almost merrily. Admission dues, he charitably thought, for exposure to alien realms. And he'd been prepared to lose again that night. But nothing like this.

"I knew it!" Izzy erupts, hands waving up and down like a traffic cop's. "I knew one day you'd bring us to ruin!"

"Quit it, Itz." Inhaling a cigarette. "I've not slept in days."

"Thirteen thousand dollars, Micah?! Why weren't you put up for adoption?!"

"You don't understand, Izzy. It was a *flush*."

"But thirteen thousand dollars?"

"Thirteen thousand three hundred, but who's counting? Listen, Izzy, I was pulling cards I didn't know existed. The twelve of unicorns, the eleven of rainbows . . ."

It had been four days since the shoot wrapped, and Izzy had been looking forward to a triumphant reunion with his brother over dailies. Instead Micah had arrived hours late to the screening. He needed the extra time to achieve the effect of his appearance: cheeks spackled with crimson stubble; hair sculpted in a mad, woodpeckerish swoop; feathery trousers out of press; shirttails dangling freely behind him; his entire aspect as ruffled and dirty as a city pigeon.

"Do you have it?" Izzy asks.

"No, I don't have it." Lighting his next cigarette off his last. "I skipped out on a meeting I was supposed to have with them last night."

"What'll they do to you if you don't deliver?"

"I don't know, Izzy. These are serious men. Serious colored men."

"How could you *do* this to us, Micah?! What in God's name were you *thinking*?!"

This was the one trait of his brother's personality—the parental scold—that Micah found entirely insupportable, and he recognized it as a form of self-punishment to have allowed himself to give Izzy free rein to this strain of moral superiority. Izzy had the luxury to be judgmental because he risked nothing, did nothing; Micah's brother could afford to be unrealistic about need and motive and outcomes because he lacked the courage that comes with simple human sloppiness.

In silence the duo jockey their way through busy midtown streets under the doleful watch of an electrified, fifty-foot Heinz pickle. A long ribbon flecked with green Coca-Cola-bottle slivers and pink bubble-gum wads, Broadway is parading with pretty girls, google-eyed kids, and cigar-chomping mugs; in the air, jabbing odors of boiling hot dogs, bright red candy, cheap wax cosmetics, newsprint, and sewer steam. To calm himself Izzy rummages a hand around in the paper bag full of novelty items he'd picked up for his nephews, identifying by touch a pair of fake plastic glasses, a toot-toot whistle, a flying dragonfly, a trick fountain pen, and a pack of black-pepper chewing gum.

"Can you get an advance from Marblestone?"

"I can't go to Arthur with this." Smacking the concavity of his brother's chest. "C'mon, Marbles has got money troubles of his own."

"Well," Izzy says, fiddling with the children's gags and gizmos, "there's one thing we could do that would settle your tab and help Arthur at the same time."

"Did I miss something? The way you described his proposal, the lunatic fat man wants to put us on a freight ship to Africa *to take nature photos*? Suddenly you've come around to the idea?"

"I don't know, the more I thought about it . . . The idea of being that far from home . . ."

"You've been reading too much Kipling. Listen, Itz, you want to see lions and tigers, I'll buy you a ticket to the zoo. I have obligations here: a wife, kids, a difficult mistress, a picture to finish. I can't go traipsing off to the jungle just because Arthur's skint. No, what I was hoping is that you might think to help me. You've always been good with money, and you certainly don't have the competing financial obligations that I do."

"Absolutely not, Micah," says Izzy, contemptuous satisfaction dripping in his voice as the pair make a turn at Forty-Third Street, elevated subway beams slicing the city into mad isometrics. "This is one debt you're going to have to sort out on your own."

Micah usually approached the limestone façade of his apartment building at 802 Fifth Avenue with the caution of a man dipping a toe into a bathtub. He was, by any reasonable measure, a terrible father. In every practical sense, Micah just wasn't around for the boys' upbringing. He didn't tend to the children when they were sick, didn't help them with their schoolwork, didn't know the names of boyhood friends real or imagined. He was, however, a thrilling presence in their lives. He showered them with fantastic gifts—hand-carved rocking horses and high-powered telescopes, Chinese checkers and chemistry sets, oversize director's chairs and miniature cars—and filled their heads with storybook visions and tales of movie stars and oil tycoons, inventors and aviators, the jewel-laden and the glamour-drenched. One night when Micah had been away in California for a particularly long stretch, Margaret and the boys were listening to an Eastman Theatre radio broadcast when the announcer introduced as musical composer a "very special guest." So enthralled was elder son, David, by the wording of this, by the concept of a "special guest"—a glamorous personage who swooped in to electrify staid proceedings—and so much did the boy identify this designation with his father that David began referring to Micah by the moniker, and the painful nickname stuck.

Arriving at the building lobby, with its stonework details like wedding-cake piping, the brothers are surprised that the elderly Italian doorman is nowhere to be found. The man's red-and-gold hat, however, sits squarely in the center of the marble floor, lonely as a buoy at sea. The space always smelled of sand and salt—powdery white, ancient, oceanic smells—but it is an unlikely overlay that reaches Micah first.

Card-game scents, starched shirts and peppermint-candy-stripe after-shave, sweet and noxious at the same time.

Like an actor in a musical number, on cue Mr. Waldo emerges from a corner of the lobby and begins striding magnificently toward its center, approaching his mark with the authority of a born headliner. He walks like a man with all the time in the world, someone who sees the bus he's meant to take pulling in to the station a few blocks ahead of him but in no hurry to catch it. Dressed in his familiar suit of candy-apple red, a solid-gold tie, and pitched at an improbable angle, a black fedora waving a velvety purple plume, he is altogether as resplendent and unlikely a presence in the great marble dome as a newly landed Martian.

In a half-lit corner of the atrium standing hovered over the crumpled figure of the doorman is Mr. Waldo's apprentice, Bumpy, decked out in dazzling bright blue pinstripes, midnight-blue snap-brim fedora, and squared-off bulldog-toed boots. In this strange environment, the young lieutenant looks hyperalert, cornered, dangerous, the air around him quickening with the movement of his hands and eyes. Micah recognizes with tightening rectal fear that Bumpy's nickname is fitting not just for his swelling of forehead but for the unpredictable, spasmodic quality of his movements. There is a hurtling, improvisatory nature about the kid, present-tensing it the whole way, as if dwelling too long on the past or thinking too hard on the future would cause all physiological functions to cease. Unlike Mr. Waldo's hardened sculpture, Bumpy's clay is still settling.

"Mr. Grand," hisses the prostrate Italian. "I tell them you no home! I tell these *mulignane* leave this place and no come back!"

"It's okay, Joe." Micah, holding his hands up, palms out. "I apologize for my business associates. They won't be here long and won't be coming back."

"These are bad men, Micah."

"Thanks for that, Itz."

"*Bad?*" Mr. Waldo purrs silkily, meeting the brothers in the center of the lobby. "Nah, we ain't bad. We're good men. Sweet. Sugarplum fairies." Then, taking an interest, "This your brother?"

"Yes. Shake the man's hand. Izzy."

"Isidor Grand."

Extending the thick-callused hand. "Byron Marcus Waldo, charmed t'make your acquaintanceship."

"It wasn't smart of you to come here," Micah says.

"*Smart?!*" Bumpy says, delivering sharp kicks to the stomach of the sixty-year-old doorman. "Who! Ain't! *Smart?!*"

Izzy runs with flapping forearms to the doorman's aid, sliding between Ellsworth's pointed shoe and the prone figure just in time to intercept another blow. Bumpy hoists Izzy to his feet, holding him by the tie like it was a noose.

"C'I cut this cherry blossom?"

"You wouldn't hurt someone wearing glasses, would you?"

"You ain't."

Izzy reaches into his bag and pulls onto his face a fake pair of frames.

"Devil his due." Bumpy laughs, releasing him. "He got me there!"

"You shouldn't have brought this business here," says Micah, ignoring the sideshow.

"Leaving aside you in no position to instruct how I conduct myself, and that El-Ray and I go wherever we please in this motherfucker, I ain't come bringing business. Santa Claus comes bearing gifts." And here Mr. Waldo presents Micah with a small ivory-colored gift box. The box is of a size that might hold an engagement ring and is tied with a girl's red bow. "Now, what could be in this here?" Rattling it, acorn sounds resonating off Rorschach-patterned marble. "Could be something you want? Or something Mr. Waldo want? . . . Could be one of your boys' fingers? Or they toes? Hey, El-Ray, which little piggy is this?"

"Pinkie-toe piggy the best!" Dragging Izzy into the center of the lobby by his shirt collar, heels squeaking over tile. "Pinkie-toe piggy ran all the way home!"

"You wouldn't!"

"I didn't." Mr. Waldo placing the box in Micah's hands.

"Listen, look." Micah fumbles for his wallet. "I have money. I can get the money."

"It's not lettuce interest me."

"What is it you want, then?"

"I want *in*. All my pencils are sharpened, my ice cubes are smooth, and I want *in*."

"I'm not certain I follow."

"I want you 'splain to me, Mr. Movie-Man, how it is you get from a couple cans of junkyard tin to people twenty, thirty feet tall up there on that silver screen?"

"The mechanics of projection are actually quite simple." Izzy's professional exuberance overtaking him. "The filmstrip passes through the—"

"You misunderstand me." Waving the science away like a lady with a fan in a balcony box. "It was a question of a more *rhetorical* nature. I got no quarrel with you personal, y'understand. No quarrel with the Moses people. Way I see it, niggers and the Moses people have lots in common, looking to find a way *in*. Wig men landed here, but niggers and the Moses people, we *made* this motherfucker."

"*Made it*, yessir!"

"And we making it still, here, right now. But what I don't understand is you got a mechanism reach *millions*. Millions people at a single go. And the best you come up with some crazy-ass cracker in a pair of glasses running 'round setting himself on fire, all other kinds of tomfoolery?"

"I think he's talking about Henry."

"Thanks, Itz."

"Seems you don't understand just what it is you *got*! Paul Robeson—a *giant*—has to run off to Limeyland to actualize himself, and here you is with actors slipping themselves over banana peels? Well, it occurred to Mr. Waldo, nobody never made a movie 'bout the story of the African continent, what all my little ancestors been through, slave times and sharecroppers, so forth and et cetera, up through to the present day. You follow?"

"I believe I'm beginning to."

"So I got to thinking. And El-Ray here, El-Ray's blessed with a touch of the poet, and we worked out a little scenario."

"That true, Bumpy?" Micah asks the fledgling screenwriter.

"Don't call me Bumpy," he says, releasing Izzy and handing the cameraman several neatly folded pages, upon the first of which is type-written:

O, AFRICA!

A Historical-Tragical Motion Picture
Scenario in Four Parts

by

Byron Marcus Waldo

&

Ellsworth Raymond Johnson

"O, Africa!," Izzy marvels, staring down at the cover page. "Good title. What's the story?"

"I trust you read that later and find out," Bumpy says with goodly authorial pride. "Let's just say a person can get a lot of reading done upstate. Learn oneself some history, locate oneself some politics."

"It's just funny about the title."

"That shit ain't funny." Bumpy shrugs. "There are no accidents, motherfucker. Little nigger associate of yours been running his mouth all over town about how the fat man's planning an expedition."

"Yes, it's true," says Izzy, surprising himself by committing to the idea. "We're considering going to Africa as soon as we finish our latest picture."

"No we're not." Micah grinding out an imaginary cigarette on his brother's shoe. "Listen, Mr. Waldo, Ellsworth, I appreciate what it is I think you're suggesting here, but you need to understand the reason I got into this business is because it beats working."

"No it ain't," Mr. Waldo says. "You better than that. Don't you understand? You got a *tool*! Sympathy, too. Why else you making time with that sweet princess up in Harlem? Early's sister?"

"Mr. Waldo connecting the dots!" Bumpy in gospel tones, punching his own head for emphasis. "Mr. Waldo is a man of wisdom!"

"I understand. Tired of white meat, go for the drumstick," Mr. Waldo says. "Stealing that sweet jelly from good ol' boys like El-Ray here."

"Where my *jelly*?" Bumpy hopping from foot to foot. "Where my jelly *at*?!"

"You mean Rose?" Micah says, his voice crossing its fingers. "I've got a dozen others like her. She doesn't mean anything to me."

"Red, Red, Red." Shaking his head back and forth, Mr. Waldo cups the filmmaker's cheek with a hand as hard and dry as tortoiseshell, a hand that eclipses half of Micah's face. "I spotted the two you together at the Honeypot. Lookit, sonny boy, I seen my share of fellas trolling round uptown, want to know what a black jelly bean taste like. But that ain't how you look at her. You're like a five-year-old running home with a Popsicle on a hundred-degree day. You want to lick her till she's gone, but you're protective, too. Nah, Red, you ain't dropping her so fast."

"Mr. Waldo," Bumpy says, "how about we pack Double-Dutch's wife and kids in the Model A, take them on a tour of his favorite haunts up in Niggerland?"

"I'd prefer it if you didn't do that."

"That's your preference, huh?" Mr. Waldo deadpans. "Well, that's worth more than thirteen thousand dollars. But like I said previous, this ain't about lettuce. Lemme ask you something, Ginger. You think it's an accident brought us together? You think it's an accident brought you to my card table? You think it's an accident brought that sorry-ass pipsqueak into my orbit talking about making movies in Africa? You think it's an accident my first job come to New York was flipping light switches for Hasids on Saturdays? You think it's an accident Lincoln named *Abraham*? Why you think the Moses people invented Hollywood? It's on account of Chooka, your crazy-Jew Festival of Lights. Moses people got knowledge about light!"

"Let there be *light*!" From the choir. "First order of business: Let there be light!"

"You a member the chosen people, Ginger. And you just been chosen for this motherfucker."

And then, incredibly, Mr. Waldo and his associate abandon the scene they've created in the lobby, stepping out into the midday scorch to begin strolling down the street on this fine Juneteenth day. They walk in their outrageous getups without shame, as if it were 125th and Lenox, tipping their hats to mink-stoled society ladies, dog walkers, hot-dog vendors, and Central Park kibitzers as they go. Micah looks at Izzy, who looks down at his brother's hand holding the gift box. The ribbon is pulled. The box opens. Inside, swathed in cotton, a tiny green Christmas light.

FOUR

Y ou rewrote it?" asks Micah, sitting on a stool, glossy strips of celluloid surrounding him and Izzy like salamis hanging from a delicatessen ceiling. Days had passed since their encounter with Mr. Waldo and Bumpy in the lobby. And, while it was a relief for the brothers to distract themselves with work, this wasn't the first time in their professional lives that the editing room came to feel like a bunker to which they could retreat from worry and adult responsibilities.

"A *light* editing job." Izzy holding a black strip up to a crook-armed architect's lamp, considering it, and discarding the frames in a nearby bin. "I just added some shot descriptions, technical cues, that sort of thing."

"The slave picture? Do they know you worked on it?"

"God no!" Threading film through the Moviola. "They're your associates, Micah. I wouldn't even know how to contact them."

"Listen, even if we were to try to make it, no one would see it. Remember a little picture called *Intolerance*? The one where Griffith thought it'd be a good idea to rebuild ancient Rome?"

"It was Babylon." Testy, facedown in the viewer. "And yes, I remember *Intolerance*. It's a mad film, but I love it."

"Right, and it finished him off! And y'know why? Because it was an *idea* picture. And people don't go to the movies for ideas, Izzy. You want to send a message, try Western Union." Micah points to an adjacent wall upon which are tacked three ancient telegrams that Marblestone had sent to the brothers soon after they'd signed on with

Imperial. The first of them reads, REMEMBER: IT'S SHOW BUSINESS. NOT SHOW FUCKING NICE.

A debt was hanging over him. Micah, who above all cherished freedom and flight, was weighed down by the prospect of having to make decisions not entirely of his own volition, afflicted by a terrible sense of the shuttering of possibilities. (He suspected that aging must be something like this: a persistent feeling of things closing off, of walls inching in.) Money. Career. Reputation. Family. Sex. The Future. These were the tarot cards he had for years enjoyed shuffling, teasing out how potentialities might be revealed through recombination and juxtaposition, only now to find the deck handled by others. Stationing himself in the tight cuboid of the editing room only amplified Micah's claustrophobia. Marblestone's money woes hanging over him, his mistress's inchoate demands pressing in on him, his dealings with Mr. Waldo hardly over, Micah forced himself to file each of these worries away for now, hunkered down, and turned his best professional attention to the editing of *Quicktime*.

Traditionally a five-month window existed between a film's production and its release, but Henry Till pictures had a tighter editing schedule. With his evangelical belief in honoring what audiences found funny, the performer had pioneered the practice of preview screenings. That meant Micah and Izzy needed to have a rough assembly of *Quicktime* ready in just six weeks in order to screen for a test group, weigh feedback, hold reshoots if necessary, and have the picture locked in time for prints to be struck and delivered for the October premiere.

They are editing one of the Coney Island sequences. Till and Mildred are relegated to the Thunderbolt's rickety last carriage. As the roller coaster traces its sine curve, Till is smacked in the face with a variety of objects from up front: a woman's stole, a half-eaten hot dog, a burning cigarette, and, finally, a man's toupee. The sequence had been a difficult one to shoot: five go-rounds on the coaster with Spiro facing the actors, operating a camera rig bolted backward to the next car, and abashed Billy Conklin seated beside him, tossing miscellany at the star's million-dollar face. Now came a fury of assemblage, judging the best takes from hundreds of feet of work print—alternating between long shots of the coaster, medium shots of the carriage, tight shots of Till, and reaction shots of Mildred—for maximum spatial coherences, velocity, and laughs.

"Well, it so happens the scenario they came up with is pretty good," Izzy volunteers. "Certainly not like anything we've worked on before."

"Even if I agree with you"—Micah offering Izzy an alternate take—"the third act degenerates into a crazy kind of revenge picture."

"A black exploitation film!" Izzy exclaims, verging on word coinage, discarding one take for excessive camera wobble, another on account of overexposed flash frames. He makes his selection and marks with a black grease pencil held between gloved fingers the start and end of the shot—sixteen uniformly spaced squares, just two-thirds of a second.

"But you're forgetting something," Micah says, crossing the words "Till, Hot Dog" from a shot list scribbled on a chalkboard. "No one will go to see it."

"I don't know. There might be interest in this kind of thing. Look at Gance, or Murnau, or Eisenstein, or Dreyer, or Oscar Micheaux."

"I do look at them. I look at those guys every chance I get. But we're not in the same league as they are. We're not even in the same industry as they are."

"Why not?" Izzy protests. "Why couldn't we be?"

Micah points to the wall upon which is pinned the second of Marblestone's yellowing imperatives—REMEMBER: THE PROPERTY MAKES THE ARTIST. THE ARTIST DOES NOT MAKE THE PROPERTY.

They are sitting on stools in front of a pair of upright Moviolas, huge industrial devices that look like oversize sewing machines. Indeed, there was something of the seamstress's art involved in film editing, its terminology reminiscent of needlework: threading, cutting, splicing, pieces hanging from pins over trim bins; women's work done with pencils and tape, glue and gloves, scissors and razor blades. For all its old-fashioned qualities, however, editing represented to Izzy the theoretical essence of cinema—the single aspect of moviemaking that could not be duplicated elsewhere.

Izzy was happy to relinquish control of the film shoots to Micah—with his nose for sniffing out and synthesizing the best of his collaborators' talents, his gift for sustaining a buzzing, partylike atmosphere on the set—and preferred the relative solitude of the editing room. It was here that the film returned to him, here where he could sift through shots like a frontiersman panning for gold, here where a procession of meaning could be welded together. Here where Izzy wielded the higher math.

And it was math: the work he performed pinned to the Moviola as theoretical in nature as it was commercial or artistic. Moreover, the grammar of film editing—the demands it exacted of viewers—was making its influence felt everywhere. Things were moving faster. Connections were becoming increasingly unspoken, subliminal. Izzy felt the impact of the new medium when tacking through the streets of Manhattan, pelleted by lighted signs and billboards, or flipping through the pages of one of the glossy new magazines, advertisements stacked atop one another like wooden blocks. He recognized cinema's imprimatur in the general daily sense one had that the thing you were engaged in doing could, at any moment, be supplanted by activities more vivid and enthralling. These crowding pressures left Izzy feeling lonely and uneasy, and he often questioned if the practice of his chosen medium was entirely healthy.

Izzy maintained a prayerful climate in the editing room because he knew he was mucking around with immutable forces. That here, working his temporal sorcery, he had entered deep into time's tickwise passage. That here time was made a liquid, fungible thing. Just twenty years before, Albert Einstein—a figure who, with his frizzy mop of hair and pool-eyed expressiveness, looked incidentally not unlike a comic film star—had worked out his theory of special relativity, and though Izzy would be hard-pressed to explain the mechanics of the idea, he knew that his own work existed on a continuum with the physicist's. The central conceit was the same. Perspective changes the object. Newtonian notions no longer apply. Distance and time are dependent upon the observer. Looking at something changes it.

"You talk to Arthur?" Izzy asks.

"No, I've been dodging his calls while he's here," Micah says. "But I spoke with Abernathy, and from the sounds of it, Marbles's story is legit. On the Ferris wheel, how bad did he say things are?"

"Bad," Izzy answers, pointing to the third and final of the mogul's proverbs—REMEMBER: PRODUCERS DO NOT PRODUCE BECAUSE THEY ARE PRODUCTIVE. PRODUCERS PRODUCE BECAUSE THEY KEEP PUTTING UP THE MONEY, THE FUCKING IDIOTS.

To a disquietingly audible trio of popped joints (back, knee, elbow), Micah lifts himself from his spot and begins pacing, thinking. "The Harlem goons aside and taking Marblestone's money problems out of it, what I can't figure is why you're so keen on this all of a sudden. You've always been a cautious fellow, Itz, and this has the makings of a very difficult trip. What gives?"

What Izzy couldn't explain to Micah—because his brother suffered from a surfeit of it—was that the answer was love. Or the opposite of love, which Izzy knew to be not hate but self-abnegation. He had decided that if there could not be love, at least let there be change, renewal, self-discovery, adventure, something, some wild blood transfusion to act as consolation. The prospect of being away from everything he knew—from New York and Los Angeles, from little editing rooms and fastidiously appointed bachelor apartments—in exchange for some alien, sun-blasted realm came as a great comfort to him. Since Marblestone had first mentioned it, after Izzy had gotten over the incident with Howard, he had thought of little else.

"It'd be different," Izzy downplays. "It'd be a new kind of picture for us. And you're forgetting—the Isidor Grand Savings and Loan is officially closed for business. You might not have any choice in the matter."

"What do we know about Africa? Besides, if we *do* go, it's got to be our decision, not because the fat man's about to lose his shirt or a gun's being pointed at our heads."

"They did threaten to do us harm."

"They suggested separating my son from his toes, Itz."

"Yes, they mentioned the removal of Benjamin's pinkie toe, it's true."

"And you'd let them do that to your beloved nephew before simply cutting me a check? What the hell goddamned kind of uncle are you, anyway?"

"I won't lend you the money because I'm tired of getting you out of scrapes, Micah. But also because they might have a point." Then, plaintively, "There's more we can be doing with all this. There are things I'd like to do."

"Things—what things? Don't forget what business we're in, Itz. It'd be worse than foolish to pretend otherwise—it'd be dishonest."

"And God forbid Micah Grand allow himself a moment's dishonesty!" Turning away, Izzy rewinds a split reel and sends through the viewer a shot of Till's face meeting a mustard-slathered hot dog. "C'mere, then." Indicating for his brother to approve the cut. "Good?"

"Good."

Micah returns to his stool. Izzy pulls the filmstrip off its three-inch core, locks the sprocket holes into the splicer, screws the strip securely into place, and prepares to make the perforation. Then the lapidary splice—a satisfying crinkly-elastic frisson as the miniature guillotine severs the magic thread. A second strip hanging from the bin is aligned with the first. Clear tape is laid across the dual frame line, and air bubbles are rubbed out with a gloved thumb. Then, pressing down on the device like a stapler, the splicer trims the excess tape off the frame edges while punching sprocket-hole perforations. Five feet of clear leader is tacked to the head of the sequence, "Till, Hot Dog" is scribbled in grease pencil, and the entirety is wound back onto the take-up reel.

"Then there's Margaret," Micah says, twisting his wedding ring around his finger.

"Margaret? You hardly ever mention her when making a decision."

"I know, but she's told me only recently she'd prefer I not go traipsing off so much."

"Or what?"

"Or nothing. Listen, Itz, appearances aside, I happen to like being married. It's a relief living with a woman without the pressures of sex."

Izzy, working fast, squeakily finishes rewinding the take-up reel and motions for Micah to look at the rough assembly. A lag in one of the cuts between one of Mildred's reaction shots—no more than a skip of a second—deflates a quantum of air from the topper with the toupee. Imperceptible to the layman's eye, it's nonetheless something an audience would register.

"Good?"

"Tighten that a hair," Micah says. "Otherwise, nice work."

"Have you heard from them since the lobby?" Izzy asks.

"Working on it. I'm not sure what to tell them yet."

"What about Arthur? You can't dodge him forever."

"Abernathy says he's got five or six months' time before the bank defaults on his loan. Says the fucking shyster's already been selling contracts for stock footage that doesn't exist."

"Y'know, were we to go abroad, it's not Arthur's financial troubles or Bumpy or Mr. Waldo that worries me."

"What then?"

"It's what none of them have considered," Izzy says, shaving a few frames from the end of the sequence like a chef slicing a clove of garlic. "Point a camera at something, you change it. It changes."

FIVE

Africa?" says Rose, lying naked on her side, the copper-penny smell of semen flowering fragrant in the room. "What do you know about Africa?"

Micah was uncertain how to explain to her that he was considering the trip. He spent the cab ride over trying to determine which might be more impressive: a show of seriousness or a cavalier absence of the stuff. In the event, he chooses to test the idea aloud in jaunty, lighthearted tones—*Arthur has this daft new proposal! Wouldn't it be wild if we actually went?*—and is surprised by the ferocity of her response. For a moment he sees himself as he fears she envisions him: one more in a long line of plunderers, a treasure seeker, a rogue trader, a safari hunter, only with a movie camera for a rifle. What did he know about Africa? What was Africa to him? A handful of Kipling stories. An undifferentiated jungle kingdom.

"Hey, what do they speak there anyway?"

"Christ, Micah, read a book!" The mound of her hip gyrating out of reach. "There are books *here*."

"I know," he exhales. "I know."

"I ran into Jake yesterday," she says about Jacob Dobie, the middle-aged barber who lives down the street, a figure whom Rose always invokes at the first signs of trouble. "He asked me to a dance at the community center next weekend."

"I think you should go," Micah says with practiced disinterest, scooping her backside into his middle and worming his way in while digging a hand into her glorious mass of hair, hair that was forever holding ticker-tape parades for itself.

"Caroline says he's about ready to ask me to marry him." Rising on him, falling. "What do you think of that, Mr. Man?"

"Sounds like you landed yourself a good one." Jostling for position, twisting, slipping, nearly snapping himself like a twig.

"He's successful, too, planning on opening another shop on 165th Street in the fall. Big, handsome man, too."

"You should do it. Were I your friend, that'd be my advice."

"You're not my friend?"

"No, I can promise you that. I will never be your friend."

I had a dream the other night," Micah says from the floor when it's over, straightening and releasing coils of chest hair with pincerlike fingers, satisfied as a pasha. "I was wearing my father's overcoat, this great big thing on me when I was a kid, and I draped it over the seat in front of me at a movie theater. And when the lights came up, a fellow in the next row started to put it on by mistake, and when I asked him to return it, he just took off running."

"So what happened?"

"I chased him for a while but couldn't catch him. Then I woke up."

"Well, show me someone who tells you his dream and I'll show you a liar."

"Maybe . . . Hey, I brought you something," he remembers, bringing up from beneath the bed a thin white box tied with a bow. He was abashed with the girl at the sales counter when he made the purchase—the expense of the gift a public proclamation of fidelity to his mistress. And he's equally tentative now—buttocks warming wooden boards, floor fluff adhering to the clammy soles of his feet—as she opens the package with childlike greed.

Gloves! She pulls one of the long black satin accessories up to her elbow, wriggling fingers into fitted sheaths. She duplicates the routine with the other, rises from the floor, and stands in the center of the room, naked barring the gloves, shimmery material marking off skin, nudity limned by boundaries, veiled fingers transformed into an immediate locus of eroticism. Then she begins pantomiming a series of activities for which she might have occasion to wear them: first accepting a gentleman's hand at a dance, then observing the stage of the Metropolitan through an imaginary pair of opera glasses, then allowing a waiter to show her to the best table in the house, then, setting herself on the corner of the bed, sampling this and that delicacy with a lobster fork, daintily attending with a napkin to the corner of her mouth. That these actions are performed as parody, informed by a knowledge of operas they would never attend, fancy restaurants they would not enjoy together, hotel rooms they would not be booked into as a couple, did little to diminish the pleasure Micah took in watching her. A lady should have a fine pair of gloves. Rose should have a fine pair of gloves. She belly-flops back onto the bed, setting musculature joyfully abounce.

His mother had worn gloves. As a boy how he had loved surveying her vanity table! How he loved slipping his hands into her gloves, because she had worn them, because a remnant of his mother's warmth lingered there, something feminine and delicate, crisp and warm, that he associated with the very best of her. What a pretty, elegant woman she had been! What horrors overtook her at the end. The white porcelain bowl full of bile by the bedside. Her stalklike arms and bruised yellow feet poking from the covers like rotting vegetation. Her eyes a pair of hard-boiled eggs peering out from skin pulled too tight like a sheet over a mattress. The most loved. The most, best loved. His parents, his own mother and father, gone ten years now, she from pancreatic cancer, he of coronary thrombosis, following shortly behind. This terrible visitation, this family catastrophe, occurring just as the twins turned eighteen, in the flower of masculine youth. No wonder magic, no wonder movies.

He sometimes questioned if he would have been a more serious man had his parents lived, if his father's example ultimately would have willed out. But once doubly orphaned, he felt freed from judgment, unmoored from seriousness, weightiness deemed the wrong kind of tribute. The scythe had swung too close, too soon, and now he felt forever on the run, dedicated to fleet-footedness, a man desirous of a life absent tragic possibilities. So, from woman to woman, picture to picture, gag to gag, never tempting the fates with a commitment to anything more substantive than pratfalls and tossed custard pies, this the surest strategy to slip the knot of adult responsibility. Would they be proud of him—of his professional regard and his boys and his material comfort—or find his life repellent? An oversize, overfed, overindulged boy taking daily delight in breaking God's commandments as casually as breathing, shacking up in the arms of a colored girl.

"Glad you like them," he says, realizing as soon as the gift is given that it's too much, too expensive, too tender, the entire apparatus of its giving and acceptance too close to the tragic thing.

"What would you like me to do with them?" she says when she's done with the pantomime.

"Play maid," he says. "I want you to get on your knees and scrub."

She looks at him squint. "You don't have to ruin it, Em. I make you feel good, you make me feel good—it doesn't have to be anything more than that."

"Don't worry, sis. It's not."

"Good, as long as we're clear on that."

She rolls over, away from him. The sun hides behind a patch of clouds, casting the brass-colored room in pearlescent shades of gray. He looks at his lover, stomach down on the bed, legs slightly apart, hair like a banquet spread after a good party, a befouled Manet draped in a sheet. Rising, he catches sight of his own naked self in the oblong mirror, slouching, baboonlike, youthful but no longer young, an overhang of waistline-inscribed belly flab, pointillist freckles stippled across his shoulders and chest. Hovering over the girl, who is this clownish figure of lust? What crazy line of continuity connects this man to the boy with a hand in his mother's glove? He would not stay here tonight and wonders for the first time if he'll return.

Jarring, tumbling noises rescue him from deeper introspection. From the next room comes crashing, glass and metal in poor negotiations with wooden floors, the sound of an excellent party or a lousy burglar. Earlier in the evening, Rose had told Micah about a series of robberies in the neighborhood, and a panicked exchange now passes between them. Suddenly feeling like a stranger here, in Harlem, he waits on her move. She removes from a bedside drawer a dark and heavy object and hands it to Micah, who has never before held a pistol.

"Where'd you get this?" he asks, surprised by the weapon's weight, heavier than a prop gun, the metal object as unlikely in his hand as a dentist's drill.

"Early left it."

Masculine prerogative dictates he's to be first through the door. In the early days of his career directing Capering Cops shorts, he had shown any number of bit players how best to hold a gun so it registers well on camera, but now Micah comes up flummoxed, one hand limply wrapping around the cold, mottled steel, the other struggling to maintain a knotted towel around his waist. He inflates his posture before opening the door.

"Put some clothes on," he tells her, "this will just be a minute." Propelling himself into the next room on waves of scrotum-tightening terror, he spots in the corner nearest the kitchen a hulking figure, kneeling down, broad back bent over milk crates.

"Up," Micah says softly, then with more conviction, "Up! With your hands! Up!"

"Relax, Em, it's me," answers Rose's brother. "Why is it every time I find you here, you're walking round the place without any clothes?"

As adrenaline drains from him, Micah physically compresses like a bicycle tire leaking air. "You're young, you'll understand these things someday."

A switch is flipped, and light lassos across the room. Refracted through thick old bottles, infusions of green- and yellow-tinged liquids cast kaleidoscopic patterns over the wall. Early, dressed in a bright purple suit and a matching fedora, looking suddenly older, taller, more fluent in the lexicon of violence.

"What's that you're wearing?" asks Rose, framed in the bedroom doorway, still gloved, a sheet wrapped around her body.

"Work clothes." Fanning out his suit jacket like a torero.

Micah nods at the bottles and their tacky, rising turpentine smell. "That's moonshine."

"That's pretty observant of you, Mr. Grand."

"So you're working for Mr. Waldo now?"

"Not *for*, Mr. Grand." Self-satisfied, removing his jacket to reveal, underneath, a pair of matching purple suspenders. *"With."*

"Listen, Early." Micah sighs. "I know those characters. You don't want to get involved with that kind."

"Oh, please, them niggers are harmless. Showed me their idea for the Africa picture, too. You gonna make the movie with them, Mr. Grand?"

"What, now you're in business with bootleggers?" Rose demands. "It's not good enough you're ruining me, you going to lead my brother down the same path?"

"That's not what I'm doing." Back to Early: "Jesus Christ, Early, I'm not in business with these hoodlums."

"Whatever mischief you're mixed up in," Rose says to her brother, pulling one of the milk crates across the scarred wooden floor toward the door, "you will *not* bring this into my house!"

"Hey, y'know I love you, sis." Pulling his suspenders out away from himself, and *snap!* "But you're not my mama."

"No, you're right, our mother's busy spinning in her grave watching you strut around like a peacock. I'm just your sister, sitting by watching you become a common hooligan."

Doors are slammed, Rose retreats to the bedroom, Early to the corner of the kitchen, leaving the shirtless wunderkind sidelined in the midst of a family feud. He looks at the boy half admiringly, confident his life is hurtling toward some terrible statistical fate. Early smiles, and Micah can't help but offer one in return, the two of them momentarily united against female outrage.

Micah enters the bedroom. In the harsh light of a sixty-watt bulb, the dreamed-of utopia is revealed in all its poverty and dinginess. Spidery stains cover the ceiling, and mouse holes burrow into the molding. There are exposed pipes and decades-old water damage, the walls bubbling and cracked from a succession of poor paint jobs over peeling layers. Dressed now in a ratty robe, she turns on him.

"Your boss still hasn't paid me," she says. Indeed, in the editing room earlier in the week, the brothers had received a telegram from Marblestone, the mogul's gift for self-dramatization rising and falling with each day's Dow: BALLS BEING SQUEEZED. LATEST PICTURE A FLOP. DEBTORS PRISON AWAITS. MAKE QUICKTIME A GOOD ONE.

"I'm still owed for the final week of shooting," she says, peeling the gloves off and discarding them like waxed paper off a roast. "Did you know I'm planning a rent party this Saturday? That the landlord's threatening to evict me?"

"It's as bad as that?"

"We had a good time together, you and I—what'd you want to know from that? What interest do you really have in my life when you're not around?"

Noting the verb tense she chose to deploy, Micah crosses the room toward the closet, opens the door, reaches into his jacket pocket, and removes his money clip. She sits scowling on the edge of the bed, holding her hand out, hating him, hating herself.

"What does he owe you? Thirty?"

"Fifty."

"Fifty, huh? Marblestone must be feeling generous these days."

"Yes, that's right."

"Okay, doll, fifty it is." He nods and begins peeling off the bills, placing them in her palm one by one for emphasis. The money, like the gloves, another prop that reinforces the dualism of the affair: a real experience, one with wounding emotional stakes, that also is a performance of itself, a piece of theater in which one is forced to play a predetermined role, the lovers buckling inside their costumes even as they recognize the refracted nature of their situation.

"Micah," she says, folding her hand over the bills once he's finished dispensing them, "I need something from you."

"Name it."

"If you go," meaning not just across the ocean but the greater distance, forever from this room, "promise you'll bring back something good."

Nice of you to put on a shirt," Early says, covering his surprise to find Micah joining him in his private sanctuary on the top of the building, rooftops and gutters being the youth's preferred settings.

"It's cold out," Micah says, tapping a pack of cigarettes, passing one to Early, and inhaling through his own a skyline different from the one to which he'd grown accustomed, the cityscape looking from this perspective more than ever like the contents of a woman's jewelry box—distant, fragile, irresolute. "How well do you know Bumpy and Mr. Waldo?"

"Mr. W I know since I'm little," Early says, lifting his legs off the tar, pulling them into himself, and beginning to rock back and forth. "He's like Santa Claus to a lot of kids around here. Holds block parties every summer, gives out turkeys to families on Thanksgiving, looks after a couple of widows in the neighborhood, that sort of thing. Bumpy I'm just starting to get to know. Spent a lot of time in and out of the pen. Taught some of the younger boys how to read, though. Passes books along to us sometimes. Poems, Shakespeare's sonnets, and whatnot."

"So one's a philanthropist, the other's an English professor? I only know them through cards."

"Well, people can be a lot of different things. You know that."

"Yeah, that's true."

"They're serious about the movie business, Mr. Grand. And these aren't patient men. Thirteen thousand dollars isn't nothing to these guys. Last month I seen Mr. Waldo slit a guy open like a fish over a seventy-dollar mistake he made on a ledger. He was white, too. A union man."

"When are you seeing them next?"

"Bumpy I have a delivery with in Hoboken tomorrow night."

"Can I trust you to relay a message?"

"Yup."

"Tell him he wrote a good script," Micah says, rising, brushing gravel off the seat of his pants. "Tell him I need time."

SIX

Poles of light drop lines into the sky. Micah, in tails, as slick and well tuned as a piano keyboard; Izzy, if not quite as roguish-looking as his brother, feeling measurably improved in black tie, monochromatic requirements having relieved him of sartorial responsibility. Movie one-sheets—images of Till atop the Thunderbolt in Coney Island, arms waving overhead, Babe Ruth in miniature standing below on the ground, hot dog in hand—are everywhere. The posters are cased in light boxes and propped on easel stands, fluttering from flagpoles and bannered across the theater entrance, an Asian temple dropped into the middle of Hollywood Boulevard. It is the premiere of *Quicktime*.

"No invite for me, Ginger?" a familiar growl asks Micah as an arm locks with his and reels him in, forcing him into close physical proximity. Mr. Waldo's face is puffy and matte, the result of four days' car travel—all dirt roads and back streets, beef jerky and poor whiskey, splinters of sleep snatched in the front seat and, just this morning, a lousy shave in a colored-owned service-station restroom, all cold water and razor pull. "No seat at the table for Mr. Waldo?"

"Good Christ, man, what are you doing here?"

"We given you plenty of time—two months to finish your picture, get your house in order, and set up the next one—so don't hand me the high hat."

"No, I'm just surprised to see you here, that's all."

"We're business partners, Mr. Grand. Come to support my business partner."

"You came all the way out here for that?"

"I'm a serious man, Mr. Grand."

"Yes, you've impressed that upon me." The naked California sunshine animates something boyish and resplendent in Mr. Waldo. The citrus spray brushes away the gangster's cobwebby obscurity and reveals new details: a fishhook scar stamped across the meat of his nose, a lotionlike thickness coating his tongue and the corners of his mouth, dry palms that look made of liquid silver with chalky scratch marks tic-tac-toe-ing his hands on the other side. He is wearing an ill-fitting bohemian-shabby brown suit, and the slant of his shoulders suggests he's preparing to go charging into windmills.

"I come here today with a business proposal," Mr. Waldo says, pressing into Micah's hand a paper napkin from the Paradise Club. Over a garish cartoon of swaying palm trees, whorling seashells, and tropical shores is scribbled in child's penmanship an IOU concerning his proposed stake in the Grand brothers' upcoming slave epic.

"Twenty percent?" Micah asks, halting the pair's progress.

"Figure five percent to relieve your debt, five percent interest, the other half for providing the inspiration for your next picture." Dusting lint from the filmmaker's shoulders like a Pullman porter.

"Keep it." Handing the napkin back to him. "It'd never hold up in court."

"Fair enough. Anyway, friends best not let paperwork gum up the works." Tucking the slip back into his handkerchief pocket. "You here alone tonight?"

"My wife's back home looking after the boys."

"And your cocoa lady friend?"

"We're through, but thanks for asking."

"Woman spins your dreidel, you shouldn't set her down," he says as they stroll along the red carpet arm in arm, Mr. Waldo answering people's gaze with a lifted regal chin.

"What about you?" Micah asks. "You bring your attack dog?"

"Bumpy? You needn't worry about him. He's a good boy, he'll do as I tell him. . . . So when are we making our script?"

"My brother's done some work on it."

"We're new to the scriptwriting game. I'm grateful for any piano tuning."

"Izzy's very fond of your pages, it's got to be said."

"But you're the decider, Red. What's your feeling on it?"

He looks at the man, reflecting on his sentimental weakness for members of the criminal element and his certainty that Mr. Waldo is made of finer, nobler stuff than himself. If he had this man's discipline and calm, he'd be a king. "It's good."

"Thirteen thousand plus interest good?"

Micah looks at the man. He has weary eyes that have seen too much and lived too much and signal five or six things at once. In another life the man might have been mayor of a city, or a captain of industry, or the dean of a midsize southern college.

"Yeah," Micah says. "It's thirteen thousand dollars plus interest good."

"Then we in the picture business together," he says, the weary face beatific. Mr. Waldo takes Micah's right hand, places it in his own eagle's claw, turns it faceup, and traces with a crooked index finger the deep "7" that's printed there. Marking their shared fate, he then spits in Micah's palm, leaving the two of them to stare at the warm, bubbling gob. "Because, understand, this ain't no bank, sonny boy. No credit's offered in this motherfucker."

Deep in the crowd, Marblestone marks Micah being accosted. Dressed in a tuxedo that looks stitched together from a couple of tarpaulins, Marblestone abandons his brood—a football-team bench's worth of wives, sons, daughters, half cousins, in-laws, tenant farmers, and forgotten serfs—and begins making a terrifying beeline for the black man.

"Byron Marcus Waldo, what brings you out west?!"

"Little Artie Marbles, I haven't seen you since you packed up the last of them nickelodeons up in Harlem. How you doing, baby?"

"Never better. Figures you'd know the golden boy."

"Yes, sir." Beaming with validation. "Mr. Grand here's my newest business associate."

"Can you get over this?" Marblestone asks, gesturing toward the assemblage. "Not bad for a little *pischer* hymie off the boat."

"Like I explained to Mr. Grand here"—Mr. Waldo radiant in the California bloom—"bringing light to the infidels, that's what pictures do."

"So you got tickets to this smoke-and-mirrors show?"

"Y'know, I just misplaced them," Mr. Waldo says, giving himself a comic patting-down.

"Come." Marblestone exhales, bullying the three of them through the crowd, past the press line to the theater entrance, where an usher barely out of his teens, still rooting acne from his chin, stands taking tickets. "We need two good seats for my guests."

"All the floor seats are reserved, sir." Swallowing hard, eclipsed in the shadow of the mogul's galactic bulk. "But there are still some seats left in the balcony."

"Listen, applesauce, do you know who you're talking to here? Arthur Marblestone, whom no less of an authority than *Moving Picture World* referred to as, quote, 'One of the great pioneers and entrepreneurs of the motion-picture industry!' end quote."

"No coloreds allowed on the floor, sir," the usher says softly to Micah, taking him for a sympathetic audience. "Theater policy's balcony only. Premiere nights especially."

"Mr. Waldo is not complaining." The peer of the realm lifting his hand in dismissal, a relaxed gesture that informs everyone that he has heard and absorbed all pertinent information and will now be moving on to more important matters. "Mr. Waldo is *delighted*."

"Very good, sirs." The usher nods, handing Mr. Waldo a pair of tickets for the upper reaches of the auditorium. "Two for nigger heaven!"

Izzy navigates his way toward the theater entrance, stopping to remove a blotch of gum from the underside of his shoe.

"Boychick," Marblestone grumbles, back in the sunshiny thick of it, having situated Mr. Waldo in the cheap seats, out of breath and leaning against an ancient stone temple dog, "there's a business associate I'd like you to meet. He's responsible for the kliegs, red carpet, security, the whole schmear."

Marblestone's man is a small, mischievous-looking character, shorter than Izzy, with shifting doll's eyes wide set in a waxworks face, and oiled, centrifugally parted hair. His affectless expression blurs into fixity like a constellation viewed through a scope as he hands Izzy an embossed business card that reads:

SIDNEY BLOAT
Dealer, Red Carpets, Fine Antiquities

"And might you know the origins of the red carpet?" Bloat asks in an indeterminate European accent, his open mouth revealing gums that have encroached too far up the shoreline and a set of nubby, uniformly level teeth, the result of too much midnight grinding. *"Der rote Teppich?"*

"I remember hearing about this somewhere." Izzy, always eager to demonstrate any nugget of knowledge that exists outside the picture industry. "Something about the railroads using them to direct people aboard, right?"

"Correct. But before its popular American usage, prior to the glamorous and fabulous red-carpet treatment, *rote Teppich Behandlung*?"

"Uh, no."

"Well, you see, the red carpet was originally implemented as a *weapon*; rolling out the red carpet was a *battle cry*, the red-carpet *treatment* a signal for certain death from above."

"Really?"

"Yes, because bundled inside said carpet, trundled inside said tapestry, *rolled* inside said rug, was a coterie of mercenaries, marksmen, private armies, jubilant assassins, soldiers of fortune, anarchist bomb throwers, a band of evil angels, and a collection of the worst, most rotten scoundrels the eighteenth century had on offer. The carpet was bad, bad, bad. And it was red."

"Huh."

"Hence the sanguine coloration."

"Right."

"And this"—opening arms wide to take in the red sea of rug—"this carpet which you walk over tonight so casually, which you traipse across with such impunity, is not just *any* red carpet but the world's *largest* red carpet, over three miles long unfurled, witness to coups, revolts, successions, surprise attacks, and, most recently, the failed Beer Hall Putsch. This carpet, which your entertainment dignitaries traverse ever so gingerly, this carpet that you take such delight in *stepping* on, upon which you stub your American tobacco and imprint your Wrigley chewing gum with abstract Kandinsky decadence, has been dipped in the waters of a thousand years of Teutonic history, drenched in the blood of German brotherhood, borne across the backs of Bavarian peasantry, all to reach you here, tonight, to be unfurled for your *Quicktime* motion-picture festivities."

"Well, Arthur always goes all out for premieres."

"This is what we in Germany refer to as *fancy-schmancy*!"

"Indeed."

"So Mr. Marblestone has mentioned to me plans of a potential Dark Continent adventure."

"Nothing's been finalized yet."

"Given the primitive moral character of our dusky friends, one suspects the opportunity might present itself to make a wide *variety* of films. Perhaps you are familiar with the periodical *National Geographic*, the periodical that exists for the promotion of terrestrial knowledge?"

"Sure."

"And have you never wondered what accounts for said publication's popularity?"

"The exoticism?" Sign-languaging a guess with shrugged shoulders.

"Oh, the American people are an innocent people! I look forward to seeing you aboard the steamship."

Inside, Micah has just thanked the cast and crew, read aloud a short telegram from Babe Ruth—who has just finished a World Series sweep and is enjoying a hero's tour of the country—and introduces the picture's star. Till rises from his seat to accept the rapturous sonic wave with no intention of wading in until an audience member shouts, "Say something, Henry!"

Micah nods across the auditorium to the puzzled actor, who, after a moment's hesitation, negotiates his row, hops down the aisle, and joins the director at the front of the theater before the heavy velvet curtain.

"Talk, Till!" shouts another fan.

"Just thank them for coming, Henry," Micah whispers through clenched dentistry. "No one's expecting Oscar Wilde."

"Well, I just want to thank everyone for being here tonight," Till manages, finding a comfortable register that fills the front third of the auditorium. "We're all very proud of this picture and hope you enjoy it, too."

A murmur wends its way through the crowd. Till's voice, while perhaps not as helium-high and ebullient as one might hope from his film appearances, nonetheless has a pleasant, oaky, midwestern resonance. Faces in the audience tilt toward Louella Parsons, Hearst's horse-faced syndicated gossip columnist, who sits in an overhanging balcony box. She stares toward the front of the auditorium, holding her pen aloft like a monarch determining whether or not to sign some royal decree, nods her approbation, and returns to her little spiral reporter's notebook.

"Nice speech, Cicero!" comes a cry from the back of the theater as the lights go down and Henry's name comes up in the credits.

"We're finished," Marblestone whispers once Micah is planted in the seat next to him. "Do you know that sitting in this auditorium tonight are parties to whom I owe more than four hundred thousand dollars?"

"Jesus."

"And those are only bankers. . . . I've not had my kneecaps broken in twenty years."

"Let's just try to enjoy the night, Arthur."

But it was impossible. While most of the movies released that year were still silent, the three top-grossing pictures of 1928 were all sound films. Most woeful to Marblestone was *Steamboat Willie*, an eight-minute short starring an indomitable cartoon rodent created by Walt Disney that had caused a sensation. "Lemme get this straight," Marblestone had thundered, slapping a copy of *Variety* on his desk after examining the weekend grosses, proceeding in a rage to rip his own shirt from his back, "we're about to get run out of business by a fucking whistling rat?!"

The curtains part like a striptease. On the screen, written in silvery light, the opening sequence of *Quicktime:* a race between Till attempting to put a horseshoe on his pony versus an auto mechanic across the way changing a set of tires. It is delightful. It is technically brilliant. And it is antiquated, Till a commedia dell'arte figure from an already receding past. The work is in opposition to the momentum of its time; there are gales of laughter, to be sure, but they do not arrive in the thunderclaps that might have greeted these antics six months ago, or even three.

"You hear that?" Marblestone moans into the quietude. "That's the sound of the icicles scraping the deck of the *Titanic*. We're sunk."

"Quit it, Arthur, they're enjoying it," Micah says, surprised at how well he can register his own murmured voice through patchy schools of laughter.

"My hands," Marblestone says, looking at his thick, callused fingers and cracked palms. "I ever tell you how my father used to lift pickle barrels for a living? In the snow he'd do it. How my heart would twist like a bagel watching him lift those heavy barrels with his frozen hands. Frozen, frostbitten hands!"

"Well, lucky for us, moviemakers work with our feet."

"If this picture fails, it's back to digging ditches for me, boyo."

"Is it really that bad?"

"Worse."

Christened in the blue-velvet dreamsong, Marblestone looks like a statue left outside on estate grounds on a cool night, something antique and forgotten that the world has passed by. Time. Work. Money. Family. Arthur. Waldo. Izzy. Rose. These the cards Micah wants to handle, the deck he wants returned to him.

"Arthur." Holding the man's sausage-link fingers in the dark. "We'll do it."

"Do what? Be clear. Say what you mean."

"Africa." Unable to renege now that the magic word has been unloosed. "God help us, send us to the jungle. We'll shoot your goddamned scenery."

Through inkwell blackness Micah can make out the contours of Marblestone's jigsaw-puzzle face, radiant with tears. "You're a good boy, Micah," the mogul says. "You're a good boy."

PART II

THE NEW WORLD

1

PAPERS AND PERSUASION

Sitting in the outer vestibule, Izzy and Micah recall similar situations from twenty years earlier; scenes outside the principal's or rabbi's office and the almost sensual prolongation that came with awaiting official rebuke for some mischief Micah had plotted and Izzy had helped perpetrate (chalk, stolen; spitballs, launched; crib sheets, concealed). An enemy of authority anywhere, Micah impersonates a swimmer trying to prevent himself from drowning, his body language that of a man trying to wrest himself free from this bureaucratic imposition. He taps his shoes, he cracks his knuckles, he hoists himself in his seat and collapses, and he buttons and unbuttons his jacket. Contributing to the illusion that they are back in elementary school are a couple of truants seated beside the Grand brothers: a middle-aged mother and her adult son—an overgrown simpleton of a man, a Harry Langdon figure in baby's bib and overalls—who are discussing their own upcoming African adventure.

Izzy and Micah's London visit so far had been an enameled affair, rich in food and drink, ritual, and attention. (Though the Great War had ended years before, the Brits they encountered still showed some excitement about being in the company of Americans, especially a pair of Yanks who'd been dunked in fame's poisoned well.) The brothers had been assured by Marblestone's European fixer, Sidney Bloat, that obtaining the permits necessary to undertake the film project in the British protectorate was strictly a formality. And "formality" was the right word for it. Even this entrance hall has a weighted, forbidding complexity, Britishly ornate with stiff Chippendale chairs, giant gemstone globes, cracked maps, and a ceiling fan registering drowsy dismissal over everything.

"Forgive the interruption," Micah says, turning up the full blast of his charm like a radiator in winter. "But did I overhear correctly that you'll soon be visiting *Africa?*"

The woman purses her lips like she's accidentally bit down on a wedge of lemon, her powdered face belonging to a woman of fifty, or seventy.

"Yes, dear boy," she says, in an accent exactly as Micah hoped she would have. "Safari. Kenya, for starters, in celebration of Martin's thirtieth birthday." Here she grips the baby boy's knee with something approaching violence, sending a fool's grin sailing across his broad white face.

"Have you been before?" Micah asks.

"Oh, just the nice bits, before Martin was born."

"Bunny!" Martin drools. "Bunny!"

"Quite a rigorous trip, must be," Micah says. "Why, if I might ask, do you wish to make a return?"

"Well, Martin has always dreamed of the wildlife, you see—elephants and rhinoceros and cheetah and the like."

"Bunny!"

"Yes, dear, I'm sure there will be bunnies," she says, then turns back to the filmmaker. "But that's not the real reason for undertaking such a journey, is it?"

"No?"

"No." Micah now puts her age nearer to seventy, the cords of her neck a disaster, the pancake makeup creasing like cellophane as she talks. "The only thing you need to know about the place, the only real reason to make such a visit, is this: Africa contributes nothing. And, at a certain point, nothing comes as quite such a relief to those of us cursed with too much civilization."

"Huh," Izzy says, lifting his head up from the floor's herringbone pattern.

"Africa, Egypt, ancient ruins, these places don't truly exist," the woman explains through a mouth that is pink, open, and benign. "Europe and America are everything now, the war saw to that. The rest are appointments on the map, in-between spaces with which to amuse ourselves. But never mind my theorizing, you'll absolutely *adore* Africa. If the Italians are like dogs, and the French are like cats, Africans are, well, Africans are *birds*."

"And Americans?" Micah asks.

"Bunny!" Martin exclaims, pointing at the twins.

"Yes, Martin, bunny. Very good, indeed."

Micah had been to England before—for an international premiere or two, and to schmooze with European distributors while keeping Marblestone's volcanic anger in check—but his brother hadn't. Jittery from the sleeper flight, a twelve-hour passage that made a mockery of the months-long crossings endured by his forebears, Izzy was vibrantly alert to the differences in color and light, clothes and food.

"Toughen up, will you?" Micah admonished on the ride into town, sensing his brother's discomfort over London's fog and rain-slicked streets, its prismatic spectrum of accents and impenetrable social cues. "You mustn't allow yourself to be cowed by these people." On the streets the homes and buildings looked thicker, more substantial, made of older, darker, more history-rich stuff, red telephone boxes the disapproving parents of squat American fire hydrants. There was the clumping of heavy shoes down cobblestone; there were weird hunchbacks and perfumed ladies with huge, crooked teeth; there were children with mature, wizened faces; there were frail coatrack men and squat dumpling women; and nowhere was a Negro to be seen. As Izzy and Micah made their way that morning from the Mayfair to the embassy, the sight of a lone man walking a gray whippet down a darkened street appeared as an emblem of the spirit of duty and sadness of the entire nation.

Izzy had never before given much thought to being American. The extraordinary set of circumstances of his having been born Isidor Saul

Grand, in Brooklyn, New York, in the millennial year 1900, as opposed to someone else, somewhere else, in some other time, had always been self-evident, something to be taken for granted as unthinkingly as eating, breathing, or sleeping. But here in London, the apprehension that he was the thing he couldn't help being—*American!*—was on a par with the birth of self-consciousness, the great and terrible shift that occurs when a child's thoughts go from "Look at that" to "*I'm* looking at that." This encounter with gentlest England, coupled with the looming prospect of the African trip, had transformed the is-ness and such-ness of his very Izzy-ness into a *thing*, a position he could embrace or from which he could retreat. To overcompensate for these unsettling discoveries, Izzy overate.

ᴮritain does not have an indigenous film industry," begins J. P. Keneally once the brothers are ensconced in the bureaucrat's office. "But what do we have in its place? History!"

A man who delighted in the scent of his own freshly starched uniform, a crisp set of stamps, and perfectly proportioned scotch and sodas served at four o'clock, Keneally most enjoyed making sport of requests from visiting foreigners. "What does a culture that gave the world Chaucer and Shakespeare and Dickens need from vulgar merchants making pictures for people whose lips move when they read?"

"I'm on the side of the lip-readers myself," says Micah. "Lets you know they're following along."

"Fair enough, but have you noticed a funny thing about your Mr. Marblestone and all your other refugee motion-picture executives? Whenever one encounters them, they carry the most curious *smell*."

"Really," Micah says, noting the way the man keeps the ends of his mustache trim and sharp, like a tiny pair of axes. "Of what, might I ask?"

"Oh, I don't know, of garlic, of onions, of street vendors and the open-air markets. Smells not dissimilar to those one encounters here in our Hampstead and Highgate sections of London. You've really never noticed it?"

"Can't say I have."

Izzy, always alert to scent, his own and others', lowers his chin by degrees to test his musky armpits.

"Nae bother, nae bother," Keneally says, dismissing the remark with a chalkboard wipe of the hand. "If you'll excuse me a moment, gentlemen, I'll gather your paperwork and we'll have you on your way."

Izzy's eyes follow the official out of the room, alighting behind the man's desk onto a framed map of Africa, a continent that in its contours resembles a giant bent knee. Bright swaths of color are applied across the terrain haphazardly, as in a child's finger painting, each cheerful splotch standing in for stories of domination, vast human machineries of rubber, diamond, tobacco, and sugarcane industries. Red. Blue. Green. Yellow. Purple. A rainbow-bright, happy abstraction, the map appears to Izzy an instrument of purest black magic. A portent designed to obscure its own meaning, the map is wholly incapable of telling its own story.

"Micah," Izzy asks, "did you find that at all funny, what he said about Marblestone?"

"He's right." Micah fiddles. "The guy sweats pot-roast gravy."

"I don't know. I think he's talking about us."

"Don't let their kooky manners get to you. What he said about Arthur is because he's vulgar, not because he's a kike."

"If you say so. But I'd rather not stay longer than necessary."

Keneally reenters with a stack of papers, trailed by a manservant carrying a tray congested with an unappetizing assortment of brown-and-white food. There are studded scones and shortbread cookies, a bowl of clotted cream and a jar of dark jam, crust-free finger sandwiches of sliced cucumber and smoked salmon, and, in the center, a whole peeled orange shot through with skewers upon which are impaled cheddar-cheese cubes, pineapple chunks, and wrinkled gray cocktail onions.

"Oh, spiffing!" Izzy says, deploying his favorite new expression and greedily grabbing a couple of sarnies.

"Curious proposal," says the officer, "making a picture in Africa."

"Well, so far as we know, it's not been attempted before."

"Not a sterling area, where you're heading. Rougher terrain the deeper you go toward the center. If my coordinates are correct, Malwiki is situated in the westernmost region of the border between Uganda and the Congo. One doubts the wogs even know they live under British rule."

"More dramatic wildlife, as I understand," Micah says. "And Sidney promises us good guides once we get there."

"And it goes without saying the natives are godless bloody buggers. You're aware, too," Keneally says, riffling through the pages, making a notation here, striking a proviso there, "that without the consent of the British government it's illegal to bring equipment, foodstuff, and arms in or out of the country?"

"Well, as we say back home," the officer's procedural opposition awakening the Huck Finn in Micah, "'no tickee, no washee.'"

"Now, let's just try one of these," Izzy says, attempting to dislodge a cheese cube from the hors d'oeuvre centerpiece and instead lifting the entirety off the tray by a single skewer. It snaps, sending the orange rolling over the fading Oriental and nibbles hopping across the floor like jumping jacks.

"Scone?" Keneally asks, ignoring Izzy's faux pas and nudging the tray of pallid food closer to Micah.

"No thanks," he says, removing from his jacket pocket a pack of Wrigley's and unwrapping with maximum aluminum-foil orchestration a piece of gum, which he begins to chew. With his entire head.

"Never cared for scones myself," Keneally says, shuffling the brothers' papers. "Too redolent of Communion wafers. Rum idea, eating a bit of corpse. Must be why our missionaries have such success with cannibals. Speaking of which: Africa! I was stationed in Cairo during the war. Had a *marvelous* time. A holiday, really. Most days I'd visit the markets around midday and enjoy a kebab. Return to the embassy and move some papers from here to there. Putter around until teatime. A game of snooker. Just before sundown I'd visit the brothels for a bit of the ol' how's-your-father? Bloody *marvelous* workers, they. Straight for the mutton! G&T at five. Then an excellent dinner. Usually fresh fish of some kind. Two or three fingers of brandy. Massive bowel movement.

For three years this was my life. But, of course, that was during the war, days of glory before Britain was brought low."

"But you won the war," goads the American gum chewer.

"Mr. Grand, the beloved England of my youth is under assault. There are cabals at work in the highest places—and your émigré motion-picture producers only accelerate the conspiracy's monopoly."

"Well, perhaps you wouldn't speak so freely," Izzy says, "if you knew who we are."

"I know perfectly well who you are: You're the Grand brothers from America."

"Originally Grombotz, not Grand," Izzy says softly, blooming under the man's gaze. "We're Jews, Mr. Keneally. Just like Mendelssohn was a Jew, and Mercadante was a Jew, and Spinoza was a Jew, and Prime Minister Disraeli was a Jew, too."

There follows a pause the approximate volume and duration of a drawbridge folding hands.

"Well, of course you are," says Keneally in that tinny British voice that instantly marks irrelevant any social miscue. "Understand, I have nothing against the Jewish race as a *people*. Just Lord Balfour and the Zionists, the ones who make such a bloody great fuss of things, you see."

"That's swell," Micah says, reaching beneath his shirt collar to withdraw a gold chain from which hangs a six-pointed gold Star of David. "Now, be a good soldier and stamp our papers, will you?"

Keneally removes a creaky ancient mechanism from a desk drawer. "Yes, I'll happily approve your permits. Besides—"

STAMP!

"—one's personal opinions on these matters are hardly important."

STAMP!

"One's role is merely to shift one stash of papers from here—"

STAMP! "—to there." *STAMP!*

"Very well, gentlemen!" Rising, saluting. "All of your documents are now in order. Enjoy your African excursion. And remember, as our forebears had it: Britannia rules the waves."

"Well, we're just a couple of kikes from Brooklyn." Micah, removing from his mouth and pressing the well-chewed wad of gum to the under-side of the man's desk. "So we're going to waive the rules."

While in London, Micah paid a visit to Benny Castor, a former col-league who in a previous life had been one of the best script men in Hollywood, as well as one of the town's leading alcoholics. With his engineer's command over the wheels and cogs of story logic, his survey-or's sense of plumb line, and his stenographer's ear for dialogue, Benny had all the tools in the script maker's cabinet. But he'd walked away from it. After the death of his father, Benny discovered that the family fortune (northwest, lumber) amounted to a few defunct mills, a failing paper-pulping plant, and a thicket of debt. Having existed until then in a booze-embalmed state of suspended boyhood, Benny, just shy of forty, took up the sadness and compromises of middle age like a new religion. Making a life project of absorbing the family scandal, he fashioned for himself a posture of noble self-defeat, quit the business, and settled just outside the British capital with his English wife, Gertrude, a woman of a temperament as mild as her peaches-and-cream complexion, and adopted a boy named Cecil. His face fell. His hair thinned. His waist thickened. He misplaced his laugh. Benny was not fun.

In the years leading up to that disavowal, however, there had been wild times: horse racing at Saratoga Springs, fully clothed leaps into outdoor swimming pools, sleeping with friends' wives in a kind of never-ending game of sexual musical chairs. And drinking, drinking, drinking—always drinking, or thinking about drinking, or planning the next drink, or recovering from the last drink—the entire appara-tus of moviemaking inseparable from a kind of alcohol-hazed masculine pounding, a knockabout adolescent rambunctiousness that very much found its way into the physical exuberance and punishment of slapstick.

It had been five years since Micah and Castor worked together on a picture, five years, really, since Micah had corresponded with Castor in a manner more significant than office-sent Christmas cards. And it was half on a whim, half as a means of testing his own precarious better nature, that Micah called upon his former colleague now.

"You're looking healthy around the middle," Micah's host said once they were situated in wicker chairs in the garden. Castor was wearing professorly tweeds and Wellington boots; bifocals hung around his chest by a chain, and a sand-colored walking stick leaned against his seat. The entire prematurely aged country-gent ensemble made Micah's palms itch. This was the man who had held Micah's prick for him when, woefully behind schedule on *Knock on Wood* and suffering through a prodigious bout of gonorrhea, the wunderkind director needed to be propped up in the men's room in order to pass a few scalding drops of urine.

"I've got a proposition for you." Surveying his friend's face for burst veins, red tributaries around the nostrils. "How'd you like to take a trip?"

"I'm skint."

"You won't be paying."

"And where," Castor asked, "would we be shooting this picture of yours?"

"Africa."

"Charming. Do tell."

"There's some jungle footage Marblestone's looking to license off to the majors and a new Henry Till picture we're looking to make. And parts of something else I'd like to try while we're down there. Something Arthur doesn't know about. One for us."

"*'One for us?'* Traipsing down to Africa on some secret project," Castor chided. "Sure you're not the one who's been drinking?"

"Certain of it. Look, it's going to be like the old days—making three, four pictures at once. I need someone there I can trust, someone who can keep track of the details while I'm running around. What do you say?"

"You know I've not given any thought to the business in years," Castor said, tracing with a steady finger the handle of his porcelain teacup. "My life here is about as far away from the pictures as could be. I like

London. I write the occasional culture piece for the papers, do a little gardening, drop by the pub, putter around. I always thought my days of adventuring were behind me."

"Nonsense." A larcenous gleam lighting Micah's eyes like a piece of coal glowing red. "In addition to my youth and my looks, clearly I've lost my powers of persuasion. Look, you're the scribbler, what would you say if our roles were reversed?"

Castor surveyed his little failing garden patch of cabbage and carrots, the village church spire, and the hills beyond that. "I'd say that travel is the way to avoid despair. . . . Where in Africa are you going exactly?"

"Deepest darkest."

"All-inclusive contract? Food, lodging, per diem?"

"Yes, the whole schmear, at least until we get to the rough. But you have to swear you'll lay off the sauce."

"That's a promise." Raising from beneath the table a cloudy brown bottle and pouring two shots. "To friendships renewed. And to the New World."

"The New World?"

"Sure"—clinking glasses—"every world's new when you've never been before."

2

UPRIVER

ONE

And then they were in Africa, having arrived by freighter from Cairo, sitting in a corner booth at the Blue Angel nightclub at the Hotel Nationale in the Belgian Congo. Rather than the twisted trees and thick jungle vines, the dark rivers and anthills, the Pygmies and poisoned arrows and elephant stampedes that Izzy had feared and longed for, the excursion thus far was redolent of routine, a roundelay of familiar faces and ritual. There was nothing particularly exotic about sitting in a corner booth in a nightclub surrounded by his brother, Henry Till, and Spiro; no strange custom the expectation of the best food, drink, and entertainment on offer; no special deliverance being waited on by silent-faced blacks in white shirtfronts. (Though how different they seemed from American blacks!) There was nothing strange about seeing Micah, insatiable Micah, eating everything, drinking everything, smoking everything, opining on everything, smiling at every young woman who crossed his path, his face betraying flickers of sadness that he couldn't gorge himself on all the world's glories at once, to devour the earth in one magnificent swallow. No, there was nothing terribly unusual about any of it at all.

"The heat is killing," Spiro complains, perspiring into his rum and Coke. "And I asked the waiter for water twenty minutes ago, and it still hasn't come."

"The climate's delightful," says Micah, khaki drainpipe trousers and flaring coat contrasting with the rest of the company's formal wear.

"Besides, dwarf, you're a son of the circus. You should know that all great adventures begin by leaving home."

"I'll drink to that," says Castor, raising a glass like Lady Liberty holding aloft her torch. "To the success of *Pot of Trouble*."

"I hope the picture's jake," says Till, "but I miss my wee chicks already."

"Speaking of chicken," Spiro says, "what's safe on the menu?"

"Bread," answers Izzy, splitting open a roll and testing its spongy warmth.

"I miss my boys, too," Micah says, attempting to buoy his star, swilling a thimbleful of scotch. "But imagine our return! I know you're just a humble midwesterner, Henry, but read the Greeks. The Greeks!"

They had traveled by car and train and ship and plane around the stretched bow of the earth, but Izzy still felt that very little had changed. Even after the panic of takeoff, gravity's forward rush that rudely pushed him into the small of his seat; even after the dollhouse shift in perspective, shaved fields seen from above as neatly lined as graph paper, parking-lotted cars like checkers on a board, telephone posts and wires dancing by like musical notation; even after the city obediently slipped into the great green cup of the Atlantic Ocean like a pea in a shell game; even after the water revealed in its depths blues within blue, purples and blacks swimming *under* the blue, architectural scaffolding of color suggesting entire inverted oceanic strata; even after the hours-long pursuit of the sun across its transit, yellow waves cresting off the silver wings and vibrating skin of that miraculously rising and dipping aluminum can; even after adjusting his watch for the time difference, entire hours of terrestrial existence impossibly lost in atmospheric transport; even after taking up temporary residence in the empyrean, even after accepting the invitation to feast upon heretical messages of clouds, Izzy, found himself still, sadly, irrevocably, Izzy.

The anticipation that he could begin at last the punishing and heroic project of smelting his crude ore into fine metal gave way to the suspicion that the trip might prove little more than a bit of rear-projection trickery: the same people doing the same things in front of different backdrops. The accommodations weren't helping any. There were tennis courts and a nine-hole golf course. There was the *Times* and the *Guardian* and the *Daily Telegraph* delivered each morning. And everyone finished work at four-thirty or five to have tea under tents, sweet-smelling yellow candles charming the insects away.

"Reminds me of the Cotton Club," Micah says, slapping one of two giant ivory elephant tusks parenthetically framing the nightclub entrance. There were berobed men in fezzes and an insectlike buzzing going on all around. There was the alien quality of the staff, their grace and courtesy absent any hint of obsequiousness, with some private withheld dignity, tucked away like a pocket kerchief. There was their language, Congolese, strong and efficient and delivered in staccato bursts like a quiet secretary pecking away on a typewriter. There was the nation's flag, the Belgian Congo having imagined for itself following annexation the simplest and most beautiful flag that Izzy had ever seen—a five-pointed yellow star on a field of royal blue.

The floor show was bizarre. There were feathers and drums and, at the climax, a man dressed in a matted ape suit chasing a scantily clad girl around the club. If Izzy was following the skit correctly, the ape had long reigned as an unseen island king until a group of treasure seekers learned of the gorilla and made it their mission to catch him. Instead the great ape kidnaps a bottle blonde the bandits have in their party. And, rather than the ape smooshing or disemboweling the girl, the two develop a connection. They grow kind of goofy for each other. Finally captured by the bandits and brought to the West, our primate hero never forgets his blonde. Shackled in chains, he never forgets her. Dropped into the alien city and exploited as a Broadway headliner, he never forgets her. The magic straw of her yellow hair, her tender stroking of his enormous engorged finger, his flared and outraged nostrils reflected in her bright blue irises. Sensing she is near, our besotted gorilla escapes and goes on a rampage, laying waste to the entire metropolis in pursuit of his girl. Finding her at last, our persistent primate pulls his paramour to the ground and forces upon her an act of interspecies love.

"Yes! Yes! Yes! Now, *that's* the picture we ought to be making!"

Micah declares, leaping from his seat to deliver a one-man standing ovation as the ape continues pumping away. "A movie about miscegenation, forget it. But the story of a girl and a giant *monkey*? Now, *that's* genius!"

"Black-and-white?" Spiro says. "I'd rather cut it off first."

"Garçon!" Castor snaps. "A pair of tweezers and a nail file, *vite!*"

"Why is that, Spiro?" Micah asks, thinking about Rose and indicating across the room a hostess standing imperious and serene. The perfect curve of her back reminds Micah of his first boyhood bicycle, her profile something he immediately wants to see cast in bronze. "I mean, look at her. She's like something pharaohs built pyramids for."

"You must be balmy from the heat," Spiro protests. "She's black as tar!"

"Do you remember that gentleman I told you about?" asks Sidney Bloat, Marblestone's advance man having joined them on this leg of the journey. "The trader who lives just outside Entebbe? He says he can't even look at the women when he returns to the Continent now. That they all look like day-old pastry to him. As a result, he can no longer eat flour or butter."

"I can see what he means," Micah says, memory pressing upon him a catalog of images: Rose on her stomach, Rose on her back, his begloved mistress standing, sitting, walking, dancing, dressing. Rose.

"I've been warned that all the pretty girls around here are gamy with clap," Spiro says impatiently. "And then there's the smell."

"What smell?" Izzy, still in mind of their encounter with Keneally, involuntarily lowering his chin by degrees.

"These nigger girls reek south of the equator."

"Well, as my uncle used to put it," Castor says, "once you get past the smell, you got it licked."

"Language, boys," Till tut-tuts into his Coca-Cola, "language."

"If there *is* some kind of smell," Micah says calmly, "it can't be any worse than the streets of Midget City."

Sensing defeat at the invocation of the site of his ruinous boyhood, Spiro turns his attention to the waiters. "Boy!" he shouts across the length of room, striking his glass with a fork again and again. "Boy! You! Boy! Some service wouldn't be frowned upon!"

Three Negroes in white dinner jackets come trotting across the room, polished floor slats answering mirrored shoes tap for tap.

"I asked for water over half an hour ago," Spiro says to the youngest of the servers, straightening his posture to appear taller than Micah.

"Wah-tah," answers the waiter, pronouncing the English word carefully, in bifurcated syllables. "Yes, sah."

"Well then, don't make a career of it!"

"Quit it, Spiro," Micah says, sloshing around an ice cube. "This is supposed to be a celebratory meal."

"All the more reason this service is unacceptable!" Spiro says, looking directly at the boy, who remains standing there uncertain whether it is appropriate for him to take his leave.

"Spiro," Micah quietly addresses his friend once the servant is out of sight, "you're offending me."

"I didn't know you were the defender of the Negro race."

"I'm not—you're offending my sense of restaurants as semi-sacred places. There are very few venues in life where you ask for something and it's brought to you. The whorehouse is one. Movie halls another. And restaurants. You'll respect the sanctity of restaurants, Spiro, if nothing else."

The boy returns with glasses of water for the group and silently begins placing them around the table, too abashed to make eye contact with anyone.

"What's your name?" Micah asks, gripping the boy's forearm as it crosses his setting.

"Sifiso."

"Thank you for your good service tonight, Sifiso," and here Micah presses a ten-dollar bill—six months' wages or more—into the boy's hand. "You'll forgive the rudeness of certain of my dinner companions."

Looking at the paper in his palm, the boy seems neither happy nor grateful but terror-stricken, convinced that such an incident must only be a portent from a malevolent deity. Somewhere, he is certain, a spell has been cast, a totem is being snapped in two, a cauldron with his name on it is bubbling over, his baby sister is drowning in a well. Looking down at the bill, the boy is certain that in a world full of misery such outrageous good fortune always carries a hefty price.

"Now, bring me another scotch and soda, please."

"Mr. Grand," Bloat whispers once the boy has retreated, the importer's dark beetle eyes disregarding all other tablemates. "I must caution you against making such extravagant gestures here. They'll go misunderstood."

"I think you should listen to Mr. Bloat," Izzy says.

"Be quiet, Itz. And you"—to Bloat—"don't tell me how to spend my paycheck, rug peddler. Just update me on the equipment situation."

"Very well," answers Bloat. "I've been able to track down a pair of lightweight field cameras and a good supply of very fast film stock, in Prague of all places. Other shipments of matériel from Nairobi have preceded us."

"Good. There's nothing another hotel nightclub can teach us."

"You talk," Bloat begins, "like a man who doesn't appreciate what lies ahead. Believe me, Mr. Grand, outside the tourist spots, Africa can be a hell on earth."

"It'll be fun," Micah says as the boy returns with his drink along with four other waiters who stare at the moviemaker, unable to discern if he is wizard, devil, or crow.

"I can assure you, only cannibals and Christians find comfort in the jungle," Bloat warns, "and you, Mr. Grand, are neither."

"You're wrong," Micah says, fully drunk, fully in possession of his faculties. "It's going to be fun."

TWO

Up the great Congo away from its mouth, where it drains into the great Atlantic, they were traveling toward the border between the Belgian Congo and the tiny British protectorate of Malwiki. They were on a rusty old steamer called the *Roi des Belges*, commandeered by Augustus Späten, a wiry German with prominent veins in his forearms. Everywhere they were followed by an overwhelming smell, powerful odors of dung and earth and green pine mixed, somehow, with cooling candle wax and schoolroom chalk, scents that were as much a physical presence in the air as gelatin wobbling on a spoon.

"Nearly the size of Europe," Captain Späten volunteers, hand-rolling loose tobacco leaves into a cigarette, acknowledging without making eye contact Izzy standing alone on the deck. "The Continent's double. True heir to the Victorian Nile."

Izzy looks out into the overgrowth and tries imagining instead the fathomless river and the vegetable tangle brimming over with cathedrals and statuary and monuments, a world of white and stone and noble thoughts.

"We're here to photograph it, you know."

"Pictures, eh?" Späten says, lighting his cigarette. "Been up and back this river twenty years or more, 'fore the annexation. Seen plenty you wouldn't want photographed. What kind of pictures you'll be taking?" he asks, removing from a holster a small pistol, which he empties of bullets and begins cleaning with a dirty rag.

"A motion picture, actually. Though I have to admit, we're not especially well versed on the history of the place."

"Its history?" Späten repeats, almost merry over the word. "Just look at a map. Africa's a pistol and Léopoldville's the trigger, there's your history." He points out to sea with the gun, squinting, aligning the sight.

"Huh," Izzy says, their speech drowning in dark waters, disappearing under eddies and depths and currents.

"Want to know the real purpose of the colonies?" Späten says, admiring a native sea hand who has come on deck and begun working a rope, stripped to the waist like a convict, exposing cords of black musculature. "It's not for the minerals, and not for the labor either, not at the core. We're jealous of their sunshine. That's what it amounts to. Too much time indoors makes us wicked."

Izzy did not enjoy sea travel, and the smaller the vessel, the less he enjoyed it. That first day, however, he sat on the prow for hours, mesmerized. As they pulled away from the port at Léopoldville and the settlements and shanties and schooners and automobiles faded behind them and they entered the dark witch's mouth of the world, at last the secret promise of the venture seemed validated to him. The only sounds were the river whisperings and birdcalls, the twitterings of tree rodents lining the shore, and the ship's metronomic *chut, chut, chut, chut.*

At first it was an effort for the ship to cleave its way through the river's topmost layer of mossy scum, a thick, oatmealy porridge. All was wilder, toothier, more haphazard than Izzy had anticipated, the earth retching up bursts of color and vine. The foliage wasn't beautiful either, but destructive, violent, amoral. After a lifetime of visiting gardens, it was as if Izzy had never before seen trees, never understood sinister arboreal logic: They demanded ascent. They'll bend, they'll twist, they'll wrap around one another, they'll burst through sidewalk pavement if necessary. But pretty they're not. Remove the sentimentality, ignore the dozen or so transcendental poems he'd committed to memory as a schoolchild, and the fact was made clear: Nature is chaos.

As he surveys the breathless fecundity around him, all illumined by the sun—that reckless card player who can't keep his hands off his chips, tossing glints of silver, purple, and green onto the dark carpet of river—the numinous quality of light, its dual existence as particle and wave, becomes manifest to Izzy. Allowing his eyes to go slack, Izzy imagines the scene through the eyes of an impressionist painter. Only color and light, thinks Izzy, loosening the grip of his vision and allowing color and light to dictate until he no longer sees sky, trees, and water at all, only slashes of color, bands of vibrating luminescence.

Unsettled by these visual experiments, Izzy reaches for his camera. It comforts him, holding his trusty Leica I single-lens reflex, its brass top cold to the touch upon removal from its scuffed leather satchel. It is received in his hands as a familiar, satisfying weight, like a wallet or a coffee mug. Prowling the deck, eye pressed to viewfinder, left hand gripping the device body, right hand cupping the lens in an inverted C, moving with something like grace, Izzy calms himself. Placing the camera between himself and the unmediated tames the space. Busy calculating F-stops and exposure times, focusing the diamond-sharp lens, winding the knurled knob between frames, considering how to crop a shot so the railings of the deck cut canted, diagonal stripes through bands of sea and sky, Izzy feels less out of his depth, technical demands quickly crowding out a sense of threat or wonder. Disorientation gives way to a soothing mechanical satisfaction, the remarkable reined in, made less so, through the act of picture taking.

And something else. Loading. Aiming. Shooting. Taking. The vocabulary of photography that of violence and possession. Framing some trees and jungle vines that look uncannily like Brooklyn telephone lines, Izzy wonders what secrets he would discover later when he developed the roll. That the jungle—experienced through his senses as forbidding, impenetrable, and innocent of its own mystery and peril—had been tamed, transfigured in a technically perfect way, into something pretty? Something was wrong with the whole project. But he couldn't help it, compulsive clicking and winding, the constant making of images, relaxed his shattered nerves.

A birdcall causes Izzy to crane his neck skyward. One thing that can't be photographed! Here the sun, lifegiver, not a brilliant source of joy but an oppressive fact to be endured, a blinding tear in the firmament that could not be looked upon too long. Had he ever really seen the sun? Certainly this wasn't the same orb that baptized his Brooklyn boyhood, that crowned him in California. This an altogether different, more malevolent God.

"You're late for the production meeting," says Spiro, strolling onto the deck barefoot, with rolled-up trousers. He also is shirtless, exposing a strongman's physique on his little frame, a torso tattooed with a Renaissance ceiling's worth of pictograms. There are squirmy anchors and swivel-hipped hula girls, verses of Scripture and polka-dotted snakes, moldering tombstones and bifurcated hearts emblazoned with the names of various women, all winding around his trunk like thread on a spool.

"Sorry," Izzy says. Then, rubbing his eyes, "Your face is a big red dot."

"It's darker below deck. You're needed downstairs. Surprises await."

Belowdecks, the cabins hold the stale smell of a summer home with closed rooms in hot weather. With Spiro leading the way, Izzy passes the kitchen and the mess, the sleeping quarters and the engine room, the utility closet and the storage facilities. An entire cargo area, too, is devoted to Bloat's red carpet, magnificently rolled and stuffed into a cabin, a full ten feet across, an obscene lolling tongue. ("One never knows," Bloat explained of its shipboard presence, "when one might need to beat a hasty retreat.")

Izzy enters the cabin. Situated around a folding table are Till (who outside his white suit and paraffin makeup could be mistaken for the manager of a small-town hardware store), Bloat (in a blue blazer festooned with giant gold buttons, looking like an admiral out of a children's storybook), Castor (soused), Micah (facial ingredients a mix of fear, confusion, and wonderment), and a passenger unfamiliar to Izzy. He is a black youth of perhaps nineteen or twenty, and even before the boy speaks or makes a gesture, even before it registers that the young man is wearing dungarees, Izzy can instantly intuit that he is not native African but American.

"Sit down, Itz," Micah says. "We've got a stowaway."

"Hey there, Mr. Grand," the youth pipes up. Hearing the boy's voice, Izzy is able to crack the context question and recognizes the boy. Early, who'd run errands around the set for pocket change. Early, whom Micah had taken some kind of shine to and paired up with Billy Conklin. Early, the kid brother of that grouchy girl from the costume department Micah'd been shacking up with for months.

"Micah, what the . . . ?"

"I know," Micah moans, rubbing the back of his neck, protecting himself from some imminent beheading. "I know."

"Three thousand miles from home and still your pussymongering threatens to bring us ruin!"

"Don't, Izzy."

"Rose's got nothing to do with it," Early says. "I'm acting as Mr. Waldo's oversight committee. Make sure you honor your agreement."

"Your sister doesn't know you're here?"

"I ain't seen Rose in weeks."

"Spiro," Micah says, scribbling down a phone number and address, "have Späten cable New York as soon as possible."

"Aye, aye," says Spiro, seafaring lingo sticking to him like insects to flypaper.

"I'm here to help, Mr. Grand. Keep things kosher while Mr. Waldo runs the show up in Harlem. Besides, the looks of it, you're traveling light."

"That's an impressive use of Yiddish," Castor volunteers.

"This is bad," Micah exhales. "This is real bad."

"Micah," his brother says, "we can't be responsible for this child."

"First off, I'm nineteen," Early protests. "Second, before you decide to drop me off at the next stop, do you have any idea what it's like being smuggled overseas in a giant *carpet*? It's suffocating, man!"

"*You* did this?" Micah, shooting a Sistine Chapel finger at the importer, who is already slipping out the door.

"On this adventure," Bloat says, "I am but Mr. Marblestone's emissary."

"Lookit, Mr. Grand, I made it this far. That has to tell you something. I'm serious about this trip, serious about the picture business."

"What about your sister? If anything were to happen to you . . ."

"Rose isn't your concern anymore, Mr. Grand."

Micah bristles at the response. "And Africa? What about Africa?"

"Africa?" Early answers, lighting a cigarette. "Africa's nothing to me."

D ay flips to night. There is rain on the water and a chorus of squawking creatures and midnight beasts. The jungle sounds different at night, Izzy registers through hammock rocking. The stars sound different, too. In the darkness there is distant drumming, percussion that grows louder and more insistent the more securely the evening's envelope is sealed, the farther the ship penetrates the continent's interior. Izzy tries affixing these strange rhythms to familiar childhood lullabies, to syncopate the spiraling repetitions into something less sinister and strange. He fears that sleep, if it even descends, will be a frail scrim. But the depths, the darkness, the heat, the rocking, the drumming—all of it blankets his senses, his bodily functions surrender, and sleep weaves its cocoon around him.

It is only when everything stops that Izzy's unconscious self registers a cessation of movement and thrusts him awake. Lighting an oil lamp, he feels his way down passageways, up stairs, and out onto the deck. There, a lone bulb on a shallow dock providing a single dot in the universe, is Captain Späten speaking English with a heavyset African dressed in a secondhand suit. The man's mouth widens into a jack-o'-lantern smile, and his arms fling open in greeting at the sight of the pajama-clad cameraman.

"Welcome," says the guide in a voice that's all honey and mellifluousness. "Welcome, Hollywood!"

THREE

I am Mtabi," says the apparition the next day as the company descends the gangplank. "Welcome, good morning, and how do you do?"

The guide has a thatch of gray hair that rises straight up from his head like a loaf of freshly risen bread and the purple-black coloring of a ripe plum. He speaks good if limited English in a voice that has trumpets and cymbals in it, a voice that carries its own conductor's batons, and is dressed in an old but well-tailored suit of wide blue pinstripes, appearing on this scorching morning dry as chalk while the rest of the crew have already soaked through their clothes.

The steamer is being unloaded by a team of boys—topless, barefoot adolescents hoisting boxes and crates off the side of the ship and tossing them onto the roof of a blasted old green bus. The bigger boys stroll along the vehicle roof like it's sidewalk pavement, catching improbably large trunks and strapping them down with worn rigging. Sitting beside the bus are a pair of weary-looking Citroëns, open-air off-road vehicles that one might take on safari.

Squinting into the sunshine, Mtabi explains that the flatulent bus will depart with the equipment immediately and drive through the night, while the crew will journey in the Citroëns, decamping overnight in a friendly village before arriving at its ultimate destination, with the final approach possible only by foot.

"The Malwiki live deep in the interior," Mtabi explains. "We'll be going far, far away."

"That's what I've been waiting to hear," Micah replies, shaking off residual grogginess and stepping forth with an extended hand, instantly establishing himself as leader of the group. "There was too much turn-down service where we were staying. The farther away from things we can get, the better."

"And of course a special welcome to Mr. Till, who can be recognized from motion-picture periodicals that reach us by foreign post!" says the guide, offering a steadying hand to the seasick star.

"You don't say?" the actor says, buoyed to learn the reach of his renown.

"We'll see our stuff again?" the more technically inclined brother asks the guide as a mechanical menagerie—light stands and scrims, makeup kits and wardrobe crates, lighting rigs and collapsible soft boxes, power generators and a small mimeograph machine—strobe past their field of vision and disappear into the back of the bus, a tarpaulin tossed over the lot.

"Oh, yes sir," says Mtabi through a smile that only wishes welcome to the world. "The bulk of your equipment will be certain to meet you in Malwiki when you arrive."

"If it's all the same to you," Izzy says to his brother, turning his back to the guide, "I'd prefer to take the cameras and film stock with us."

"Good idea," Micah agrees. "I bet things go missing a lot around here."

"I can both read and write," Mtabi continues, addressing the brothers' backs as the twins rummage through the equipment, siphoning off essentials. "When just a boy, I learned English from a burgher. A great man, a burgher king."

The guide goes on to explain that he has performed the task of taking Western tourists and business concerns on expeditions through the continent for twenty years or more; but never before so large a group, and never to meet the Malwiki. A long time ago, Mtabi explains, before he was fully grown, he had visited Malwiki together with his father and uncle and had befriended their ruler, King Mishi, who keeps five wives and has fathered twenty children.

"Sounds like he has his hands full," Micah says.

"Beg pardon?" Mtabi asks.

"Your king. Sounds like a guy who swims in the deep end of the pool."

"King Mishi is a great man. A man of wisdom."

"I'm looking forward to meeting him. Is he expecting us?"

"No, sir. Apart from missionaries, the Malwiki have not seen white men in many, many years."

"Mm-hm, mm-hm. What about cameras? Have the villagers seen them before?"

"No, sir," says Mtabi. "But King Mishi is familiar with many Western advances."

And here the guide explains how the Malwiki sovereign had in the decades leading up to the Great War earned his education as a citizen of the world, first schooling in Djibouti, the old Red Sea port town on the Horn of Africa. Mishi then worked as a servant in a diplomat's office in Cairo, then on the Mediterranean as a deckhand on an old galleon, picking up English, Spanish, and French as he went, ultimately attending a nondenominational school in Portugal, where he familiarized himself with works of Shakespeare, Homer, Chaucer, and Lewis Carroll and even set foot inside some of the Continent's great cathedrals and museums before finally returning to his remote native land to take up the responsibilities of the throne.

"An adventurer like us," Micah says admiringly. "Saw the world, then found his way back home. See, Henry, what'd I tell you? The Greeks!"

Let's take Jesus off the dashboard," says Castor the next morning from the front seat, removing from the control panel a glued religious figurine. "He's got enough on his mind."

The guide doesn't drive. Instead he navigates in the lead car sitting next to Spiro, who reaches the accelerator pedal with the help of a wooden block, while Micah, Izzy, Early, and Till follow behind with Castor at the wheel. There are fields of hard clay and openmouthed caves, prehistoric peaks and calcified vegetation. Gnats are everywhere, and there are occasions where they're met with clouds of insects that resemble gangs of chimney sweeps covered in soot. There are undifferentiated hours of cracked earth and brown mesas, hours spent driving through heat as thick and substantial as cake batter. Once, in the doldrums, Early spots a giant gray boulder that suddenly becomes animated and begins kicking up clouds of dust. The big rock revealed to be a fan-eared elephant, Izzy gets off a series of shots as the animal lumbers away into the distance.

"We leave the vehicles here," Mtabi says after ten hours of driving, the mid-evening sun as unyielding as its noonday twin.

"This isn't Malwiki, is it?"

"No, sir," he answers Micah, signaling to some underbrush. "Yedig, raisers of cattle. We rest tonight. Reach Malwiki tomorrow day."

The company walk another hour at least, carrying only the provisions they need for the night, marching over difficult terrain through a continuum of light and heat. A kind of viscid, cotton-candy stickiness clings to them, a second skin of coagulated sweat and dirt that provides strangely sleek insulation. While the men munch on hardtack—thin, unsalted biscuits used as military rations—Micah closely watches Mtabi, who is expert at finding gourds and prickly plants to chew for moisture. "Keep your sights on him," Micah instructs Early. "One like him is worth a dozen back home." When the smell of fire and dried dung reaches his nostrils, Mtabi informs the group, "Not too far now, sir."

A six-foot-tall herdsman, slender as a rope of licorice, materializes silently and begins walking alongside them, mimicking their progress from a bluff several yards above. His ovoid face is almost expressionless—a near-faceless face—and the only clothing he wears is a short leather skirt with a beaded belt that holds a sheathed blade and other wooden instruments. He is darker than anyone they have ever seen, as black and graceful as a musical note, and lyrical, too, in motion.

"Ah, Yedig!" says Mtabi, scampering up the bluff to greet the herdsman. What follows is a Lower East Side–worthy pantomime of gesticulation, chest smacking, cocked heads, the pointing of fingers, and, gradually, some wary nods. Once the herdsman is pulled near, the company sees that his torso and arms are decorated with an elaborate pattern, a beautiful and ghastly design comprising hundreds of healed, raised scars that look like braille.

"Dear God," Izzy says, groping for the camera as Mtabi brings the herdsman near.

"That's what we came here for," says Micah, a smile rising through glittering facial sweat as he steps forward to greet the man.

The herdsman leads the way to a group of children by a watering hole, four unclothed boys with exposed bellies and members. Never before having seen white men, never having known slacks and shirt-sleeves, pith helmets and corked hats, the boys begin screaming and launch themselves behind hot rocks. The herdsman, whose name is Arnewi, explains to the frightened children that the men are important makers of pictures who have come from the great lands to the west.

Slowly, the bravest of the boys emerges from behind the stone. He looks at each of the travelers in turn, fixes like a missile on Izzy, and makes a straight line for the cameraman. The boy pokes a finger into Izzy's midsection, the digit sinking a considerable way into the pad-ded softness it finds. The inquisitive, froggy-faced boy keeps jabbing at Izzy's stomach, throwing the switch on his ticklishness and causing him to jerk wildly. Enjoying the puppet-on-a-string effect this is having, the boy begins to poke Izzy even harder, all over—thigh, calf, buttocks—laughing uncontrollably all the while, disarming the other three boys, who come out from hiding.

"What gives?" Izzy asks, pinwheeling away from the boy.

"He says," Mtabi translates, "that you look made of stone but in truth are soft like rotting fruit."

"Gee, thanks a lot, kid." Izzy reaches into a pocket and pulls out a melted, half-eaten bar of Cadbury chocolate he'd been hoarding since London. He breaks off a few small pieces for the boy and his friends that they accept with reluctance. They sniff the pieces, carefully holding the bits to their faces and withdrawing spasmodically, like pigeons pecking at seed, until, finally, the most adventurous of the group places a dark morsel on his tongue and allows it to dissolve there. Keeping suspicious eyes squinted on Izzy as the chocolate melts, the first boy bravely begins to chew. Another child, upon the foreign food's first contact with his taste buds, throws himself onto the ground and begins shuddering with convulsions, calling out words to the translator between spasms.

"Is he okay?" Izzy asks. "Are they going to be okay?"

The boys are dancing around the men now, Early patting them on the heads, determining how different, or not so different, their kinky hair might be from his own. Licking clean his smeared fingers, the leader of the group speaks to Mtabi.

"They believe you to be messengers from the sky," the guide reports, "and this offering to be manna from heaven."

"Tell them it's true." Micah beams. "Tell them we're messengers from the sky."

The Yedig live in a small compound of twenty or twenty-five circular clay domiciles with conical roofs. Poles covered by big leaves rib the ceiling of each hut at intervals like hoop skirts, and in the cross-woven thickness one can hear small creatures scratching and chirping and tweeting, the giant nest serving as a kind of amphitheater.

Retiring on thatched mats in their hut following a meal of cold baked yams and a fermented, beerlike drink called pombo, Izzy busies himself fiddling with one of his father's kaleidoscopes, splitting the world of wonder around him into gemlike fractures, while Micah works on some letters home.

"Can you develop the pictures we've got already?" Micah asks, having deemed the postcard from the Hotel Nationale as unsatisfactory and sterile a representation of what they'd seen so far as a world's-fair diorama.

"Yeah, we've got the chemicals for it," Izzy answers, putting down one of his keepsake optical devices. "Setting up a darkroom shouldn't be too difficult."

"Good, I'll include some pictures, then."

"To whom will you be sending them?" Izzy asks, aware that he has no waiting postcard recipients of his own.

"To *whom?* Margaret and the boys. Arthur. Various and sundry other professional and personal interests. Why?"

"I'd rather not be party to that last group, I don't think."

Micah looks at him squint. "And why's that, kid?"

"I'd like to try making a clean slate of things while I'm here."

"Which means what? No longer aiding and abetting your no-goodnik brother?"

"Something like that."

"You're being a child, Itz. First, that kind of moral posturing is a form of vanity—it's too easy by half. Second, things are through between Rose and me. Is it a crime to send her a note?"

Izzy puts the camera down and looks at his brother. "Well, you should plan on making it a wedding card, then, because while we're out here playing summer camp, she's back home getting married."

"How do you know that?"

"Early told me."

"When is it?"

"Saturday."

Micah counts out four days with his fingers, then lets the digits loosely curl back into a fist. "Well, we've all got our jobs to do, then, don't we? Just print the bloody pictures, will you?"

"I'm going outside."

Night. Something to be inhaled. Sweet eucalyptus smells. Even in the darkness, a linear crispness outlining all things. Ten hours behind us in New York. Thirteen in Los Angeles. Perspective changes the object. Less than a minute passes before Izzy hears from behind him the sounds of his brother's wide-legged stride.

"You know I can't stand being left alone, Itz. C'mere, sit with me for a second." And here Micah links arms with his brother and drags them both down to the crusted, coffee-colored earth, the better to lie back and examine the sky. Eyes lifting moonward, Izzy sees the pin-cushion firmament crammed with stars. Infinity spread out before them, expressed simply and without shame, like a child's connect-the-dots drawing. Time made visible, devouring itself. Izzy turns back to his brother, whom he hates and loves. The desolation and comfort that come with being small. The local and the cosmic. Micah's hand. This, the person the heavens had conspired to make closest to him in all the world.

"Do you ever wonder what it'd be like if everything were taken away?" Micah asks. "Money, family, love, the striving, the wanting, the *things*? All of it?"

"You're forgetting"—Izzy, digging his nails into cool grains of earth—"I don't have all the things you do, Micah."

"Yes, that's right." Rising, smoothing dust from his pants, and melding into the night's thick pudding. "You've been more successful at leading a life without complication."

3

FACES

ONE

After rising early, eating a simple meal of porridge and juice, and wishing the Yedig farewell, the members of the company march back to the vehicles, reload their supplies, and begin the journey farther north, over calcareous white stone and great rectangles of sunlight, jungle greenery bristling in the distance as fine as fur. Mtabi was expert at discerning where they were and where they were headed, based solely on the direction of animal footprints, the position of the baking sun, and his uncanny reading of radiant objects and color.

While the light was extraordinary—reminiscent of the greatest red and yellow ecstasies of Manet, Monet, and Matisse—Izzy recognized that the extreme dryness and heat were dangerous for the film and feared that their supply of stock would combust in its aluminum cans. During the drive he occupied dull hours cleaning his camera with an air gun and a soft camel-hair brush, trying out various hypotheses of how best to preserve the footage once they'd set up camp.

"Reminds me of cornfields," Till says after a four- or five-hour stretch of undifferentiated flatlands, "without the corn."

"No more driving today," Mtabi calls from the lead car. "We leave the vehicles in Bundini, walk to Malwiki. A word of warning: Our laborer friends will likely have treated themselves to a small gratuity."

After killing the car engines, the men push the two Citroëns a few hundred more yards, cover them with tarp, and leave them in storage outside the grass hut of a friend of Mtabi's who had received the balance of their equipment and provisions the day before. Inside the hut the brothers find much of the company's canned food and costumes stolen. The bulk of the film equipment, however, though clearly having been sifted through, remains more or less intact. The crew then assembles the wheeled crates and carts into a kind of caravan held together by straps and begins the arduous work of hauling the heavy equipment on foot, Spiro out front, stripped to the waist, a belt gripped between his teeth, like an Eskimo dog pulling a sled.

They come upon the Malwiki three hours later. On the outskirts of the village, the tribespeople are engaged in a great festival of warriors. Rather than interrupt the ceremony, the company decide to remain hidden behind a large tree several hundred yards away. There is a group of perhaps twenty grown men, several of whom are covered in a kind of ash-white paint, forming a wide circle. Musicians stand at readiness, fingers pressed to strings, mouths fixed to instruments. There is complicated drumming, and, viewed through the camera scope, a xylophone made of animal bones. The men begin stamping along with the drumbeat, and one village elder steps forward and begins dancing. Moving nimbly, he keeps his torso stationary while arms, head, and legs dart this way and that. Other warriors join him. The dance takes the form of a succession of attacks and retreats, spears flashing through thick clouds of dust toward the center of the ring, with fluttering robes, animal skins, and outlandish feathered wigs creating a spectacle unmatched by anything invented in Hollywood. There are bare-breasted women dressed in fantastic skirts of colored glass beads and younger girls whose small, firm breasts remain immobile as they dance, even when their movements grow increasingly provocative and wild.

"Eyes, you getting this?" asks Micah, enraptured.

"All of it," Izzy answers, screwing a telephoto lens onto the Leica. "Mtabi, what can you tell us about what's going on?"

"Rain dance," the guide answers, kneeling to the ground and coming up with a handful of parched earth. "Drought."

"Lookit," Early says, spotting some felled cattle just off the center of activity, rib cages visible as fork tines through thin layers of fat, muscle, and skin.

"Conditions not look good," Mtabi tut-tuts as the dancing grows more unruly and desperate. At the conclusion of the dance, the village elder points at one of the men, the tallest and most muscular of the warriors, and indicates with a bangled hand the mountain range beyond the tree where the company is hidden. The warrior nods, accepting this dangerous commission, and begins walking directly toward the crew's hiding place, spear held as erect as a radio antenna.

"Eh, you will allow me, please," Mtabi whispers to Micah, "to do the talking." Taking a deep breath, the guide steps from behind the tree and greets the tribesman as casually as if he's just run into a neighbor on the sidewalk, trying to ignore the business end of the spear pointed at his groin. Mtabi speaks, faster and in coarser tones than he'd used with the Yedig, while the tribesman frowns through the conversation, pointing with the spear for emphasis. The commotion draws the attention of the dancers many yards away. The drumming slows and comes to a halt, as one, then another, then the entire group of village members crane their necks to see what's happening.

"We've been found," says Early.

"What *we*?" says Spiro, mapping escape routes, committing to one, and shimmying up a tree trunk.

The entire congregation, forty or fifty of them, converge upon Mtabi, spearheads glinting in the sun. The guide's speech becomes more rapid and desperate—the pleading tones of a crumb-covered kid discovered next to a toppled cookie jar. Micah, Izzy, Early, Castor, and Till emerge from behind the tree, hands raised, palms up, a clumsy gang in a heist gone wrong.

"Mtabi, explain!" Micah orders as a spear inches closer. "Talk to them!"

"Just a moment please, to formulate the proper response."

"Words," says Till, who has said so little since they'd first arrived, rendering a dismissive single-syllable verdict against everything that threatens his world-conquering fame. In his white safari suit and shiny desert boots, the silent-movie star looks like a specter, a dignitary from beyond the clouds. The translator turns to Till at once, exclaiming that near-universal word of negation, "No, no, no, no! No, sir! No, no, no, please, sir, allow me first to introduce!"

But it is too late, and a spear is brought to the neck of the sixth-best-paid actor in Hollywood. The warrior, hair shorn in a decorative pattern and trunk covered in that strange ash-white stuff, lowers his weapon, leans in with suspicious eyes, and inhales the air surrounding the visitor. He sniffs Till's neck, then pulls back, sniffs a shoulder, then pulls away, reaches for the man's hand and sniffs that, too, continuing to circle him, inhaling the foreign body and frowning the entire time, jerking himself away from the actor like he's a hot stone. Till, skin papery thin and patchy in the unrelenting sunshine, licks parched lips. He reaches into his jacket and removes a red handkerchief, holding it halfway out of his breast pocket for effect. The color delights the young girls in the circle, as most of their beaded dresses are a similarly sanguine shade. Sensing a softening in the crowd, Till removes it to its full length.

"Christ on a bike," Micah mutters, "he's doing a magic trick."

Till brings the red kerchief to his forehead, dabbing here and there at perspiration. He continues pulling it from his pocket until a yellow kerchief, tied to the first, announces its arrival. Feigning surprise at this improbability, Till gives another tug. A green kerchief tied to the yellow, then a purple after that, then blue, an endless stream of color and fabric, which he yanks from his pocket hand over hand over hand, an entire rainbow-colored bolt of fabric emerging from his quickly deflating jacket. One of the girls emits a shriek of laughter from the back of her throat, a high, trilling *la-la-la-la-la-la* sound that could be interpreted as a signal of either horror or approval.

Till reaches for the warrior's spear. At first the tribesman withdraws, but then—with twenty or more spearheads pointed in the direction of the star's jugular—through a gentle laying on of the hands Till is able to persuade the warrior to allow him to make an inspection. Once in possession of the spear, which is perhaps four feet in length, Till considers what to do with the prop. Using the weapon as a baton, he begins playing parade bandleader, twirling it in front of him, behind, tossing it free in the air, windmill style, catching the stick and landing on one knee.

"Tough crowd." Till sighs at the lack of response.

"Mtabi, explain to them please that we're artists," Micah says, "here at the pleasure of the king, that sort of thing."

"Malwiki want to wrestle," Mtabi translates. "When strangers arrive, before they meet the king, Malwiki determines character through sport."

"I'll wrestle the bloody savages," calls Spiro from above, springing out of the tree like a squirrel and revealing himself in all his barechested glory. "Lemme at 'em!"

At the sight of the midget—twin cobra tattoos slinking across his back, tracing the blades of his shoulders, and meeting at the base of his neck—the village children erupt in screams, running around in circles with arms flapping like chickens. Mtabi quickly explains that Spiro is no underworld demon and that his bodily decorations are the rough equivalent of Malwiki cicatrix patterns.

Held at spearpoint, the company and its equipment are brought to the center of the village—a far bigger and more complex arrangement than that of the Yedig, with large retaining walls, a series of wells, perhaps seventy or eighty cinnamon-colored thatched huts, two or three granaries, and several more complicated linked edifices farther away. The ash-covered warrior—whose name is Yani and whom the company, even terror-stricken, recognize as a model of human perfection—stares in bewilderment at Spiro.

"Let the bastard know," says the enraged midget, "that Queensberry rules most definitely *do not* apply."

"No translation for that in Malwiki."

"Keep things copacetic, will ya," Castor says. "We've got to gain their trust."

"Eh, Izzy," says Micah, recalling from Spiro's résumé a three-year stint with Sam Spectacular's Magic World of Midget Wrestling, "I think the time to summon the movie camera is upon us."

Lifting the lid of the brass-handled trunk, the cameraman feels like a priest in biblical times entrusted with safeguarding the Ark of the Covenant, the device in its sarcophagus a cool and indifferent God, happy to wait things out a millennium or two. Mtabi explains that Yani, who is now waving a flag around the wrestling circle, is one of the best wrestlers in the tribe, flag holder being an honored position. A village elder intones an incantation and sprinkles ash onto the fighter, who moves about calcimined in his coat of chalk, peculiarities of light making him appear as white as a wedding sheet.

"He looks to be a fighter of great competence," Mtabi warns, noting around the warrior's waist a belt made from goatskin tails. "A man of many feathers."

"Feathers?!" Spiro says, bouncing on the balls of his feet, fists flying before his face, fastening his gaze on Yani, taking the measure of the man. "He's nothing but a peacock!"

Two pubescent girls trace on the ground a large circle of chalk while others begin stamping their feet and uttering syncopated cries. Yani spits on the ground, claps his hands together three times, sending plumes of powder high up into the pungent day, and positions himself in a squatting stance, while Spiro springs about, jerking his neck from side to side, working out knots of tension and bad vibes. The village elder blows into long antlers—five low shofar blasts—and the match begins.

"Eyes, how're things looking over there?"

"Working as fast as I can," Izzy answers, unzipping a lightproof black changing bag, steadying the portable darkroom flat on his lap, and bringing inside the camera and a sealed film can. He pries open the tin disk and feels for the start of the filmstrip like peeling a roll of masking tape. Finding it, he opens the film chamber's door, snaps the supply reel into place, and seats the magazine. Then he threads the crinkly stuff between the film-gate aperture and pressure plates, wraps it around the sprocket wheel, slots it into a notch in the take-up reel, winds things tight, shuts and locks the chamber door, and lifts the camera from the bag. "Got it. Early, tripod." Wooden legs are brought out and umbrellaed open, camera screwed atop stand, eye pressed to optic, hand clamped to

crank, and the shutter begins flicking open and closed sixteen to eighteen frames per second, just as the wrestling match begins.

"Dwarf!" Micah warns from the sidelines as Spiro stays true to his
word as a gifted dirty fighter. Feet are stomped upon, hands are bitten,
eyes are gouged, hair is pulled, and delivered above and below the belt
are a series of titty twisters and crotch punches. "Play nice!"

Yani protects himself by making full use of his height advantage,
using his long limbs to leap over the diminutive technician, eluding
bull-like charges with fast feet and in one instance, if midday vision
wasn't fooling them, palming the midget in one hand and spinning him
like a basketball.

Izzy lifts the apparatus, moves a few yards closer, jams the insectoid
legs into the wrestling circle's perimeter, and wheels the turret around
to the wide-angle lens. In the private movie temple of his mind, the
place he frequented most often, Izzy can imagine these mad visions projected in black and white on Broadway screens, the events unfolding
before him already receding into the past.

"Henry," Micah says to Till, "whenever you're ready to join the
action."

"Oh, no, sir!" begs Mtabi. "Wrestling sacred to the Malwiki. Must
not be made into mockery."

"Fair enough," says Micah as Spiro is tossed out of the ring. "Thanks
for keeping things kosher on the cultural front."

Yani circles the ring, working out kinks in his shoulders and thighs,
taking inventory of his injuries, making a careful study of his pint-size
opponent. His expression is relaxed, superior, languid. Looking at the
wrestler's musculature, Izzy gains a better understanding of how bodies
work, how tissue connects to bone, limbs to trunk, the whole mario-
nette business.

Kicking up dust with hooflike feet, his face contorted in expressions of midget rage and indignation, Spiro charges headfirst for the
African. Instead of dodging, Yani squats and takes up the position of a
baseball catcher, aiming to cup Spiro's head with both hands, flip him
over, and bring him down hard on his back. Anticipating this maneuver,

Spiro uses the wrestler's limbs as a stepladder to climb up his forearms, bound off his biceps, scale his shoulders, and slide down his back. Getting between the warrior's knees, Spiro grips his ankles and brings the champion down flat on his face. Spiro then rolls onto his opponent's back, straddles the powerful spine, grabs both of the man's ears, and brings him facedown into the sand. Shocked and gagging on dry earth, Yani is incapable of thrusting Spiro off his posterior, and the latter begins mashing the champion's face into the earth. After a while of this, a village elder enters the ring to signal that the match is over. Spiro dismounts and begins jumping up and down, an openmouthed dwarf, the whites of his teeth as prominent as that of his eyes, chanting, "I am the greatest! I am the greatest!"

"He calls it official—little fellow has defeated Yani," Mtabi translates, "a champion not beaten in six harvests."

"The greatest," Spiro taunts, "of all time!"

"Not since Tunney and Dempsey have I seen such a display," says Castor.

"Even more significant than the result, sir," Mtabi explains. "The king confers upon the new wrestling victor a private meeting and the granting of a wish."

Yani rises dustily. He looks at Spiro with neither bitterness nor resentment but admiringly, a smile whistling across his face like a teakettle. One of the girls brings Yani his spear, which he presents to Spiro, laughing and smiling the whole time. Then Yani speaks.

"He says you must be members of a great warrior tribe," Mtabi relates, "from lands beyond the mountains."

"Tell them we're from America," Micah says, jerking a thumb over his shoulder, "great land from the West. Now, enough pussyfooting around. Take us to their king."

TWO

They are brought to the far end of the village, past the *lawapa*, or village center, which opens up like a dam once they have passed the square to encompass dozens more huts than they'd originally spotted. Leading them is Talli, a long-faced counselor who oversees the tribe's trading with foreign parties and the distribution of goods to the village. Dressed in flowing wizard's robes, Talli possesses the close-set, unblinking eyes and pursed lips of an inquisitive goldfish. During the walk Mtabi warns that the counselor, like the king, has been educated abroad and is a fluent speaker of English.

Walking through the greater village, Izzy appreciates the screwy logic of nature—how the relentless repetition of forms allows the alien to rhyme with the familiar. Just days before leaving for the trip, Izzy had come across an uprooted downtown city street, its surface made rubble, construction workers and electricians having excavated and exposed networks of pipes and wires like surgeons working on a varicose leg. Izzy stood for a moment peering into the pit, experiencing anew the recognition of how it's the cording together of sewage, electricity, and subway systems that make the city run, a complicity of inner workings that mimics the body's own circulatory, nervous, and respiratory systems. Systems within systems—the city resembling the body, the body resembling the city.

And so it is here. Taking in the village, Izzy spots a series of shapes and structures that wouldn't be out of place along a row of Lower East Side tenements. Sheets of fabric hanging from clotheslines drying in the

sun. Bison horns like bicycle handlebars parked outside huts. Kids playing some ancient version of stickball. Giant flower buds popped open
like umbrellas in a thunderstorm. Recognizing the familiar so far from
home, Izzy wonders whether things precede forms or forms precede
things, whether he exists in a world of things or has finally been delivered to a world beyond them. After a few minutes of walking, Talli leads
them through a gate to an enclosed compound and into a large, dark
building adjoined by smaller ones stacked together like dominoes.

"I've met some big shots in my day," Micah says, "but never a king."

"Oh, King Mishi is a man of wisdom!" Mtabi says with delight.
As they walk, the guide explains the layout of the place, how prior to
meeting the king visitors must first make their way through the living
quarters of his wives, this being a way the king advertises his potency
(the beauty of one's wives, more than physical strength or wealth, being
the true measure and advertisement of one's powers and purchase on
the world). It is notably cooler and darker here, and the company begin
to get the impression that they are traveling underground. There are
curtained hallways and tangy curls of incense, turrets for interior running water and dried flower petals arranged on the floor in decorative
patterns. The walls look slick, viscid with humidity, like bars of chocolate left too long in the heat.

Then the wives! They come upon three of them sitting in a large
room, with the youngest, perhaps sixteen, first to greet them. The
child bride's arms are as slender as tapered candles, and the inventory
of her youthful beauty includes a cinched waist, a ballerina's neck, and
miniature-chandelier breasts. Her face is edible, succulent, cheeks bursting like ripe fruit, dark eyes like plums, small nose some rare undiscovered berry. Barring a dozen or more tightly looped earrings fringing
her ears, silver bangles adorning her ankles and wrists, beaded necklaces and belly chains, and hands elaborately dyed with henna, she is
standing before the men entirely unclothed. There is nothing brazen
about her nakedness, and when the men enter the room, the buttery
bride does nothing to cover up. Also sitting in the chamber are two
older-looking women, perhaps in their late twenties or thirty, who do

not meet the strangers' stares. Across their abdomens are streaked chalky white markings, which Mtabi explains indicates that they are menstruating, during which time they are considered unclean and may not be touched or even looked upon.

The queens have lives that are free of duties, the guide continues, apart from caring for the children and performing a few chores like fetching water, the splendor of their languor a testament to the king's prowess and the surety of his rule. The youngest and prettiest of the wives welcomes the guests. In blessing she places a cool, dry hand atop each wanderer's head, spending the longest time considering Early, the foreigner who most closely resembles her in age and color. She gets very close to the young man, placing both her hands on his shoulders, gently squeezing them, then laying her flat palms on his chest.

"Boss," says Early, covering with a satchel his phenomenal physical reaction, "I need to take a hall pass."

"Stay put, kid."

A gong sounds outside the courtyard, and Talli rises. Following the emissary down a long, dark corridor, slats of light breaking through at evenly paced intervals, the crew feel like the Tin Man, the Scarecrow, and the Cowardly Lion out of the pages of L. Frank Baum, prowling the halls of Emerald City. At the end of this passageway, a heavy wooden door is reached, unbolted, and pushed aside.

It is dim inside the chamber, and at first they cannot discern him, sitting at the far end of the room on a simple wooden throne. Then, akin to images cloudily resolving out of chemical pools in darkroom trays, the outline of royal lineaments begins to sharpen into focus. Light glows on King Mishi's forehead and face, illumination passing through bands like phases of the moon. His head is spherical and free of bump or blemish—a specimen that would cause a phrenologist little trouble—and adorned with tight peppercorn-style hair. The lips are thick and sensuous, like a pair of sausage links on a breakfast plate, but the nostrils are delicately tapered, the eyes long-lashed and near to womanly.

On first inspection the Malwiki sovereign appears sleepy and disinterested in the visitors, but this only in the way of a lion digesting an antelope. Thickly muscled across the shoulders and back, King Mishi shifts while seated on strong legs and small buttocks, his bare feet like the roots of a great tree trunk. He wears a splendid dashiki of purple and gold, royal garments that articulate each current of movement from the torso down to the legs. He acknowledges the visitors slowly, expending no more effort than absolutely necessary, but it is clear that, even sitting and at rest, he is in possession of a kind of physical genius, a man on close speaking terms with grace, expert at enacting drama out of somnolence, silence, and stillness.

His is a great physical presence, or *muntu*, as Mtabi had earlier explained the word. The size of humanity in oneself, the measure of vitality and fullness of soul, the place one occupies at the table of earthly radiance, *muntu* was the Malwiki's most important concept. Everything possessed a degree of it, even things inanimate—a dress or a piece of pottery could be described using its terms—and if one's life could be thought of as an unfolding story, that narrative found its meaning in the enlargement of *muntu*. Conversely, one's *muntu* could be depleted through acts of smallness, fear, and cowardice, or through the accumulated burden of living with diminished possibilities. But that kind of squandering is hardly in evidence here. Waves palpate across the distance between host and guests. The walls vibrate like a just-whacked tuning fork. The room buzzes.

"Today I feel good as ripe shit!" pronounces the king in a voice that is all bass, the woodwinds section of the orchestra, a voice with forests and echoes in it. "Is that you, Mtabi? My eyes have not rested on your forehead in many harvests."

"Yes, King," Mtabi says, stepping forward with evident pride. "I am most happy to see you."

"Then why not leave behind your Western clothes before taking an audience with your king!"

"I beg pardon." Mtabi trembles. "These are work clothes."

"And is there not work to be done here, among your own people?"

"I do beg forgiveness, Your Highness."

"You should know your king better," Mishi says, a man enjoying his own joke. "Do you not remember my gibes and gambols from when you were a boy? Has the weight of years pulled down the corners of our mouths so? You are welcome among the Malwiki in any garment you choose. Now, let the warrior who has defeated Yani present himself."

The assistant cameraman takes a step forward. "Oscar Dimitrios Spiro, at your service."

"Ah!" the king responds, delighted by the midget. "Proof of an interesting proposition. Trust not the container but the thing contained. The same basket that holds grain to feed the village might also keep a poisonous snake. Your *muntu* is very great, very strong."

"Thanks, King."

"I am sorry to have missed your victory. Wives, many wives . . ."

"Thanks, again, Your Grace," Spiro says, "and I'd be happy to defend the belt for your pleasure anytime you like."

"Indeed!"

"King," Mtabi ventures, "please allow me to introduce the other members of my contingent."

"Micah Grand, American moviemaker." Leaping forward, a pony racing out of the gate. "And this is my brother and ace cameraman, Izzy, and international comic star Henry Till, and Benny Castor, our cracker-jack production manager from London, and the delinquent here is Early Letty, descendant of one of your very own African tribes, must be, who resides in the great city of Harlem, New York."

King Mishi frowns. "Most turbulent *muntu*, the speechmaker."

"That's what I was hoping to talk with you about."

"Will the brother please step forward."

"Greetings, Your Highness," says Izzy, Leica wagging around his neck.

The king makes an examination of the siblings. "One egg," he asks, sounding like a greasy-spoon waitress taking a breakfast order, "or two?"

"My brother and I are twins," says Micah, "if I follow your meaning."

"Solomon's baby, two halves of the same loaf," the king pronounces in a verdict that leaves the brothers looking at each other with fresh eyes. "Each *muntu* takes its spirit from an animal in nature. Mtabi is a giraffe, gentle yet strong, with eyes forever on the horizon. You"—pointing at Spiro—"are a great and poisonous snake. You"—addressing Till—"appear to be a gentle jackrabbit in the fields. You"—turning to Castor—"are a loyal and watchful turtle. You"—now Early—"a crab washed upon the shore, approaching all things slantwise."

"And my brother and me, Your Excellency?" asks Micah, as desperate for news as Moses waiting on Mount Sinai.

The pull of an idea tugs at the end of King Mishi's line; cautiously, he hauls it in. "You are a bird who displays all his feathers on the outside," he says to Micah, "and you are a bird who hides his feathers on the inside," he says to Izzy. "Both capable of taking wing, only in different ways."

"Huh," both brothers say in unison.

"Talli informs me of your plans to introduce modern mechanisms to the village," King Mishi says, switching subject and tone. "The Malwiki are unfamiliar with many Western advances, and I fear these will only sow confusion. Mtabi, what is the whites' true purpose here in Malwiki? Answer your king!"

"King Mishi," Mtabi answers, "these are serious men who have come from far, very far, to make moving pictures of the Malwiki."

"Movies?" A single eyebrow lifts on the king's forehead. Talli leans close and cups a hand to the ruler's ear, a confidence that is swatted away like a fly. "I have seen the flickers during my travels and studies at university."

"Then you're on board with the program?" Micah asks.

"A senseless parade of images, sound and fury, bursting through the fort of one's imagination, crowding out contemplation. The very opposite of well-considered rule."

"That's a good point, King," Micah says. "But we're no quick-change act, believe me. When we take a picture, we think about what it means."

"It's true, sir," Izzy interjects in spite of himself. "I know that things change when you photograph something, that you have a responsibility to it."

The opposing eyebrow rises on the king's forehead, forming a steeple. "I would like to talk with Hiding Feather more about this theory later."

Micah barrels ahead. "I'm uncertain about the pictures you saw during your travels, but our project isn't some run-of-the-mill studio job or adventure serial, I can assure you. We've come to tell the story of Africa, of your people, from slave times to the Civil War right down to present-day generations in America."

"Ah, Lincoln," says the king, "the ancient."

"Yes, that's right," Micah repeats, proud that the name of the sixteenth president is familiar on the far side of the earth.

"The first Great War, your nation's Civil War, waged for future generations," the king says, pointing at Early, who shrivels under the regnant forefinger. "But back to your motion pictures. My fear is that once created, such representations cannot be erased."

The king then describes how Malwiki culture forbids the making of graven images. And it was true, the only pictorial representations they'd seen since their arrival were the ritual scarrings that were considered outward expressions of gratitude. The king also explains, however, that he is obligated to honor the wish of the new wrestling champion, who promptly asks that the crew be granted six weeks' time to film with the full cooperation of the court.

"As you wish, Mr. Spiro," says the king. "Before you are dismissed, however, Outward Feather, have you read the poet Yeats? You do not strike me as one slouching towards Bethlehem to be born, rather galloping full tilt. Who is to say you will not trample the Malwiki en route?"

"Well, you have my word, Your Highness," answers Micah. "And the seriousness of my intent. That's all I can offer, really. Listen, Mtabi's informed us that the tribe is in the middle of a drought. How about this? After we decamp, we'll arrange to have provisions sent your way. Whatever you need: food, water, supplies, the works."

"One should not make promises that one is not prepared to keep."

"This one I'll keep. Meanwhile, we're on a pretty tight production schedule, and Henry here is needed back in Los Angeles in a few weeks' time, so we really appreciate your okay on getting things moving."

"Are you at all Bible-read?"

"A little."

"In the New Testament, there is a betrayer figure with raven hair, is there not?"

"Yes, there is," Micah says, running fingers through his wavy red mane. "But we're Jews—our God's older."

"Ah, Hebrews. Great people of the Book. These, however," King Mishi says, pointing at Izzy's camera, "are not books. I have seen in nickel theaters bandits shot by gunfire only to be resurrected in the next showing. I have seen men and women kiss with lips large as oases. I have seen Africa portrayed by a painted backdrop, a soldier with a rifle, and a camel on loan from the zoo. I have seen the man in the moon assaulted in the eye by a ship sent to the stars. These images have lodged in my mind's eye like stickiest sap. I cannot rid myself of them."

"You sound like a real fan."

"Your cine-film machines capture events as they unfold, then re-arrange these pellets of space and time at whim, is that correct?"

"Yes, King," says Izzy, "it's called *editing*."

"What are your thoughts, then, Hiding Feather, on the relationship between cinematographic pictures and deep time?"

"Movies and time?" Izzy repeats, his interrogator's eyes consuming the entire prospect of him. "Motion pictures occur in time, they're a medium of time, it's true."

"And what is time?"

"I don't think I can answer that."

"You sculpt without insight into your material," the king says, near to sensuous in his calm. "With your cine-film machines, you propose to make a new reality, to pull stitches from the very weave of time. You propose the creation of new frameworks that will instantly supplant all others, the promotion of an undifferentiated continuous present."

"I think we're talking about the same thing," Izzy speaks up, "but coming at it differently."

"Continue."

"Well, where we're from, things are moving very fast. Faster every day. It's getting more and more difficult for a man to stop and hear himself think."

Izzy's mind flashes forward to the return to his dark apartment. There would be back issues of the *New Yorker* and *Vanity Fair* to read and stacks of newspapers gathering outside in the hall like crumpled leaves. There'd be the latest phonograph records to catch up on and sheet music to peruse. There would likely be a string of invitations from Howard to this latest show and that private screening. There'd be the arrival of the new season's suits at Brooks Brothers to browse through and another meeting of the cinematographers' union at which to discuss DuArt's latest tricolor-film processes. And if those and countless other invitations, items of interest, and other distractions didn't occupy his time, just pull the blinds and there would always be the twinkling, insomniac city begging for attention. All the things! The things! The terribly interesting things!

"Yes, I am familiar with some of the Western manias of which you speak."

"And I think it's only natural to want to try to arrest things as they are." Izzy struggles, his voice faltering even as his thoughts clarify. "And there are only a few things that can achieve that kind of stillness. Art is one of them."

The king considers Izzy very carefully, in such a way that the cameraman thinks all his organs might burst.

"You'll have to forgive my kid brother, King," Micah interjects, breaking the spell. "Sometimes he talks when he should listen. While we're Socratizing it, though, mind if I ask you a couple of questions?"

"As you wish."

"What do you make of America?"

"Land of becoming, not being."

"C'I ask another?"

"Very well."

"How do you please so many wives?"

"Certain questions," King Mishi says, curling his fingers toward himself to admire his manicure, "answer themselves by being asked. Next."

"So in theory I've come all this way to relieve a debt, but I don't think that's really why I'm here. I suppose what I mean to ask is whether it's possible for a man to know himself? His own intentions? In his own time?"

"This depends on the clarity of his *muntu*."

"Okay, then, so how does one go about cleaning it up?"

"This is not something one charges straight into, like a ram against a fort."

"But how can a person square the deal with himself? With others?"

"Yes," Izzy asks, "how does a person become himself? The thing he's meant to be?"

"Perhaps it is the investigation of these questions that has brought you to the Malwiki." King Mishi smiles, looking from one brother to the other like a lighthouse guiding two ships into harbor.

THREE

They had assembled back in the brothers' hut after their audience with the king, as depleted from the philosophical working-over as from their travels and time-zone derailment. The company had transformed the space, the largest and most expansive of the guests' accommodations, into a makeshift production office. Script pages were tacked to posts; shot lists, sketches, and storyboards lined the inside like wallpaper; tin film cans were stacked in corners like dirty plates; and a bruised pair of trunks provided countertop space for an Underwood typewriter, coffee cups, flasks, ashtrays, opened packages of saltines, and cans of Italian sardines and American tuna fish.

Candles are lit. Food is passed. A bottle of Pepto-Bismol is passed around. Micah, his head in mosquito netting turbaned like that of an Arabian sheik or a high priest, lands on another slave story—his favorite Jewish holiday from childhood. Signs and wonders. The full glass of wine placed at the center of the table. The front door left open for Elijah, slipping unseen through the neighborhood. In this religious frame of mind, Micah locates in one of the trunks a talisman, carefully wrapping Mr. Waldo's small green Christmas light in a handkerchief and placing it on the cool, dry earth.

"Our first order of business," he says, staring hard at Early as he smashes the bulb underfoot, making a crunchy sound like mashing fistfuls of shredded wheat. "Mazel tov to your sister on her wedding. I hope Rose and her barber friend had a swell day."

Faces look to Micah, awaiting instruction. He had decided on the walk back to the hut that he wouldn't try competing with King Mishi in the theoretical department but would instead call upon the organizational component of his talent, the compulsive jigsaw-puzzle-solving and model-airplane-building part of his professional brain. "Gentlemen, I'd like to remind you before we begin that between the years 1908 and 1912, D. W. Griffith made *four hundred* pictures. Now, we've got a light job of it by comparison, but still we've got our work cut out for us," Micah says as Izzy distributes mimeographed lists of assignments, random script pages, and a catalog of shot lists from other directors' pictures, a dozen or so films that include the next installment of Numa Pictures' *Tarzan* serial, an agrarian drama from MGM called *His Daily Bread*, and a Fox kids' film called *Mr. Maslansky's Animal Menagerie*. "Izzy, I'm putting you and Early in charge of the B-roll project. As many apples as you can pick."

"Done," arrives the answer with military efficiency, his brother a lesser officer on a frozen Russian field.

"Good. Arthur's committed to these licensing agreements, and I'd like to help preserve the man's half-good name."

Rumor of the seriousness of Marblestone's illness had come to Micah just days before they'd shipped out. News of the whispered, initialed disease that, like the holy deity, was too terrible to be invoked by name, the great- and many-souled *macher* said to be diminishing by the day, melting away like a snowman under an August sun.

Barely twenty Micah had been when he first showed up at the Vitagraph lot, a kid with a notebook filled with sketches, a motor mouth, and a face still full of freckles whom Marblestone somehow trusted to put in the director's chair. "This kid know what he's talking about?" the classically trained actor asked Marblestone, who searched the postadolescent's face for glimmers of princeliness, stirrings that corresponded with the producer's own kingly self-conception. "Yeah," Marblestone said, "I think he does."

"Till," Micah says, turning his attention to the pale-faced star, who had not been holding up well since the company decamped from Congo, his chalky complexion now attributable less to pancake makeup than to some creeping intestinal ailment, "you heard it from Mtabi—it's your coattails we've flown in on. I figure we can shoot about half of *Pot of Trouble* here on location, but we need you in fighting trim. Can I count on you to deliver the funny?"

"There's a little thing us Protestants refer to as a work ethic."

"Good. Spiro?"

"Aye, aye," says the bare-chested assistant, picking threads of citrus from his teeth with a scimitar.

"Get the lay of the land, see which villagers have star quality. Bring me back some faces."

"Arrrrgh," answers Spiro, headed for the exit with the blade between clenched teeth.

"Not their *heads*, dwarf, *faces*! Faces! Now, before we retire for the evening, gentlemen, there's one last thing to discuss." A new tone enters Micah's voice, a syrupy quality that's equal parts soothing and medicinally insistent. He addresses them now not as a friend or a colleague or a fellow artist-laborer-in-arms but in the tones of a bank president looking over a balance sheet. It's the voice of political candidates and captains of industry, the distinctly American voice of a man who, through force of will and self-invention, could double assembly-line productivity, get girders strung up over a cityscape, coax a desert derrick to erupt in tar. "There's another project we've committed ourselves to in Africa," Micah says as Izzy begins distributing among the men crinkly onion-skin mimeographs of Bumpy's film treatment.* "I'd like each of you

---

*   **"O, AFRICA!"**

**A Historical-Tragical Motion Picture
Scenario in Four Parts**

by

**Byron Marcus Waldo
Ellsworth Raymond Johnson
& Isidor Grand**

to review those pages in your quarters tonight. More than gathering Marblestone's B-roll, more than *Pot of Trouble*, that scenario you hold in your hands is the reason we're here."

PART I: THE OLD WORLD

A montage history of slavery through olden times.

The HEBREWS of Egypt being worked to death in the Sinai copper mines. Siberian SERFS toiling in the hard Russian soil. VEILED FEMALES of the camel lands being sold into amorous bondage. An image of the globe in chains.

ZOOM IN: The Western Coast of Africa. Circles identify the Slave Coast countries: Senegal, Sierra Leone, Congo, Angola, Dahomey, Western Nigeria.

CLOSE-UP: A polished black boot sinks into fertile soil.

FADE IN: A peaceful village. Women at work in the fields. Men with spears hunting game. Naked-bellied children playing. Huts dotting the landscape like Morse code.

CLOSE-UP: A musket fires.

Scores of tribespeople set running in every direction. Images of white-uniformed soldiers rounding up the villagers. A row of Africans standing in the sunlight shackled in dungeon chains, each of their faces a portrait of grief. A demonically laughing soldier lighting a thatched hut on fire as a family crawls out of their domicile on their bellies. In the distance, the village in flames, swirls of smoke blacking out the scene.

FADE IN: Ships leaving port. Below, the cargo hold. In the dark, MEN and WOMEN in heavy shackles, packed tight as matchsticks. The ship rocks. Pools of blood and human waste slide across the floor.

TITLE: "From 1500 to 1850, Ten Million Men, Women, and Children Transported Across the Atlantic."

Belowdecks, the strongest of the SLAVES manages to pick the lock of his chains and break free from his bonds.

TITLE: "But Not Without a Fight!"

The slave creeps up onto the deck, sneaks up behind the ship's CAPTAIN, and drives a nail into his neck.

FOUR

Among the many sights Izzy was encountering here that he had never seen before: a collection of uncircumcised dicks, the rope's length and earthworm-shaped tips of these easygoing organs forcing upon Izzy mental comparisons with his own cold and vulnerable mushroom cap. As the village men go about their work unashamed, Izzy wonders if the Bowery bathhouses are at all like this: venues for nudity untrammeled and unashamed. As he did when present at Marblestone's Christmas Eve orgies, Izzy finds himself at a painful remove, an observer rather than a participant, comically overdressed in the African sunshine amid a riot of mass nudity, walking around in the steam heat buttoned up in his three-piece wool suit while everyone else in the crew dons cotton T-shirts and khakis rolled up to the knee. "I'm much more comfortable this way," Izzy explains to no one in particular. "Added layers act as a natural coolant."

TITLE: "More Than 250 Shipboard Rebellions Occurred During the Crossings."

The slave throws the officer's body overboard and raises his arms above his head, triumphant.

TITLE: "But This Is an Exception to the Rule."

FADE IN: 1619. Jamestown, Virginia. NATIVES dropped off by DUTCH TRADERS. Slaves working in tobacco and cotton fields. A heartbreaking wilderness sunset, the land still radiant and new.

FADE OUT.

Chief among the things Izzy busied insulating himself against was Cri, the nineteen-year-old prince widely acknowledged as the favorite of King Mishi's many children, who had, since the production team's arrival, made himself something of a group mascot. At first they mistook for a naïf the slender youth puppydoggishly trailing along beside them. It was only once they returned to the brothers' hut on the second night and the prince insisted on crossing the threshold and attending the production meeting that they understood that his presence had a more formal component. This was the prince's first exposure to a world beyond the Malwiki. Ushering the company around the village grounds, sitting in on their planning sessions, directing the camera crews toward prime spots of flora and fauna, then reporting everything back to his father's aide, Talli, all this constituted the prince's first diplomatic mission.

In the same way a newborn's parents might stare for hours in amazement at the working parts of an infant's eyes, nose, and mouth, so Izzy was entranced by the transparency of Cri's face. The revelation surprised Izzy, who made a living appraising faces, envisioning how they would look made gigantic, how light might flatter their planes and

---

PART II: THE NEW WORLD

FADE IN: 1776. WIG MEN signing the Declaration of Independence.

TITLE: "We Hold These Truths to Be Self-Evident, That All Men Are Created Equal."

FADE IN: The auction block. The beam and the post. The lash raised high. Families torn asunder. Husbands taken from their wives. Babies pulled from their mothers' breasts.

Slaves picking cotton in the fields. Lighter-skinned blacks, respectably clothed, up at the house fetching pitchers of lemonade. Slaves singing and dancing to religious spirituals in "hush harbors."

A SLAVE teaching a group of children how to read and write using a stick to draw the letters of the alphabet in the earth. He is discovered by his MASTER.

folds. Regarding the boy and taking in the simple, elemental fact of his features—the functional brilliance of their hardware—Izzy considered the relationship he had to his own plain but not unhandsome visage. There was the purely mechanical work, his daily caretaker's rounds— meadows to shear, hedges to brush, weeds to pluck, grouting work to be done on orthodontic stones. But there was also his philosopher's inves- tigation of it: his face as a field of inquiry and interrogation, the ques- tion that he posed to the world. A burden he lived behind—something to puzzle and fret over, a screen to monitor for signs of aging and ill humor, a mask he met in mirrors upon which he could try on expres- sions or attempt to rid of emotion entirely—rarely was Izzy's face ever something that simply *was.*

Cri, on the other hand, carried with him the terrifying lack of self- consciousness of the very young or the very old. Picking up and putting down various foreign mechanical objects, Cri's teacup fingers moved only slightly, like those of an expert typist, suggesting his father's delib- erate conservation of movement to which the prince added grace notes of childlike glee and discovery. When he took delight in something, Cri smiled; when unhappy, the prince frowned; when bored, he quit the

---

CLOSE-UP: The slave at the whipping post. CROWDS jeering.
The slave's FAMILY weeping. He exposes his broad, naked back,
welts risen thick and crosshatched.

TITLE: "The Civil War, 1861–1865"

A montage of battles from the War Between the States. Weary
soldiers and the battlefield dead, corpses stacked by the
uncounted hundreds. ABRAHAM LINCOLN, in stovepipe hat,
delivering the Gettysburg Address.

TITLE: "We Here Highly Resolve That These Dead Shall Not
Have Died in Vain—That This Nation, Under God, Shall Have
a New Birth of Freedom—and That Government of the People,
by the People, for the People, Shall Not Perish From the
Earth."

FADE OUT.

scene. The outer and inner man in him very much in harmony, Cri had yet to learn his father's skills of political calculation and withholding.

Making introductions the first day of filming, Mtabi informs the group that the prince's name is derived from the king of Christianity, a philosopher and poetic genius whom King Mishi greatly admired. In recognition of this tribute, the boy had stamped across his right shoulder a three-inch-long cross, a sluglike keloid scar prominently knitted upon the boy's plum-black skin.

"Praise be," says Castor, who upon seeing the tattoo pulls a simple wooden cross and some scuffed rosary beads from the satchel around his waist.

"I didn't know you were practicing," says Micah, in opaque sunglasses.

"Didn't know what'd we'd come up against out here," Castor answers. "Like this lunatic script you've decided to spring on us."

Their work has begun. The Grand brothers have never shot documentary films before, so they decide to spend the first few days simply following the Malwiki at work and play, allowing the villagers to acclimate

---

PART III: MAGIC AND DUST

FADE IN: On a Mississippi plantation, SORI, a young African boy, is maimed by his master, MR. WILLIAMS.

A series of DISSOLVES takes us through the generations as SORI's son, WALTER, a sharecropper, works the fields following Emancipation. Sori's grandson, JACKSON, the spitting image of his grandfather (to be played by the same actor), heads up north.

TITLE: "Harlem, 1928"

FADE IN: A montage of Jackson working a moonshine operation out of a nightclub on 137th Street. A Robin Hood figure, Jackson takes from the rich and gives to the poor; here he is dressed as Santa Claus handing out books and Christmas presents to children at an orphanage.

to the presence of the camera and to the phantoms following their steps like a corps of servants. In addition to helping them get their bearings while building up the vault of B-roll, the group agrees that easing into the life schedule of the village would allow them to discover promising situations into which they could drop their comic star.

True to form, *Pot of Trouble* has no script, just a handful of gags they're still working out. The basic premise: While on safari, Till's character—a novice traveler who fancies himself a great adventurer—is accidentally separated from his fiancée and their traveling party and quickly runs out of food and water. Wandering from tribe to tribe searching for nourishment, our hero lands in every kind of jungle bungle imaginable—shrunken heads, poison darts, quicksand, Pygmy warriors (a supporting role for Spiro!)—eventually ending in a boiling pot of jungle broth, becoming the very meal he sought.

A gag is developed for Till. That morning the crew watched four tribesmen begin construction on a six-foot-tall retaining wall; by midafternoon one pair is left to finish the cementing work. Dressed as an explorer from colonial days, the Till adventurer character will come along and try to help but soon lose all his gear in the drying earth-dung construction.

FADE OUT.

FADE IN: The back of a pickup truck winding its way down a dusty road. Jackson, dressed in a black suit and tie, approaches a deserted plantation at dusk.

Jackson discovers OLD MAN MR. WILLIAMS, drunk and asleep in a rocking chair on the front porch. Jackson approaches silently. Standing over the unconscious figure, he taps the man on the cheek.

TITLE: "You Old Man Williams?"

The man stirs awake, too drunk to understand.

TITLE: "Who Are You?"

Jackson leans in toward the man's ear.

TITLE: "I Said, Who the Hell Are You?!"

Izzy frames an establishing shot, Early clacks the clapboard, and Till approaches the work site from stage right as the tribesmen continue hoisting fistfuls of wet earth and pressing them into the wall. Their backs to the movie star, the tribesmen are oblivious to Till, ignoring the actor completely.

"You've got a good setup, Henry," Micah encourages as the actor moves into frame. "Now earn your paycheck."

Till steps forward and begins shaking one tribesman's hand, pumping his arm as furiously as a used-car salesman greeting the first customer of the day, while the other villager backs away and quits the scene in disgust. Till then pantomimes the suggestion that he might help the tribesman with the wall. Completely confused now, the tribesman stares directly into the camera, speaking loudly and pointing angrily at the brothers.

"Okay, cut!" Micah calls. "Goddamn it, what's he saying, Mtabi?"

"He does not understand the making of work for show," Mtabi translates. "He believes this to be a sign of rank dishonesty. That such grand gestures are reserved only for King Mishi at times of public speaking or storytelling."

Micah gallops into the shot. "Okay, okay, okay. Explain to our friend

---

Leaning closer.

TITLE: "My Name Is . . ."

Close enough to inhale the man's breath . . .

TITLE: "Get Off My Property, Nigger!"

TITLE: "My Name Is Jackson *Sori*!"

Jackson jams a blade into the man's overstuffed belly and lifts, lifts, lifts, rising all the way to the neck, gutting him like a fish. Dead. Dead. Dead.

A series of dissolves follow Jackson's pantherlike movements around the property as he plants explosives on the porch, in the stables, in the dining room, in the cellar.

CLOSE-UP: Jackson lighting a stick of dynamite the size, shape, and color of a Coney Island hot dog.

here, please, that this *is* the time of storytelling. *That the time of storytelling is upon him.* Explain that to him, will you, Mtabi?"

The guide translates, then relays the response. "According to Malwiki philosophy, every effort must feed some result. Food feeds the mouth, music feeds the ear, sights of home and family feed the eye, the warmth of bodies feeds the genitals. He believes Mr. Till's expenditure of effort feeds nothing."

"Tough crowd," Till says, flipping quarters between his fingers like Jacob's ladders. "Eh, tell him King Mishi sent us to help him put up the wall in earnest."

The tribesman agrees that Till can help with the wall and that the others can watch and record, so long as their efforts don't impede his work. Benny comes up with the idea that Till will accidentally step on an anthill, triggering a procession of insects that go crawling up the funnyman's leg. So is born the "ants in the pants" sequence, a career highlight that would find its way onto Till tribute reels. With both Till's and the tribesman's backs to the cameras, the comic's upper half continues the work of building the wall—hoisting what is handed him, spreading silt, smoothing wet earth—while his posterior sashays, thrusts, and clenches in expressions of befuddlement, terror, and relief (this Saint Vitus' dance

---

CUT TO: The Williams plantation engulfed in fire and brimstone, whirlpools of black smoke filling the southern sky.

FADE OUT.

PART IV: HOME

FADE IN: Jackson in his office, his violence appeased. Meanwhile, out in the streets, the ghetto is inflamed. One of Jackson's LIEUTENANTS, hopping mad.

TITLE: "Police Killed One of Our Own! Jackson, What Are You Going to Do?"

JACKSON THOUGHT BUBBLE: THE HEBREW PEOPLE being led by MOSES across the desert to the Promised Land. From high atop Mount Pisgah, the prophet espies Zion, but he is denied entry.

CUT TO: An ARMY of angry young men taking to the streets of

a none-too-subtle jab at Chaplin, who—walking away from the camera in picture after picture—had the most famous ass in movies).

"This is good," Micah says once Till fully commits to his ass dance. "This is what we came here for."

"Eh, Micah," Izzy says after the take is through, "we could use a couple of close-ups of our man here."

Micah sidles up to the tribesman, links arms with him, and begins leading him away from the retaining wall, closer to his cameraman brother, their postures mimicking the sharing of a private on-set moment between the director and a starlet.

"He says he does not trust red rooster," Mtabi relays after the tribesman violently breaks links with the filmmaker. "He demands to know the purpose of this machine. He believes the camera robs him of precious layers of *muntu*. He fears your cine-film machine to be a thief of souls."

The tribesman is now standing in front of the camera, staring into its black, inquisitive eye.

"Do the Malwiki ever use spices to preserve food?" Micah asks.

"Yes, sir. There is a smokehouse beside the granaries where they make the beef jerky."

Harlem. Jackson addresses the CROWD in statesmanlike tones as the film bursts into sound.

JACKSON: Brothers and sisters! We must neither return to Africa nor endorse violent uprising. Instead the time has come for us to awake from the nightmare of history. The hour has arrived for us to honor Lincoln and to ensure that our second American Revolution was not fought in vain but might truly be won at last. Though our ancestors arrived in chains, we must now break free from the bondage that confines us all.

Images of a black-and-white fraternity of MEN and WOMEN: candlelight vigils at the footsteps of the Lincoln Memorial, SCHOOLCHILDREN learning together in rural red schoolhouses, WHITE FOREMEN shaking hands with BLACK WORKERS on the assembly line, integrated military PLATOONS marching in formation, BLACK DAY LABORERS being served at integrated diner counters.

"Okay, good, explain to him please: Just like salt preserves certain foods, we're trying to capture an idea of him as he's standing before us right now."

"He does not understand the making of him into jerky."

"Fucking actors! Everywhere I go!" Then, quietly to Izzy, "Can you use any of this?"

"No, he's staring straight into the lens."

"Listen, does anyone have any photos, program books, lobby cards, that sort of thing?"

"I've got one," says Spiro, producing from his trouser pocket a laminated photo of himself sandwiched between two naked ladies of the night. "This one's called 'Lucky Pierre.'"

"He's scared enough already!" Micah says, smacking Spiro atop the head. "Photos? Does anyone have any photographs our man here won't mistake for dispatches from the underworld?"

"This one's called 'The Rusty Trombone,'" says Spiro, volunteering another.

"Leave us, dwarf!"

"I have a copy of *Photoplay* back at camp," Till answers.

The tribesman sits on the ground dejected until Till comes jogging

---

CUT TO: An unnamed northern city. YOUNG PEOPLE of mixed races at a music hall, the trepidation on display more a product of natural adolescent shyness than of learned prejudice.

A blues record plays as a BLACK BOY crosses the space and offers his hand to a WHITE GIRL. She takes it. He leads her onto the dance floor. He pulls the girl in tight. She leans in. There is heat rising between them. They dance, their bodies responding to each other with grace and instinct. With grace and instinct, too, the boy screws up his courage, leans in, and the two lock together in . . .

IRIS SHOT

. . . an interracial kiss.

THE END.

back with the movie magazine. Micah flips through the periodical like a man at the racetrack scanning the morning tip sheet and quickly finds what he's looking for: a photo of Till standing beside Babe Ruth accompanying the review of *Quicktime*.

"Explain to him that this picture of Henry here was taken eight months ago," Micah says to Mtabi, holding the magazine next to the actor, who assumes the same pose as his likeness in the photograph. "And he's still here! He's still here!"

"*Muntu* going strong," Till confirms, patting himself on the chest.

Mtabi offers the magazine to the tribesman, who looks at the photo, to Till, and back again. He runs his fingers over the photograph's glossy black-and-white halftone pattern. He examines his fingertips and rubs them together, bringing the photo closer to his eyes for inspection, registering with wonderment how the image of the man dissolves into a meaningless catalog of dots the closer it is brought near, then materializes into recognizability when held farther away. He attempts this same experiment with the person of Till standing before him—leaning in close and taking a step back—then offers his conclusion.

"He insists there are *two* Mr. Tills," Mtabi translates, "one standing before us, the other trapped in the photo. He is more scared now than before."

"A fucking *close-up*!" Micah howls, smacking Spiro atop the head with the rolled-up magazine, consigning the shredded and distressed thing to the coffee-colored earth. "Halfway around the globe and we can't get a fucking *close-up*!"

"Lemme straighten this joker out," Spiro says, cracking his knuckles. "You'll get your close-up."

Stepping out of the shade and into the light, Early takes up a position out of frame and immediately adjacent to the camera. "I want to talk to him," he says. "Mtabi, help me out, okay?"

And here, with the translator's help, Early begins asking the tribesman questions about life in the village. Early speaks plainly about his own life of petty criminality in the great cities of the West—hustling for change, the squalor of gin joints and the numbers game, always feeling watched but not seen. Early compares himself unfavorably to the wall the tribesman has spent the day building. He suggests that his own foundation is rotten but that he's working to repair himself from the top down. He shares, too, his sense of amazement over the Malwiki's peacefulness and good-naturedness and how this experience, just days old, has enlarged his view of the world and his own sense of place in it. The tribesman is relaxed, intelligent, generous in both listening and response, and for the duration keeps his eyes fixed on the youth—that is, at a thirty-degree angle from the camera's eyeline.

"Get it?" Micah asks.

"Got it," Izzy answers. "Good."

"He still does not understand your interest in the Malwiki," Mtabi says after a few minutes of this, once the sequence, close-up and all, is safely in the can, "but appreciates the conversation with the youth and thanks Mr. Till for his help with the wall."

"Don't mention it," says the actor, collapsed on the dirt, placing a fresh pair of horn-rims on the million-dollar face.

"Nice work, Early. Now, Till, back up on your feet," Micah orders. "Once more, with feeling, please."

The shoot breaks for the day; the wall remains standing. Micah looks out at the landscape that would serve as their back lot over the next weeks and months. Ale-colored hills and grounds the color of tea with too much milk poured in. Barren. In its way not unlike the city, crowded together with buildings, offering another kind of barrenness. He is exhausted after this first day of filming, eyes sunken and pouched with a papier-mâché puffiness. Things were worrying Micah, a new experience for him. There was Marblestone's illness and the debt hanging over Imperial and what all that might mean for him professionally. There was Rose and her marriage to the barber taking place half a world away. There was Izzy's growing independence and Micah's sense that he was losing his ability to control his brother. There was the prospect of doing justice to the violence and madness of Mr. Waldo and Bumpy's script. Micah had never had ambitions toward serious-ness, about love or work or anything else, and he experienced all this worry like a physical object, a tethered ball he had to keep kicking in front of him, something he wanted to discharge but couldn't rid him-self of. He kept coming back to the threat and challenge of *O, Africa!* The wrangling of atrocity into images. This a job for Micah—who had twice failed history as a boy!

He allows his eyes to rest on the wall, baking like a piece of pot-tery in the late-afternoon sun. Stare long enough and it doesn't look solid at all. Seems flat against its surroundings, like a notebook sitting on a desk or a kite hanging against the sky. He blinks, returning the structure to substantiality. There's mud with roots and weeds mashed in and tangled up like a woman's hair with too much shampoo. Micah picks up a smooth stone, a tan pebble, and places it in his mouth to stimulate saliva production. He begins to suck, with his tongue run-ning the rock between the underside of his bottom lip and his lower teeth. Stone on stone. Empty your head. Don't think. Be like the vil-lager over there. Be the day laborer. Be the bricklayer. Put up your wall. Think no more than taking a brick from one pile and putting it on top of another. Then another. Then another. Until the wall is up and you can go home. Exhausted. To sleep. And awake to another pile of bricks. Repeat.

"You look like a Rodin sitting there like that," says Castor of the frozen-profiled filmmaker.

"Trying my best not to think, actually," says Micah, spitting out the stone.

"I'd forgotten how much I missed the physical part of filmmaking," Castor volunteers. "It's like carpentry or athletics—the thinking comes through doing."

"You're right," Micah says, rising from the ground and making a loop around the perimeter of the retaining wall. "But I feel lousy about today. That close-up of our man there, he thought we were stealing something from him. I wonder if he doesn't have a point."

Castor considers this, taking a swig from a silver flask. "It was never really a matter of logistics, was it? What I mean to say is, once the place was decided upon and the paperwork squared away, it's all about establishing trust. They don't have to understand what we're up to exactly, but if they're not with us on some basic level, it's going to show. . . . Look here, I've made some notes about how to attack this *O, Africa!* scenario."

Micah accepts from Castor the pages along with an oily helping of liquid heat and in silence begins circumnavigating the wall once more. He walks in a line, avoiding cracks in the parched ground, careful to maintain the integrity of his mother's back, thinking to himself how little usable footage they'd managed to shoot that day.

He ambles over to Early, who since their arrival has proved himself a marvel of feline unobtrusiveness and an indispensable camera assistant to Izzy, the pair of them working hand over hand like teammates bound together in a tug-of-war.

"I'm going to let you in on a secret, kid. No matter what the specifics, the making of every picture's really always the same."

"How do you figure?"

"Well, at the outset you imagine it to be like some fantastic ocean liner. It's perfect and gleaming and full of passengers, and its course is charted flawlessly. And then you set sail, and first the compass cracks. Then the boiler blows. And then the cargo hold gets waterlogged. And then you have to start throwing wardrobes and supplies and engine parts overboard. And the farther out you get from shore, the more you come to realize that the ship is just this crummy old vessel and the whole endeavor becomes about how you can guide the leaky goddamned thing back to dry dock."

Early wipes his face and neck with a soiled T-shirt. "Sounds like anything else. You plan what you can and do your best with the rest of it."

"Yeah, maybe. Anyway, you did good out there today, kid. You were the only one who knew how to read the situation."

"Just doing my part."

Micah lights a cigarette and inhales, smoke meeting and lifting his flagging consciousness, intoxicants slotting into thought patterns as comfortably as a car sliding into a perfect parking space. "Did you mean those things you said? About life back home and the rest?"

"Listen"—Early spits on the ground—"whatever these jungle boogies need to hear from us to get the job done."

FIVE

I t's a hundred and twenty degrees, Mr. Grand," Early teases Izzy. "Take your jacket off."

"I can't," says the tweed-covered cameraman, tugging at his vest buttons. "It's melded to my skin."

"I never knew there was such a thing as a seven-piece suit."

"Well, live and learn."

The cameraman and his assistant are wandering under a blue enamel sky about four miles from camp, disturbing eggshell silence as they crackle across twigs and dried brush. Traveling light, with a handheld field camera and a minimum of supplies, the two set out that morning determined to knock off as much B-roll footage as possible. After walking awhile, Izzy sets down his equipment, plants himself on a hot rock the size and smoothness of an automobile hood, and unfolds the crude map that Mtabi provided for them. He serves himself a cup of coffee from an aluminum thermos, removes from a pocket four packets of sugar, rips them open, and pours.

"You want some coffee with that?" Early asks, watching the granules waterfall into the cup.

"Leave my sweet tooth out of it and concentrate on what you're supposed to be doing," Izzy says, having demonstrated to Early that morning how to load a fresh roll of film with the camera in a changing bag. "Can you feel the lead?"

Early works his fingers inside the black canvas tote. "Got it."

"You're dexterous."

"What's that?

"Good with your hands."

"Mr. Waldo says so, too. He and Bumpy brought me 'round to the warehouse in Jersey the other night, showed me how to work the Bunsen and tubing. 'Lead burns red and makes you dead.'"

"I imagine making moonshine's not so different from working in a darkroom."

"Suppose not," Early agrees, securing the lid on the camera and removing it from the bag. "Mr. Waldo and Bumpy aren't only interested in whiskey and running numbers, though. They're looking to *diversify*. That's why they sent me—to ensure they make a righteous entrance into the entertainment business. Speaking of diversification, you spend much time around Micah and Rose?"

"No, but they don't exactly make a point of being seen out together." Looking at the boy, Izzy recognizes for the first time in Early his sister's skeptical, frowning face, only blacker. The nose is rounder and less aquiline, the hair more densely woven, but still the siblings have been manufactured from the same human stuff. There are womanly traces in the boy, too, of Rose's extravagantly long eyelashes, elfin ears, and pillowy lips. Looking at Early, it occurs to Izzy how hopelessly beautiful Rose is; that Micah had the wit to uncover her heartens Izzy enormously.

"What do you suspect they see in each other?" Early asks.

"What does anyone see in anyone?" Izzy says, attempting a seen-it-all tone that doesn't come natural to him.

"I mean"—talking mostly to himself—"Rose knows her way around. She's got to know there's no future in it."

"Micah's never really talked to me about your sister, if that's what you're asking. But listen, Micah's someone who likes having a lot of balls in the air." Izzy recognizing the observation to be true even as he formulates it in speech. "He's one of those people who need to create disorder around themselves in order to think clearly."

"I guess that's all beside the point now anyway," Early says, consulting his wristwatch. "If I've got my math right, she's married already."

Looking like a lost groomsman, a small, slender animal coated in black-and-white fur comes out from hiding, slinking its head around the corner of the rock formation. Eight or nine inches long, with a wet nose and a striped tail like a gondolier's shirt, the thin little creature looks unabashed, happy to share the space and the sunlight with the strangers.

"What is that, some kind of rat?" Early asks.

"I think you'll find it's a lemur."

Early mounts on his shoulder the Akeley and screws a macro onto the lens turret. "He's got a funny face. I'm going to get in close." Early squats to the ground near the lemur, which rises on its hind legs as if readying to take a bow. When the animal pivots to the left, Early shifts to the right; when it bobs its head forward, Early pulls back, the two locked together like expertly matched boxers in a ring. Watching from this short distance his apprentice's hands, eyes, and feet working together in concord with the mechanical apparatus, Izzy marvels anew at how picturemaking combines the technical and the artistic, the industrial and the athletic, the modern and the atavistic. How it's not every day that new modes of experiencing the world come into being. He returns his attention to the map.

"So Mtabi promises this is the spot, that if we're patient, we'll spot herds." Looking up, Izzy sees perhaps a hundred yards away three gazelles standing stiff and proper as small-town matrons posed on a church step. The antelopes are preternaturally calm, the three-member tribunal staring unblinking across the expanse at the filmmakers, unable to speak yet communicating nonetheless in that pristine and urgent way that animals sometimes have.

"They're making me nervous," says Early.

"Good actors are like that sometimes. Really still."

"But nothing doing—better to shoot them running."

"Sure."

"Okay, hold this." Early hands Izzy the camera, withdraws from his dungarees a tangle of red, white, and blue wicks, strikes a match off his heel, then lights the sizzling mess of firecrackers and sends it hurtling into the air.

SIX

The crew hadn't seen their host since they commenced filming the week before and worried that they'd fallen out of favor with King Mishi. Then, on the afternoon of the seventh day, Talli, the court's chief counselor, visited the set of *Pot of Trouble*. Just as Till emerged dripping from a giant cauldron, Talli leaned in to whisper words to Mtabi, his mouth drawing a distinct line of disapproval, suspicious eyes gathering all light toward him, and doleful, fantastically long earlobes lengthening as he imparted his message.

"There will be a great feast in the village center tonight," Mtabi relayed after the counselor departed. "The king requests the honor of your attendance and in particular asks that you bring the cine-photo camera."

Spiro makes his entrance first, carried in on high, Cleopatra style, in a heavily decorated chair held aloft on poles; with his iron-filing stare and his arms folded regally across his chest, the wrestling champion appearing the realization of his dream self. Talli follows next, taking his ceremonial place beside the empty throne, features as fixed as the leading in stained glass. Then perhaps twenty of the king's children assemble, ranging in age from babies just a few months old carried by wet nurses to strong young warriors in their early teens. The king's wives arrive next, including a few older women the company has not yet encountered who wear large metal and wooden disks in their lips and ears. The plates stretch and distend the women's skin, in some cases pulling their lips several inches away from their faces so they jut straight out like opened cash-register drawers or tugging their earlobes into giant hollow loops that swing as freely as bird perches. When the women take their seats next to Castor and Spiro, the men turn away from this monstrous distortion of feminine beauty.

"Every time I feel close to understanding them . . . ," says Spiro, who since their arrival has himself taken a pirate's piercing.

"Signs of great beauty," says Mtabi.

"Strange idea of beauty, that," Castor grumbles.

"Not meant for decoration originally," Mtabi explains. "Intended to make the women ugly, so Arab traders wouldn't sell them on the coast. Meaning changes over time."

With this explanation serving as overture, the women join in a circle and begin chanting and stomping, hopping on coal-red feet to a variety of skin drums and fossilized percussion instruments. They work themselves into a near-orgiastic fervor in their effort to conjure the man of the hour, who finally appears in the distance.

King Mishi is covered in ceremonial robes and headdress, as if recently returned from lands beyond the sun after communing with his forebears. First acknowledging the faraway crowd with the smallest bow, the king then enters an animal pen near his compound that houses the royal family's private livestock and appears moments later coaxing forth a mighty bull. Izzy is filming it all, opening the aperture wide to accommodate the fading blue light of the magic hour. Zooming in with the telephoto lens as the king begins the long walk to the campgrounds, Izzy sees that the king is wearing a lion's mane on his head—the two sets of eyes stacked close together as unsettling as watching a person open his mouth while doing a headstand.

"What's with the tiara?" Micah asks Mtabi.

"Only a hunter who has killed a lion with a spear, without assistance from others, may wear the lion's mane."

The king ushers the ox into the center of the convocation, stroking the animal's sides while coaxing him into position. The animal's hooves are like large cracked stones, and his smell is a mixture of dung and clay and honey. The bull is massive, with a bristling, thick coat and heaps of musculature piled atop an undergirding of sinew and bone, as gloriously well proportioned as the hills and valley of a great river landscape. The assembly quiets, and at this closeness it becomes conversant with the animal's breath, synchronizing itself to the calming rhythm of the bull's intakes and snorting, dust-filled exhalations. In the firelight all are captivated by the forces of *muntu* emanating from both beast and master, who clearly loves him.

The king slits the animal's throat. It occurs suddenly and without warning, the act performed as indifferently as a bank teller opening an envelope: A blade issues forth, a line is drawn, and a spray of arterial blood spasms from the animal's neck. So quickly does it happen, so casually is the murderous rite performed, that the congregants have no time to register shock. The beast falls on its front legs, and the king continues stroking its mane, comforting the dying animal as its black eyes begin to cloud milkily, its breathing slows, and its hind legs finally shudder and collapse.

Long knives are brought out. Spearmen rise from the group and jab at the carcass here and there, thick red and black blood matting the fantastic brown coat, seeping through the fur like wine rising through cheesecloth, the animal now covered in large punctures. From its curled lips issues forth a frothy white substance that distends distressingly like elastic and reaches the ground, where it gathers and soaks into the parched earth. The king's forearms and hands are now coated in blood and mammalian thickness, exhaustion mapped on his face, something of the bull's passivity and force wedged into his expression. He turns to face Izzy, who has been preserving it all, the sacrifice and its aftermath, with the magic instrument.

"Now he has achieved immortality."

"Yes," says Izzy with bile-scalded breath. "We'll make sure of it."

The tribesmen, wives, and children all look expectantly toward the sky as the bull's *muntu* expires and is absorbed into the ground, the universe left a fraction of a degree duller following this departing essence. But the vault does nothing to acknowledge this gift, offers nothing in return except boundless blue with stripes of white clouds that look like fat streaked through bacon.

"The bull is the mightiest animal of the Malwiki," Mtabi leans in and whispers. "This ritual sacrifice made to appease the rain king is very much a last resort."

Micah holds a hand to his mouth as the tribesmen complete the butchering of the carcass, but it is more out of empathy with the king than horror over the fate of the slayed bull. Though his wives continue chanting and stamping and wailing—the youngest rending their hair and clothes, some of them bathing in warm animal blood—the king begins to mark his retreat, making his long march home. In the distance, diminishing, viewed from behind, he might have doubled for one of the sad Jewish salesmen that Micah, as a boy, watched from his window each morning, leaving their homes with heavy suitcases.

SEVEN

As the crew grew more familiar with village ways and began taking their meals together with the tribe, Cri, the king's favorite son, became known to the company as the friendliest, most ubiquitous of the Malwiki. His very appearance around camp was an event as happy-making as the summertime sounds of an ice-cream truck jingling down the street, a kite taking the wind, or the opening of a city hydrant on a hot day. "Did you see the prince today?" "Do you know what the prince did?" "Did you hear what the prince said?" were the constant refrains of the village chorus.

The prince had limbs that bent as easily as blown glass, tapered fingers as long as candles, and a forehead that curved like an incandescent bulb. He also was in the habit of touching whomever he encountered. He would eat food with both hands and offer the beslobbered, slime-covered digits for others to lick, pass a pipe while gripping one's thigh, ask a question of you while cupping the back of your neck and fixing his stare upon you like a wax seal. All of these actions he handled with great affection, all accomplished with immense, unblinking, wide-spaced eyes. Izzy, who could not tell whether he was one of Cri's true favorites or a mere recipient of the prince's promiscuous sociability, found these tendencies of touch both heavenly and disconcerting.

The prince had fixed upon the cameraman from the start as a focal point among the production company's members and made it his ambassadorial mission to acclimate Izzy to his new surroundings. With Cri leading him through the village square by the hand, Izzy resembled a transfer student being shown around the high-school cafeteria by the varsity football captain. While the cameraman's native unease and reticence kept the flag of his social skepticism flying high, after a few days of this attention Izzy's wariness began to subside.

In Izzy's imagination the features of the landscape were inseparable from the contours of Cri's hand. There were muscular hills and dry dorsal plains, thin vegetation streaking out across flat fields and rocky formations marking the outskirts of the territory. By way of these hand-holding expeditions, Izzy had in those first few days touched Cri more than he had any other human being since childhood. If their contact were to be limited to that, the cameraman told himself, it would be enough to sustain him for years.

Instead Cri helped Izzy out of his suit. Surprised to see the cameraman dressed so formally after his first days in the village, Cri fingered with incredulity the scratchy, hot material, which gathered the sun's rays and splintered in the heat like rope. It was with a forgiving laugh that the prince forced Izzy to shrug free from this cocoon, pulling the cameraman's arms out of their casings like shucking stalks of corn from their skins, attacking the buttons of Izzy's oxford shirt, working each tiny tortoiseshell disk through its slot, then rolling up Izzy's thick sleeves and wool trouser cuffs to expose skin that was white, supple, and unblemished. As simple as that.

"Why does he keep touching me?" Izzy asks Micah one night after they've retired to their hut, its curved, sloping walls mocking the brothers' rectilinear luggage, equipment crates, and thought processes.

"It's just their way, Itz."

"Yes, okay, fine, I know that, but what am I supposed to do about it?"

"Do whatever the hell you want," Micah responds with impatience. "Do you even know? Do I need to diagram it for you, Itz?"

Micah had known for a long time that Izzy was a twist, a sexual proclivity that didn't particularly bother Izzy's brother, who had encountered his share of industry fruits. To Micah, anything that expanded upon the body's catalog of desire—any variation on that comically limited repertoire of expression—was good news to him, good news for the humanity business. He was almost certain, however, that Izzy had never acted upon these urges. It pained Micah to think of his brother dooming himself to live a life without touch. Especially given Micah's belief that sex was one of the truest portals of discovery a person had available to himself, the surest passport to locating other people's secret selves. Micah had tried talking with Izzy about all this on a few occasions, usually around holiday time or when they were invited to some industry function that Izzy would invariably attend unaccompanied. When prodded on the subject, however, Izzy was as fragile as an Easter egg: press too hard and he might permanently crack.

There were ways to live like that, a life could be made for oneself—Micah knew a pair of puffs who lived together as bachelors in Hollywood—but his brother lacked that kind of bravery and brazenness. Dutiful, serious, self-abnegating Izzy! What was most troubling for Micah was how he couldn't tell whether his brother's grim and purposeful hollowing-out was a way of masking his secret or an expression of the very core of his person. Izzy was an orderly guy—someone most at home in a mechanical world of machines and darkrooms and chemical baths. And sex was madness. Sex with women, sex with men, too much sex, not enough sex. The whole thing was an unruly disaster, the great swamp from which we spring and spend our lives looking for a clean patch of water, a happy spray of sunshine.

If Micah puzzled over his brother more than another sibling might, it was because they were twins. As King Mishi had suggested, Micah believed that Izzy was in possession of missing pieces of himself—that the payload of spiritual and temperamental gifts had been divided evenly between them in the womb—and so he chose to interpret his brother's fate as an inversion of his own. It was for this reason that Micah felt a special sense of responsibility for Izzy's sadness and sobriety and took his own excesses and profligacy to be a necessary counterweight to his brother's temperance. In fact, Micah nicknamed the worst of his alcohol-induced shakes and tremors "the Izzies." Confronting his achy, blue-lipped self in the cold-tiled bathroom some hungover Thursday, unable to meet his own bloodshot gaze in the mirror, he'd often find himself saying, *"For you, Izzy! I did this for you!"*

If the opportunity for experience presented itself to Izzy—especially out here, where no one could see—Micah wished his brother would take it. At times Micah even found himself envying what homosexuality might be like, an entirely alternate system of values and secrecy. In his imagination it seemed like a higher form of male bonding, a realm separate from love, from institutional pressure, from emotional bargaining or dubious promises of fidelity, marriage, children, stability, responsibility. Rather, this would be an altogether other world of men, applying male ruthlessness and efficiency to the arena of physical contact and release. What could be better? (Indeed, there was something masculine and matter-of-fact about Rose's approach to things carnal that he admired very much.) No, it was never his brother's inclination that Micah found untenable. Micah could forgive Izzy's faggotry, but his unhappiness was inexcusable.

Izzy had been found. A shoulder squeezed in passing would keep him cradled in warmth all night, some popping *cluck-cluck* words delivered in his direction would send a smile sailing across his face, an after-dinner tousling of Semitic curls would bring on sharp summer storms of happiness. The beautiful boy seemed to experience the world through his fingertips. Such facility with touch, such an infant logic to it! And why shouldn't you touch everything and eat everything and see everything? Izzy thought, rising from his mud hut into a van Gogh night of swirls and whorls, blue moonlight printing everywhere negative images of trees, leaves, huts, and stones. Pretzeling himself on the parched ground, belly covered in ooze, Izzy was left to wonder if the prince was thinking of him at that moment, too.

On the ninth day, Izzy comes upon Cri bathing. Though the nominal reason for the expedition is for the cameraman to relocate the steamer trunk full of exposed film closer to the bathing pond and its surrounding cool clay earth, Izzy is familiar with the villagers' schedule and knows when and where the king's son washes.

The prince is kneeling on some stones before a reflecting pool,

washing himself without soap, when Izzy arrives. The drought has robbed
the bathing pond of most of its water, and the boy stands in its center
naked, liquid ringing his ankles like a pair of dirty socks. The water level
is low, and what remains of the stuff is coated in a scummy film, similar
to the lathery residue lining a sink after a shave. The pond walls, though,
are rich in mineral deposits, and each time the prince scoops up handfuls
of dark substance to pour over himself, traces of glittery particles streak
across his skin, like glass-flecked city pavement reflecting light.

Izzy has seen Renaissance paintings of similar tableaux: mythic
scenes of flawed human specimens stumbling across perfect bathing dei-
ties, and he wonders if he will be transformed into a fawn or a tree for
this transgression. Instead, spotting him in the near distance, Cri waves
happily to Izzy, motioning for him to come closer. Izzy does not move.
The prince gestures for Izzy to remove his striped cotton pajamas and
join him for a wash. Izzy looks around, then unbuttons his top and casts
it aside. Cri cocks his head impatiently, and Izzy quickly removes his
trousers and then the rest of his garments, standing for the first time
unclothed before another man.

Naked and white, Izzy feels like a boy; only the hair covering his
legs and belly and chest is not childlike. Cri frowns. He then wades
over to where Izzy is standing, rising from the pool wet and gleaming, covered in gold dust like an amphibious god. Without preamble,
he takes Izzy's penis in his hand and goes into a careful study of it,
curious about the organ's lack of foreskin. The prince pinches the head
between forefinger and thumb like a Boy Scout testing the resilience of
a campfire marshmallow and begins running his thumb back and forth
over the ridge like a lighter that's difficult to strike.

"In my religion . . . ," Izzy begins, his explanation trailing off as the
biblical organ of patrimony grows bigger and he leans, quaking, into
the princeling, both arms collapsed around Cri's shoulders for support
as the boy continues tugging at the organ's length, pulling Izzy's penis,
gripping it in his fist, stroking it up and down, tugging him this way
and that, until Izzy's first hand job is complete.

EIGHT

In New York Izzy had often wondered, What *is* happiness? A good meal? A successful picture? The physical pleasure of zigzagging through busy midtown streets? Feelings of goodwill toward others? (It always amazed Izzy how Micah could be so phenomenal a shit, such a callous betrayer of people and principles, and still appear in the pink of self-content.) Happiness now revealed itself to Izzy not as a thing but a place, something topographical in nature, a physical distance that could be surveyed and brokered. The familiar hues of misery had for so long been a comfort to him, grays and blues and blacks soothing in their very unchanging coolness. Not so the brilliant and balmy humidity of happiness—climates temperate and temperamental that could explode into epiphanies of sunshine or thunderstorm erasures.

The old world had the texture of history to him now, a yellowing photo robbed of currency and significance. Cars, streets, newspapers, many-storied buildings, the mass desiring of the entire ambition-drunk metropolis—all seemed to belong to some imagined past already receding behind him. He felt as if awakened from deepest sleep, a revenant revived to find the world not rocketing toward some crystal future but cast back to some simpler past, one pared down to body and earth and communal bond. If he could strip himself of everything known, all the assumed premises—how to button a shirt, fold a newspaper, hail a cab, make a bed, scramble an egg, settle a bill—he would. Physical sensation had become all. Everything had become color. Language replaced by dialogues carried on among cadmium, canary, cerulean, crimson. Green had its own vocabulary, earth and mustard their own lexicon.

This internal reengineering was accompanied by a physical transformation: Izzy had become leaner, his posture improved, his skin now glazed and coppery with lines of seriousness sun-inscribed across his brow.

"You have become less a shadow," King Mishi observes during one of their private meetings, "more a man of solidity."

Izzy treasures these visitations. Once the king granted his consent for the crew to begin filming and their work began in earnest, the monarch asked little of them apart from regular progress updates from the cameraman.

"Your brother has traits of natural leadership, it's true," the king observes. "His light is great, though he could benefit from shining it inward more often. However, I am curious about you, Hiding Feather. How have you been enjoying Malwiki hospitality?"

Izzy wishes he could draw for the king a picture of himself stepping out of a too-tight suit or smashing a set of iron castings that had bound him, so grateful is his dancing heart for being a guest in the court of the king.

"I am very happy here."

"And the buggery?"

"*King?*"

"A long tradition among the Malwiki. From the ripest shit there often blooms the most fragrant flower. You have been enjoying such private moments with the prince, correct?"

The cameraman looks at the ruler like an astronomer who's stared too long into the wrong end of a telescope.

"A king has many eyes. You have brought other eyes to the village," Mishi says, nodding toward the camera hanging from a strap around Izzy's neck. "A phenomenon I noted visiting theaters and museums during my student days in the West—people are often happier to watch than to participate. I find your personal role in this endeavor intriguing, too: serving as watchful eyes to your brother's mouth. Perhaps your time among the Malwiki will help right this imbalance."

"I think so."

"Yes, it is clear that each day you turn over new topsoil of the self. Do not forget, however, even during your time of great unbinding, the Malwiki experience deep suffering."

"The drought, Your Highness?"

"Yes," the king says, still bristling from the failed ceremonial sacrifice of days before. "The drought."

It was true: The foraging expeditions to dig new wells, with tribesmen traveling through dangerous territories as far as two hundred miles from the village, had yielded nothing. The granaries were in good shape—the year's harvest of dura had been a strong one—but with each passing day food supplies diminished further and word would come of another cow or boar expiring from malnourishment.

Sensitive to these conditions, the members of the company were diligent about limiting themselves to their rations. Till was first to fall ill, the star laid out in the village infirmary under the care of a red-eyed, wild-haired witch doctor and declared out of commission as a diarrhetic epic wormed its way through his system. It took just a week before the crew had gone through most of its water supply and began dipping into the village's reserves. Everyone was suffering. Skin blistered and peeled like whitewashed fences; limbs were fabulously scratched and bleeding from pointillist bug bites; windpipes frayed as dried cornstalks left in abandoned fields. In sum, the company looked like a discarded set of dolls in an orphanage: worn, filthy, torn, impossible to imagine having once been clean and bright objects of adoration.

Though the place had helped Izzy shatter the old dichotomies— good/bad, beautiful/ugly, civilization/primitivism—as his senses adjusted to the undifferentiated jungle, he had to admit that much of what he encountered stank of death. Even here, on his long walk to the king's underground chambers, Izzy had noted in the corridors smells of decay, lifeless trees and ribbons of dead and deliquescent roots, clouds of flies and maggots wriggling over rocks. What unnerved him was his fascination with it all. Izzy sensed how freeing it must be to live inside physical or moral wreckage—how embracing the abject thing, the disgraced thing, the unwanted thing, would relieve one's life of meaning and responsibility. He marked with disquiet his attraction to this kind of abandonment and the danger of aligning himself with such a proposition.

"I have not seen the land so hungry for drink since I was a boy free of whiskers," King Mishi continues. "Many men, many kin, perished then."

"What can we do to help? Micah promised we'd arrange to send for supplies once we get home, and he meant it."

"This proposal is generous and most welcome. But if the earth is truly in revolt, she will swallow these gifts much like a boa devouring a pig."

"Surely there's something we can do!"

"I wonder if the solution does not rest," says the king, pointing a *muntu*-heavy finger toward the camera swinging from Izzy's neck like a clock pendulum, "with that."

NINE

Your village is being destroyed!" Micah booms through the megaphone, at last the military leader he had dreamed of incarnating, responsible for the movement and deeds of great blocks of men across distances of space, fields and faces made real. "Your village is being destroyed!" he repeats over and over, his voice growing more strangled and constricted as he goes. "Your village is being destroyed! Your village is being destroyed! Your village is being destroyed!"

They are filming a massacre, the ransacking of a nameless West African village and the taking of its people into bondage, fifty of King Mishi's most able-bodied men and women relieved from work details standing in for ten million. Early and Izzy had pieced together a tracking system with some long poles and electrical tape, a rig they use for the first shot of the day, one that took several hours to stage. It is the longest tracking shot they have ever attempted, an uninterrupted, two-minute-long take of all fifty Malwiki villagers lined up side by side, hands and feet bound in chains, the camera registering each of their faces in turn after they had been rounded up by traders, then panning to the slave ship, a matte painting that would be added during postproduction back in New York.

"Your village is being destroyed!" Micah repeats, walking down the line, the camera wheeling along beside him, eliciting grimaces and tears as Mtabi translates the terrible words. On the first take, an older tribesman, upon hearing the news, breaks free from his chains, springs from the line, and goes running in the direction of the village. So convinced is he of the literal fact of the white man's words that when he reaches the empty village and recognizes it to be still intact, it is this imagined paradise, this familiar heaven on earth that he believes to be the fantasy. Only the children, accustomed to games—to the establishment of and adherence to rules that require standing in patterned formation—immediately recognize this as some higher form of play.

"Why is he smiling?" Micah asks Mtabi upon reaching a cat-faced seven-year-old boy whose toothy grin ruins a take. The director hovers over the boy, casting him in shadow. "Why is he *smiling*?"

"He finds it amusing that even the elders are playing along."

"Ask him what's his favorite toy."

The translator relays that the boy's flute is his most prized possession.

Micah picks up the nearest stick he can find. "Tell him when we get back to the village, his flute—*your flute?*"—snapping the stick in two—"is like this! Now, back to your marks. Let's do another take."

And once again Micah delivers the terrible news, only this time when they reach the flute-loving boy, he is weeping uncontrollably, each facial orifice transformed into a delivery system for snot, tears, and wails. "Your! Village! Has! Been! Destroyed!" Micah bellows in the heat, repeating the words so many times the phrase becomes an abstraction, a kind of bleating Morse code, no longer recognizably a proper English sentence, the terms of the deal recounted phonetically, syllable by syllable, blip by blip, which only increases the ferocity of Micah's delivery.

From behind the camera, Izzy recognizes the dark magnificence of what is unfolding before them, a sculpture in time, the creation of a spatial and temporal event that even in its present unfolding is somehow archetypal, *found*, a record of faces never seen before that promises to become instantly familiar. Faces. A mother weeping, her face slick as a birth scene. A boy looking down at the dry ground with studious incomprehension. A girl, hair arranged in fantastic tight braided patterns, staring beyond the clouds. An old woman, the puckers and flaps of her face like a folded umbrella forgotten in the corner of a restaurant.

A man, his face riddled with the record of some ancient lunar acne. A rabbinically bearded elder, facial hair thick enough to store a comb or pocketwatch. A teenage youth, Early's age, a cartoon wisp of fuzz penciled across his upper lip, looking defiantly ahead, eyes narrowing into the sun. A middle-aged man who could pass for a Harlem building superintendent, one nostril snarling upward as the camera makes its pass. An old crone, whose chin boasts the sharpness of a second nose. A young wrestler who betrays no emotion across his slightly lopsided face, product of a difficult delivery. A girl looking down at her cuffs and weeping, not knowing how long the enforced immobility of her quick-moving hands might last. Cri, at the exact apogee of the lineup, the prince's normally expressive features blank. Talli, the king's adviser, looking saurian and severe, a single cocked eyebrow the fig leaf covering the depth of his displeasure.

A cherubic-cheeked child, eyes bright and clear as marbles. One of the village's most fearsome wrestlers, face flat as a nickel. A mannish-looking woman, with shorn hair and a giant beaded, looped ring through her left nostril. Another woman with a fantastically long face, like a piece of pulled taffy or a funhouse-mirror reflection. Yani, his posture and bearing the very definition of the dignity of athletic accomplishment. A perfect boy, handcuffed hands ingenuously brought to his cheeks, just below the eyes, like a child playing peekaboo. An aristocratic-looking woman of perhaps thirty whose profile wouldn't look out of place on the cover of the *New Yorker*. A boy with almond-shaped, Asiatic eyes. A centurion guard, an unsmiling figure standing outside Buckingham Palace. A thin farmer with long, exposed horse teeth. A seventy- or eighty-year-old man, his expression heavy-lidded, worldly-wise, and reminiscent of one of Micah and Izzy's uncles. One of the queens, unaccustomed to labor of any kind, visibly hot and impatient over being taken away from her cool underground chamber. A hunter with jangly limbs that look assembled from Lincoln Logs. Faces, one after another, a generous enough human sampling to make them question how many faces there are in the world *really*. Faces.

"How's it look?" Micah asks after the third take.

"Good," his brother answers, troubled over how the re-creation of something horrific can be so aesthetically pleasing.

Micah turns to Early, who's been pushing the dolly and has the best sense of whether or not the shot will be usable. "How'd it feel?"

With a flat palm, Early slices a horizontal loaf of air. "Smooth, no bumps."

"Okay, let's wrap the shot."

The crew begin breaking down the rigging for the next setup. Going about their work, they are oblivious to the disorientation that lingers around them. Most of the tribespeople remain fixed, standing in line rictus-mouthed, or wander around still shackled in prop chains, afraid to look behind them at the destroyed village center, confused about what to do next.

"You think it looked like this?" Early asks, lighting a smoke and tossing the pack to Micah, whose head is in need of a good throat clearing.

"What?"

"In olden times, the roundups?"

"Well, if it didn't," Micah answers, feeling bolstered by the cigarette packaging's crisp, cellophane-wrapped rectitude, "it does now."

It had taken days to erect the hut. Since they would have just one chance to destroy it on film, this sequence had been especially well planned. Izzy circles the structure with the camera like a prop plane corkscrewing during a bailout, in rehearsal laying out his marks on the ground with Dixie Cups. Castor is dressed in a white uniform with sparkling gold buttons and red piping, his beefy gut and gin blossoms a caricature of imperialism. His face is red and hot in the noonday sun, sweaty wisps of white hair atop his balding head lending him the look of a poorly poached egg. Castor steps into his mark.

"I'm to go here?" he asks, a hint of aggression in his voice. "Like this?"

"Yes, that's correct, Benny," Micah answers, plucking from the air the note of opposition in Castor's voice and turning it over in his head, determining how to either quickly derail it or use it to his advantage in the scene.

"Because I'm having some difficulty puzzling out what we're doing here."

Micah squints into the light. "Just worry about hitting your mark and we'll be fine."

"Sure thing, boss," Castor says, breath sending waves of honey and cherries and black olives wafting in their direction, his face green-tinged and froggy, misery packed into his cheeks.

Early consults a light meter. "The light's really good. We should start."

"Okay, let's do a take of this thing."

Spiro ignites the gasoline-doused, rag-wrapped end of a torch, sending barbecue smells sparking in all directions. He hands the living thing to Castor, who attempts to set the roof of the hut ablaze. A feathery breeze frustrates his efforts, the torch's flame flicking and whipping about like a washcloth on a clothesline. While some individual spokes of straw blacken, the dry thatch is slow to catch fire, and Castor, as he goes about this difficult business, holds in his face the dispassionate expression of a banker sitting for his portrait.

"Okay, N'golo!" Micah calls through the megaphone. First the tribesman chosen for his wonderfully hangdog expression, then the village women portraying his wife and daughter, emerge from the burning building. They have been instructed to crawl out of the hut on their bellies. They are not natural actors, and despite Mtabi's many explanations, they inch across the dead grass with all the emotion of a restaurant patron trying to recover a lost earring by feel.

Frustrated at the roof's refusal to cooperate and his acting partners' lack of attentiveness, Castor goads his director. "Any pearls for me, boss?"

"Yeah, Benny, pretend it's me down there."

"Now, why would I do that, old boy?"

"Because, *old boy*, you know why you're out here? You know why I brought you along?"

The thatch catches at last, ribbons of smoke beginning to curl around his face. "No, pray tell."

"Because I wanted to keep someone around who's a bigger bum than I am. I needed someone here I'd feel better against by comparison."

"I'm afraid you're getting perilously close, Micah, to crossing a line."

"Play nice, fellas," Spiro suggests from the sidelines. "We have just one chance to get this right."

"Sorry, dwarf, I was under the impression I was working with adults," Micah says. "Everyone knows Benny's a drunk and a failure. My hope, at least, was that this trip might put something back where his spine used to be. But how does a man who's halfway talented just *give up*? That's what I want to know." And here Micah begins to catalog all of his colleague's deficiencies: the debt, the default on the family business, the infidelities and marital distress, the inebriated lost years and squandered professional opportunities, the commonplace, unforgivable shame contingent upon being a bright and flawed human being.

A captive audience member of this unfortunate biographical recitation, Castor looks from one man to another, his face engorged like he's just taken an unmanageable drink of something and doesn't know whether to spit or swallow. Each of the crew members looks away, all occupying themselves with pieces of technical business. Castor looks down and begins to pantomime kicking N'golo in the stomach, over and over again, pulling his boot just short of connecting each time as the women claw at the earth and weeds and as the walls of the hut now finally come ablaze, sending triangular licks of flame up behind them. Once Micah taps into this wellspring of violence in Castor, the scriptwriter seems to grow larger, inflated, an emboldened physical presence. Hatred flows from him easily, in cresting waves, as Micah continues egging him on.

"You're not even better than that man on the ground there."

"You go to hell, you good-for-nothing no-talent," Castor says, kicking at the prostrate African again and again, sending up billows of dust that mingle with the belching smoke and flame, obscuring the figures in painterly thickness. "You and that black bitch of yours."

"All right, Benny, now's your chance to let rip," Micah coaxes. "Out here where no one can see!"

As Castor kicks at the man over and over and over, the women playing N'golo's wife and daughter let loose great yawping wails, authentic cries and howls that balloon up into the African sky. They hurl themselves between Castor and N'golo, clinging to the officer's heels, imploring him, their faces bright with tears, to stop.

"It's a good lesson, Benny," Micah goads. "All the way here to find we're no better than a bloody wog crawling along on his stomach."

Castor raises his prop rifle and, leading its aim a foot to the left of the African's head, fires into the earth. Terrified by the loudest, most disruptive sound he's ever heard—one more wrathful than thunderclaps—N'golo freezes and flattens himself, arms outstretched like glider wings. On camera the action registers as a point-blank shot to the head.

Izzy looks up from the viewfinder, a monocle raccooned around his eye. "Fucking hell."

"And . . . cut!" says his brother, charging into the frame, the space sizzling with sinister vibrations. Helping N'golo to his feet, Micah presses both sides of the man's face with flattened palms and stares straight into his dilated eyes while Castor remains off to the side, shrouded in smoke and shame.

"Look at me, look at me," Micah says to the African in a private voice that is all patriarchal reassurance, a voice reserved for fireplace seductions and feverish five-year-olds. "Mtabi, quickly, please. Tell him we're sorry that we frightened him. But it's important that we make these pictures to show the world. Tell him that, will you, please?"

"Oh, bloody hell," Castor says, tossing the prop to the ground in disgust as Spiro and Early extinguish the hut with heavy blankets and buckets of earth. "Now you're a humanitarian, is that it? You incorrigible bastard!"

Ignoring Benny's words, Micah steers N'golo toward the scriptwriter, forcing the African to face his acting-partner executioner. "Explain to him, will you please, Mtabi, that Castor is his friend, that we're all friends here. That this is the time of great storytelling."

There is a long silence during which the man processes this information. Then N'golo's body answers with a jolt, a shudder that spasms from the crown of his head to the heels of his feet. It is an exorcism that asks the ground to absorb the bad *muntu* of the preceding moments. When N'golo finally speaks, it is very softly and gently.

"He thinks he understands," Mtabi translates. "He knows something of the slave routes of many generations ago and believes you to be storytellers of grave importance."

Micah exhales. "Good, I'm glad he understands what it is we're trying to do here."

"But he hopes for your own sake that the cine-camera absorbs some of this bad *muntu*," Mtabi adds. "Because he felt this thing. He really felt it."

Filming goes on all day, past the magic hour, into crimson dusk. Micah and Izzy have storyboarded the action meticulously, dividing the fifty tribespeople into units of fours and fives. As an additional safety precaution, the brothers decide to direct the actors to pantomime at half speed and undercrank the camera, similar to how they'd shoot knockabout stunt work in their comedy pictures. They film the scene from on high, in homage to similarly framed battle scenes from *The Birth of a Nation*. In the distance, Spiro snakes around Early and Castor, costumed as imperialists, hacking away at natives, striking them again and again and again, the Kabuki slowness of their actions accentuating and making strange the violence. It is something medieval and terrible out of a Hieronymus Bosch triptych or Goya's *Disasters of War* series, both visual inspirations that Izzy shared with his brother before filming began. The fields should have been bloodied, the grounds soaked, so sad had the time of storytelling become, so remorseless its verisimilitude.

Micah, ravaged by sleeplessness and sunstroke, held aloft by ambition and adrenaline, is everywhere at once, demonstrating to this costumed native how to strike a blunt machete against another's leg, illustrating to Castor how to hold a rifle in close-up, using Mtabi as a stand-in to teach two natives how to fall to the ground more poetically, lining up complicated shots for Izzy, hoisting Spiro on his shoulders to frame high-angle compositions of the destruction, thrusting a print of *Saturn Devouring His Son* into the pop-eyed faces of bewildered children. This is the mad dream realized, seen through Micah's dark-ringed eyes, pupils the almost-no-blue of fine glass.

Izzy had witnessed versions of this mania in his brother before, the need to size up and overtake any situation—playgrounds, detention halls, street corners, boardrooms, car dealerships—and win, cajole, torque, twist, and bend people to his will. It was these forces—Micah's animal energy and dynamism and blindness—that bound the company together and mediated the epic strangeness of the endeavor. The king was right to recognize some regal affinity in the man: In Micah's presence you felt better, safer, the impossible placed within closer reach. But Izzy had never before seen his brother put his talents to such demonic use; this the scabrous, gravelly underside of the charm and ease that allowed Micah to swim through life as frictionless as a seal. After twelve hours of filming—his twin's hands and face caked in mud, his shirt a gray windshield rag, his hair a nest aflame with grease and sweat—Izzy experienced Micah's manic energies for the first time as a terrifying, obliterating force and wondered if his brother wasn't in perpetual flight from some terrible void. Even while marveling at his brother, how Izzy hated his twin for his constant thrashing about, his narcissism and moral slop! How Izzy resented Micah's tornadic ability to sweep up everyone in his path.

"Is this what we came for?" Micah asks as the crew silently break down the equipment.

"We got some good stuff today," Izzy understates, taping up the tenth can of film and labeling it with the word "Massacre."

"No," Micah says, his voice a sharpened pencil. "Did you get what you want?"

"Better," Izzy answers.

"Mr. Waldo and Bumpy would be proud. My sister, too," Early says, circulating a canteen. "From the look of things, the king also approves."

"What makes you say that?"

"He's been watching the whole time," Castor grumbles, nodding to the top of a bluff, perhaps a third of a mile away from the production site, where King Mishi sits on a simple wooden throne, purse-lipped Talli whispering admonishments into the royal ear. It is too far off for Micah to read the king's expression, but in that moment he feels himself the monarch's intimate, two practitioners on equal terms with forces of magic and the collective psyche.

Micah points to Mtabi. "Promise the king that we'll return to show them the film when it's done."

"You're going balmy, man!" Castor exhales, hands on his hips, kicking at the dirt.

Micah stares across the expanse at the king's ill-tempered adviser. "Say it in their language so everyone understands."

And as the translated words are delivered by Mtabi, the first pitter-patter of rain, soft as elves' feet, wings its way down from the heavens. The drops strike thatched huts, bounce off crosshatched greenery, and are swallowed by gulping brown earth. The group looks up in unison as the swirling sky darkens at once, like melted chocolate added to cake batter, and a blue bolt of lightning—the first the Malwiki have seen in six months or more—traces a broken spine across the sky. There is a rumbling overture of thunder, followed by a conductor silencing the orchestra. Then rain begins to fall in earnest. It comes in bursts of Christmas tinsel and tossed blue blankets, waterfalls and rivers of the stuff, dams broken and bathtubs overturned from above, accompanied by slaps of contact louder than planks of timber felled in the forest. It comes in pails and buckets, pouring and sluicing around corners and bends, a pronouncement delivered right out of the heart of the firmament. Exhausted from their long day filming, at first the Malwiki think this is just another conjurer's trick, another Hollywood effect, placidly accepting it as yet another manifestation of the magic that has enveloped them since the Westerners' arrival. Then, slowly, registering this as the real, the actual, the thing itself, nature's long-awaited judgment on the worthiness of all their ways, the Malwiki throw off their false shackles and begin singing in the rain.

See, what'd I tell ya!" Micah booms, bursting, unannounced, into the king's private sanctum, trailing a fluttering parade of dignitaries and outraged wives. "I knew we'd do some good around here!"

Outside the king's quarters, the sound of raindrops continues tap-dancing on dry earth. Pots and pans of clay, metal, and glass have been left outside huts to gather rainwater, and even from the cool interior of the king's underground chamber one can register water's entire sonic range, its splashdowns in all keys.

"What does Hiding Feather have to say about this development?" the startled monarch asks Izzy, a devoted pupil who, in just days, has earned advanced degrees on the subjects of love digital, oral, and anal.

"I'm not certain the old rules of cause and effect still apply, Your Highness," Izzy replies, beaming. "But I'm glad it's raining!"

"Indeed."

The director steps forward. "Your Majesty, on this auspicious occasion might I put in a special request?"

Micah asks permission to shoot a lion. Not slay one but photograph one, venturing deep into the veldt to capture the big game in its native habitat.

"Let's leave photographing the birds and zebras to my kid brother," the director says. "I'm the captain of this company. It's only right for me to go up against the big cats."

"No, this will not do!" says Talli, the counselor betraying to the group his fluency in English. Outraged by the impudence of this re-quest—the king serving as lowly guide for decadent Westerners!—Talli quickly catches his mistake and reverts back to his native tongue. The counselor's high-pitched protestations are accompanied by a flurry of gestures, winged bats flapping from the end of either arm, but King Mishi lifts a silent hand against his adviser.

King Mishi raises in salute to the filmmakers a chalice filled with cool rainwater. He drinks. "We will plot this expedition as you wish. But with the understanding that the lion, the rhinoceros, the mastodon of the fields, these creatures you so admire, might not respect this as *your* time of storytelling."

"It'll be dangerous, is what you're saying?"

"Oh, yes." The king smiles.

"We brought the rain, Your Highness. What's a little kitten to a couple of fellas like us?"

TEN

Sleep came difficult to Micah here. When it did arrive, the second hand on Micah's wristwatch prompted a recurring dream. He is standing in a large ranch-style house, and an announcement is made that he has just five or ten minutes left to live, which sets him running through the place. As he runs from room to room—a succession of rooms like you'd find in the compartments of an overnight train or an ocean liner—there is the persistent sound of ticking clocks, and the announcer's voice provides updates: "You have five minutes left to live," "You have two minutes left to live," et cetera. And each room is occupied by different people from Micah's life: his parents, Izzy, school pals, professional associates, Margaret, his sons at various ages. And in the final room, sitting alone on a bed wearing her pair of satin gloves, is Rose.

To Izzy everything was waking dream. Once love had visited him, Izzy made no attempt to deny it. He walked around shirtless, with peeling shoulders, shirttails wrapped around his waist like a skirt, and a feather—a gift from Cri, the boy with a whisper for a name—fastened behind one ear. In the evenings Izzy had taken to bringing the prince back to the brothers' shared sleeping quarters, where they held each other like pliable pieces of cooling candle wax. If they didn't dare engage in congress in Micah's sleeping presence, still Izzy's brother would sometimes wake in the night, thinking of Rose and be comforted by the sight of his brother cradled spoonwise.

Izzy had wings, wings of his making and his choice. The former limitations and self-doubts were revealed as sand-castle monuments, imposing-looking but insubstantial edifices that could be knocked down with the slightest prodding. It went without saying that Izzy was the vessel (Cri was a prince, after all!), and if his first time was indeed painful, he felt a kind of flowering in himself as it went on, sensations that coupled pain and pleasure and itching and scratching and tightening and expansiveness and rippling and calm and pain and then no pain. He was on his knees, then on his side, then on his back, in a cool field at night. Cri was gentle but showed a determination in sex, too, that he kept hidden from daily view (a purposefulness that would serve him well, Izzy thought, in his future role as king). If the boy could have entered Izzy and pushed *through* him—subsuming him and passing to the other side—the cameraman felt he would have.

A catalog of sensations new to Izzy: the warm, inviting pliability of skin; the pleasant tacky quality of sweat and saliva and semen; the bristling of little hairs where Izzy didn't know he had any (at the base of his back, the rims of his earlobes, the fantastically sensitive stretch between his scrotum and anus). There were the improvisatory demands of the act, its shifting, problem-solution dynamics; a dissolving of self-consciousness accompanied by a heightening of the senses. There was the miracle of a beating heart, another human clock ticking away under his. There was the preposterousness of his cavity sealed like a ring over the boy, honest enough for a wedding vow. There was the senseless repetition of the procedure—pull it out, try again; pull it out, try again; pull it out, try again—a facsimile in miniature of a lifetime's trial and error. There was the rising, the falling, the grappling. There was the way the act dramatized its attempt to get at the bottom of itself. (If you intellectualized it, if you described the mechanics of it, if you tried frontal-lobing it, it made no sense at all.) There was the fragility, too, of grasping another's corporeal shell, an awakening awareness of the body as bone and gristle and muscle, a vulnerable container carrying a collection of spuming, gurgling organs. Tracing the delicate line of Cri's collarbone and the hollow it formed against his chest, Izzy appreciated just how fragile a body is and how sex is, among other things, an act of bravery, a test of resolve.

His parents visited him during the act, the first time their ghosts had appeared to him in years. They were there with him that first night Cri entered him, were with him as he wrapped the boy's arms around his shoulders, were with him as he nuzzled in the prince's armpit and inhaled his musk, were with him still as he greedily sucked on Cri's fingers. Did they know? For all their boundless love, had they been aware how much pain he had been in? Did they know him at all, these strangers who'd birthed and raised him? Was it sickening or happy-making for them to see him entwined in contortions like these?

"Hi there, Bean," his mother said as if she'd seen him just yesterday, calling Izzy by his childhood nickname still, the pretty lady in a dress he remembered from boyhood instead of the ravaged, cancer-stricken skeleton from the end. "I'm glad you're finally learning how to wrestle. I always did wish we'd been more encouraging about you taking up sports." There was no fooling his father, who watched the coupling poker-faced. A flicker of bodily disgust twitched across his mustache as the two men continued grappling—this from a man who had sawed open cadavers.

For Izzy, even out here in the jungle, being buggered by a black boy, his parents dead over a decade, how important their approval was to him! How important still, to be thought of as a good boy! Could his parents understand the necessity of the project, the entire apparatus of this stripping-away? Had they wished that their own lives had been bifurcated by some similar jolt, a severing from the systematized demands of household chores and office work, child rearing and holiday making—the thin chain of events called life that could, so easily, through accidents of history, have been replaced by other, equally valid catalogs of memories, irreplaceable loved ones capable of having been played by other, equally essential casts of characters? A comforting and terrifying prospect: the thought of his parents as other than his parents, a life lived without his world.

When it was over and the spirits had retreated, with broken language and hand gestures Izzy tried explaining to Cri how he'd been visited by his mother and father. The prince was unfazed. The Malwiki believed with little fuss in a spirit world, one that required neither palm

reader nor séance but that spun all around them, a cocooning continuum of community and feeling that extended across the divide between
living and dead.

"It must have been good to see them," Cri offered, responding to the
news as if Izzy had mentioned running into a neighbor down the block.
"Were they happy to find you here?"

"Yes," Izzy answered, sprouting another beanstalk, "they were."

A toast to my sister's wedding," says Early, raising a mason jar to the
union of his sister and the fifty-three-year-old barber who lived up
the street. Izzy is off somewhere with Cri, and Till is still laid up in the
village infirmary, so on this night before leaving for safari, it is Micah,
Mtabi, Early, Castor, Spiro, and the midget's contingent of four teenage
handmaidens lying around a campfire under a bluff, covered in thick
woolen blankets, passing around bottles and sitting out the rain, pro-
tected by the landscape's overhang.

"He's no oil painting," Early reports of his new brother-in-law, who
at that moment was standing knee-deep in hot towels and hair clippings
half a world away, "but he's a good man."

"And Rose?" Micah asks, accepting a cloudy bottle of rye from Castor. "How does she feel about him?"

"Rose plays those things close to the vest." Early smiling, stumbling
backward, and landing on his rump. "But he can take care of her."

"Well, your sister's a big girl," Micah says. "That's one of the things
I admire about her."

Castor retrieves from a satchel a flask of brown bourbon. "To para-
phrase the words of our friend Oscar Wilde, the first glass makes you
see things as you wish they were. The second makes you see things as
they are not. And the third makes you see things as they really are, and
that's the most horrible thing in the world."

"Fair enough," Micah says, draining his third shot. He waits for the
alcohol to do its work, for the binding of the pages of his personality to
loosen. Rose. It is worse that he should receive news of her wedding out

here, in her imagined homeland of antelope and sunshine and yams, out in the unmediated world. She was very much with him these days. Each time he passed something beautiful or odd or uncanny he'd note it for her, thinking how he would like for her to have seen it and how he might describe it to her upon his return, congratulating himself, really, for how deeply she might appreciate his own appreciation of things. Rose. If he were honest with himself, he'd never liked a woman more, never felt more himself around a girl, the two of them tuning forks humming at similar frequencies. He pressed his mind to deliver a metaphor that would strike at the heart of her appeal. She was the cool side of the pillow. The sugary milk left at the bottom of the cereal bowl. A perfect piece of blue sea glass found on a beach. She was gone, is what she was. He was out here in a delirium, and Rose was off getting respectably married to some black dude in Harlem, and Mishi had ten wives and Spiro had a harem and even his brother was off getting laid and Micah hadn't once turned to stone since their arrival. He wanted all things in all ways, he didn't want to give anything up, and he never pitied himself more than when surrounded by other people's happiness. He passes the bottle.

"Well, good luck to your sister and her barber friend," Micah says, rising to investigate a wardrobe filled with props and costumes. It's a great wooden coffin of a thing, more easily kept outdoors than in one of the huts, and as Micah sifts distractedly through its contents, he is reminded of being a child playing hide-and-seek in his father's armoire. Inside, there are colonial-style hats and seafaring helmets, ruffs and frilly things, plastic shackles and chains. The stuff of dress-up and make-believe. Micah screws a helmet onto his head and places a bolt-action rifle and a realistic-looking prop version of the same on the ground before him. He considers both of these items with a quizzical expression—one the authentic article, the other its simulacrum. Then he picks up the longer of the pair, and—in a sudden sequence of simultaneous and well-executed movements—loads the rifle, raises its scope to eye level, presses its butt against his shoulder, and places Castor squarely within his sights.

"Wedding toasts aside," Castor says, slowly redirecting the rifle muzzle with the back of his hand, "I've taken a closer look at the revised production schedule. *O, Africa!* is the real reason we're here, isn't it?"

"I came for the sea air."

"We're a thousand miles inland."

"I was misinformed." Micah puts the rifle he's holding back into the wardrobe, leaving the other on the ground. He plops down onto the nearest blanket and with his bare foot begins nudging a shiny black disk across a wooden checkerboard. "Look—I win! I win!"

"Okay, Micah, you win. But I'd like to talk to you seriously for a moment about this script treatment of yours."

"That's fine, but must we be serious?" Micah asks of an empty, upturned bottle. "Aren't some things too serious to take seriously?"

"Yes, now, putting aside how you brought us out here under false pretenses," Castor says, "if we're to continue shooting this epic of the Negro race, have you given any thought to the veracity of the thing?"

"The what?"

"Historic accuracy."

"Oh, forget about all that. . . . Look: An elephant in the distance, Till slipping on a banana peel, a slave roundup—it's all the same to me, just something to see." Micah recalls the schoolboy essay exams he'd turned in filled with stick-figure drawings of Washington chopping down a cherry tree and Ben Franklin summoning bolts from the sky.

"But you know something about the topic, right?" asks Early, ogling the backsides of some of Spiro's leavings, the dwarf having disappeared among lissome brown limbs.

"Your sister has some books in her apartment . . . but books won't tell us how to make the movie work. Rose cares deeply about these things, but she can't do what we can, she can't imagine it like this. It's not about the facts. I can tell you more about the slave trade, how the world really operates, from looking at this checkerboard. . . . We're *moviemakers.* . . . Images are our authority. . . . Seeing is believing. . . . This is what will be."

ELEVEN

The hours-long walk to the Citroëns was the first time the monarch and the movie director were together away from the eyes of the court, and witnessing the king out in nature, beyond the scrutiny of ceremonial duties, came as another form of instruction. Even more than the prospect of the hunt itself, Micah was delighted to have this uninterrupted stretch of time with the king: walking along paths, tracing hills, hearing him hum traditional songs as they went, watching how the man kept cool, a marvelous body moving through light and heat. It was like accompanying a sommelier down into a wine cellar: Everything about Mishi was expert and liquid; in the king's company everything was big-barreled.

For the day's expedition, the king dressed in a flowing gown of metallic gold thread; in motion he looked like an admiral butterfly, light bouncing off the white-and-yellow royal lineaments.

"Nice duds," Micah says. "How's the *muntu* coming?"

"Developing nicely," the king says, responding to the compliment with a happy gastric sound and a fragrant fart. "Keep working at it."

"Glad to hear it. Listen, what do the Malwiki make of all the filming? I know the other day couldn't have been much fun for them."

"Perhaps the rain has already washed away the memory," Mishi answers slowly, referring to the re-created village massacre and the series of counseling sessions held in his private chambers in the days since. "I have for many years tried to protect my people from such visions, but the machinations of the world change so quickly. As with any advance, one must ask oneself whether it is better to be oil or sand. . . . Ah, look, our friends the giraffes!"

Looming just ahead of them are two skyscraping beasts, munching on leaves high up in a tree, their priapic necks crossing each other like sabers, their hoofed and snorting presences stronger, more masculine and fearsome encountered in this proximity than at the zoo or under a circus tent.

"Oh, what we learn from animals!" the king marvels. "Each with its own signature upon nature, each its own vibration of *muntu*, each offering a reflection of human character as surely as every shadow casts its own penumbra. Take, for instance, the giraffe—always peering into the horizon, ambassadors of foresight and preparedness for the future. How much they have to teach us about ourselves!"

"Yeah, all that and their necks," Micah says, "tell us everything we need to know about being men."

Izzy preferred not speaking much around Cri, but he had grown entranced with the Malwiki language. Though it had a much smaller working vocabulary than American English, Malwiki had deeper poetic properties and greater associative depths. If the language lacked English's ubiquity of metaphors and similes, it was because the individual words themselves, granted the full authority of physical objects, were inherently figurative.

"Everything is everything," Cri explained when Izzy asked how the word for "sun" (*tangu*) could be the same as the word for "moon." Rather than assign the Manichaean dualities of the West—where things were good or bad, black or white, spirit or flesh—the Malwiki placed little stock in the binary. The word for "brain" was the same as the word for "thinking" and "memory" and "invention" and "the school." "Heart" was at once the proudly beating pump, the blood that the organ pulsed through veins, emotions of love and friendship and fidelity, and the faith that bound the community, all at the same time, each concept conversing with the others. Everything was everything.

"Your speech is so simple." Cri chuckled. "So slow-moving." Placing one pebble in front of the last, Cri attempted to illustrate to Izzy the English-language bricklayer's approach toward building and concretizing meaning. He explained how this quality was true of every foreign language he'd encountered: how the desire to achieve specificity and linearity was a means of evasion, a way of hiding behind curtains of words, of using them to obfuscate or circumvent the mystery of things.

The way Cri understood it, filmmaking had much in common with the Malwiki tongue, with action occurring simultaneously in front of them and preserved in a perpetually unfolding past, time folding back on itself, head conversant with tail. Cri understood immediately that their cinematic endeavors were enchanted undertakings. Cameras were dream boxes from heaven. Lenses eyes of gods. Filmstrips sacred scrolls. Without ever having seen a movie, Cri suggested that were you to crack open a person's head, ribbons of celluloid, ticker tapes of memory, are what you'd find pouring out.

It was because of this intuition that Izzy felt comfortable enlisting Cri's help behind the camera after Micah left Izzy in charge of shooting the shipboard slave revolt. That morning they'd already staged in King Mishi's underground chamber scenes of the slave ship's holding area, with men and women shackled in shadow, bodies pressed together and made abstract, sinister.

It was the first time that Izzy had worked on set without Micah, and he was able to monitor how his shooting style differed from that of his dervish brother. Izzy took longer with his actors and worked toward achieving a greater sense of verisimilitude in performance style. Early was assigned the part of the mutinous slave, digging at the nail holding his chains to the floorboard until his fingers drew blood. When the prop didn't immediately pry loose and Early asked him to call "cut," Izzy kept the camera rolling and instructed Early that he'd have to find a way to pull the nail from the base, leading to a fiercely realistic piece of acting on the part of the amateur. Izzy also held shots for a beat longer than his brother might have, offhand moments bracketing the takes and candid revelations as important to him as the scenes themselves.

Shooting a sequence by himself allowed Izzy to recognize how alive he was to the possibilities of location shooting and the opportunities for visual discovery it provided. Working with twelve villagers in the cold half-light, he was thinking of shot transitions from Eisenstein's *Strike* and *Battleship Potemkin*, he was thinking of Goya's pitch paintings and van Gogh's *Potato Eaters*, he was thinking of Christian iconography and Mathew Brady's Civil War photographs. Though they had storyboarded the sequence in advance, once Izzy was immersed in the chiaroscuro of the king's chamber, he had the inspiration to dissolve from the long rusted nail—a nail held diagonally in the slave's bloody hand like the very key to history's redemption—to the slanting deck of the ship. This morning, for the first time, Izzy felt like a movie director.

They'd set aside provisions for the safari the night before, Micah manfully taking it upon himself to help prep for the trip, drunkenly and in haste. There were canisters of gasoline and canteens filled with water. There were maps and field guides. There were canvas totes and duffel bags packed with cans of waxy insect repellent and sanitary supplies. There were binoculars and flashlights. There was a field camera and cans of film stock. There was the rifle and some flares.

Now the ark of imagery was filling. Before setting out into the veldt, on the outskirts of the village they had seized upon zebra and crocodile, distant herds of dwarf antelope and water buffalo traveling like motes through blocks of sunshine, wickedly smiling crocodiles with forepaws raised like cornered bank robbers, baby elephants with rubberized limbs and jump-rope trunks, large birds that opened and folded their wings like spoked umbrellas as they rose and dove.

"The lion is king, this is true," Mishi explains after relaying the story of his first killing, the act of a brave and unruly seventeen-year-old that led to his ascension, a terrifying yet humorous story of nighttime battle involving a coconut to the head, a fisherman's net, and the future king's being doused in pungent floods of lion urine. "But he is also much like a spoiled child, an infant accustomed to receiving his mother's teat each time he cries."

"Should we come across one," Micah asks, loading a fresh magazine in the changing bag as they drive, "how close should we get?"

"For your cine-film preservation project?" Mishi holds thumb and forefinger together like a chef deciding how much salt to add to a pot of stew, then spreads wide the distance between the digits. "We'll see. Wait for a signal from your king."

The set for the shipboard slave rebellion, which wouldn't have passed muster on the auditorium stage of an elementary school, looks convincing enough when seen through the viewfinder. A platform the dimensions of a king-size bed, an old piece of railing borrowed from Späten's ship, a white sheet for the ship's sail, all of it docked at the lip of the bathing pond, doubling for the Atlantic. Framed correctly, edited cunningly, augmented by postproduction trickery, there'd be a ship where there was no ship. This thin slice, this cardboard cutout, would carry the authority of oceans.

Playing captain was Spiro. Planted atop a costume crate, photographed from below, the first assistant director with his flinty, long-distance stare looked authentically seafaring, the gray in his face the color of a man who hadn't seen a woman, a citrus fruit, or a strip of land in many months.

"Feels like we're kids playing dress-up," says Early, stripped to the waist and covered with berry juice, lash marks blooming across his spine like a perverse family tree. "Just making things up as we go."

"That's a good sign," says Izzy, who recognizes the feeling: doing all the prep work so you could be relieved of it and be fully in the moment, alive and in sync with a world of spinning plates, where the off-the-cuff, the spontaneous, the improvisational, ends up flicking at the important stuff—*becomes* the important stuff.

"Arrgh, slave!" Spiro says, standing with hands on his hips, his shooting coat flaring behind him magnificently in the wind. "Why did Lincoln pick his nose?"

"Fuck you, midget!"

"To free the boogies, arrrrrgh!"

"Midget, I'm going to drive a *nail* into your neck this next shot."

"Save something for the performance," Izzy suggests, laughing to himself that here they were, a gallery of misfits—a black kid, a Jew fairy, and a circus freak—halfway around the world, pulling levers on the American culture machine.

With Till out of commission and Spiro and Early appearing in nearly every shot in this sequence, Izzy was depending on Cri to serve as best boy, meaning the prince would be responsible for handling props, taking meter readings, and negotiating reflectors for lighting continuity as the sun wheeled around the afternoon sky. Watching Cri begin to grasp how and why they were shooting things in fragments, out of chronological order, at variable focal lengths, inviting the prince into an understanding of Izzy's visualization process and the secret pride he took in his technical expertise—it all afforded the cameraman a kind of voluptuous pleasure. Izzy, sensing how Cri was understanding the fundamentals of montage, how discontinuous units of dramatic action would later be stitched together through the miracle of the new art, was beginning to believe that the mad project had the potential to transcend language and culture.

"Shiver me timbers," Spiro grumbles, watching Izzy and Cri go about their work with unabashed affection. "The jungle is atwitter with rum, sodomy, and the lash!"

"Yes it is!" Izzy says, the headlights of his soul all lit up, kissing the African boy on the nape of the neck as he brushes past. "Yes it is!"

The lion is sleeping when they come upon it in an open yellow field. King Mishi is first to spot the animal, uttering a single, satisfied syllable: "There." They steal up to it slowly, killing the engine and leaving the automobile doors ajar as they exit the vehicle a few hundred yards away, dust clouds ringing their trouser cuffs as they step into the scene. The Akeley is in Micah's hand, the rifle in Castor's. Though the situation is one of tremendous displacement, the men feel safe in the presence of the king, who moves with a dancer's surety toward the astounding vision, his glinting yellow robes rhyming with the lion's coloration, the gold of cold beer at a ball game on a sunny day.

With the animal lying on its side, its torso rises and falls like a baby's cradle, and the men are lulled and disarmed by the gentle rhythm. Afforded the luxury of examining the lion at rest, they first appreciate the animal less as a living being than as a startling contribution to the physical universe, things made more interesting and threatening for containing impressions of the uncanny and disjunctive.

Waves of color bring finer definition. There are oranges and whites and pinks and blacks—deepest black around the eyes and snout and feet—the rough, porous pads on the underside of the animal's paws suggesting something prehistoric, cracked, crumbling. The lion's mane, however, looks soft and cottony—what you might use to pad a basket before sending a baby down the Nile. Then the arrival of shapes. The animal's face is enormous—the head half the size of its body—and a surprising, elongated distance exists between its close-set eyes and boxy snout. The tail, the thickness of Micah's forearm, has a life independent of its owner, swatting away lake flies and swinging regularly even while the animal is at rest. In its length the lion is as big as a good-size sofa, its shimmering velvet suggesting a couch you might find in a sitting room at Versailles.

Raising twin forefingers like conductor's batons, King Mishi indicates that the others should stay put while he makes an initial investigation, sun-dried grass and twigs on the ground crackling like hay as he approaches the animal. His heart keeping steady percussion, a powerful memory of fear-conquering returns to Micah: daring himself as a child to sit in the front seat of the Chase Through the Clouds at Brighton Beach. Time's same unwinding occurs to him now. He recalls the slow, sinister cranking as the roller-coaster carriage yanked uphill, dragging him toward the pivot of fear. The conjoined, rising sense of dread and exhilaration as he inched his way up at that unlikely angle, street life, seascape, and buildings disappearing from his field of vision as he was pulled higher. Then a terrible leveling-off and a moment of looking out from that marvelous height as he was pushed far over the tracks, seemingly set free of the rails. And, finally, a roaring animal release, relief bursting from him like clouds of confetti as he lifted a few inches up and off his seat, gasps flying free as he punched his way downhill, the awesome sense of transcending ancient forces and fears as, the first drop triumphantly surmounted, he rocketed along reborn a faster, better, braver Micah.

The camera lends him courage now. Micah raises the Akeley to his face, sockets his eye to the viewfinder, and begins operating the instrument. The otherwordly vision is immediately tamed, subdued, made less threatening, through the distantiating filter. And it is as soon as Micah begins cranking the mechanism, as soon as frames of emulsion start making their Icarus pass through the shutter to get stamped by light's imprint, as soon as that inch-wide rectangular frame is tossed over the animal's image like a net, that the lion's sleepy eyes open and it lets rip a yawn that wouldn't be out of place during a late inning of a dull ball game. Rousing itself, the beast lopes somnolently, its head upright, duly taking note of the strangers and their varying distances from itself. He looks weary, heavy-lidded, like a middle-aged accountant handed a folder of tax returns to file just before day's end. The animal remains complacent, drowsy even—nothing more than a big house cat sitting on a windowsill contemplating a bird on a telephone pole—until it registers that it is being photographed. Locking eyes with Micah through the mechanical intermediary, the animal communicates its outrage with a slowly raised lip that exposes a terrible length of incisor. Having made its displeasure known, the lion inhales, bringing the volume of its chest to full immensity. Then, slimming itself, the animal rears back on its hind legs and catapults through the air.

"King!" Micah shouts, tossing the camera to the ground as Mishi dodges away from the animal in a yellow blur.

"Bloody hell!" Castor cries after taking up the rifle and, with impeccable aim, firing a stage blank into the dust.

Upon the introduction of the prop—an anachronistic bolt-action rifle standing in for the musket they were unable to secure from Imperial's prop department before shipping out—Cri immediately makes the connection between the camera and the weapon, christening both with the same Malwiki word. Both are instruments that rely on good optics and quick reflexes, both hard-lined forms one scarcely finds in nature, both implements of possession and domination.

With Izzy needed as an actor in the scene, playing the role of first mate, Cri has been charged with operating the camera for those handful of shots. For all his shyness, appearing on film wasn't something that Izzy disliked. Rather, he looked upon these rare occasions as opportunities to learn more about the nature of performance. Appearing in the scene, however, required some additional prep work on his part, and the night before, the cameraman created an animated flip book of the sequence, which he uses now, isolating several pages at a time in order to reference compositions and approximate shot durations. Once Izzy is in costume and light-meter readings are taken, the pair review the previous night's English lesson, repeating back to each other the words for "stop," "start," and the numbers one through ten. Cri stands in for Izzy as the cameraman blocks the scene, adjusts the aperture, and demonstrates a short panning maneuver.

"Good, good, good," Izzy says from behind the camera, shooting the rehearsal, his hand habitually churning the crank even after the scene is satisfactorily blocked and Izzy feels secure in Cri's abilities as camera operator. "Now, if you'll just hand me that prop."

Action precedes thought. Castor throws the rifle tomahawk style at the animal's hindquarters; the prop ricochets off the animal's left buttock and lands like a twig.

"In the car, now!" Castor turns and sprints toward the vehicle, first one in, leaping into the driver's seat, slamming on the gas as hard as he can, gripping the steering wheel hand over hand and interjecting the automobile between the lion and the other three men just as the beast begins to charge. Everything is viewed in flashes, events hopping in the periphery, but there's enough visual data to comprehend in the workings of the lion's musculature the enactment of some magnificent rope-and-pulley system, some marvelous lock-and-tumbler number, some murderous demonstration of cause and effect.

The lion rams into the Citroën, grotesquely smashing the driver's side—more billy goat than cat—its mane close enough for Castor to inhale loose dander and a not-unpleasant smell that mixes hay, mustard, and freshly sharpened pencil. The vehicle swerves at a forty-five-degree angle, the driver's-side door accordions in on itself, strips of metal gouging Castor's leg, all accompanied by fairy-tale sounds of spraying glass.

Jelly-legged Micah wraps an arm around King Mishi's waist, hoists him into the vehicle, and dives on top. With Micah, Mtabi, and the king all squeezed into the backseat, the Citroën exits its spin, tires aligning and exerting renewed traction confirmed by four corresponding puffs of smoke. The lion leaps and latches onto the side of the vehicle as it peels away.

Gaining a foothold on the running boards, the creature begins pawing wildly, half attacking the passengers, half sloppily trying to improve its grip. Rearing up, it takes a swipe at the king, successfully removing a segment of his shoulder as neatly as a chemist lifting a weight from a triple-beam scale. There is a delay before the blood arrives, the wound deciding what its reaction might be. Then red sparks everywhere, liquid fire flowing from an iron mine, and blood—with its almost-no-smell—is suddenly ubiquitous.

Castor veers wildly from side to side in an attempt to shake the animal off the car. The lion's snout—a wet, livid thing—pushes itself just inches away from Micah, who presses a Thanksgiving handprint against the animal's cheek. The moment is intimate, the contact relaying a message about the inadequacy of the match-up: so encrusted and vivid the animal's face, so tough and wiry the thick whiskers, so ancient and unyielding the undergirding bone.

The vehicle brakes, and the lion comes tumbling off, rolling over itself like a Chinese acrobat. Halting, the grizzly, pumpkin-headed thing performs a top-to-bottom shake, ridding itself of this indignity, and suddenly everything stops. The auto and the animal face each other, perhaps twenty yards apart. Contemplative and stone-faced, the animal is now the physical manifestation of a single idea. There is not enmity but a terrible lack of affect in the lion's eyes as it sits there, splashing gravel and determining which verb it will unloose to bomb, blast, steam, slam, slice, slash, smash, cleave, wreck, dismantle, and destroy the vehicle and everyone in it.

"Go! Go! Go! Go! Go!" Micah yelps. Castor grinds his foot down on the gas pedal, and the automobile belches its response: a sputtering engine and a hood hissing steam. Micah and Mtabi grab whatever they can—canteens, Baedeker books, gasoline tins—and begin hurling them at the animal. The objects glint off its back like streamers in a victory parade. The camera lies on the ground not a hundred yards away, black celluloid spilling out of the cracked chamber door. Its unspooled shiny filmstrip attracts the lion, which saunters over to it and begins playing with the tangle like a kitten with a ball of black yarn.

"Drive, Benny! For fuck's sake—drive!" Micah hears himself exclaim as the lion, irritated by the clingy jumble wrapping around its limbs, coils up again. This is it, Micah thinks as the animal springs through the air in a perfect parabolic arc that eclipses the sun, this is what we came to see. (That, and how odd for Goldwyn to have picked a lion as cinema's mascot. Why this particular animal? What about its ferocity relates to the nature of the motion-picture business? And he thought of Rose's wedding. Was it tacky and impoverished or a joyful affair? Had the day been a happy occasion or a lonely-making one? And he was thinking, too, of imaginary headlines in tomorrow's *Variety*: A GRAND MEAL: *IDIOT DIRECTOR, DEVOURED*.)

"Got it!" Castor says as the ignition catches, the vehicle peels off, and the beast crashes and conforms into a self-made crater. A moment later the lion is galloping behind them—its shifting weight and springy limbs far better attuned to the variable terrain than the shocks and rigid carriage of the boxy automobile—the animal gathering speed while the vehicle stop-starts, recovering and recalibrating after every molehill and dip.

"Sir," Mtabi interjects, a model of polite composure still. "I feel it important to note that a ravine lies ahead."

And, sure enough, a few hundred yards along, the plains stop altogether, the ground dropping away and the landscape resolving into sky, in what, it is impossible to determine: a cliff or a pit or the very end of the flat world itself.

Castor jackknifes the vehicle around, charging directly toward the lion, which continues sprinting, looming up larger and larger. Then an explosive hiccup signals that the engine has failed again.

"Get down! Get down now!" Micah screams, pulling at his friends, all of whom take up the curled postures of the unborn. All except King Mishi, who, damp with blood, rises like a spirit to face the beast. Confronted with a noble adversary at last, the lion bares its teeth as it leaps. Even in his crouched position, eyes squinting from terror and glare, Micah—his observational habits asserting themselves instinctively, visual acuity never finer than in Africa's irradiated light—believes he can see *inside* the animal's cavernous mouth, that he can discern in that self-sustaining micro-universe an insect, a gnat or a small beetle, cleaning one of the beast's teeth. From the perspective of the insect—busily removing some plant fiber or string of antelope muscle—all this furious activity is extraneous frippery. The bug has its job to do. Just as the lion has its job. And the filmmakers theirs. Apart from offering a profound insight into the nature of relativity, the vision makes, even Micah must admit, a not-bad note on which to go out.

But not today. King Mishi, all silken composure, lifts his spear and holds fast as the lion descends. He leans back, as far back as a deep-sea fisherman braced in his chair, holding his ground as the beast comes crashing down across the hood of the car. With the sound of a great head of cabbage being chopped in half, the weapon thrusts far into the

animal's torso, just below the white curtain of neck, the weight of impact causing the front wheels of the vehicle to rear up, then smash back
down to the ground as the lion's limbs splay across the automobile.
Deeper and deeper the king plunges the weapon, exerting more might
as the lion grinds down onto the car hood and drapes across the backseat as it expires, beginning to regain some of its earlier expression
of somnolence. The king, slippery with his own blood, stares down
his nemesis as he feels the spear rooting through stratified layers of
muscle and sinew and bone. The animal's breathing—heavy and hot
on their heads, offering its own form of benediction—gradually slows,
then stops. After some time the men rise from their huddles. One of
the lion's limbs rests on Mtabi, the paw cupping the translator's shoulder like the hand of a father acknowledging his son after a good showing at school.

"You okay?" Micah asks Mtabi.

"Yes, sir." Lifting the heavy extremity off himself by his fingertips.

"Benny?"

"Yeah, I'm good."

Micah looks to King Mishi, who sits slumped and closemouthed in
a corner of the vehicle, apparently breathing from the lips of his open,
palpating wound. For a long while, King Mishi does not speak or make
any movement until, meeting the eyes of the filmmaker, he grants him a
small smile. At this signal Micah bursts out weeping, hot tears mixing
with blood and water and sprayed gasoline.

The carnage is deep. Tourniquets are applied, stinging bourbon is
used as antiseptic, and wounds are dressed with fresh bandages. Though
the lion's weight causes the automobile to sag considerably; though the
animal continues issuing the message of its mortality the whole way,
covering the backseat and floor in inches of warm blood; though Micah
is sitting close enough to the animal to receive its residual heat and feel
its bristles brushing against him, King Mishi insists that they bring
the carcass back to the village, that his people should bear witness
to his trophy, that the animal's skin should be stripped and its heart
eaten. Rumbling through the darkening veldt, the Citroën looks like

an ambulance from the Great War zooming through the Italian front under bordello skies.

"We took the wrong gun," Castor repeats over and over. "We took the wrong blinking gun."

"It's my fault," Micah says. "I packed the prop by mistake."

"Blanks!" Castor says, smacking his free hand against the ruined dashboard, his bloodied palm crosshatched with gashes and embedded slivers of glass. "Blanks! You dragged us halfway around the world to pit us against a lion with a bloody toy."

Cri spent his days smiling, the kingdom of sunshine dancing on his face. He smiled through the worst of the historical re-creations, and he smiled today, too, all through the filming, right up to the moment the rifle went off.

Days and months and years later, Izzy remained convinced that during that flash, time had indeed stopped, that the universe had folded in on itself, and for that instant he could plot the progression of the shell leaving the gun barrel in a puff of magician's smoke, could chart through the air its demented trajectory, a straight line just a few meters long that in transit made some unholy wager between life and death. Izzy was certain he could divide the moment when the projectile hit Spiro's face—the impact, the explosion of brainpan, the spattering of bone and teeth and skin and tissue and viscera, the snapshot of an expression erased, a human face erupting into instantaneous abstraction—into its component parts, its discrete millionths of a second.

Izzy's bowels turn to ice water as Spiro rockets backward off the crate, and the narrative meaning of what's just occurred affixes itself to the permanent chronology of time. Early hunches over, grabs his stomach, and vomits steaming volumes into the earth, hands pressed on the ground in front of him, head lowered like a quadruped's. Cri, who has no idea what's just happened, clumsily points the rifle to the sky, confused as to how to proceed until Izzy gently relieves him of the weapon. The cameraman is surprised to find the gun still smoking and warm with Cri's touch, like a serving dish you'd pass to the person sitting next to you at a dinner party.

"What are we going to do?" Early says, directing his words to the ground, having erected an invisible wall between himself and the corpse. "What are we going to do, Izzy?"

TWELVE

The rain returned and continued unabated, pouring and flowing and streaming and washing over everything. It rained so much that the damp kingdom attracted frogs and toads and grasshoppers and algae and paramecia and other forms of aquatic nuisances and pestilence, all threatening to overrun and pollute the Malwiki's hard-won supply of fresh water. The huts were leaking terribly, too, and the Malwiki were cold and chilled under darkened daytime skies, wandering around the tropical pudding half dazed, drenched, and bedraggled.

The burial was held in the rain. In its imperative to return the body to the earth as quickly as possible, the ritual reminded Izzy of Orthodox Jewish funerals he had attended as a child. Draped in ceremonial robes, fingers wrapped in crinkling, bright-colored snakeskin, a painted wooden decorative mask placed over his face, Spiro was laid to rest not far from the site of his wrestling-match victory over Yani. Spiro had no surviving family, and the group did not entertain the thought of transporting the body to a final resting place in America. Better to bury him here, where he would forever be remembered as a champion and an honored guest.

Spiro's small wooden coffin had been elaborately decorated with all manner of carvings relating stories and legends from his life as the Malwiki had come to understand it. There was the hero's birth into a strange kingdom of little people, his adventures abroad on great sea vessels, caravan crossings over the Russian steppes, jalopy journeys to Tijuana, his glorious career as a maker of stories and as acrobatic master of the dream box. Certain of these drawings were based on fantastic tales Spiro had relayed to the villagers during their days together and nights spent swaddled in nests of Malwiki women. Others were based on the tattoos that twisted round his torso, angels and devils and hula girls and peg legs and ship's anchors and white whales. These coffin scenes were unified by a snake motif, an ouroboros wriggling its way around the bamboo box and devouring its own tail, signifying the soul's birth, death, and ultimate reclamation.

King Mishi, ashen-faced and convalescing still, is first to speak, praising the wrestling champion's athleticism and heroism and the special message his life held for the Malwiki about trusting essences over appearances. Afterward each member of the production company places a small tribute in the casket beside their fallen friend: a pair of spectacles from Till, an unopened pack of Camels from Early, a hip flask from Castor, Micah's pocketwatch. Izzy is last, placing beside his friend's strong, folded hands a brass kaleidoscope from his father's collection and a photo he'd taken of Spiro on the deck of the *Roi des Belges*. Then the casket is closed, and Yani approaches to fasten a ceremonial spear over its lid.

The next speaker is an unexpected one. Rip-cord thin, his physiognomy a distillation of the man's severity and ambition, Talli rises like a shade to deliver a speech that is more rebuttal than eulogy. The rains swell during Talli's peroration, plinking across the adviser's shoulders like sparks of electricity. Though Mtabi does not provide translation, it is clear that Talli's speech is a rebuke, a condemnation of the interlopers for bringing doom down upon the Malwiki. And it is from Talli's lips that for the first time during the ceremony the name of the prince is spoken, sending a shudder through Izzy, who has not seen Cri since Talli and the royal guards came across the horrific scene of reckoning and ferried him away. Whether as a matter of penance or punishment, the prince's whereabouts are unknown; Mtabi has relayed rumors that Cri traveled to the mountains to seek the forgiveness of the gods, while others have suggested he is being held in a jail beneath the royal palace, awaiting the verdict on his deed.

The rains continue through the ceremony, gaining in intensity as the funeral progresses, an invitation for slithering snakes and hopping frogs, which gravitate toward the casket. Women are weeping and stamping their feet, some of them rending their clothes like Hasidic Jews. Others are shivering in the cold, their sanguine mourning garments clinging to their bodies, bright wet reds lending them the look of hatchlings, river creatures coated in birth slime, a reminder of aquatic origins.

The casket is finally lowered, returning Spiro to the squirrel world. The frozen tableau reminds Izzy of his family's first sitting for a professional photograph a quarter century before. All of these photos were vaguely similar, vaguely sad. Families visited the photographer with the same solemnity with which one appealed to a doctor or a fortune-teller: Tell me how I am, tell me *who* I am.

"You mustn't move," the kindly portraitist instructed, generously obscuring Izzy's hands behind Micah so the boy could relieve his nervous energy across knuckle and palm. "If you do, the photograph will be ruined." Though the exposure time seemed endless to the fidgety child, it was the first occasion during which an adult not a schoolteacher or a family member had asked Izzy to participate in some serious undertaking, and Izzy brought all his four-year-old's concentration and fixity to the task.

It was this image of his parents that had appeared to Izzy that day in the field with Cri, his mother and father looking out at him from that formal studio portrait taken twenty-odd years ago, goggle-eyed, having done all they could to prevent themselves from blinking, less a Jewish family from Brooklyn than a stunned school of netted fish.

"It's a way of preserving the present," his father explained afterward, "like your mother canning peaches for the winter."

No it's not, Izzy thought now, witnessing shovelfuls of African earth being laid atop his fallen friend, the cameraman tempted to memorialize the scene with nothing more than its vanishing visual imprint. It's so they'll remember what you look like when you're dead.

THIRTEEN

Soon their last hours with the tribe were upon them. Under a tree as bent as the crook in an elderly man's arm, Izzy and King Mishi sit high on a bluff overlooking the village as it continues being battered by waves of wind and rain. It felt to them all that entire seasons had transpired since the company's arrival, but the truth could be measured by a single moon passing from ripest fruit to thinnest melon slice. They couldn't stay.

This was a pact unspoken between the men until the day after the funeral, when Micah told Izzy, "I've made contact with Bloat. Späten will be here in two days. You should tie up any loose ends."

No one had touched the film equipment since the dual disasters with Spiro and the lion. When Izzy went to retrieve the trunks, buried in a trench near the spot where he had first spotted Cri in the bathing pond, they were covered in mud and slime, a wormy welcome for a pirate plunderer. Izzy had wished everything to be washed away, but upon inspection the film cans appeared safe and dry.

It was King Mishi who had requested this final private audience with Hiding Feather on the morning of the company's departure. As he sat on their privileged perch, Izzy was reminded of his meeting with Marblestone atop the Wonder Wheel those many lifetimes ago.

In the days since the lion attack, King Mishi has recovered much of his strength, drawing vitality from the fallen animal and shaking off a dangerously high fever like a man shrugging out of an overcoat. His left shoulder was badly mauled, a cornice gouged from a mighty doorframe, but this only seemed to add to the glamour of the man, as some ancient statues improve their nobility through lost noses and limbs.

"If you look inside me, this is what you would see," King Mishi begins, holding his hand out flat against the landscape and watching clusters of rain perform their chaotic dance, then turning his hand over and sweeping it across the ravaged view of the village, "this grim magnificence."

A lava-colored frog leaps into Izzy's lap. It's small, no bigger than a dime, with brilliant black polka-dot patterns on its rump, bulging eyes, and self-satisfied cheeks. Izzy guesses from the frog's phosphorescent color that it's poisonous, but wanting to remain as close to nature for as long as he can, he allows the animal to sit there, inhaling the earthy earth.

"I did not have to return, Isidor," the king says, calling the cameraman by his name for the first time. "After I completed my schooling in the West, there were opportunities never to look back. But home proves a powerful draw no matter how far one travels. Even if one departs physically, home is not something one easily leaves. I suspect that in time you will discover this to be true as well."

"King, it would bring me the greatest happiness were I allowed to say good-bye to Cri."

"When Talli reconvenes the council, the prince will be judged and punished. Until then, not even his father can intervene. My most favored son, and I am powerless to help." Water streaks across the king's face; in the rain it is impossible to distinguish the work of clouds from that of lachrymal glands. "You have developed great affection for each other."

"Yes, King."

"This is where all good things live," King Mishi says, placing a hand over the Westerner's heart. "You will reside there for the prince as well."

"Thank you."

"Our time together grows short, and there are many things I wish to tell you."

"We never meant to hurt you—" Izzy blurts.

"But by pointing your cine-film machines at the Malwiki, you *claimed* us. Do you not appreciate that even now? With your camera hanging around your neck like a talisman even as we say good-bye to each other, do you not recognize how the Malwiki will be left so very different from how you found us? How with this invention you slip the lock of time, how with this device you remake yourself as a god? That is not a crime, Hiding Feather, it's a sin. Do you understand?" He holds Izzy's hand between his own. "Only time is God. Time is God. Time is God."

PART III

MAGIC AND DUST

1

IN THE COURT OF
THE CROWN

POT OF TROUBLE 1929 77m/BW *w.:* Henry Till, Mildred Mack, Ernest Morrison, Marion Lewis, James Wintz. *Dir.:* Micah Grand. **VHS, DVD $19.98** *IMPERIAL* ******½

Shoddily made, with a distracting preponderance of cheap-looking rear-projection shots, Henry Till's final silent picture finds his "glasses" character pursued through a patently phony, corrugated-cardboard, back-lot Africa. While there are incidental pleasures here involving a lost expedition and stolen idols, snapping crocodiles and garden-hose snakes, shrunken heads and cannibal kingdoms, they are all of a stripe that viewers have seen done before, and done better.

If the film distinguishes itself at all, it is for an offhand bit of business involving Ernest Morrison (aka *Our Gang*'s Sunshine Sammy). The iconic instant of the film—familiar from Academy Awards tribute reels and civil-rights commemorative specials—has Till's explorer character sharing a bubbling cauldron with the child at the picture's climax. The pair of them sweating profusely, Till drags a finger down the boy's cheek: "It doesn't run!" he marvels about the boy's dark skin. Innocently repeating the act, the boy answers the man with, "Neither does yours!"

This challenge is, one suspects, the timid and humorous flip side, forty years before the fact, of "They call me *Mr. Tibbs!*" and the hothouse atmosphere and bursting attitudes of 1960s American cinema. If there is a great subject here—the terrible treatment of blacks in silent pictures—it is sidled up against only to be eschewed, like a shy schoolboy who brings himself to the dance but is unable to separate himself from the gymnasium wall. The resultant slapstick, while serviceable, is doubly disappointing given that the man in the white suit, at thirty-two, is at the pinnacle of his athletic artistry.

MICAH J. GRAND (1900–1973), b. Brooklyn, New York

1923–1925: more than 100 two-reel pictures (including *Bothered Blue, The Kenosha Kid, Think Big, American Idyll, Knock on Wood, All the Marbles, Crazy Chester Followed Me!, Drop the Soap,* etc.). 1925: *Sweet Thirteen.* 1925: *The Cat and the Canary.* 1925: *Mr. Bosley's Busy Ballgame.* 1925: *Scaredy Spooks.* 1926: *The Pink Parasol.* 1926: *Bedtime Story.* 1926: *Mama's Boy.* 1927: *Under the Bandshell.* 1927: *Girls' Night Out.* 1927: *Cops and Robbers.* 1927: *Nine Lives.* 1928: *Penthouse Sweet.* 1928: *Hopping Mad!* 1928: *Moonshine Madness.* 1928: *Home Sweet Home.* 1928: *Quicktime.* 1929: *Pot of Trouble.*

What are we to make of the tradition of cinematic brothers, those fraternal pairs who begin with the wondrously named Lumières and extend through to our modern-day brothers Boulting, Coen, Dardenne, Farrelly, Hughes, Polish, Quay, Scott, Taviani, Weitz, even, very recently, the siblings Wachowski? Does the bond of brothers—so much competitiveness, so much child's play—provide some distillation of the roughhouse rivalry, the big-baby boyishness, that characterizes our great infantilized industry-art?

So Micah and Isidor Grand (nés Grombotz), twin sons of a Jewish pediatrician from Brooklyn. Isidor, the more technically minded of the two, pulled from optometry school to serve as director of photography for his brother's pictures. And Micah—as big-spirited, precocious, and anti-intellectual as Welles, separated from the more prodigious artist by just fifteen short years and a premodernist sensibility—a teenager hustling his way onto Brooklyn's Vitagraph studio lot, charged with helming two-reelers by the time he'd turned twenty, his first feature at the ripe age of twenty-three.

If Grand is little celebrated, little known, the question begs to be asked: What to make of the midlevel directors of the silent era, the journeymen and craftspeople who sprang up and pressed the medium forward an inch or two when the movie industry more closely resembled factory work than picture making? How best to honor those poets of pie, kings of custard?

For Grand was a talented shooter, restricted neither by literature (there's not an adapted play, story, or book in the bunch) nor by the early silents' predilection to film a popular stage performer's "act." Looking at the Grand brothers' pictures from the mid- and late 1920s, one is struck by the boldness of their camera movement, the confidence of compositions, the fluidity of action, all of which, in their agility and elegance, both mimic and honor the filmmakers' finest leading man and on-screen collaborator, the redoubtable Henry Till, the least deviant, least sexed-up, least narcissistic of the great silent clowns. In *Quicktime*—with its justly famous tour of the old Coney Island and its delightful cameo by Babe Ruth—some pinnacle of silent film artistry has surely been reached. We are here within hailing distance of Keaton's train, Chaplin's boot.

What, then, to make of this? For the directing half of the duo, a final film at thirty and still four decades of living after that! Though the career appears tragically foreshortened by the coming of sound, Mr. Grand enjoyed his forty more years, if not as a second-tier auteur ripe for rediscovery, then certainly as a professional-minded, hardworking artisan. His was a worthy, varied career. Despite the fact that Grand must now be considered a lesser light, he was a wunderkind still, whose flaring and cooling might illuminate the present.

After the feature work dried up, there was some noteworthy, albeit improbable, agitprop theater in the 1930s and '40s (including the legendary original Off-Broadway production of *Landlord!*). There was, later in the 1950s and '60s, erratic yeoman's work in television, often in collaboration with his brother, for shows that included *The Philco Television Playhouse, The Outer Limits, Route 66, Marcus Welby, M.D.,* and *Owen Marshall, Counselor at Law.*

There also was work that was better than good: The Grand brothers were there with cameras on the steps of the Lincoln Memorial for Marian Anderson's historic concert in 1939. Six years later they were among the first to bring to the world documentary proof of the death camps. And they returned to the shadow of the sixteenth president again, twenty years later and not quite yet elderly, to record Martin Luther King Jr. recount his great dream and its suggestion of a new America that might lie open and in wait. A sophisticated visual and moral intelligence, then, belied by a relatively thin filmography.

One last thing: The tale of the tape is framed by curious feature-length bookends, 1925's *Scaredy Spooks* and 1929's *Pot of Trouble.* If in the first picture Till's "glasses" character engages in the usual race-baiting inside the sheet- and flour-filled confines of a haunted house peopled by minstrel-show servants, in the second one, set in a Hollywood back-lot Africa, there are stabs at a tentative reconciliation of the races that still jangle.

More provocative still is the rumor of sequences for a film shot on location in Africa and of a very different picture straining to be made. Let the record show that Grand, his cameraman brother, Till, and a small film crew did in fact sojourn in and around the Congo region for some weeks in 1928–29. And from that trip the Grand brothers promised to generate a catalog of stock sequences of the African bush for the financially imperiled Imperial Pictures to license to other studios for use in adventure serials and sword-and-sandal beefcake. Let us also submit into the record that during this journey Grand's longtime first assistant director, Oscar Spiro (after whom, legend tells us, Hollywood's holiest totem is named), was accidentally killed, bringing the endeavor to ruin.

What occurred during the making of the mysterious African project? What shape was it meant to take? How did it come to be lost? What these queries suggest most profoundly, perhaps, is that Dream City contains within itself a counterhistory of films lost, pictures collapsed, projects forestalled, fantasy collaborations that never were, and movies neither brave nor insistent enough to force themselves into existence.

2

RAZOR BLADES AND LEMONADE

ONE

It was only once Micah had returned—after sorting through a Santa sack's worth of mail and Marblestone's telegrammed entreaties; after bills were paid and checkbook was precariously balanced; after lonely, dutiful love was made to Margaret and together at Benjamin's bedside they endured a vomit-ridden dark night of the soul; after his first hot bath and a proper shave; after all the hooks and clasps that yoked him to his terrestrial existence as a twentieth-century American husband, father, and professional had taken their measure, weighted his resolve, sunk into him, and deposited him like a wriggling fish onto the deck of his daily routine—only once he found himself standing in the browning half-light of Rose's apartment-building hallway on West 140th Street, not knowing whether she'd still be living there or not, only then did he consider how little the experience might have changed him, how a shedding of skins might also prompt the regeneration of the same.

The thing that guided him here like the North Star was something he had never mentioned to her. On Rose's windowsill was a small framed photo of her around the age of five or six, outrageously tomboyish and Afro-headed, looking away but smiling, fiddling with the brass buckle of her pretty blue Sunday dress. Past the accumulated unhappiness and adult disappointment, beneath the layers of bruising sexual experience and learned expectation that had settled over her like sediment, he'd caught glimpses of that girl. Generally Micah loathed indulging in that kind of sentimentality—the world was a blisteringly tough place, childhood an idyll, illusions best left for the screen. But he'd catch her looking at him sometimes in a certain way with what could only be described as hope, and there it was: the tenderness they allowed to pass between them despite themselves.

She drove him nuts. He had traveled halfway around the world to escape her and invisibly pay homage to her and complete the project of pushing her from memory, and still he couldn't stop thinking about her. At the outset he was confident they understood the situation in outline: the transaction that was taking place, what each was getting from the other, the contract they had signed. It alarmed him how his emotional equipment was outmatched by the weightiness of this lift. It enraged him to be caught in the gears of this self-perpetuating crazy-making machinery, the whole nagging thought apparatus that just wouldn't quit. It humiliated him to have become someone who spends his mental hours weighing outcomes and consequences, like a man circling a billiards table lining up endless series of shots he never takes.

She had taken up permanent residence in his skull, like some terrible tenant who wouldn't stop complaining. Even three thousand miles away, there was no escaping her dominion. How he hated her for rupturing his certitude and well-being and ease! He'd had better-looking women. He certainly didn't trust her. She was a grouchy broad and a world-class pain in the neck. He didn't like her entirely. He loved her completely.

If she's in, keep it light. Make like a knock-knock joke, he instructs his folded hand as it disrupts her peaceful door. *Micah who?* Exactly!

Her chin is sharper than he'd remembered. His first thought, looking at her beautiful frowning face, is that you could chip ice on it, which makes him crave a drink. Looking at her through a sliver of open doorjamb, he notices how her eyes turn Asiatic when she looks at him, and he marks, too, the determined tilt of her nose, like a speedboat planing through water. She seems unfazed to find him here, his skin now almost as dark as hers, twelve pounds lighter than she'd seen him last. Taking in all of her—her facial moles, her skeptical mouth, her questioning eyebrows, the Egyptian eyeliner, the light brown curls descending like streamers from her dark hive of hair, the modest glint of wedding ring on one of the fingers she brings to her mouth—his months-long menagerie of imaginings superimpose themselves upon the actual. She strikes him now, as never before, as a real-life heroine, a brave woman who a hundred years ago would've crossed the frontier by herself in a wagon train, single-handedly fended off a pack of Comanche with a water pistol, given birth alone outside under a bowlful of stars, then opened a can of beans with her teeth, strung a guitar with catgut, and sung songs to her baby by campfire.

"You got a haircut?"

"No," she answers, uncertain whether she is directing the word to his query or to the more general question of him.

"You had your hair crimped?"

"Try again."

"You let your hair *down*."

"Thanks for noticing. What are you doing here, Micah?"

"Is that any way to treat a friend?"

"You promised never to be my friend, remember?"

"Yes, that's right. I left my watch."

"Why are you here, Micah?"

"You don't understand." Having shouldered his way inside the apartment, the magic amber-lit box as he'd remembered it, but littered, too, with foreign objects—a stained brown jacket hanging slack on a wooden hanger, suspenders draped over a chair, a bottle of whiskey on the kitchen table, a large pair of boxy black shoes—all stamps of another man's presence. "It's special."

"You came for your watch?"

"It was my father's." Not addressing her, making a show of looking around the place, overturning and sifting through a tin soup can filled with pennies. "It's got sentimental value."

"I've heard of that." Rose gathers and smooths the hem of her dress. "Micah, I'm married."

"I know. Consider it one more thing we have in common."

"I didn't say you could come inside, Micah."

"Well?"

"Well what?"

"Can I come inside?"

The two of them clamped together again, how he missed her! How her eyelashes spread like Oriental fans when she closed her eyes. The smoothness of her skin, how it blushed and darkened around the buttocks and labia. The sink into her gluey depths echoed by the revelation of his own substance, shockingly white. Her unself-conscious wonderment at things—how, when he urinated after it was over, she'd marveled over the organ of micturition and procreation both: "It's like a train conductor switching tracks."

She told him everything: how Marblestone had stiffed the nonunion workers of their pay; about the latest police raid at the Honeypot; about the humiliating rent parties she'd been forced to throw, endurance tests replete with endless aluminum trays of macaroni and cheese, oxtail stew, red velvet cake, and gossipy neighbors; about the terrible desperation and self-betrayal she'd felt over finally accepting the marriage proposal of Jacob Dobie, the fifty-three-year-old barber who'd been pursuing her for more than a year; about the squalid nonevent of their City Hall wedding, wildflowers swiped from flower boxes for a bouquet, a Bronx-accented court officer the couple's only witness. "The dress you saw me wearing in the doorway was the one I got married in," she says, showing off the modest engagement ring planted on her hand, stone no larger than a shining snowflake, a chip of glitter embedded in the sidewalk.

"Why'd you do it, hon?" he asks her. "Why'd you marry him?"

"How can you ask me that, Em? I wasn't expecting any proposals from you, now, was I? I'm thirty-one; I don't make a sale now, who's going to buy it?"

"I'm sorry, honey."

He told her everything: about the light show of Africa; about the dignity and grace and generosity of the people he met there; about *muntu* and Malwiki notions of deep time and the spirit world; about the lion attack and Spiro's getting killed; about her own brother's gradual emergence as a serious young man; about how Izzy had found happiness, at last, in the arms of his African prince; about how he had checked in with her constantly in his mind.

"That's easy," she said, having nestled into his armpit during storytime. "It's easy to feel those things when you're apart. You can always make things work when you're alone in your head."

And there was the thing she didn't have to tell him. The beat of his heart, the beat of her heart, the merging of those two marching bands, and dawning recognition of still fainter percussion. That and the pleasing roundness of her abdomen that she'd tried to mask. Three months apart wasn't a long time, but still.

"Don't worry," she says, "it's not yours."

"You sure?"

"Yes, I'm sure. I wouldn't have let that happen between us."

They'd gone for it a second time, dorsalwise (Micah, mindful of the child, taking in the view), when the bedroom door opens a crack. For so large a man, Jacob Dobie makes practically no sound at all. Instead he quietly takes up a chair in the corner of the bedroom as Micah, eyes closed in rapture, continues working on his wife from behind.

"Micah," Rose says, gripping the back of her lover's thigh.

He opens his eyes and pops out of her, slick and upright before them all, the persistent asparagus the room's throbbing focus of attention.

"Slip that back in, son," the man says in a voice rich with burned tobacco leaves and swill and dark polished wood. Biting his lower lip and nodding in appreciation, he folds his hands across his chest as he nestles back in his chair, as relaxed and untroubled as a man taking up his favorite spot next to the radio after a long day's work. "Got to finish what you started. Daddy taught me anything, it's that: got to finish what you start."

"Do as he says, Micah."

"That's right, son. You look like someone who can walk and chew gum at the same time," Dobie says, crossing his legs and—was it

possible?—reaching into the night table, removing a bottle, and pouring himself a drink. "Listen to the wife."

They both keep their eyes on Dobie sitting in his chair as they
resume the act. Stretched across the length of the barber's wide forehead is a horizontal line as deep and insistent as a mouth, from which
all the man's facial expressions appear to be rigged. Dobie's cheeks are
lightly mottled, like brown arts-and-crafts paper where drops of water
have spilled and dried, and above his lip resides a patch of mustache that
looks like it was penciled in that morning by a cartoonist, a thick black
bar that glistens vaguely wet. After he's shrugged out of his checked
suit jacket, the man exposes a great dignified gut that's rounded but
firm and without flab, a prideful stomach that announces to the world
that its owner would never go hungry.

"Just so we clear, Eagle Scout," Dobie says, stretching his long legs
straight out in front of him, swirling his drink and sniffing its mystic
brown vapors. "Man who don't know what his bride up to a cuckadoo-
dle. I *know* what my Rose been up to. I'm privy to everything happens
in my house."

God Almighty! Micah thinks—working himself into a pleasurable
rhythm despite himself—not another one of these! When would Micah
stop encountering these characters, these proscenium-faced men—these
ghouls with great, gargoyled, Grand Guignol masks? Marblestone, Mr.
Waldo, now Dobie—this tribe needn't say nor do anything to broadcast
aggression or threat; it was all mapped right there on their epidermis.
You're not talking about human beauty or ugliness or even anatomi-
cal necessity with these characters. Instead their features work as cartoon projections of personality: noses that thrust and jab, eyebrows that
punctuate like typewriters, assaultive eyes and mouths that poke you in
the chest. When would these men—these lunatic men with their terrible, insistent faces—stop haranguing him?

Dobie begins to undress.

"Moviemaker," he says, standing and kicking off an enormous pair
of black shoes, broadcasting to Micah that he knows some facts about
him, that his name hasn't gone unspoken in the apartment since Dobie

had begun sharing the address. "I'd ask if you gift-wrapped the package, but that doesn't much matter nowadays."

Dobie scoops out of his suspenders—each loop diving away from him and smacking against his thigh in suicide leaps. Then up come the shirttails. He goes after his shirt buttons with nimble fingers, as expert as a society matron wielding a lobster fork, and Micah begins to sense what an excellent barber the man must be. Next the belt lashes off in a single stroke, its clanging brass buckle suggesting a deadly double life. Off come the heavy wool trousers, accompanied by a musty, shameful locker-room smell. Down come the boxers, the jaundiced T-shirt is lifted overhead, and Dobie stands before them completely nude. Even partially obscured in the dark, it is clear he is a powerfully built man; thick-armed and stocky-legged, with skin marked by unexplained scars and large ashy patches. Micah—inside the man's wife still—climaxes and dismounts just as Dobie takes up residence at the edge of the bed, causing that side of the mattress to sink.

"If you're finished up in here," Rose's husband commands, slapping her nearest thigh, "why don't you go the next room, put on some cocoa."

Dobie stares at Micah's shriveling member with its exposed mark of Abraham, slick with his wife's slime. Micah stares at Dobie's veined purple thing.

"Yeah, I heard of you, moviemaker," Dobie says as his wife exits the room. He is spilled out on top of the covers, as resplendent a physical presence as an Alaskan grizzly.

"I've heard of you, too," Micah says. "Would it be all right if I put something on?"

"You spend all afternoon rocking-and-rolling with my wife, engaged in all kinds of skulduggery, you going to ask my permission to get dressed? You go ahead, do what you like."

Micah remembers that relations with Rose started in the other room and that all his clothes are scattered there. So he rises from the bed, reaches into the closet, and pulls out the first thing that greets his hand. He can't explain why, but Micah feels safer, less ill at ease, wearing the man's bathrobe. It's crumpled and brown and smells of cod liver oil and cologne, and Micah cannot imagine the barber—a person who drapes protective aprons around his customers—bringing harm to him while he is wearing the man's own clothes.

"Back down on the bed, son," Dobie instructs, folding his hands across a barrel chest covered in curly black wire, his body heat and weight erasing the faint imprint of adulterous elbows and knees. "You got some good fuck in you, I'll tell you that straight off. Most white boys I seen in the army just hit that honeypot fast as they can, only take but a minute. But with you, I could tell, you and Rose's got *chemistry*, you're trying to *communicate* something, take your time. I see that, I think, *watch* that, let they mind they business, enjoy they fuck, see if they can't *get to the bottom of it*. Sit in the corner, fix myself a drink, see if we can't discuss the situation like equals. *Honey!*" Dobie barks into the next room. "Is our refreshments ready?"

"Not yet!" Rose calls back in a voice different from the one Micah recognizes.

"Save some of that hot water! Bring me a bowl of that and my razor and shaving brush." Turning to Micah: "You ever have a hot lather shave?"

"They're not my favorite."

"Well, you're going to get a proper one today." Dobie rises from the bed, lifts the wooden chair from its corner, and slams it down in the center of the room, making four exclamation points where its legs connect with the floor. Naked still, he hoists the adulterer off the bed and drops him into the chair like a sack of potatoes. Rose reenters the room, now also dressed in a bathrobe. Over one forearm hangs a towel. A porcelain bowl of steaming-hot water presses against her middle, and around it her hands hold a folded straight razor and a sudsy brush in a shaving mug.

"Rose . . . ?"

"Don't worry, Em, he's a professional," she says, placing the tools on the nightstand. Her eyes are steel, her mouth a nautical horizon. "Just promise to stay very still."

Rose takes her leave, and Dobie begins to whip the black badger brush around the inside of the shaving mug like he's beating an egg. "Rose is past thirty. She's no spring chicken, I got no illusions about that," he says, continuing the conversation as he clockwises generous helpings of hot lather over Micah's face and neck. "No illusions about her arriving to the ball with a past that isn't folded into the present. No illusions that the past don't breathe the *air* of the present."

The barber returns the brush and mug to the nightstand and retrieves and opens the black wood-handled razor—as simple and elegant an implement as a fountain pen or a pocket lighter. He takes up his position behind the chair—the man's soft privates brushing against his guest's back—and begins waving a thick, weapon-wielding arm in front of Micah's face. "You go with or against the grain?"

"With."

"Good," the barber says, the first impeccable stroke down Micah's right cheek making the sound of a skater's initial push out onto the ice. "You got some ingrown hairs there you should be mindful of." He switches sides, swooping down the planes of the left half of Micah's face. Next Dobie pinches together the wings of Micah's nostrils, lifts his nose, and begins scraping away at the ill-defined territory between his jaw and neck. "Careful your chin doesn't grow a second cousin down there."

"Thanks."

"So a piece of advice my daddy gave me I'll pass along: Some women worth killing for but ain't worth dying over."

"I've met a few of them."

"You ever been to Europe?"

"Yes."

"Well, in Eye-talian cultures"—scratching at one side of his mustache—"there are powerful men keep in their lives important ladies who's not their wives. They have a word for it in Sicily. You been to Italy?"

"Uh-huh," Micah says without moving his lips. "You?"

"Harlem Hell Fighters," Dobie says, stanching a nick with the towel. "Little blood there, my apologies. Anyway, I know Rose is more than just another lay for you. I know you and Rose got *history*. But I want you

to know I chased that girl for years and won her honorable, and she's . . .
well, she's my Rose. Leave the sideburns long, right?"

"Yes, please."

"What I'm saying is this: I'm a man of the world, too, about as much
as a colored man can be in this piss pot, and I'd rather accept the known
than be fearful of the unknown. So long's I know whose potato she's
peeling, I'll run my marriage best I can, and my business best I can,
and when the baby come, if you like you can be a silent partner in that
enterprise, too."

Dobie finishes his work, wiping stray stripes of foam from Micah's
cheeks and neck with a warm towel. Micah's face stings with cold.
"There, you been laid, shaved, and filleted all in the same day. What I
say sound like a fair proposition to you?"

"Does Rose know exactly what it is you're suggesting?"

"*Know?* What *know?* The world is what it is, what's to know?" Dobie
says, bending down to retrieve his boxers, giving Micah a view of his
powerful haunches. "Just leave the back door free. Leave that pudding
for me, son. Some things got to belong to a husband alone."

TWO

They worked together in silence. After weeks of riotous stimulus, the return to the editing room came as a sanctuary, offering monastic quiet and concentration that was itself a form of prayer. The brothers were relieved to find themselves back in this ascetic arena. They worked twelve-, fourteen-, sixteen-hour days, cataloging Marblestone's Noah's Ark of stock footage, putting together a rough assembly of the location sequences for *Pot of Trouble,* and working most diligently and worryingly on the roundup, village massacre, and slave-ship passages for *O, Africa!*

Izzy had initially been inconsolable following the brothers' return. He ignored Howard's entreaties to meet for drinks, limited spoken communication to monosyllables, ate hardly at all, bathed little, slept less. Once, confronted with a bar of Palmolive soap as white and substantial-looking as a boiled chicken breast, Izzy sniffed it, then began eating. Micah was so worried about Izzy that a few days after their return he'd installed him on his family's living-room couch, his brooding brother's newly brown and slim form an immediate object of fascination to Micah's sons, who at first mistook their uncle for a dusky native their father had smuggled home in a box.

"Prove you're Uncle Izzy," Benjamin pleaded, fingering the stranger's brightly beaded African necklaces.

"I can't," Izzy answered, his head a crate packed with cotton. "I don't remember what it was like being Izzy."

"What's your name, then?"

"Hiding Feather."

"Then where's Uncle Izzy?"

"I'm not here."

If since their return Izzy had been as listless and withdrawn as a tortoise, there was one thing over which he couldn't mask his anticipation: the arrival of the developed reels. As for a virginal groom approaching his wedding night, expectations mounted. What would he find? Would the brothers be greeted with something revelatory as anticipated, or would the reels come back damaged, ruined, blown out? It was only once the work print came back from the lab and they began the arduous labor of sifting through all they'd shot that some atavistic reflex took over and Izzy was able to replace his catatonia with fierce concentration and critical discernment. This was craft. After everything else had left him, after all the old ways had been hollowed out, what remained was craft. Terra firma to which he could retreat, his mechanical certainty was the shoreline that absorbed the waves of his erratic emotional state. Sitting in the editing room in his brilliant red dashiki, though he looked like an unemployed Coney Island swami, bangles and beads clanging as he went, Izzy could function so long as he was working.

The editing facilities were situated on Forty-First Street and Fifth Avenue, near the epicenter of the brothers' lost, glittering city of white. When they arrived back in New York in early February, in the post-holiday gloom Manhattan looked as tired and lonely as an outdoor pool in midwinter. But that was just street level. Lifting their eyes by degrees, the brothers found the metropolis in the midst of convulsions, the city's vertiginous skyscape tarpaulined in struts and girders, ladders to some imagined empyrean, a child's game of pick-up sticks writ large.

"It's not about better views or more office space," Marblestone suggested to the boys one time he was in New York, zipping through the city's canyons in a crowded yellow cab. "It's the old child's game with the building blocks: 'How high can I make it so it won't fall down?'" They were zooming along Lexington, all the lights falling for them like dominoes, each of them a brass-buttoned marching-band leader bracketed on either side by brick and steel walls of brown and gray lined with relentless shoppers and businessmen and matrons in overcoats and furs and fedoras carrying bundles and newspapers and suitcases and umbrellas, and Marblestone loved them all.

Though the sixty-story Woolworth Building still reigned as the tallest building in the world, Micah and Izzy could on clear days mark from the editing room's window the progress of the Bank of Manhattan Trust building downtown and, over on the East Side, the skeletal frame of the Chrysler Building on Forty-Second and Lexington, its silver silhouette gleaming like an ancient spike. Most days, however, the blinds remained drawn. They worked dispassionately, never once referring by name to lost ones as they encountered them through the Moviola, but always objectively, as in, "I like what he did there" or "I prefer the way he steps into the light in that take."

They lost all sense of time. Keep him working, Micah thought. Keep him busy and the work will bring him back to you. Familiarity will crowd out the exotic. Indeed, the work had already returned Izzy's appetite to him. Micah had set up a military cot in the corner of the room, and the brothers took turns sacking out for an hour or two at a time, but the noshing was nonstop. The editing-room floor—a checkerboard tile littered with congealed Chinese-take-out cartons, halved pickles, milk-shake spills, crushed coffee cups, rinds of toast, accordioned straw wrappers, balled napkins, and smashed cigarette butts—came to resemble an archaeological dig fossilizing their diet.

Izzy had turned a corner of the suite into a shrine. There was a map of Africa overlooking wooden figurines, reliquaries, small finger drums, beaded bracelets, and the blunted copper head of a wrestling spear. Every time the winds of exhaustion whistled near or visions of the sensual paradise he had left behind threatened to get supplanted by other thoughts, Izzy would sit before this pond and bathe awhile in its colors. On the windowsill adjacent to this memorial, he arranged a collection of hourglasses, a half dozen of them, each bigger than the last, lined up in a row like a series of Russian nesting dolls, the first one good for counting off fifteen seconds, the next thirty, then a minute, two minutes, five. Filled with timeless blasted particles of rock, these wizardly ornaments suggested both an accurate means of measurement and the quarry of things limitless. Izzy put the hourglasses to good, practical use clocking sequences and gauging film time to real time. But it was more for symbolic reasons that, remembering King Mishi's final words to him, he wished to keep these reminders of the finite and the illimitable near at hand.

"Izzy?"

"Yes."

"We haven't been outside in three days."

Izzy interrogates an empty oyster pail of egg foo young. "Has it been three?"

"Margaret's getting worried, we're running out of oxygen, and my balls are turning blue. How're you holding up?"

"I'm okay," Izzy lies, pressing a thumb upon a single frame he had excised from a discarded take, the oils from his fingerprint forming a perfect palimpsest over a close-up of Cri's face, the color, pliancy, and texture of the prince's skin the product of several centuries' worth of African sunsets. "But the thought of never seeing them again is just impossible."

"I know."

"We made a promise, Micah."

"And I mean to keep it. We'll meet with Sidney to talk provisions as soon as he circles back east. In the meantime, let's finish our work here and I'll make the trip out west," Micah says, crushing an empty box of Camels underfoot, contributing to the impasto below. "I gotta get some smokes. I'm going outside—wish me luck!"

Consulting his wristwatch in the elevator, Micah is surprised to find it just after 3:00 A.M., the inexhaustible city at this hour quiet as a moon. Not even newspaper stands would be open. Hitting the lobby, he sniffs himself as the doors open: tobacco, coffee, dried sweat, an overlay of aftershave, an alchemy of smells that occur when men coexist in cramped quarters for too long. He can feel his eyes sunk deep in their sockets from lack of sleep and knows he looks like hell. Without fuel from cigarettes or sauce, Micah worries that his synapses will quit making cognitive leaps. Thankfully, Donnie "Shago" Moody, the colored night doorman, is sitting reliably at his station enjoying a smoke.

The night watchman's desk is situated down a hallway perpendicular to the elevator bank, so as Micah approaches, he can see the doorman in profile without being immediately spotted himself. Shago can, however, hear the clackety-clack of Micah's heels across the marble floor and answers the sound by visibly flinching. He stubs out his cigarette, puts his doorman's cap atop his broccoli sprig of hair, straightens up a few pertinent inches, and places both hands flat on the desk, the dingy uniform against the ramrod posture lending him the look of a comic figure out of Shakespeare. Turning and recognizing Mr. Grand shambling down the hall—rather than a surprise late-night visit from the building's management company or some senile dowager needing help with her dog—Shago exhales, loosens a measure of physical tightness, and relieves himself of some height. After months away from home, Micah is grateful for the lesson: confirmation that in America every black leads a double life.

"What's shaking, Shago?"

"And a fine evening to you, Mr. Grand." Rescuing his cigarette butt, the doorman's practiced tones of survival and supplication giving way to the man's true voice, a rolling, tumbling thing. Across Shago's cheeks are a collection of weird moles and growths, specks of cocoa drying on a kitchen counter, that light up when he inhales. "Cutting your latest picture?"

"Yeah, been holed up for a few days," Micah says, airing out his jacket of hamburger grease and stale fart. Shago packs the carton tight and passes it to the filmmaker. "You're a prince at midnight," Micah says, shaking off the compression bends and recognizing with a shock his own weary expression warped and reflected in the lobby's brass piping.

"Mr. Grand, let me ask you a question," Shago begins, leaning in with a light. "Speaking hypothetical now, if a person was inquiring around about an individual—a bad dude from uptown, say—would that information be worth something to someone?"

"Depends who's buying," Micah says, peeling a dollar bill off a roll and laying it in Shago's leathery palm.

"Flank's a fine cut of steak," says the doorman, "but no sirloin."

The filmmaker adds two more singles to the pot.

"Papa likes them potatoes *crispy.*"

And a five.

"Pour some gravy on them biscuits, baby, you'll get it *all.*"

"All right," Micah says, laying another Lincoln across the man's hand. "What's the rumpus?"

"Coupla coon-ass black-ass jackaboo motherfuckers looking for you, Mr. Grand," Shago says. The doorman proceeds to fill Micah in on recent goings-on uptown, relaying how during the few short months the filmmaker has been away, the twenty-two-year-old Bumpy has broken ties with Mr. Waldo and taken up with Stephanie St. Clair, the Martinique-born Frenchwoman known as Madam Queen or Queenie, who has become the dominant player in the numbers racket uptown. Shago explains how Queenie lured the wild child away from his brokenhearted mentor, Mr. Waldo, who has fallen deep into debt, dejection, and addiction. First St. Clair assumed all of Mr. Waldo's business interests. Then, taking Bumpy under her wing like a mother hen, St. Clair transformed the young thug into a freshly minted prince of Harlem, unleashing his gang of enforcers across the midnight city and consolidating power uptown just like Dutch Schultz had done for the Jews, Lucky Luciano for the Italians.

"Mr. Waldo's no longer running the show?" Micah asks.

"Byron Marcus Waldo's fortunes are as flat as a tire."

"I'm away for three months, no one notifies me about the change in management?"

"The young dude talking up how he's in the motion-picture business now," says Shago, explaining how Bumpy has been asking about the filmmaker since he got wind of Micah's return. "Says he got *points.* Says he wants his piece of apple pie—with a slice of American cheese."

"Huh."

"Pardon my French, Mr. Grand," the doorman marvels, "but you making a *movie* with these motherfuckers?"

"It's complicated."

"You a respectable person, Mr. Grand. What are you doing getting mixed up with these characters?"

"Let it drift," Micah says, stubbing out his butt and scribbling on the back of a note. "Listen, here's another five-spot. This is the direct line to the editing room: At the first sign of Bumpy or any other dudes with lapels like pelican wings, I want you to call that number, okay?"

"Can't take that," Shago protests.

"I just gave you ten bucks."

"Thirteen, but who's counting?" Shago says. *"That's* Christmas dinner, thank you very much. I take *that*"—pointing to the rejected bill—"I'm on the payroll. Therein lies the distinction. Mr. Waldo, he's old-school—a person can cut deals, talk sense, wiggle-waggle. But this next generation coming up, Bumpy and the crowd he runs with, is *wild,* man. They will slice you up like banana over cornflakes soon as look at you twice. Brothers like that are like pigeons—lay down with them once, you mate for *life.* You understand? You see each other ten years from now, you *still* make it, it's never over with that kind. Lemme offer you a piece of advice, and I'll provide it free: It comes to fellas like this, there are exits, but there are no escapes."

F our pieces of correspondence reach Micah care of the editing facility during the brothers' hibernation. The first is a telegram from Marblestone, summoning Micah out west to screen the Africa footage ASAP. (WELCOME HOME BOYCHICK. WHERE ARE MY LIONS AND TIGERS?)

"Bellyache better," begins the second post, a rare handwritten note from Henry Till, who is as terse a wordsmith in print as on camera. "Had Marblestone to the house," continues the letter that Micah keeps hidden from Izzy. "Half the man he was. V. ill. Till."

Third is a notecard that had been slipped without notice under the editing-room door days earlier. Printed on engraved stationery bearing the calligraphy initials "S. St. C." and a return address at 131st Street, the message inside the card reads simply and cryptically, "Wednesday at noon." It is only after his conversation with the doorman that Micah understands this to be a royal summons, an invitation from Stephanie St. Clair that he would be wise not to ignore.

"This is the beginning of the end," Micah says of the final and most elaborate of the missives, a gilt-edged invitation from Academy of Motion Picture Arts and Sciences president Douglas Fairbanks explaining that *Quicktime* has been nominated in the category of Best Comedy Direction as part of a new industry awards ceremony to celebrate the best films of 1927 and 1928. Micah folds the gala-event subpoena into a paper airplane, which he sends sailing across the room. "Once we start pinning medals to our chests, forget it."

"Maybe," answers Izzy, who agrees to stay behind in New York to work on the rough assembly of *Pot of Trouble*, while Micah travels to Los Angeles to attend the awards dinner and review the stock footage with Marblestone. To Micah's mind this is no bargain: forty years' desert travel by donkey preferable to the forty-eight-hour futurist ordeal involving overnight trains and jumper planes—bad back, stiff joints, and constipation his almost certain rewards for making the trip west.

"You want to take a look at this?" Izzy asks, rewinding a split reel. They've been working all day on the slave-roundup sequence, and he readies a rough cut for his brother. Izzy stands huddled over him as Micah presses his face to the viewer, eager to gauge his brother's physical reaction to the winnowed selection of shots, the braiding of light and dark, the rhythmic cutting and metronomic pace, the entire heightened, deterministic reassembly of experience.

Micah has been handling Africa footage all week, cataloging hundreds of takes in a spiral notebook, wielding the grease pencil, trimming fractions of seconds like a topiary gardener pruning pine needles; he is a professional who prides himself on call-and-response powers of detachment and engagement, but still, viewing the assembled sequence comes as a shock. Have such faces as these ever been seen before, in this way, in all their dignity and ranginess and human singularity? He is viewing their work—a reiteration of land, sky, water, and faces—and it is at once naturalistic, archetypal, and consummately strange.

Through the viewer pass before them friends and colleagues, a magic foreign land, a temple of radiance, a parade of history written in light. Through the little screen, horrors assemble themselves, wiping across the kingdom of enchantment like clouds building toward a storm, swells at sea, plague made visible. Though the brothers themselves have orchestrated what they are watching, though they have choreographed and been present for the staging of it, Micah is unprepared for so unsettling a realization, unprepared for his own reaction to the full flower of imagery written in bone and blood. The footage fulfills the requirement of all great work: It widens the availability of experience a lane, restoring to the world a degree of the uncanny while confirming that, yes, *this* is the way the world works. The recognizable is made shocking; the unfamiliar is made proverbial. When it is over, Micah steps down from the stool and puts an arm around Izzy's back.

"Well?" his brother asks.

"It's good work," Micah says. Then, taking a breath, "Goddamn it, it's important."

THREE

I have been spending more and more time in the Americas," begins Sidney Bloat in his crypto-European accent. It has been three months since the brothers last saw him before departing from the Congo. Upon learning of the importer's visit to New York just before Micah is due to leave for L.A., they had arranged to meet for dinner at the Mercantile—a smart, clubby, smoke-filled midtown restaurant within walking distance of the editing suite. Bloat was already seated at the table—nattily dressed in a blue velvet blazer and royal purple cravat, his dark hair and mustache longer and more cosmopolitan-looking than they'd remembered—when the brothers made their unkempt, unshaven, cavernous-eyed appearance.

"How's America been treating you?" Micah asks, extending his hand while settling into his chair.

"America?" Bloat replies, his pointed nose performing figure eights around the rim of a brandy snifter. "America is like the prettiest girl in class. One smile from her and you're hers. One smile from her and you're ruined."

"And New York? How've you been finding our fair city?"

"If other cities are nouns"—repeating the aphorism he'd coined since his arrival—"New York is a *verb*."

Bloat is in town to promote the license and distribution of *Pfefferminz*, miniature toy dispensers of pelletlike peppermints that have become all the rage in Vienna. "The figurines are inspired by characters from folklore, myth, and legend," Bloat explains, placing one of the harmonica-size novelty items in the center of the table. "Ancient Greek and Roman gods and goddesses, prophets and oppressors from Testaments Old and New, Hans Christian Andersen's diffident mermaid, Sir Gawain and the Green Knight, the rogues' gallery from *The Canterbury Tales,* Quixote and his faithful Sancho Panza. I consider this my small contribution to world culture—a way to popularize the canon of great literature while simultaneously keeping clean the breath of befouled, grubby children."

"I don't get it," Micah says, fumbling with a hand-carved porcelain Grendel.

"Here." Bloat pulls back the monster's head and elicits a squeal of delight as a rectilinear-shaped chalk-white candy emerges from the creature's gaping neck. "You pull back the character's head like so and voilà—*Pfefferminz!* My plan is to popularize them in the Americas with notables from your motion-picture industry: Chaplin, Keaton, Arbuckle, Fairbanks, Jolson in blackface, Little Nemo, even Walt Disney's irritating singing mouse."

Micah begins working the hinge, examining how the candies are stacked and loaded into the cylinder's chamber. "I get the toy part, but not the decapitation routine."

"Americans truly are comical in your innocence! To the children of Europe, *Pfefferminz* makes perfect sense. We've even a special bejeweled line of PEZ dispensers featuring all the great crucified, beheaded, pitch-forked, and assassinated figures in world history, from Jesus to Marie Antoinette, Rasputin to Archduke Ferdinand. The kiddies there make the connection intuitively. To what do you awaken from the nightmare of history? Candy!"

Izzy maintains a wary silence during these opening salvos and *Pfefferminz* small talk. Though he was still uncertain whether or not he could trust the man, once the meeting was planned, Izzy could think of little else. When finalizing arrangements with Micah, Bloat intimated that he had news of the Malwiki. Now, seated next to the importer, Izzy can feel his forehead gleaming and is uncertain whether this is from anxiety or because his chair is positioned in front of an immense fireplace showering him in waves of warmth.

"So what service may I provide the brothers Grand?" Bloat asks. "Where might your next intrepid adventure take you?"

"Well, as Micah mentioned when we left Africa"—Izzy's ill-lubricated voice a car skidding over ice—"we promised we'd send some provisions."

The importer's left hand resting on the saltshaker, his right on the pepper, he leads the pair in table-waltz miscegenation. "And you mean to make good on this pledge?"

"We mean to, yes," Micah says.

"And may I ask why?"

"Because we love them," Izzy blurts.

Micah leans forward and places a conciliatory hand on Izzy's forearm. "What my brother means to say is we'd like to thank the Malwiki for the hospitality they afforded us during the shoot."

"You know, the Europeans have an expression: 'What happens in the forest belongs to the trees,'" Bloat says. "The sun makes us say funny things, do funny things. No one expects you to honor something you might have uttered in passing, on a lark, least of all to an ill-educated people whose language you do not share."

Izzy shrugs free from Micah's hand. "We very much mean to honor those things."

"I see," Bloat says, eyeing Izzy carefully. "You know, Isidor, everything has an end—only sausages have two."

"Well, it's not really for you to say how we choose to spend our money, is it? I mean, who *are* you anyway, Sidney? You're a glorified errand boy who dresses like the bathroom attendant at the Oak Room."

"Easy, Itz."

Izzy leans back in his chair. "Apologies, comment withdrawn."

"That is unnecessary, I assure you. One gets paid with neither compliments nor contrition." Bloat considers his next few words carefully before addressing Micah alone. "If you *would* like provisions sent to the Malwiki privately, without British approval or under the aegis of some goodwill agency, there are two things I will need to perform this action: The first is a good deal of money, the precise sum to be determined dependent upon the list of goods you will provide. The second is a set of forgeries of all required paperwork, which will take me a bit longer to procure and will also cost you a considerable sum. Before we proceed, however, you should be made aware of certain conditions that have come to exist in your jungle haven since your haste-filled departure."

"Conditions?" Micah asks.

"Yes, following the unfortunate and suspicious death of your colleague—"

"Spiro's death was an accident!"

"As you wish, Isidor . . . But what is it that Viennese witch doctor Mr. Freud proposes as it relates to humor? 'There are no jokes'? Well, as it relates to the Malwiki, it appears there are no accidents. Apparently they believe that every action offers a window onto some secret aspiration. As far as they're concerned, the prince struck Mr. Spiro down in cold-blooded vengeance. And so it follows: Gods need to be appeased, monsters need their meat."

Micah, the brother with hands warmer to the mechanisms of power, asks the next question. "What'd they do to the boy?"

"As far as I understand it, Prince Cri was the king's most favored son," Bloat begins, drawing the words out slowly, cautious as a barber shaving the neck of a duke. "It really is something out of the Greeks: The sovereign, King Mishi, offered himself in return for the absolution of his firstborn."

"What are you saying, Sidney?" Izzy asks.

"King Mishi is dead," Bloat says blithely. "Apparently there was a supremely *ambitious* court adviser who carried out the action with some alacrity. This *adviser*—Talli, I believe his name is—has now assumed control of the village. From what I could gather from communiqués on the western coast, things have quite fallen apart, which should make the importation of pirated shipments an *interesting* proposition to say the least."

"Mishi . . ."

"It was me," Micah volunteers. "It's my fault. I did it. I swapped out the guns by mistake."

In his hands Izzy holds a glass of water so tightly it threatens to compact into a diamond. "You?"

"Izzy, you have to forgive me. I was sozzled. It was the night of Rose's wedding."

"You did this?"

"Izzy, you have to listen to me for a minute. Everyone was goofing around. I was mucking about in the props crate."

"*You?*"

"Oh, I'm afraid the Malwiki's tale of woe does not end there," Bloat continues, nodding acceptance to a waiter's pantomimed suggestion of coffee all around. "This boy, this *princeling*, guilt-stricken over the death of his father, seeing the destruction his actions had wrought, took his own life, accomplishing it in much the same manner as your American southerners traditionally dealt with unruly slaves. He hanged himself." At the arrival of these last four syllables, Izzy turns to face the fireplace and vomits, a madras-colored arc landing on the logs with a splash, extinguishing the flames. The fire doused, the dining room takes on acrid smells of ash and bubbling innards, the air filled with dark streaks of smoke as a team of black busboys scurry about the table, busying themselves with shovels and sand and fresh linen.

Micah wraps his arms around his brother, and, though Izzy remains silent, his back spasms in lizardlike bursts, an insensate reptile jerkily making progress up a tree, the spinal column cranking and releasing, cranking and releasing. Micah holds his shuddering brother tight, relieved not to have to engage his face.

"You. You. You."

"Izzy, I'm so sorry."

"Micah, you killed us."

"Oh, now I'm afraid we've made a scene." Bloat holds a white cube of sugar just above his coffee cup's waterline. He allows the crystals to turn grayish brown as they grow saturated and crumble into the porcelain cup. "You mustn't take the news so hard, either of you. Consider your time among the Malwiki for what it was. An idyll. A Gauguin adventure. Prospero's dream. And remember, for the future you must always remember, the road to good intentions is paved with hell."

FOUR

Awareness. That's the word that occurs to Micah as soon as the giant black man opens the door. The manservant's head is shaved, the smooth, round dome and globular shoulders contrasting with the sharp hypotenuse threat of his lapels. For all that visual information, Micah is principally aware of the fact that Troy, the man greeting him, is black—a circumstance that sets in motion a series of cogs and wheels of assumptions and associations prior to any further discovery. Troy, in turn, is aware of the man's awareness, the pair of them shrouded in mutual awareness that any exchange that occurs between them will proceed from this first predestinating fact. Micah, exhausted by his awareness of all this awareness—this tyranny of awareness—is tempted to turn around and go home.

"I believe I have an appointment with Madam St. Clair," Micah offers instead, presenting the calling card.

Troy lifts the note to the light, runs his fingers along the calligraphy's crenellations, and asks in a Japanese-gong baritone who he might say is visiting.

"You the moviemaker mixed up with Ellsworth?" he asks upon Micah giving his name.

"Yeah, I know Bumpy."

"Don't call him that."

"Noted, thanks."

Massive hands spin the filmmaker around, exposing him to 131st Street at noontime. While nighttime Harlem is a place familiar to

Micah, in daylight the neighborhood feels foreign, populated by people unknown to him. There are young mothers wheeling broken baby carriages and old ladies trundling grocery bundles, there are children who live and go to school here and young, serious-looking pamphleteers—an entire world of commerce and community and identity independent of the familiar nightclubs that is so alien, so improbable-seeming, as to be otherworldly. Micah doesn't have time to investigate these thoughts too thoroughly, however, during his patting-down at the hands of the giant. Facing the street—sky casting its stone-colored verdict of agreement with the avenue's architecture—Micah realizes that he is being frisked for a gun.

"Wait here," Troy says, opening wide the heavy door and leaving Micah to stand in the vestibule. The expanse resembles the lobby of a midsize hotel or a public library. There are fresh-cut flowers in lead-crystal vases and original oils on the walls, bolts of proscenium velvet and a fountain whose persistent tinkling triggers in Micah a sudden need to urinate. Clattering cutlery and the sounds of service staff moving around in rooms beyond the lobby call Micah's attention down the hall, and his perspective widens to take in a sliver of sitting room where he can spy maids and menservants dressed in monochrome going about their work. Only they're white. She's appointed the place with white servants. The mischief of that.

"This way," the giant says, stomping back into the lobby. He leads Micah down a series of linked hallways not unlike the network of underground passages that brought the moviemaker to his first audience with King Mishi. Being ushered in to visit another kind of dignitary, Micah allows some spring-heeled jauntiness to enter his step. White servants for a black queen! Worlds within worlds. So many New Yorks, so many Americas, going on everywhere, at the same time. Different rules, different notions of class and wealth, the variety and vulgarity of the national dazzle dream. Just open another set of doors, Micah thinks, registering how the place smells of butter and flour, like a working bakery, familiar smells of Sabbath challah.

Micah has a long-standing weakness for outlaws. His first exposure to the illicit spectrum was at the hands of his Uncle Morty, his father's older brother, who was some kind of bookie or loan shark. Following some bruising, unspoken family business, Morty was never allowed in the house again, and the boys rarely saw him at all outside Yom Kippur services and family funerals, where he'd walk around handling a fat wad of bills held together with a strained rubber band. He'd peer down at you through bushy eyebrows like two parted curtains when he spoke, no matter what the subject—school grades, ball-game scores, the holidays—making the conversation feel instantly freighted with criminal intent.

"Nice day, huh?" he'd ask conspiratorially, a man with the inside dope on the mechanics of sunshine, a direct line into the managers of clouds. His nephew loved him. And when Micah announced his intention to leave school and go into show business, it was the example of Uncle Morty that Dr. Grand invoked like a curse, an invitation to ruin, Micah's father pursing his face as he uttered his disgraced brother's name as if he'd just taken a swig of curdled milk. It was only later that Micah could appreciate the inheritance the man had bequeathed him. Every picture was some kind of gamble, and Micah credited his uncle for leaving him equipped to handle schnorers and sharks, shysters and schnooks, moochers and big shots. Troy waves an arm into the sitting room. "Madam Queen, may I present Micah Grand."

Seated on a daybed in the center of the salon like a figurine atop a wedding cake, Stephanie St. Clair does not move as the filmmaker is introduced. Her frozen expression brings to mind certain Renaissance portraits, her gaze confident that prolonged examination will only bolster her mystery and power. She is outfitted in a dress that looks applied papier-mâché style, patches of silk and cotton layered in strips like some fabulous mummy. She waits before speaking, allowing Micah to continue to see what his investigation might uncover, similar to the way two boxers afford each other a quiet moment of sizing-up before the start of a fight.

St. Clair's face follows the formula of every successful business model: It takes in more than it gives out. While the frown lines run deep and

the nose wrinkles suspiciously, her dark eyes are wells of delight, dancing with merriment as the filmmaker steps forward and, with a flourish
of unexpected gallantry, lifts her wrist and kisses the back of her thin
hand. Despite the drabness of the day, the room quickens, attuned to the
hostess's good mood.

"May I offer you a refreshment, Mr. Grand?" St. Clair asks in a lilting voice that defies the cues of English punctuation. "I recommend the
pink lemonade."

"Lemonade'd be fine, thanks."

"Troy, a pitcher of lemonade and some all-butter *cookies*," this last
word delivered with the erotic suggestiveness of a wicked stepmother
proffering a poisoned apple. Upon the henchman's leave-taking, St.
Clair gestures for Micah to be seated in a nearby armchair upholstered
in red fabric that matches the color of the filmmaker's socks.

"I enjoyed your last picture."

"Thank you," Micah says, convincing himself for a moment that this
is a visit with a fan. "We were all very proud of it."

"Do you know who I am?"

"I believe so, yes."

"Tell me, please, what you've heard."

Micah, uncertain whether playing smart or dumb will earn him
honors on this test, begins. "Well, you were born in the Caribbean."

"*European* France, but go on."

"And came to America about twenty years ago."

"In 1912 to be precise. Seventeen years in your great country. Please
continue."

"And when you first arrived here, you got involved with the Forty
Thieves."

"*Mon Dieu*, Monsieur Grand! What would a little old colored lady
like myself be doing getting mixed up with those ruffians? However
would an immigrant woman of color even *begin* to insinuate herself with
one of the Five Points gangs? What a fantastic tale! But, please, do go
on with your story."

"As I understand it, Madam Queen, with all due respect, you're one of Harlem's leading numbers runners."

"Your tale grows more extravagant by the minute!" St. Clair exclaims. "Could you imagine amassing any kind of wealth from playing three little numbers? These are wild rumors that have gathered around me like so many leaves on a lawn. Now, do you know why I summoned you here today, Mr. Grand?"

"I suspect we must have a connection in common, but I'd like to hear it from you."

"I envy you," she says, lifting a small trinket, a jade elephant, off the coffee table. "I've never been to Africa. I don't enjoy travel, but mostly because I believe that the struggle remains rooted here, in this country, where we are all"—her pointer finger tick-tocking between them—"both artist and clay."

"Where's Waldo?"

"Byron Marcus was a friend for many years." Accepting a tall glass of lemonade from Troy, who has returned to the room and appears almost balletic balancing and setting a silver tray. "And an admirable businessman, too, before he allowed himself to get mixed up with that devilment. I ask you, Mr. Grand, why bother to emancipate ourselves only to choose to enslave our minds?"

"I'm a moviemaker, Madam Queen. That's the question, isn't it?"

"I have never seen a man more broken over his habit than Mr. Waldo."

"I'm sorry to hear that. I was developing a fondness for him."

"Drink your lemonade while it's cold."

Micah, who is not thirsty and needs to urinate, takes a large swig.

"Why so impatient, Mr. Grand? I can assure you, I'm the most interesting person you'll encounter today!" St. Clair says, taking from her cookie a bite the size of a tiny crack chipped from a porcelain figurine. "Have another sip. Only *taste* it this time. Think about those little lemons ripening in the sun. The texture of the rind contrasting with the softness of the pulp. The sugary and the tart, the sour and the sweet. Let the *drama* of the fruit play out over your tongue. Now try again."

Micah swallows, his head filled with fairgrounds and fireworks and ballparks and circuses, cotton-candy days when his greatest desire was to devour the world.

"There is bliss all around us if only we awaken to it. That is why I have no sympathy for Mr. Waldo if he chooses to blot out the world like a fool. I have no trouble ridding myself of a sentimental attachment. And I have no compunction when it comes to collections either. Mr. Grand, I'd like you to have a look at this." St. Clair lifts from the coffee table a heavy embroidered photo album and begins flipping through its pages, each black leaf holding in place with individual mounting corners a smattering of receipts, train and movie ticket stubs, and newspaper clippings that document her exploits. Reaching a page toward the middle, she finds the item she's looking for. Carefully, she removes a slip of paper from its pinning and passes it to Micah. On the crumpled, coffee-cup-ringed napkin from Mr. Waldo's Paradise Club is etched a palimpsest of scratched-out names, numbers, and notations that culminate in "Micah Grand, 20% interest in 'O, Africa' movie. I.O.U."

"With all due respect, Madam Queen," Micah says, returning the napkin to its new owner, "I wouldn't wipe my mouth with that."

"Is it true you lost a portion of your next picture to Mr. Waldo in a poker game?"

"Yeah, something like that."

"And it's true that it was Mr. Waldo who brought this original inspiration to you, is that not correct?"

"Strictly speaking, yes."

"And a film with the title *O, Africa!* now exists?"

"Certain sequences do in raw form, yes."

"How much of the film exists, Mr. Grand? Be precise."

"Perhaps a third of the picture. All of the location stuff."

"And this being the first such film to be shot on the great continent of Africa, the footage is imbued with some historic import, is that not correct?"

"Yes, I suppose you could say that."

"How good is it?"

"Excuse me?"

"How serious an artist are you? Is the picture better than your usual monkey business?"

"It's good," Micah says, settling back into his chair. "It's unlike anything anyone's ever seen."

"Now you've set my mouth watering, Mr. Grand!"

"That's just the lemonade talking."

"Oh, you're devilish! What would you say the picture is worth?"

"I can't put a figure to something that doesn't exist yet."

"How much does one of your Mr. Till pictures usually make?"

"Let's see, our biggest hit would have to be *Hopping Mad!*" Micah says with pride, "and that pulled in about one, one point two million, depending on who's counting."

"So let's extrapolate. You see, all of Mr. Waldo's former business concerns have fallen to me. It's now my burden to look after each of those investments."

"Yes, I appreciate all that, but a scribble on a napkin's not exactly a binding agreement. There're studios, distributors, exhibitors, ways in which these things are formally done. Even if I wanted to, I couldn't just transfer partial ownership of the picture."

"Mr. Grand!" St. Clair says, bursting into helium fits of laughter. "Perhaps you don't appreciate the full significance of my name. In any queen's kingdom, tribute must be paid."

"Feudalism," Troy contributes.

"I believe you've made the acquaintance of Ellsworth Johnson."

"Bumpy?"

"Don't call him that," Troy warns.

"As I understand it, Ellsworth is the picture's coauthor. I've read his poems," she says, smiling sweetly. "My Ellsworth is a gifted child in so many ways."

Micah handles the napkin as a new parent might a soiled diaper. "And you're suggesting this means what exactly? That Bumpy—"

"Don't call him that."

"That *Ellsworth* now owns twenty percent of the picture?"

"Ellsworth is a princeling I took up in my arms like Moses sent downriver. Princes share in the fruits of their queen's kingdom."

"Feudalism," Troy repeats, a man having found religion in a single word.

"Think of it this way: You see that pitcher of lemonade? Let's suppose you have a batch of lemons and I have a batch of lemons. Maybe your lemons originate from a different region than mine, maybe they're a little bigger or a little smaller than mine, maybe they're more or less tart. Maybe even—because of certain accidents of history—you're able to bring more lemons to market than I can. What that napkin means is that if ever I decide I'm thirsty—or should ever my associates decide that *they're* thirsty—no matter where I am, no matter what I'm up to, no matter how full my pitcher might be, I will *squeeze* your lemons. *I'll squeeze them up!* Now, tell me exactly the status of my investment."

"The reels are on a mail plane to California."

"Why would you ship the film away from your investors?"

"I'm due in L.A. next week."

"You have a very smooth face for someone so accomplished," St. Clair observes. "No imperfections, no marks. It always amazes me when successful people have faces with no scars. But then, things have come very easily to you, haven't they, Mr. Grand? Now, tell me again please: Where is my investment?"

"Like I said, the footage shipped out yesterday."

Although the weapon is a small one, Troy appears instantly bigger with a gun in his hand, an inflated hot-air balloon crowding the room.

"Repeat that," says the clock puncher with a pistol.

"The reels are on their way to California," Micah says in a rush. "Even if I wanted to, it'd be days before I could call them back." The moviemaker remains fixated on one of Troy's gold-filled teeth even as the fist-wrapped weapon rears up, comes down, and ricochets off the side of his head. Though he appreciates the restraint exercised by the muscleman—the proportion of the blow containing more knuckle than steel—the pain is apocalyptic. Colors vibrate, patterns pulse, a ringing rises in his inner ear, and everything turns noxious as Micah recalibrates and attempts to steady himself in his chair. Troy puts the gun back in its holster as quickly as a housewife clearing away the good china and resumes his position with hands folded in front of him. A comforting warmth spreads across Micah's lap.

"You pee yourself, Jew-man?" Troy asks.

Micah covers his lap with the same handkerchief he's using to stanch his bleeding temple.

"Banana-peel dick?"

"Beg pardon?" Micah asks the strongman.

"You a son of Abraham?"

"I'm Jewish if that's what you're asking."

"Banana-peel dick."

"If I understand your meaning, you're referring to circumcision and the Hebrew people's covenant with God."

"Let's see it."

"What?"

"Banana-peel dick."

"Madam Queen?!" Micah, a schoolchild begging a teacher to acknowledge some playground injustice. "They shipped the cans out this morning. I'm due in California in three days' time to review the footage with the studio head. As soon as the scenes are edited into a reasonable assembly to show you, I will. And when the picture's ready we have every intention of giving you your share of profits. This is where things are. This is the way things are done. This is what I'm trying to explain to you. Things take time."

"Madam Queen?"

"Yes, Troy."

"I shoot this Jew?"

"No, not today," St. Clair says, taking another squirrel's bite of a cookie. "Mr. Grand, you are a charming conversationalist, and it was a pleasure making your acquaintance. I do hope you appreciate that the only thing keeping your obituary from the evening's paper was your presence here this afternoon. I am known to be a patient woman. That virtue is the leash restraining the hounds of hell. Were I in your shoes, I'd make every effort to screen that footage for your good investors at your earliest convenience. Otherwise my patience has been known to slacken."

3

HOLLYWOODLAND

ONE

A chocolate replica of the award sits at the center of the table, wrapped in gold foil glinting light. Every table has a candy trophy, so that even if you didn't win one, at least you could *eat* one. The award recipients had been announced weeks earlier, and the papers published the winners' names the day before, but still the white hall hums, a collective agreement to preserve anticipation.

In the moments before Douglas Fairbanks and William C. DeMille take the podium, the primary question is one of tonality. How would the evening play? Would this be the real thing? Or was this self-congratulatory business simply more silliness, gold stars passed out to millionaire schoolchildren? In a propped-up town lacking tradition, a kingdom of stucco, would the awards ceremony *take*?

Apart from the awards themselves, so far the evening had been not dissimilar from other industry gatherings, dinners, premieres, and schmoozefests—thick with sycophancy and bad blood, heavy with amorous humidity, sex suspended in the air like pollen in a field before a good rain. It was true about most any kind of gathering: One person, you have an opinion. Two people, there's politics. Plant six at a table, you can start calculating crosscurrents and rivalries with a slide rule. A roomful of guests will collect insults, offenses, and slights like cashmere picking up lint. This room held three hundred, the entire industry pretty much accounted for in the hall, inflated personalities floating big as parade balloons.

The gloomy German actor Emil Jannings, who had performed

acrobatic eyebrow maneuvers in Murnau's *The Last Laugh*, was in Europe and unable to accept the evening's inaugural award. But after the first few trophies had been handed out, the first earnest speeches delivered, the first invocations made to God and country and the newly dead, Marblestone knew. These were amulets. Magic feathers plucked from mountaintops. Peas pressed under princess mattresses. The industry's self-love transmuted into tribal art. Within a year everyone would be greedy for one. All Marblestone wanted to do was grab one of the chocolate-candy doubles, peel away the gold foil like the wrapping on Hanukkah gelt, and swallow its decapitated head in one wolfish gulp— but the therapy had neutered his appetite.

"It's spreading," came the doctor's tombstone diagnosis weeks before. Of course it's spreading. One doesn't need a fancy degree to know about manifest destiny. Spreading, driving, conquering, dividing— this is what great and terrible things do. The doctor might well have said, "Go west," the national prescription and America's moral imperative that Marblestone had followed over a lifetime. The land, the light, was heartstoppingly beautiful in those days. Limitless. Light buttering everything it touched, giving birth to the land as it spread. Sunshine an expression of God's love. At night you couldn't see where the horizon ended and the sky began. The ocean, the Pacific, not the pale, puke-green frozen sea they'd labored to cross but the waters of sunshine. Let there be light, the first exhortation. Then chase it, go west, an eleventh commandment. A purity begging to be defiled. The first tracts bought up in Laurel Canyon and Casaba Field and Antelope and Coyote Hills and Buttonwillow. Little more than frontier towns. Eucalyptus smells. Clapboard houses. Tin lizzies. Endlessly seesawing derricks. Rigs close together as peppercorns in a mill. Sawdust-covered soundstages. The whole thing a novelty, an adventure, a mass improvisation. No different from the bootstrappers, prospectors, wildcatters, and speculators, the crouching American primitives of a generation before, scooping gold out of the ground with saucepans, hands literally dirty with money, hands callused and covered in grime and black. Now, thirty years later, soft hands to cradle awards. Progress.

Onstage, Douglas Fairbanks—as quick-witted and effortless a master of ceremonies as could be, comfortable in his skin as a cheetah—has just presented a special award to Warner Bros. for *The Jazz Singer.* The corners of Fairbanks's mouth crinkle as he reads off a card praising the breakthrough talking picture that's revolutionized the industry.

This award makes the room's mood uneasy, *The Jazz Singer* being a picture the town loves, hates, and fears in equal measure. Apart from the film's bringing down the gavel in favor of sound pictures once and for all, there's this: It cuts too close to the moguls' nightmare image of themselves. There's just too much of the sweaty striver about Jolson for everyone to feel comfortable. *I want! I want! I want!* the performance screams, and, though it's a kind of triumph, it's a strenuous one.

"What do you think?" Marblestone asks the profligate, surrogate son.

"Picture's okay," Micah says. "Jolson's not my favorite."

"Me either. But they don't get it, why the picture's such a sensation," Marblestone says, recalling seeing the picture at a private industry screening and blubbering through it like a thorn-stricken lion. "A *Jew*, in *blackface*, married to a girl named *Mary*, singing colored music on *Yom Kippur.* We're telling stories to each other we don't even see what they mean."

"You're overthinking it, Arthur. It's just a cheap melodrama with music."

"Sure, kid. And how'd the Jews make it to America?" Marblestone asks. "Yiddle by yiddle."

Marblestone's dinner jacket, now several sizes too big, hung on his mastodon frame like a sheet draped over a fossil at the Museum of Natural History. This night would be the last of these for him. Looking out over the banquet hall of the Roosevelt Hotel, the mogul decided to take the evening for a memorial service, the funeral of his choosing, the shiva he had lived to see.

He'd been out to the hotel the week before. The air in the hall was expectant. Good ballrooms always quiver a little when no one's around. Outside, a spiral staircase was being loaded off a truck—how surreal, how apt a symbol, a staircase spinning around, connecting nothing to nothing, wheeling about under the California sky. Inside the hall a pair of carpenters worked on some chairs in need of refurbishment. What's lonelier than peeling white paint? Marblestone thought at the sight of one chair in particular—a leg suffering from a fracture, custard-colored stuffing spilling out from its ripped-open seat, gilt peeled away at the arms—that had brought him close to tears. But tonight everything gleamed.

A team of colored waiters in natty white dinner jackets begin plating appetizers: pink shrimp, puffed up with pride, lined up like high-kicking Ziegfeld Follies girls. The waiters are wearing red, white, and blue striped bow ties that echo the patriotic bunting decorating the hall and lend the place the look of a political convention. As he completes his round, one of the servers hovers over Micah and Rose longer than over the other guests, and a weird moment of recognition passes between them.

Micah's eyes follow the server as he departs, pupils paranoia-ing to pinpricks. "I think I know that one."

"Just because they all look alike . . . ," Rose jokes.

She's elegant in full makeup, all dressed up—and she'd obviously gone to some trouble having her hair done that afternoon, the swarm of spirals now straightened, chemically treated, frozen stiff as a Hasidic woman's wig. Marblestone allows himself to be moved for a moment by his protégé's ability to discern and tease out beauty in people and places others might overlook. But still, why did he bring her here? More pressing, if Marblestone was correctly reading the rationale behind Rose's choice of Empire-cut dress and the careful arrangement of her shawl and handbag, what the hell could Micah be thinking? A colored kid? Mayer kept a doctor on the payroll to take care of that kind of thing, and Marblestone'd rather pass a cactus through his prick than ask a favor of that fucking monster. Still, he'd asked if Micah wanted his help taking care of the problem, only to have the boy wonder insist that the baby wasn't his.

"You think this menu is an accident, boychick?" Marblestone asks, nudging across his plate a prawn the size, color, and curl of an embryo.

"The whole place is an accident," answers Micah. "Hollywoodland is a brilliant goof."

"That's where we disagree," Marblestone says, scanning the room for the shrunken-apple faces of Cohn, Mayer, Schenck, and Lasky, terrorizing dealings with each of them flash-carding through his memory. "You think Jews gravitated out here by mistake? To the desert—the *biblical* desert—with nothing but sunshine to recommend it? Read your history, boychick, there's a little number in there called manifest destiny."

"Right. Pioneers get the arrows, settlers get the land."

"Sure, there's that," says Marblestone, who's seconded by a chandelier jingle. "But heading west is an instinct, too. It has to do with mortality, catching the last of the light before it slips behind the horizon."

"I never took you for a poet, Arthur."

"Well, human beings are *complex*, kid. You're an artist, you should appreciate these things."

"Tonight's festivities notwithstanding," Micah says, "I've never made claims for myself as an artist."

"That," Rose says, publicly billed for the evening as Micah's personal assistant, on a special trip out west while Margaret stayed back in New York taking care of the boys, "lets you off the hook too easily, Mr. Grand."

"Mr. Grand's the name of my father," Micah says, his prick happily hopping a beat, a needle skipping across a record, each time she addresses him by that salutation. "Call me Micah."

"Well then, *Micah*," pipes in Merian C. Cooper, clearing his throat from the other end of the table, "leaving aside the terribly sad business with Mr. Spiro, rumor has it that some of the footage you captured during your African excursion is really quite something."

Cooper, one half of a producing-directing team with Ernest B. Schoedsack, has a reputation as one of Hollywood's leading crackpot exotics and on-location loonies, and he's got the résumé to back it up, including a nine-month stint in a Soviet prisoner-of-war camp as a volunteer member of the Polish army.

"Well, Africa was grand, but we never did get close to an elephant," Micah offers, referring to the wild stampede climax of *Chang: A Drama of the Wilderness,* the picture shot on location in the jungles of Siam that's been nominated tonight for Best Production.

"Oh, you must make it a point to shoot an elephant sometime," Cooper says. "There's something about them that's very humbling. They carry history in their wrinkles."

"Well, next time we're in the bush," Micah says, hoping to switch the subject. "Before we decamped from Congo, though, we saw a nightclub act I highly recommend about a blonde falling in love with a giant ape."

"A girl and a gorilla, did you say?" Cooper asks, eyes widening at the news, a lost dream having found its correspondent, Skull Island beginning to map its coordinates.

"Micah's being modest about spending their time in nightclubs," Marblestone interjects. "I had the privilege of reviewing the footage this afternoon, and true as I sit before you, I can assure you no one's ever seen anything like it. It's a vision of Eden before the fall, and we're taking offers from all the majors as we speak."

Marblestone was lying. While Micah, Rose, Till, and the mogul had indeed convened at Imperial's dilapidated screening room earlier that afternoon for a viewing of the B-roll footage, what emerged from the projector instead were schlocky soundstage tests for *Pot of Trouble.*

Upon their arrival the reunion mood had been ebullient, celebratory. Having spent their first night in a hotel room together following the grueling, days-long journey by train and plane, Micah and Rose had emerged into powdery Los Angeles sunshine bright-eyed and raw from a morning romp (Rose ringlet-haired, three months pregnant but not too obviously showing, Micah excited to be having intercourse with a pregnant woman not his wife). The filmmaker was happy to be reunited with his chalk-faced star for the first time since their Dark Continent adventure and was relieved, too, to be afforded this brief reprieve from oppressive worrying over his brother. He was even looking forward to seeing the boss.

Though warned by Till in advance about Marblestone's physical deterioration, Micah was ill prepared for his first sight of the big man. Arriving on twin canes, each step as tentative as a hatchling emerging from an eggshell, Marblestone brought the room to quietude, the kind of hush normally reserved for visiting dignitaries. The wagging gray head with its dark eyes and bushy mustache combined with sticklike legs, angled elbows, and thin canes hanging loose from the bent bow of his back lent the mogul the look of an unhappy tarantula. An old, broken arachnid, but still a spider with some power, some poison, left in its sacks.

"You owe me sixty dollars," said Rose, breaking the silence.

"All business, I like that in a man," Marblestone said, peeling three twenty-dollar bills off a thick green roll and lowering his frame into a plush chair to the sound of joints cracking.

"What's got you, kid?" he asked Micah, who remained standing in the aisle after all the others had taken their seats.

"Nothing," Micah answered, recognizing in his mentor's countenance the death-haunted aspect of his parents near the end. "Just, it looks like you've lost a few tons."

"Yes, Micah, it's called *dying.*" Then, shouting, "Cheech, the bitter herbs!"

A smiling Mexican emerged from behind the steel projection-booth door, nodded greeting to them all, and began packing a small tobacco pipe with a dry, oregano-looking substance.

"I've a progressive doctor," Marblestone explained, receiving the bowl as if it were a reliquary. "Says it stimulates the appetite."

Holding a lighter to the instrument, he greedily sucked, keeping his mouth closed for a length of time before releasing a dragon's plume of smoke. A pungent smell filled the room—Christmas pines and urine—an aroma familiar to Rose and Cheech, foreign to Micah and Till, who took up the bowl next.

"So listen, Arthur," Micah said, "in addition to the location footage and scenes from *Pot of Trouble,* we shot some test sequences for another thing, a project we've had kicking around for a while, a new kind of picture for us."

"As long as you brought me back darkies and voodoo dolls, I'll be happy," Marblestone responded to the news, gripping one of the arms of his chair, which came free in his hand. "But your footage better be good, kid," the boss continued, launching the upholstered piece of wood across the room. "Your livelihood and the future of Imperial depend on it. Then again, any *chazerai* looks better on this stuff." Marblestone relaxed into the chair, merging with its fleshy folds, fingers laced across his stomach like a man in a casket, and his features began to lose their fixity. While the drug did little to help him eat, he was grateful for the insight it gave him into the mysteries of time, the calendar having recently become his chief obsession. Obituaries were now the first section of the paper to which he turned in the morning, graveyard arithmetic his new favorite pastime. He compulsively checked his watch and made certain all the clocks in the office kept accurate count. Once the intoxicant began charting its course, he felt able to negotiate his way cross this slipperiest of dimensions, to get on top of it and influence its direction like a man steering a stagecoach. He relished the accordion tricks the drug performed with temporality, amplifying and contracting its parameters, how malleable and accommodating it made appear the linear progression of this terrifyingly rigid-seeming yet mutable governing force.

"You know why time was invented?" Marblestone asked, mental processes floating from the orchestra to the mezzanine to the balcony. "So that even misery might come to an end."

"Oh, gosh," said Till, the churchgoer having fallen off his seat and now doggy-paddling across the floor. "Oh, golly fucking gosh."

"Slip me some happy, Em," Rose asked with lyric familiarity after Micah had taken his first few puffs.

"This is what all the fuss is about?" dismissed Micah, passing her the pipe. Turning to his mistress, he began making a close inspection of Rose's hair, pinching a curl between his forefinger and thumb, straightening it, letting it spring back into a coil, and repeating the procedure, marveling at how this maneuver could be performed all day, that Rose had many, many, many more hairs just like it—thousands of them, tens of thousands, millions—that weeks and months could be spent laboring at this investigation, free-associating on the mysticism of the spiral, the spiritual generosity of that questing circle. From there he began noodling the centrality of snake imagery in Western myth: the serpent in the Garden of Eden, Perseus and Medusa, phallic snakes and vaginal caves, how nothing ever really changes in the stories we tell ourselves. Then the sight of Rose naked, bursting in the California sunshine across white linen this morning, their first deliverance together to an alien bed. Then the fact that for all his years of womanizing (and, it occurred to him in this moment, that he and every pussy hound he knew had a deep and abiding fear and mistrust of women, their sexual power, their secret knowledge of men's pathos and gratitude), until a few hours before he had never really stopped and taken a moment to really stare at a cunt. And my God!, what a thing it was, the entire inverted temple palpating and exposed! And then the audacity of getting down and licking and lapping its folds like it was an envelope that held within itself life's very secret! Then the thought that every woman had one of these pulsing between her legs—that no amount of clothing or decorum or propriety could obscure this self-evident fact. And then the syllogism's terrifying conclusion: If Rose is a woman, and every woman has one of these, why her? Why Rose, who, on paper, when one examined the facts of the thing, was an absolute disaster?

"Nope, this stuff is doing nothing for me," Micah said, continuing to play with her hair.

"Give it time, boychick," Marblestone said. "Cheech! Milk and cookies, then let's start this picture, pronto!"

Marblestone braced himself for a sublime encounter, the realization of his longed-for vision of conquest, the liquid dream of jungle topiary, the African sun as malignant as the Old Testament eye of God. Instead, as the image flickered to life, he found himself watching a pith-helmeted Till skipping over a hundred-meter dash of hot coals, cheered on by white actors in blackface, a painted scrim pinned behind them a synecdoche for everything cheap and ignoble about their banana-peel art. "What is this shit?" Marblestone snorted.

"That's a mistake," Micah said, springing from his seat and barreling into the projection booth. "Cheech, where are the cans that arrived yes-terday?" Micah went to inspect the first, then the second, then the third of the aluminum containers, garbage-can lids that cast their own visual verdict on their junkyard art. Izzy had done a sloppy job of relabeling, the words "Africa B-roll" appearing in grease pencil on little strips of masking tape that, once peeled off, revealed the words "Pot of Trouble" written in permanent marker on the metal disks themselves. Micah unspooled one of the reels and examined its introductory length. Izzy had even swapped out the film leads.

"That's it, just those three cans?"

"*Sí.*"

Putting in a long-distance call to his brother as the agreeable pro-jectionist looked on, Micah received no answer at the editing suite. "I'm calling home," he announced through the projection-booth por-tal, watching as Rose used an emery board to work a fingernail into a dagger. Micah listened as his wife relayed that, no, she hadn't seen her brother-in-law in *days* but that Izzy *had* packed a bag the other night and explained he'd be working around the clock during Micah's trip and also that she hoped Micah was having a *wonderful* time in Los Angeles with all of his *friends and colleagues* and could not *wait* for her husband's return.

"Why is Margaret such a cunt?!" Micah demanded of Cheech, bringing the heavy black phone down with a clang.

"I do not know this woman," Cheech noncommitted, continuing to arrange chocolate-chip cookies on a silver tray in the pattern of a Jewish star.

"Ahhhhh, you're just being a gentleman, Cheech!" Micah said, already dialing Shago Moody, the night doorman at the editing facility.

"Remember that steak dinner?" Micah began. "There's a whole cow in it for you if you can tell me where my brother's hiding."

"Keep Mabel in the stable, Mr. Grand. I ain't seen Mr. Isidor for days," Shago reported. "Cleared the place out from the looks of it, though."

"That's what I'm calling about: There were some reels of film he was in charge of shipping to California while I made my way out here. Did anyone else get their hands on them?"

"No, Mr. Izzy arranged the shipping of them cans with me, personal. That having been said, some of Bumpy's crew were sniffing around here the day after you left. Mr. Grand, that gang is on your backside like a tick on a bloodhound."

"What'd you tell them?"

"Those that know don't tell, and those that tell don't know."

"I'd say that's largely true." Nodding to the worldly-wise Cheech and hanging up the phone. Lifting a ribbon of celluloid to the light, Micah held by his fingertips an image of Till in blackface, attempting an escape from death by boiling chicken soup. He disgustedly jammed a fistful of baked goods into his gob.

"Where's my footage, boychick?" Marblestone boomed at the movie-maker as he emerged from the projection booth coated in sweat. "Where are my lions and tigers?"

"Screw your footage, Arthur," Micah said, spraying cookie crumbs across the screening room. "Izzy's gone missing."

"What do you mean?"

"He's gone! He's run off with the Africa footage and is who-knows-where."

"Any leads where he might be? Any contacts at the bathhouses?"

"I'll make some more calls, but, no, not really. . . ."

The boss allowed the note to hang suspended, determining whether the moment might break comic or tragic.

"I don't think Izzy would do himself in, if that's what you're worried about. He's too self-dramatizing for that—he'd only kill himself if he could be around to see your reaction."

"How can you be sure?"

"Because he hates your fucking guts! I have a brother—I know about these things."

"Arthur, I don't know what to do. I can't make a move."

"That's just the grass talking, Em," Rose contributed.

"Look, Micah," Marblestone continued, "you're a long way from home. The city's a big place, and Izzy's a big boy. If the *faygeleh* wants to disappear for a while, he chose the right place to do it, and there's not much you can do about it from here. Is the footage as good as you say it is?"

"Better."

"Izzy won't harm it, then. He's the only one of us who mistakes this schlock for something like art."

"What would you have me do, Arthur?"

"Do your job, Micah. It's called 'show business,' Micah, not 'show fucking nice.' Not 'show me all about your fucking family problems.' Showing is the first prerogative. And showing is what's required of us tonight. This thing now is a few hours away. It doesn't matter if the footage is here, or in New York, or lost at sea. Our job is to get out there tonight and sell, boychick. *Sell!*"

Yeah, like the big man says, Coop, the footage is jake," Micah says, retrieving himself from flashback. "Much more colorful than your Siamese coolies."

"Well, I look forward to seeing it," Cooper says diplomatically.

Onstage, Fairbanks has just presented a special award of merit to Charles Chaplin for producing, directing, writing, and starring in *The Circus*. Silver-haired and already past forty, trademarked baggy pants replaced by black tails, Chaplin is as slender and elegant as a figure lifted from a chessboard. The Little Tramp has declared his allegiance to silent cinema, and the trades have reported his commitment to shooting his next picture—something familiarly Dickensian about a millionaire, a hobo, and a blind girl—without dialogue. Chaplin is perhaps the only film-world persona powerful enough to press against the sonic tide, and indeed there is something grave and militaristic about the man in person, the suggestion of comedy eked out in thumbscrew increments.

"He's not what I expected at all," says Rose, powdering the sides of her nose, the white particles leaving a fine, chalky dusting, like Turkish delight. "Sounds like he's got a plum in his mouth."

"That voice," Till says quietly, "will have audiences dumping tea in Boston Harbor."

The table of twelve agrees. Seated with Micah and Rose are Marblestone and his wife, Masha; Till and his five-months-pregnant wife, Emily Davies; Merian Cooper and his date, a dimpled redhead who looks like she's just stepped off the *Mayflower*; the screenwriter, former Chicago newspaperman, and Broadway playwright Ben Hecht, whom everyone finds agreeably hard-boiled and sour; Hecht's wife, another Rose; and the starlet and socialite Fay Wray, along with her movie-star-handsome screenwriter fiancé, John Monk Saunders.

It's a good table at which to be seated, the group acknowledged with unspoken nods upon first taking their chairs. While there are bigger stars in attendance—Errol Flynn and Myrna Loy, Janet Gaynor and Charles Farrell—Wray is one of the best-liked ingenues in Hollywood. The soft-spoken midwestern Saunders, meanwhile, is credited with the story for *Wings*, the Great War aviation epic that has won the top award of the night. Plainly smitten with each other, the two are set to be married in a month, the wedding earmarked as one of the biggest events on Hollywood's summer social calendar.

For his part the kind-eyed, broad-nosed Hecht picked up an award earlier in the evening for the original story to Sternberg's brutish *Underworld*. During the course of the year the writer has earned a reputation for savaging the industry that has made him rich, and he doesn't disappoint tonight. The scenarist plants the trophy in the middle of the table; with the two placed side by side, it's difficult to discern which is the award and which its candy double. To Hecht, who'd scored the trophy and ten thousand dollars for one week's work, they're both false idols. Years before, the screenwriter had received a telegram from another writer friend, Herman Mankiewicz, imploring him to try his luck out west:

MILLIONS ARE TO BE GRABBED OUT HERE
AND YOUR ONLY COMPETITION IS IDIOTS.
DON'T LET THIS GET AROUND.

Hecht keeps the telegram on his person during business meetings and script readings and finds the words burning a hole in his dinner jacket tonight.

"When tonight's over," Hecht says, "we'll have to go home and wring the personality out of our clothes."

"Mayer really pulled it off," Marblestone agrees, making eyeball revolutions around the room, flitting on Schenck, Swanson, DeMille, Gary Cooper, Clara Bow. He looks over at the next table, where Jesse Lasky looms above a young actress like a construction crane at a building site. As the kingmaker admonishes her, impressing upon her some vital career guidance, life lesson, or sexual tutelage, she blinks slowly and tries to absorb the information, darkly shadowed eyes framed like mollusks in a shell. The girl's tongue protrudes from her slightly parted lips, upon the lower of which rests a tiny baby's bubble, the secrets of the universe shimmering and bouncing across this stretched skin of spittle. Staring at her lips, Lasky is momentarily silenced. This, then, the secret of beauty: You don't really want it to do anything; you don't really need anything from it other than to be allowed into its hypnotic proximity. The secret of beauty residing in its childlike certainty of itself: You just want it to be.

"It's worth remembering, everyone," Marblestone says, "that the world is run by grown-ups, who are just children, grown up." A colored waiter, cocoa skin beautifully offset by formal white dress, stands at the head of the table and asks Hecht, "Water for the table, or would anyone prefer one of tonight's other offerings?"

"This is Los Angeles." Hecht chuckles. "Don't go spending water like it's money."

The waiter looks at him confusedly.

"Yeah, sure, kid, water all around."

Micah has been drinking for the entire table, hoping that the alcohol would neutralize the effects of the marijuana. In the event, the booze only compounds with interest the filmmaker's panic and self-loathing. Worse, the teacups of medicinal-smelling gin remind Micah of his father's doctor's bag, that depthless black leather satchel with its vials and syringes and bottles nobly clanking against one another. Thoughts of his hardworking, responsible, abstemious father cast in relief against his own self-congratulatory nonsense work send Micah deeper into a funk. What would Dr. Julius Grand make of the evening's proceedings? Imagine Dad's reaction to a bunch of bums pinning medals on their chests for making easy lays and earning a million bucks. Fancy Dr. Grand coming home with a trophy for Best Strep Throat Culture, Finest Earwax Removal, Noblest Vertebra Realignment. Surveying the table's bounty, Micah wishes he were a maker of things, real objects of material substance: airplane engines and X-ray machines, horseshoes and barrels, bowling pins and spools of yarn, candlesticks and blown glass. This shame and self-pity make him drink more.

But the real reason Micah keeps signaling waiters over to whisper illicit orders into their ears is to confirm his certainty that he knows them. From the Cotton Club, from the Paradise Club, from card games played around Mr. Waldo's poker table, from the halls of Madam Queen's mansion, from Rose's apartment-building stoop and nighttime strolls down Harlem's wide boulevards. It is impossible, it is preposterous, but it's true. Micah is convinced that every shrugging, loping black threat he has ever encountered on the streets of New York City has assembled in this festive hall, that the entire service staff is composed of Madam Queen's emissaries posing as waiters, watching for a signal to strike. As a team of invisible black servers encircle his table and begin plating entrées, Micah believes that his ears have tuned in to some higher, rarefied, secret frequency.

"They're here to kill me," Micah says, too loudly, to Rose, who directs her response to the table.

"We know you didn't win," says Rose, "but no one's trying to *kill* you."

"Waiter, I can't eat this," Marblestone announces about the jumbo squab Périgueux, admitting, for the tenth time today, that despite his every best effort the therapy has robbed him of his appetite. "Listen, do me a favor, bring me a couple of slices of plain Wonder Bread, a sour pickle, and a glass of chocolate milk." Then, after the waiter departs:

"When Masha and I first passed through Ellis Island, they put new arrivals in holding pens where they fed us hot soup and bread. Only everyone was used to the hard, dark stuff, like pumpernickel and rye. We'd never seen anything like spongy white bread before, so at first we mistook if for cake. Imagine that—being served birthday cake your very first meal in this country! Cake! Gold bricks would pave the streets! All the stories were true!"

"Wonder Bread." Hecht chuckles. "An appropriately named product."

"They're here to kill me," Micah repeats, a wishbone dangling from his mouth.

"Keep it together, Em," Rose whispers. "Two puffs from a cigarette, I swear."

"And you?!" Turning on her. "How could you have done that to your hair?"

"I thought I'd try something different for tonight. I thought you'd like it."

"It's fucking awful!" he says, reaching for it and being repelled by the aerated, frozen mass.

"Okay, leave my hairstyle out of it."

"No, I needed your hair tonight. It has *answers*, goddamn it. It's like Samson . . . all my strength comes from it. I needed that glorious fucking Brillo pad."

"You're having a bad reaction, is all. Calm down. Focus on something nice," she says, planting the table's centerpiece in front of him. "Here, look at this."

"Bee-you-ti-ful!" cries cotton-mouthed Micah at the ridiculous explosion of floral sexuality, blushing petals and reaching stamens like some fantasy out of H. G. Wells. Under closer inspection the plant begins to turn malignant and mean. Whatever the drug was doing to Micah, he didn't approve. Too much naked exposure to the potentialities of things beneath the visible. You enter a room and it looks safe, but who's to say the arrangement on the table isn't deadly poisonous, that its flowers won't spray you in the face, that its vines won't wrap around your neck, that your mistress doesn't hate you, that the waiters aren't all

secret agents, that every space one enters isn't charged with murderous threat? "Flowers! Such beautiful . . . Gah!"

"Shh!" Rose stifles him, working on a pornographic strawberry. "Talk to Arthur's wife. No one's spoken to her all night."

"You're right," he says, turning to face Masha Marblestone like a knight charging headlong into battle. "I will speak to her!"

Micah had met Arthur's wife on just a few other occasions but had never before really engaged her in conversation. If his blinkered eyes weren't deceiving him, on this night the mogul's wife had attended the banquet outfitted in her wedding dress—a yellowing Miss Havisham number, festooned front and back with fish-scale sequins. The intervening three decades having done little to alter her heavily built, round-shouldered figure, she sat next to him beaming like a mermaid bride.

"I was a seamstress and washerwoman," Masha begins after Micah asked her to describe how they met, "at the house Artie would frequent."

"The house?"

"Where deh women make deh V," she says, spearing an entire new potato with a fork, lifting it, and nibbling at the vegetable as she twirls it clockwise. When she is finished, she drops the utensil into her handbag, where it joins a smuggled soup ladle, a pair of lobster forks, a set of linen napkins, melting pats of butter wrapped in aluminum foil, and a shattered champagne flute. "This is where I trained Artie in deh tenderness."

"The tenderness?" Micah repeats, a man in solitary imploring a jailer dangling a key.

Mrs. Marblestone, encircled in a nimbus of light, blows out a candle and drops the waxy staff into her bag. "Deh tenderness, deh sweet stuff, was like the rising sun to him." With dancing medieval fingers, she paints for Micah an entire world of pictures, a world of the Ostjuden, the Eastern European Jews of the Austro-Hungarian Empire, a benighted world of peddlers and cobblers and apothecaries and poisoned wells and lanterns that clanked together as children walked along forest paths. The dumpling bride paints spun-sugar pictures of their wedding day—an occasion that in her telling of it had burned away the clouds, had brought knotted, dormant trees to bloom, had sent the first locomotives whistling through the valley. A union that had, through its revelation of love, foisted modernity onto the shtetl. "They still celebrate our anniversary there," she relays with modest pride. Adventurers shot from their own cannon, their love could propel them but one place. To America! America! America! Washington, Jefferson, Lincoln, all those battles and parchments and monuments mere prologue to the Marblestone marriage, backdrop historic pageantry for the main-stage event of their union.

"It's all true, everything she said," Marblestone concurs. "There exists in Germany a turn of phrase for America that was bandied about by the military during the Great War: *Das Land der unbegrenzten Möglichkeiten.* 'The land of endless possibility.'"

"With Artie," says Masha, her sixteen-year-old's face shining through her old-woman's face as she looks at her husband, "everything was possible."

Settings are cleared and coffee is served. From across the hall—as Lewis Milestone picks up his trophy for Best Comedy Direction for *Two Arabian Knights*, the category that had brought Micah a nomination and all of them to the ceremony—Rose watched one of the colored waiters framed in the oval porthole of the swinging kitchen doors. The waiter is now dressed in street clothes, wearing a fantastic brown checked suit with yellow paisley tie and matching yellow derby, and when their eyes meet through the windowpane across the ballroom, Rose cannot help but think how handsome the young man looks. The night is winding down—there are only one or two more awards left to be presented—and Rose figures the waiter is being let off work early. She continues thinking about how elegantly dressed the young man is, how fine, until he mouths in silence a vile two-syllable word, a word that travels across the length of the room and lands like an ice pick in her heart. As the hall envelopes Milestone in applause, the young man leers at Rose, licking his chops like a fairy-tale wolf. He points a spindly finger at her and mouths the word again, only slower this time, to make unmistakable that the odium is intended for her, to let it be known that he is not fooled by her secret identity, and to confirm that Micah is, impossibly, correct in his suspicion that they are in no small danger.

"We should leave now," Rose says, squeezing Micah's hand, glancing at the watch he'd given her, registering the time as five minutes before the witching hour.

"I know," Micah says, resting his fingertips atop the boss's hand, Marblestone's once-massive mitts now priestly thin with fine bones risen too close to the surface. "I'm sorry I couldn't win one for you."

"I won't need it where I'm going, boychick."

"It's that bad?" Micah asks, too young to be twice fatherless.

"I shit my pants now like a baby, Micah. Yeah, it's bad. Hey, Ben, pass the tinsel."

The Award of Merit, a foot-tall bronze knight holding a Crusader's sword, glows like a gyroscope. The figure stands ramrod straight atop a five-spoked reel of film, each partition representing a different branch of the academy. The table falls silent as the totem is passed hand over hand.

"He's heavier than he looks," Marblestone says, taking possession of the ready-made relic. "Seems like this town bought some prestige at last."

Hecht smiles grumpily. "'And fools, who came to scoff, remained to pray.'"

"You know who he looks like?" asks Micah, amazed by the sensation of metal coolness and smoothness baptizing his fingertips, recognizing in the figure a resemblance to his fallen friend.

"My God, you know, you're right," says Marblestone.

Till passes it back to the boss. "What's an award without a nickname?"

"Well then," Marblestone says, rising on wobbly legs to bless the table with the trophy. "To Spiro."

The tablemates raise their coffee cups. "To Spiro."

"No, wait a minute," Marblestone says, correcting himself. "To *Oscar.*"

TWO

The lobby was large and dim and full of marble columns aflicker with the lickety lights of many candles, the mausoleum gloom heightened by Micah's worry over Izzy's flight, sadness about Marblestone's imminent departure, and thoughts on the nature of his own sepulchral art. The insistent grip of Rose's hand, too, spoke of the place's eeriness. Fortunately, the effects of the drug were beginning to diminish, and with them came the lifting of his conviction that he had been followed to the opposite side of the country by an army of angry black manhood. Micah and Rose strode across the lobby, she pulling him, he pulling her, shadows casting long Dracula patterns over the black-and-white checkerboard floor.

"We're too late," Rose says, squeezing Micah's hand as she sees standing guard by the doors, his back facing them, a figure in a brown checked suit and a yellow derby.

"What's the matter, Red?" asks the wild-child dandy, revealing himself in full face and half smile, holding from his neck one of the night's coveted gold awards. "Can't recognize a colored person out of uniform?"

The months spent under Stephanie St. Clair's wing have been good to Bumpy, who seems cooler, more composed, less hopped up on his own rabbity youthfulness than before. He holds his head proud and high, a natural-born aristocrat whose every scrap of knowledge, every experiential gain, is spontaneously snatched. Even as a terrible threat hangs between them, Micah cannot help but find the gangland prince admirable.

"The waiters?" Micah asks in wonderment.

"That's right," answers Bumpy, and from the great twin marble staircases come strutting and waltzing and cruising six of his West Coast confederates, a gang of whistling, humming, terrifying Negroes brandishing razors, brass knuckles, cat-o'-nine-tails, and assorted medieval weaponry. All of them wear black slacks and white dinner jackets that make them look like the half-moon cookies Micah gets for the boys at Jewish bakeries on the Lower East Side. As poised as a gaggle of southern debutantes or Broadway chorines, they sail into position, descending the stairs, physical grace inseparable from physical threat. Making malicious show of their high-Kabuki strutting, two of them plant themselves in front of each of the entrance doors while the rest perch on the staircase, awaiting a signal. An oceanic mirror at the back of the lobby duplicates the room. In it Micah is able to register the entire orchestration of doom; in it he has trouble recognizing his own face.

"Come to see my business partner pick up an award," Bumpy says, thumping the base of the Oscar in his open palm like a policeman's billy club.

"I lost."

"I know. It'll pass."

"Thanks."

"Dumb motherfucker left this in the kitchen," Bumpy says dismissively, nodding at the award shining in his hand. He instinctively points at Rose's belly. "Hey, I know you, you're Early's sister."

"No, you're mistaking me for someone else."

"Sure thing, sis," he says, tossing the trophy tail over head to one of the goons.

"What's this for, El-Ray?" asks the henchman—the shortest, most extravagantly conked and rabid-looking of the gang—catching the award with a metallic clap. "Someone win a race?"

"Nah, man, out here they hand out trophies for getting they picture taken." Bumpy smiles, plucking a familiar scent from the temperate night air. "You motherfuckers smell like reefer!"

"It's medicinal," Micah says. "Where's Waldo? I've not heard from him since I got back."

"He's dead," Bumpy says briskly, confirming the news in the reflection of his gleaming black patents. "He's gone. I forget more in a day
than that fool ever had to teach. Now, where's my picture, Red?"

"It's not here. I think the footage is back in New York."

"No, no, no." Eyes shunting back and forth like traffic signals. "I paid
your little faggot brother a visit, only *nothing* was there. *He* wasn't there.
That's why I come out here."

"Look, listen, Izzy's not been himself since we got back."

"You think I give a rat's ass hearing about your brother's hemor-
rhoids? D'you understand who you're indebted to now, Red?"

"Yes, I had a meeting with Madam Queen." Micah points to the red
bruise on his forehead. "I understand we're in this together with her
now, I know that."

This whole time Rose has been making a careful observation of
Bumpy, trying to determine just how different, and to what degree, he
might be from her brother. "Why're you listening to this chump?" she
asks, testing a theory, using the exasperated tone of a schoolteacher
presiding over a third-grade tussle. "It's been a long night, fellas. Nice
meeting you all and hope you enjoyed the party, but we're going home."

The shard of toothpick Bumpy has been jostling between his two
decks of teeth stills itself like the leg of an animal caught in a hunting
trap. "Hold out her arms." He shrugs, looking at the floor, almost doleful. With a nod from him, the two men guarding the door step forward,
grab Rose's hands, and pull her arms outstretched, crucifixion style.

"Now, what do we have here, Red? Shut out your business partner,
but look who you bring to the ball instead." Bumpy begins stroking
Rose's cheek with his pointer finger, the tapered digit of an artist or a
musician. "Hmmm, what big eyes you have! Better to see what can't be
scrubbed away, my dear."

"Don't you touch me!"

"Hmmm, and what big lips you have! Better to suck this cracker's
joint!" He presses harder now, leaving a fluorescent imprint on her skin
as he drags the digit down her cheek. "And what fine banana skin and
straight hair you have! Better to pretend you are what you ain't. How

do you see under all that pancake?" he says, smiling at the sight of his finger coated in chalky powder. "How does *he* see *you*?"

"Get your hands off me, you black son of a bitch," Rose says, kicking and whooshing like a kite in a windstorm as the goons struggle to hang on.

"Let her go, Ellsworth," Micah says, pleading with his voice to keep from cracking. "She's got no part in this."

"Now you're just talking foolishness, Red. What you think our script's about, son? You steal that fine jelly from hardworking boys like us and then you going to tell me she got no part in this? Fucking her's like eating a piece of Ebinger's blackout cake—you're going to tell me she's got no part in this? Baby, everything you *touch* is mixed up in this. Everything you *love* is mixed up in this. Doesn't that earn your acknowledgment yet?"

"Yes," Micah says, allowing the word of affirmation to envelop them like a passage of Talmudic text. "Yes, I understand. Just tell me what you want."

"Easy, Red. I want *in*. Ellsworth wants his piece of pie."

"And I'm working on getting it for you. With a slice of cheese."

"That fine American cheese, huh? Listen, Red, if you don't want somebody writing the rules on your back," he says, flashing an unopened switchblade as casually as a husband might reach across a nightstand for a pair of reading glasses, "stop saying stupid things."

At the sight of the strip of silver, some single, final, errant leaf releases its intoxicants into Micah's bloodstream and Bumpy's metaphor materializes before him. The mark of Cain. Hester Prynne's crime ironed onto her breast. Your sins written on your very human skin, across one's arms and breast and forehead for all to see. What an elegant and terrible system of retribution! The rules written on your back!

"You know what tonight's missing?" Bumpy asks, the polished instrument in his hand revealed to be not a switchblade but a mouth harp. "Nice to see Chaplin and Fairbanks and all—though they're shorter than they look—but you know what the festivities been *lacking*? Party without music, t'aint a party t'all. Fellas!"

Bumpy snaps, and with that command the two smallest of the goons, each poised on opposing spiral staircases, leapfrog like the Nicholas Brothers over the heads of the hoodlums standing in front of them, landing in full splits on the cold tile floor. Bumpy reaches into a pocket and sends a handful of sand to the floor, the better to scat and slide, initiates a reedy C chord, and begins to sing:

"The Rules"

[To the tune of Ma Rainey's "Misery Blues."]

I love my brown skin, indeed I do
No use playing by other people's rules
I'm gonna tell you, just what I done
To live my life and have my fun

[On one knee, arms open wide in supplication,
like Al Jolson in *The Jazz Singer.*]

Busboy or a porter or a shoeshine boy
How's that mean niggers ain't slaves no more?
Ellsworth's screaming, he's almost cryin'
Because the world, it isn't mine

[The award is tossed back to Bumpy, who presses
it close to his cheek for the chorus.]

[Chorus]

Learned me some rules
Ain't in no school
Got to be versed in them
Miserable rules

[The trophy is passed between the dancing gang members,
who lob it among themselves, pantomiming stickups
and prison rapes, accosting Micah and Rose.]

You serve up that gruel
'N work like a mule
World spins to the tune of
Miserable rules
The kind and the cruel
The burnt and the cool
Will brand on your back them
Miserable rules

[Bumpy laying hands on the award for the final verse.]

So protect your jewels
[smiling wickedly at Rose]
And sharpen your tools
[nodding to his enforcers]
Be on your guard 'gainst
Miserable rules
Gots to rebel 'gainst those
Miserable rules

"Nice song," Micah says at the conclusion of the first Academy Awards musical number.

"What song?" Bumpy asks.

"Look," says Micah, no longer convinced of the actuality of what is transpiring, the concrete reality of events unfolding around him, "this is a very unusual way to conduct business."

"*Conduct business?*" Bumpy repeats, face corkscrewing around the phrase, speaking with his mouth but translating through his body. "And how exactly would you have me *conduct business*? What'd you have a nigger do? Make an appointment with your secretary? Visit the bank, ask to take out a loan? Go off sniffing drainpipes? I see you and the fat man at dinner together, but where's the seat at the table for Ellsworth?"

"Things change," Micah says, giving voice to a thought he hasn't until this moment articulated to himself. "It takes time, but things change."

"Motherfucker, change is what goes jingle-jangle in my pocket. Know what doesn't change? Every time I look in the mirror expecting to see someone like you, I see someone looks like he crawled out the ass of America. *That* don't change. That's what you motherfuckers never understand; hos, hootch, and horns are the only things you left us. Talk to me about conducting business—that *is* my business. I'm in the stay-black-and-die business."

"Bumpy," Rose spits, "you're just a common crook."

"Don't call me common."

He winds up the award from its base like a batter at the plate and delivers a roundhouse to Rose's pregnant stomach. A sickening flat thud, the sound of a sandbag dropped from a great height onto a haystack, sends Rose crumpling to the lobby floor.

"I am's what I am," Bumpy says, sending the award sailing across the room again then snapping together the loose night air with the click of a popped-open switchblade. "That's more than I can say for you."

Darting in like a varsity-team fencer, Bumpy punctures the uppermost part of Micah's right arm. Even during the phenomenally slowed moment in which he is attacked, Micah appreciates the fierce athletic splendor of Bumpy's form, the cloud of electricity he carries in the air that huddles around him. A portion of Micah's white dinner jacket begins turning deepest red, a red that, in its spill and spread, announces all previous incarnations of the color to have been impostors.

Swooning, Micah consults the lobby mirror to confirm the occurrence of all these events. It registers upon him that his site of injury echoes that of King Mishi. As he kneels to the floor, thick drops of blood begin patterning tile like sauce on a plate; the pain comes flooding in, but at a remove. *Yes, this is excruciating!* shy nerve endings scream into the cool night air. *But brace yourself, because worse might be in the offing.*

There passes instead a fermata of stillness that allows the molecules between all of them a chance to absorb their terrible knowledge, to do whatever fizzy subatomic rearranging needs occurring. Micah huddles beside Rose, who is unblinking and impassive, as pitiful and cold as a seashell at the bottom of a well. Meantime, the dinner just concluded, end-of-evening sounds of clattering tableware, jostled chair legs, and farewell chatter begin to move toward them like a fast-approaching storm.

Bumpy folds up his knife, and the hooligans scatter behind him, the smallest among them leaving the trophy on its side at the foot of the stairs, as the lobby begins to spackle with familiar faces of the famous and fabulous. "I'm just a song-and-dance man, but this is one number we're going to finish together, Ginger."

Then, all smiling Sambo obsequiousness, Bumpy sidles up to an elderly couple entering the lobby. Without prompting, he links arms with the woman in her mink stole and claims the coat of her husband, whose eyebrows lift like pup tents at the young Negro's touch. "Hallo, ma'am, sir," Bumpy says through keyboard teeth. "Allow me to show you good people to the door!"

THREE

It has been days since Izzy set foot outside the editing room, and drifting through stone-colored midtown streets, astrally alone, ignoring the puzzled stares of passersby startled to see a man walking down Broadway dressed in a bright red dashiki, he notices how intemperate the weather in New York has become. Catching his crimson reflection in a sheet-music store's window, he acknowledges that he looks not entirely of this world.

Conferring with this red-chalk smear of himself, Izzy recalls the occult message that has pressed itself upon him during sleep. The words, which seemed ripped from a poem or an ancient scroll, occurred to him in a series of dreams (dreams of birdmen in flight; dreams of giant black spiders and terrifying winged cockroaches; dreams of unstoppable, overflowing toilets; the recurring dream of shattered teeth, being pulled from his mouth one stringy root at a time). A warning about the actualization of deepest dread, the message was one that Izzy inscribed on every available surface since its visitation. Across editing-room notebooks, table, and walls, even, in grease pencil, across his own forearm, he scrawled it, and he repeats the words to himself now, staring through his own whispered reflection on newly strange streets.

THE THING YOU FEAR MOST IS THE THING THAT WILL HAPPEN.

He had experienced a version of the thought years before, during his inaugural takeoff from Brooklyn's Barren Island Airport, during which every sudden dip, every unexpected elevation, every sputtering mechanical gurgle, registered as a portent of doom. Say the plane skids off the runway or you fall from the sky. What then? What is the thing you're most afraid of? He looked across the aisle at an elderly man, perhaps in his mid-seventies, who seemed not at all alarmed by the jolts and jostles. Why? Because the distinguished thing isn't so far off for him. Blown engine today or not—tomorrow, next year, ten years from now—the great inevitable makes its gains. Why should its realization ever come as a surprise when we all, everyone, spend our lives speeding toward the bottom of that well? The thing you fear most is the thing that will happen.

If the message was true—as Izzy believed it to be—if religion was just a set of stories we tell ourselves, if the soul did not persist after death, if we were not to be reunited with our parents and loved ones after death in some cottony white playground, if life was indeed a business nasty, brutish, and short—the question became one of resignation. How to construct meaning in the face of the inscrutable? Dr. Freud, whom Izzy had lately taken to investigating, argued that the answer lay in love and work. But too many days—even days spent in the presence of loved ones, days spent doing good work—felt vacant. What then? What binds us together? A grinding repetition? A dull sense of duty? Could questions, as King Mishi suggested, provide truer consolation than answers? Could questions themselves—and the rarefied shape they take in the form of narrative, the stories we tell each other over and over—be the answer?

What question, what comfort, what distraction does Izzy find himself walking toward this late afternoon? After many months of silence and separation, Izzy's friend, the Broadway publicist Howard Rubin Mansfield, tracked him down and insisted that the filmmaker take a break from his editing-room labors to have a look at some foreign Bible picture he couldn't stop raving about.

O unhappy man! Izzy thought upon arriving at the screening room and finding Howard waiting for him, alone, his face as tightly knotted as the loop of his necktie. How could he ever have mistaken the man's mordant humor for anything other than dimmest sadness? Situated across Howard's lap like a stadium blanket is a small, well-manicured spaniel that looks up from the publicist's waist with a half-expectant expression, as if Howard has already told him lots about Izzy.

"My life's companion," Howard volunteers, introducing Bruce. Uncertain what would be an acceptable form of physical greeting after so long a time apart, Howard uses the dog as an excuse not to rise from his seat and instead offers none. "The only creature on God's green earth I'll happily take shit from. Ha-ha! You're looking well, Isidor," he continues, his speech keeping a step ahead of his thoughts, "modeling the indigenous fashion, I see."

A bright red handkerchief the same color as his tie and expensive socks warns off approaching happiness like a stop sign. Even at rest his shoulders are scrunched too high toward the neck, gathered tension and denial causing the body to torque around itself like vines climbing a university dormitory wall. A life lived in code, hope measured in earlobe tugs and colored handkerchiefs. If the man seemed permanently gloomy—a person for whom every cloud has a cloudy lining—his expression nevertheless holds the serenity of a man who doesn't dare happiness.

"What is it we're seeing?"

"Not one for chitchat," Howard responds, stung. "Still acclimating from the trip, I gather. That's fine, that's fine. Yes, well, the picture's called *La Passion de Jeanne d'Arc*"—a thousand Frenchmen instantly felled by Bronx-flecked pronunciation—"and I've never seen anything quite like it. You know Dreyer?"

"The Scandinavian?" Izzy, carefully removing Bruce's teeth from his hand. "He's the real thing."

"Yes, well, I believe this picture marks an enormous leap forward for your fledgling cinematic art. The images are something like the equivalent of grain alcohol, and the film contains what I consider to be the single greatest performance ever committed to celluloid. At the risk of embarrassing myself further, I shall say no more until our immersion in it is complete. Rocco," Howard snaps to the Italian projectionist. "Lights!"

Izzy has not seen a film in a theater since before they left for Africa, and he is ill prepared for Carl Theodor Dreyer's treatment of the story of the Virgin of Orléans. With its religious theme executed in a manner as rigorous as a Flemish canvas, with its ascetic storytelling style, its intertitles lifted verbatim from court transcripts of the martyr's trial, and its parade of faces—faces in all their particularity and peculiarity; faces held in extreme, near-clinical close-up; faces forced to yield up their mystery like grapes submitting to a winepress—*The Passion of Joan of Arc* imprints each of its images upon Izzy's consciousness like a watermark.

Heart beating perhaps twice over the course of the film's eighty minutes, Izzy is thunderstruck by the picture's compositions and camera movement, its hypnotic patterning and sublime reiteration of forms (the shadow from a windowpane falling as a crucifix across a prison-cell floor); the uncanny medieval implements of torture (the saws and winches and spiked spinning wheels); the undercurrents of unabashed eroticism (Joan, dressed in men's clothes with close-cropped hair and the frisson that passes between her and Antonin Artaud's priest). And Izzy is knocked sideways by the lead performance of Melle Falconetti as the nineteen-year-old martyr—which appeared to be not so much a performance as an act of conjuring. But it was through Dreyer's decision to tell the story as a catalog of close-ups that the picture achieved a kind of purity and saintliness. The insistence on the primacy of the human face—the director's belief in the essential dignity and strangeness of every actor's set of features—came through as less an illustrative storytelling choice than an inevitable spiritual imperative. The absoluteness of it, the actuality of it! *The Passion of Joan of Arc* wasn't a picture *about* something; it wasn't a performance or a staged re-creation. It was the thing itself.

"Do you see?" Howard asks once Joan's martyrdom is complete and the lights come up to reclaim the two of them for the twentieth century.

Howard has hoped his friend would recognize the latent plea in showing Izzy this particular film. He has hoped that Izzy would interpret the
picture's message as being one about unnecessary self-punishment, that
by way of its deliverance they might find it in themselves to forgive each
other for being who they are and appreciate that they are no longer con-
demned to live in a medieval age of martyrs and visions. Several times
during the picture, Howard had to stifle himself from crying out about
Joan and her lovelorn priest, *Look how happy they could have been together!*

Howard carefully folds his damp handkerchief. "Now do you see?
Now do you see what I mean?"

"Yes, I think so."

"It's been a long time, Izzy. How about we go for a drink and get
properly caught up?" Attuned to the scent of pheromones, Bruce yelps
his assent.

Izzy's face is matted with perspiration and tear tracks. "Thanks, but
no," he answers. "There's somewhere I have to be just now. But thank
you, Howard, very much, for sharing that picture with me."

Izzy kisses the man's clammy bald head, which tastes unmistakably
like cork. They have been watching different films. A soul fallen from
love into nothingness, Izzy leaves the screening room consumed with
thoughts of immolation, visions of martyrdom, grand gestures realized
and engulfed in flame. He would depart tonight. He makes the decision
walking the few blocks from the screening room back to the editing
suite, recounting the shepherd girl's final, silent prayer before burning
at the stake. *("Dear God, I accept my death gladly, but do not let me suffer
too long.")*

Never did New York seem more alien to him. Never before did the
city seem to exist as a dream of itself. The singing of trees and trucks,
the siren calls of construction, the tinkling of silverware escaping
revolving restaurant doors, the howling of wind down avenues, the snarl
of subways emerging from elevated caves, all of it melding together in
some strange and beautiful and necessary music. All this he realizes he
would have to abandon.

Keys do not know they're keys; they await some lock's recognition.

Defining themselves through action, that's their beauty. Returning to the editing room just moments ahead of the thumping arrival of Bumpy Johnson and a collection of Harlem's most feared gangsters, Izzy silently surveys his prison cell. The wrought-iron industrial machinery, the hanging glossy strips of immortal stuff, the rows of hourglasses, the map of his beloved home, and, new to the room, a series of mockups he had printed the week before, posters advertising sinister and imaginary films of the crew's African exploits. Recognizing at last the materials that lay before him the entire time—the clay he daily shaped in his hands, medium of magic and dust—the key slips its bolt, tumblers fall like toy soldiers, and the sound of the door closing behind him rings out like a consummation, confirmation that he knows what he must do to set things right.

4

THE RETURN

ONE

Arthur Marblestone died, and Micah found a room in Till's house and cried very much. Though Marblestone had served in no army, he insisted on being buried with an American flag draped over his casket and had made arrangements for there to be a twenty-one-gun salute. The funeral—conducted in Hebrew, afforded moderate coverage in the trades—marked the second of two deaths that delayed Micah's return to New York.

Micah had done his best to avoid everything related to the physical fact of Margaret's pregnancies—using as distractions work, drink, and philandering—but with Rose's miscarriage he was right there. There was lots of blood. There was the revelation of women as fluid and ocean and moon. And there was Micah's surprise at the shifting, liquid nature of his own feelings. As Rose recuperated in Till's compound with its great, year-round Christmas tree and chronic yuletide cheer, her look was as far away as that of Manet's barmaid, a kind of level, distant passivity, her mood a fort that Micah found difficult to breach.

"I never got to feel it kick," she said after several days of silence. "I don't know if I was ready to become a mom, but it would have been nice to have felt it kick."

"Well, being a parent's no picnic."

"You think I'll ever meet your sons?"

"That's not really possible, no."

"I'd like to be a mother someday."

"You will be."

"It won't be yours, though, will it?"

"No, it won't."

When he wasn't at his mistress's bedside, Micah spent his time in California hustling on behalf of Imperial's failing fortunes and talking up the Africa footage that might no longer exist. Fulfilling his final role as surrogate son, Micah also helped Masha Marblestone sift through the ruins of her husband's estate, the big man's heavy oak casket clattering behind it a chorus of claims and accusations like tin cans clanging down the street after a couple of newlyweds. With Marblestone now gone, Micah was aware of how fully exposed he was professionally. If he was thought of as Imperial's A-list director—and a filmmaker who was yoked to a genuine box-office force in the person of Henry Till—Micah also knew he was deemed a second- or third-tier talent by the major studios. Being judged too young, too brash, too profligate, too ungovernable had never bothered him so long as Marblestone considered him his prize pony.

Thumping away like a bass line through this song of personal and professional anxiety was Micah's worry over Izzy's whereabouts. As days of silence calendarized themselves into a biblical week, Micah became convinced that Izzy had somehow managed to wing his way back to Africa. Micah was at least three days away from New York, putting him seven or ten more from the Dark Continent. And Bloat, the man most likely to hold a lead on Ariadne's thread, proved impossible to reach.

Howard was the last man reported to have seen Izzy the night after Micah flew out west, and the publicist had no pertinent details to add to the missing-persons case beyond Izzy's strangeness of dress and manner, his general uncommunicativeness, and a screening report concerning the private viewing of a foreign film.

"Your brother seemed very moved by the picture," Howard said about his friend's reaction to *The Passion of Joan of Arc*, sounding more resigned than saddened by the news of Izzy's disappearance. "I've seen other friends of similar temperament do terrible things to themselves. I do hope Isidor is wiser than that and chooses to take the long view."

Returning to New York at last, half suspecting to find Izzy hanging from the editing-room ductwork, Micah was instead greeted with a message for him from his brother, scrawled across the wall in Izzy's inimitably nervous hand in thick, foot-tall block letters:

THE THING YOU FEAR MOST IS THE THING THAT WILL HAPPEN. YOU WATCH, MICAH.

"Fucking little cocksucker," Micah said to no one in particular. Pinned to the center of the floor, sealed in an envelope marked "SSC," another message awaited the filmmaker. "Watch your lemons. The time for tribute draws near," read the card in Madam Queen's familiar, tight calligraphy.

"Little fucking cocksucker's going to get us all killed!"

The room had been ransacked, every shaving of celluloid cleared out of the bins and swept from the floors, all the reels and spools emptied of their contents. Each of Izzy's prized hourglass figures had been emphatically smashed, the tile covered in splinters of glass and dunes of dust. Even the room's ancient, immobile projector—a piece of industrial hardware that had formerly presided over its corner of the room like a ship's anchor or a railway water tower—had gone missing, leaving behind a clean, bright rhomboid of floor. The only remaining piece of equipment was a Moviola, which loomed over the empty scene like a tombstone.

"I shall have to hang a shingle," Bloat said in a phone voice dripping with sugar and arsenic once Micah was finally able to make contact. "From all appearances I am now in the brothers Grand business. Apologies for being so long out of touch. The *Pfefferminz* trade has been booming!"

For a price Bloat confirmed that, yes, he had booked passage for Micah's brother to make his way back to Malwiki the week before. For another fee the smuggler would happily make arrangements to have Micah met at the Brooklyn Navy Yards as early as tomorrow afternoon for a similar return trip. Additional sums would ensure that word would reach Mtabi and the translator would meet the moviemaker in Congo.

"I can confirm that your brother was traveling abroad with a good deal of cinematographic-industrial equipment—much more than what you took along for your first expedition," Bloat reported for a final figure. "The transport of this tonnage to the interior presented a set of hitherto-unheard-of logistics and challenges, but given how Isidor made clear that money is no object, my associates were able to assist in this endeavor as well. After that, I'm afraid the trail grows cold."

Izzy! So ill prepared for life, so in need of reality training, able to touch only the surface of things, like a spoon skimming the top layer of hot soup. The thought of Izzy undertaking alone so rash and dangerous a trip—his attempt to big-picture it, to reconcile all the strands of his fears and uncertainties in one bold move—no good could come of it. Worse, in his solipsism, his willingness to read the collapse of the village and a people's collective fate as a backdrop for his own awakening, Izzy had put himself, his brother, Rose, Margaret, and the boys in no small jeopardy. *"You fucking little cocksucker!"* Micah repeated, pulling together passport, paperwork, and bills into his leather travel satchel. *"I should leave you out there to rot!"*

Instead Micah committed himself to his brother's pursuit. He did not know what he expected to find, but if Izzy was out there, Micah pledged himself to his brother's care. The decision made, the boys kissed good-bye, the bank account emptied, Micah propelled himself forward from train to ship, from ship to plane, from plane to chartered boat, by boat upriver, from cities and hotels to shanties and huts to the desolation of the inner continent, following a bread-crumb trail of memory the whole way, surrendering himself like a man toppling into deepest sleep.

When the brothers were young and magic had first begun to fan its cards across their imagination, they would put on performances in the basement for relatives and friends. The sets, costumes, and props were fashioned from children's stuff: cardboard boxes and sheets of construction paper, swatches of felt and yarn, cotton balls and Popsicle sticks. But even in the hands of a pair of ten-year-olds, the entertainer's will to amuse and delight, the need to believe and foster belief in others, the compulsion to transform the quotidian, to offer intimations of a world beyond the visible, was ancient and formidable.

Borrowing his father's oversize top hat, Micah ran the show, his role as master of ceremonies preordained. It was left to Izzy, then, to play quick-change artist: here impersonating an overgrown, bucktoothed rabbit; there an unsuspecting volunteer lifted from the audience; here a human piggybank from which coins of different size and value were pulled from various orifices; there, in his mother's dress, a damsel, distressed, squeezed inside a box, awaiting the blade. Even in Izzy's dream life, Micah appeared as an impresario forever in need of an audience and a subordinate upon whom he could impose his will.

A wandering spectacular that never left home, "Micah and Izzy's Traveling Medicine Show" always ended with the boys' favorite sketch. During the "Topsy-Turvy World" portion of the program, the light switch on the familiar was flipped and some comfortable everyday norm was inverted, upturned. In this nonsense world, words and sentences were spoken backward, landscape photos were displayed in negative, pitchers of water were colored green with food dye, egg cartons were opened to reveal a half dozen chirping chicks. In this world of opposites, day became night, past became future, good became bad, black became white, boys became girls.

Most profound for Micah was the dawning precognition that the conjuring of make-believe, the construction of a kingdom of paper and cotton balls, was neither an exaggeration nor inconsistent with the world's spectrum of reality. Shadow play was no less substantive, magic no less real, for knowing how the trick was performed. Or as Micah explained to Izzy upon introducing him to a ventriloquist's dummy named Otto, "Just because he's fake doesn't mean he isn't *real*."

The Grand brothers' intuition told them that their children's play, their first paddles into illusion's undertow, was of a piece with some ceaseless planetary music. The talking puppet, the rabbit pulled from the hat, the ace of spades peeled from the top of the deck, these silly contrivances were on a continuum with the cosmic. Make-believe, the topsy-turvy, the world of inversion—that *was* the world. And it was the memory of his first experiences of magic as real as dust that came swimming back to Micah now as he returned to Africa like the fulfillment of a Möbius strip.

The smells reached him first. Odors of putrefaction, of rotten eggs and curdled milk, of fish heads with dried-berry eyes, of dead things given over to decomposition. Then the flies, clouds of them thick and black as smoke, windborne armies of Beelzebub, following them everywhere like a procession preceding a diplomat's entrance. Only a few months had passed since he was here last, but Micah might well have been an old man returning after many decades to the playground of his youth to find it overrun, smaller than memory had it landscaped, sadder than childhood could accommodate.

Everything about the return seemed off, askew, like a plumber's level that wouldn't right itself. In the distance vibrates the stamp-size village, as unmoored from the real as a woodcut illustration from a children's book: inky, black, elemental, monolithic. Ahead he makes out the presence of some British soldiers, rifles strapped to their backs and pointed upward like radio antennas, as out of place in their red-and-white starched uniforms as crocodiles cruising the Arctic floor.

"Bad things have befallen," says Mtabi, recently reunited with his employer and similarly weighed down by sadness. "Many bad things since we last made visit."

"Is Izzy here?" Micah asks the loyal guide, repeating the question he has posed like a prayer countless times since their journey began.

"I do not know, sir."

What happens to a place when you leave? Does it go on without you or continue in your imagination unabated? What responsibility do you owe it? A few yards ahead of them, a small figure sits silent and still on the parched earth. At first they mistake it for an armadillo or a muskrat. Moving closer, they recognize it to be a child, a boy of perhaps seven or eight, wearing no clothes. He looks on the verge of starving: bones squeezed too close to the skin, the bodily rigging all too apparent, a drawing awaiting a watercolorist to lend it some substantiality. Reaching him, Micah recognizes the boy as Liwiki, one of the most curious and delightful of the village children, whom the company had filmed at play with his friend Souleyman. Recognizing the Westerner, Liwiki struggles to sit up, head and shoulders resting atop a distended midsection the shape of a comic-strip dialogue balloon. He stares unblinking at the group of foreigners. The corners of his mouth are coated in a white crust. Micah kneels down and offers his canteen. He is uncertain whether or not he has license to touch the child, whether or not it would be improper to begin stroking the boy's head, moving slowly with an open palm from his forehead to the base of his skull, a placating gesture that helps soothe his own boys to sleep when they're sick. He does, the warm, skin-to-skin contact making the return trip real to him at last.

"So this is Africa?" says a third voice.

"Sometimes," Micah answers Rose. "Sometimes."

Bringing Rose had occurred to Micah as a necessity, something preordained rather than a question to be deliberated over. Leaving her for an indeterminate length of time so soon after the miscarriage seemed a terrible cruelty. He feared for her safety back in New York in ways he didn't worry about Margaret and the boys (the murder of a colored woman in Harlem seeming well within Bumpy's vocabulary of violence, the slaughter of a Fifth Avenue matron and her two white sons something perhaps not even the gangster would dare). And if the journey led, as Micah suspected it might, to Izzy's death, that destination was one Micah did not want to face alone. Were he called upon out here to dredge up some reserves of heroism, it would be good to have her watching. Rose's gaze brought out Micah's better moral posture.

"I have a husband, remember?" she shot back when he first made the proposal, sitting up in bed in Till's guesthouse, the old fire returning to her voice.

"Yeah, the man gives a good shave."

"He likes you."

"I like him, too. Only man's ever seen my pecker hard."

"Only man he's seen laying down with his wife. Speaking of which, why not ask Margaret?"

"Because I like you better."

"Really, that's news to me, mister. Sometimes I wonder how you tell us apart."

"The difference between a wife and a mistress?" Micah mused, gripping her hand. "A wife is someone you keep secrets from. A mistress is a secret you keep for yourself."

"That's the difference, huh?"

"Yes, doll."

say!" exclaims the mustached British officer, picking up his pace as he begins walking alongside the group. His face holds an alarmingly parboiled look, the color of corned beef left too long on a plate. "Mr. Grand! Still drinking from the dregs of the colonial cup?"

"Remind me how I know you," Micah asks, woozy from the heat and unable to pin a name or context to this unexpected recognition.

"J. P. Keneally, at your service." Said with a salute by the British panjandrum from whom Micah and Izzy had gotten their paperwork in the London embassy. "Have you forgotten your friend from Merrie Olde?"

"Yes, of course," Micah says, recalling his unhappy encounter with the bureaucrat and concluding that all Brits look alike. "My brother, is he here? Is he alive?"

"He's gone beaming bloody mad, is what he is! Thinks he's one of the darkies now, running around without any clothes, talking gibberish, says he's never going back."

Micah exhales. "Then he's alive."

"If you call this living," Keneally says with expert comic timing. Apart from the stray British soldier pacing back and forth, the village seemed weirdly depopulated, not so much the place he had come to love as its abandoned fossil record. Other than the sick child they'd left in a soldier's care, they had yet to encounter a single member of the tribe.

"What's going on in town?" Micah asks, nodding toward the village in the distance.

"Just a spot of mismanagement on the part of the bloody wogs," Keneally reports. "After their king died, the savages couldn't be trusted to run a bath, much less a country. So the powers that be put yours truly back in the field."

"Interesting. This is Mtabi, our guide." Distractedly introducing his companions. "And this is Rose."

Keneally licks each pen stroke of mustache. "I say! An honor and a pleasure, Mrs. Grand!"

Micah chooses not to acknowledge Keneally's mistake. His discomfort is of a piece with the embarrassment he'd felt as a child whenever he'd run into a schoolteacher while with his parents. Only who was responsible for this anguished sense of dislocation? His parents were still his parents. Mtabi was still Mtabi. Rose was still Rose. Of course it was Micah—kaleidoscopic, fragmented, unresolved Micah: Micah the moviemaker, Micah the son, Micah the brother, Micah the husband, Micah the father, Micah the lothario, Micah the child, Micah the man-child—who feared being found out by figures from these disparate contexts. It was Micah who experienced the shame that comes with knowing he would never get his warring personas to reconcile.

"Respectfully, Mr. Grand," Keneally says as they walk, "I suspect that anything shy of a tranquilizer dart will prove incapable of bringing your brother back to his senses."

"Take me to him."

"And that your presence here might go over something like a lead zeppelin. I've seen cases like this before, amongst military men whose constitutions consist of, shall we say, stiffer stuff than your brother's. Going native can be a powerful intoxicant. Pardon me, madam, they simply have to bugger it out of their system."

"You take me to him now, Keneally."

"Very well, Mr. Grand, very well. But there's no mystery where he is." The officer smiles creepily. "He even rolled out the red carpet for you. Just follow that bloody rag. It'll take you to your blessed brother."

TWO

In their haste Micah and Rose had failed to make proper preparations for the return trip to Africa, instead simply taking the valises they'd brought back with them from Los Angeles. It was for that reason Micah now found himself walking down a red carpet dressed in the slashed and bloodstained dinner jacket he'd worn for the Academy Awards ceremony, and Rose trailed beside him in formalwear, barefoot, swollen brown toes lined up in rows like chocolates in a box, a pair of agonizing heels held by their straps, her emotive hair having exploded in the tropical heat like a champagne bottle uncorked.

Micah had never seen Bloat's red carpet unfurled at its full length before, and it appeared now in all its ugly grandeur, perhaps half a mile outside the village center, a red lane of death opened wide. The earth, vegetation, and thatched huts all around them appeared painted in blacks, whites, and grays, rendering vulgar the carpet's phosphorescent red—color of blood and battle, of edible berries and wine pressed from black grapes, of the roulette wheel and the billiard ball—the rug's declamatory brightness a rebuke against the brittle condition of the village. The color of the runner was also weirdly inconsistent, with dappled, stippled blotches and sprays streaked across its threadbare thickness, and here and there the carpet emitted a moist squishiness when they stepped, a fetid tackiness beneath their feet.

"It's like a movie-theater floor," Rose says, cautiously taking her next sticky step.

Mtabi removes a candy wrapper from his heel. "What kind of tapestry is this, sir?"

"It's called a red carpet. They roll it out for special occasions."

"Such as the commemoration of a good harvest or the anointment of a royal heir?"

"Yeah, something like that."

"And with Providence this grand threadwork might bring us to your brother?"

"That's what we're hoping for, yes."

"I have also met *your* brother," Mtabi says, turning to Rose, rolling up his suit sleeve and pressing his forearm against hers. "Early is much darker than you! I believe he truly enjoyed his time here."

"That's what he said."

"Tell me, Miss Letty, what is it like to be of African descent living in the land of Henry Ford and Coca-Cola?"

"What's it like?" Rose repeats, wondering how to answer the kindly guide. She thought of stories her grandmother had told her of being a sharecropper's daughter, visions of southern night skies streaked through with comets out of the book of Revelation. Of growing up thinking "nigger" was a word as commonplace as "radio" or "flower" or "hamburger." Of the first time she had seen her father casually abused in a restaurant outside Philadelphia, the waiter knocking the man's hat off his head as he passed. She remembered being warned by the neighborhood grocery-store manager not to touch anything on the shelves because her color might rub off and staring in wonder at a carton of brown eggs, amazed that the store would carry what was surely the product of black chickens. She remembered a thousand acts of kindness and cruelty. A world of limits and markers and daily precaution and delight and secret language and singing and rapture, too. A daily existence that once in a while offered flashes of clairvoyance, a sense of privilege in having some clear conception of what America—the place of it rather than the idea of itself—really was. She thought of her grandmother in the kitchen, making red velvet cake for the Fourth of July. "All that white! All that white!" The woman's face creasing like a newspaper when she said things wicked, mixing cups of sifted flour, sugar, eggs, and buttermilk in a big aluminum bowl. "Needs some dark," she said, bringing two tablespoons of cocoa into the mix. "Reach inna back the cupboard, honey, and bring me them beets," she instructed seven-year-old Rose. "Needs some red," her grandmother said, carefully straining the purple-red vegetable juice and noisily stirring the bowl like a witch brewing a potion. "Needs some blood," she said, and here the woman held her pointer finger straight out like a staff, pricked it with a clothes-pin she kept on her apron, squeezed the tip until a drop of the stuff bubbled on the fleshy bulb, and let it drop into the batter. "That's the love," she said. "That's what holds it together. Can't be the Fourth with-out some blood!"

"Living in America's a difficult thing to put into words, Mtabi."

"Sometimes, like the birds of autumn," the guide suggests, "one must leave a place in order to see it clearly."

As they near the entrance of the king's compound, the carpet becomes covered with small strips of bark. Stubbing her toe on one of the strange pieces of wood, Rose picks it up and recognizes that these aren't fragments fallen from trees at all but uniformly die-cut chips, each decorated with different striped markings and patterns, single, double, and triple lines etched in quarter-inch bark.

"Look there, sir." The guide is first to spot it, a giant photograph pinned to the side of a thatched hut, a poster as black and shiny as the back of a scorpion.

Micah hops off the carpet and approaches the image. It is an enor-mous image of King Mishi sacrificing the bull, the two-foot-by-four-foot one-sheet capturing the beast in midfall, bloody gash in its neck as deep and irrevocable as a first slice of wedding cake. In the bottom third of the movie slick, a credit block touts a picture titled *Monsters Need Their Meat* as an Imperial Pictures Production and a "Grand Brothers Boondoggle." In bloodred letters, the words NOW SHOWING! stenciled in a strip across the top.

"Fucking hell, Izzy," his brother moans.

There are other handmade posters, glistening photographic reproductions adorning the sides of huts and hugging tree trunks, some
stretched tight as sails, others waving gently as flags. There is an image
of King Mishi nobly looking out over the land (*The Trials of Abraham*)
and the beloved prince standing next to the camera tripod (*The Passion of Cri*), of Malwiki wrestling matches (*Sport of the Ancients*) and the
peaceful harvesting of dura (*Food Co-op*), of Spiro in his captain's costume (*Memory of the Fallen*) and Till in his pith helmet (*Brewing the Pot*).
There is even an image of the twins themselves, arms wrapped around
each other's shoulders, smiling into the sun together like Tom and Huck
(*Blood Brothers*). Each of the billboards is emblazoned with proclama-
tions that announce TONIGHT ONLY! and COMING SOON! and FROM THE
STUDIO THAT BROUGHT YOU *SCAREDY SPOOKS*!

Mtabi shields his gaze from the image of the fallen monarch. "This
kind of conjuring is very bad voodoo."

THREE

They follow the red carpet through the deserted village, past the big gates and through underground tunnels, to the great hall of the king's chamber. Cast in pearlescent light, at first the space seems occupied only by a camel whose sphinctered lips look like they're whispering silent thoughts. Staring into the creature's cello-like face, for a moment Micah allows himself to believe that his brother has metamorphosed into this benign and secretive beast.

"Any sign of him?" Rose asks.

"No, not yet," Micah says, eyes adjusting to the dark as he moves toward the far end of the hall by the vacant wooden throne to throw open the shutters, "but he could be anywhere."

The room holds a musty, clotted scent, a smell reminiscent of empty mason jars or old slippers pulled out from under the bed. Gray shafts of light illuminate large, unhealthy-looking motes that squiggle around the space like it's a petri dish. Absent the animating force of King Mishi, the hall is revealed a dank and gloomy affair.

Were Izzy not lying in the opposite corner wound in a filthy bed-sheet, were he wearing clothes, were his scalp not shorn, were his figure not emaciated—with stalk-thin arms and an exposed rib cage—if he looked less like a broken puppet, it would have been easier for Micah to distinguish his brother from the surroundings. Izzy, warped, diseased, a sliver of personhood, connected to selfdom by mere filaments, but still, irrevocably, Izzy.

"Argh, Micah, I really don't want to talk about it," says the sheet-tangled figure in a voice indistinguishable from the one Micah knew as a teenager, when Izzy improbably stumbled ahead of him into puberty.

"Good Christ! Rose, get some water."

"Yes, Rose, get this man some water!" Izzy says, hurling a chamber pot at his brother, a spray of waste and a clang of copper halting Micah's advance.

"I think I'm going to be sick," Rose says as a rivulet of drool winds its way toward her bare feet.

"Why do people love the smell of their own shit?" the phantom figure asks, folding back into the gloom. "But not the smell of others'?" Izzy has learned to love defecating out here, outdoors, squatting away anywhere, leaving excremental traces of himself everywhere, wiping himself with handfuls of mulch, sometimes choosing not to wipe at all. It was all shit. The world was a giant factory of entropy, waste, decay. And we experience that not-so-secret truth as individuals every day. Couldn't they see that?

Micah's eyes now fully adjusted to the theater of blackness, he begins to make out additional details: empty cans of film—shiny doubloons, silver dollars, dozens of them—stacked in a far corner of the room; a primitive-looking wooden table his brother must be using as a kind of workbench; drained cans of condensed milk, baked beans, rotting fruit rinds, and empty medicine bottles. There were startling details of Izzy's person to discover, too: clumps of hair indiscriminately deracinated across the bloodied scalp; his face covered in pitch or ash, black as Jolson's; and, stranger still, twining across the torso, too many to count, a map of bruises or scratches, patterned strings of them, small, black, almost indiscernible, wending across his back, wrapped around his neck and wrist and shins. Eventually these shapes sharpen out of the fog, revealing themselves to be neither cuts nor contusions but the most familiar figures of all: 4, 3, 9, 1, 2, the Arabic numerals string themselves together in random-seeming combinations, marking themselves across Izzy's bruised and injured body.

"Why did you come here, Micah?"

"To find you. To make sure you're okay."

"Everything you've ever done is for you. What'd you really come here for?"

"To bring you home, Itz. To bring you back with the film."

"Oh, the film! The film! Always an ulterior motive with this one," he says, wagging a finger at Rose. "You'll get your picture, Micah. I've been working on it out here, back at the scene of the crime. Is that my friend Mtabi?"

"Yes, sir," says the translator, whose immanent calm in the face of these unnatural circumstances convinces Micah that the guide must have enjoyed a life even stranger, better versed in unnatural circumstance and human variety, than the filmmaker had originally suspected.

"Come here, Mtabi, I want to talk to you for a minute," Izzy says, sitting up and running his eyes over the African's rumpled blue suit and purple tie. "My father—may he rest in peace—first showed me how to knot one of those. I've been thinking about them a lot out here: the dead." And here Izzy curls his face up toward the translator like some deep-sea creature breaking to the surface, a blowfish about to spit its poisonous message of defense. "Mtabi, I always wanted to ask you what you make of the people you work for as a guide."

"Make of them, sir?"

"Yeah, what you think of them."

"I do not know how to properly answer your question, sir. Their job is to look, my job is to show."

"But what do you think they come here for? Really?"

"Some come to see the animals, some to hunt, some come for rubber and diamonds. Most think they know a place by seeing it. But they see nothing. To know a place, one must live the worst of it."

"And what's the worst of it, Mtabi?"

"Izzy," his brother says, "that's enough."

"Don't listen to him, Mtabi. He's not the boss anymore. Tell me the worst of it."

"That was a long time ago."

"Tell me, I want to know."

"Ten years ago our youngest son died."

"What of?"

"Diphtheria."

"How old was he?"

"Two. He was two."

"And there was nothing you could do?"

"No, sir. We traveled far, far for medication, but it was too late. This is the thing in life that has weighed heaviest upon my heart."

"I never knew you had that sadness, Mtabi. I'm sorry to hear that. You know, in the West, there are inoculations for that sort of thing."

"Yes, I have heard of such miracles."

"It's no miracle, Mtabi. It's there, it's a thing, it exists. *You just don't have it!* In other words, apart from your son's death being tragic and untimely, it had the added benefit of being wholly unnecessary. That's not injustice, Mtabi, that's *comedy.*"

"That's *enough*, Izzy!" Micah barks, lunging for his brother. "You won't insult him like that."

As soon as he reaches him, Izzy snaps at Micah like a turtle and bites his outstretched hand.

"You rabid little faggot!"

Izzy ignores his howling brother. "I didn't mean to insult you, Mtabi. I've just been thinking about the nature of suffering since I returned. Who gets what. Accidents of geography and time. Like me. You heard it straight from my brother: I'm a repulsive little Jew fairy. But out here I was happy, even if it was just for a little while. Do you understand that?"

"I think so."

"But *institutionalized* suffering, the kind that turns people into numbers, that doesn't even allow them to suffer *uniquely*—the forces at work that allowed your son to die unnecessarily—that's got to be the worst kind, don't you agree?"

"Yes, sir."

"One more thing I've been working on. Tell one person something, it's a secret. Tell a few, it's a story. People start believing you, it becomes history. That's what we were doing out here, Mtabi. Numbers, do you understand?"

For the first time in as long as they've known each other, the guide looks past clothes, custom, and context to see his clients simply as men.

"I do not know the personal significance of numbers," Mtabi says. "I only know my son."

"Listen to me, Izzy, you're talking gibberish now," Micah says. "We've got food and antibiotics, and we're going to get you out of here, all right? But I need you to understand this: I've been stabbed, I've been hit in the side of the head with a gun, I've been subjected to a hot shave! These fellas back home aren't kidding around. They want what's theirs."

"Or what? They'll bring harm to someone you love? Too late for me, Micah. You made sure of that."

"Izzy, where's the goddamned negative?"

"Strange word, that."

"*Izzy!*"

"Yes, *Micah!*" Spitting his brother's name, and suddenly it's twenty years before and they're back in their shared bedroom. "You should have left me here, you really should have. Why didn't you leave me here? I could have done it. A little while longer and I think I could have done it."

"How could I let you? I wouldn't."

"I know. Twins and all the rest of it . . . Well, you pays your money and you takes your seat. C'mon, then, you've come all this way. I want to show you something."

FOUR

The filthy bedsheet has fallen away several paces behind Izzy, who now walks beside the other three with a naked body encrusted in sedimentary layers of dirt, rotting foodstuff, and excrement, the organ of procreation wagging before him a mere hopeless tentacle.

"Itz, put on some clothes, for Christ's sake."

"Nothing I've not seen before," says Rose, marking that Izzy's penis at rest is thicker, longer than Micah's. She registers for the first time, too, that even with Izzy in tatters, the brothers look very much alike, their strides naturally complementing each other and seesawing into an easy, metronomic rhythm. In the daylight dazzle, Micah notes Izzy's strange tattoos coming into relief, armies of black ants that emerge from navel and armpits and crawl across his limbs and shoulders and back, insects that gain a jangly, noble mobility as their keeper continues walking.

"What's with the numbers, Itz?"

"Time codes. Best way to keep track of them. I've been working hard out here."

"Listen, Itz, you should know this," Micah says, trying to reach him with news from home. "Arthur's dead. Mr. Waldo, too. Bumpy's running the roost now."

"Marblestone?" Izzy says, engraving in air each of the name's three syllables. "I loved the man."

"Me, too."

Izzy steps around a puddle of mud. That the maneuver is performed conscientiously, daintily—in such a way that suggests his brother is still in there somewhere, that toothed gears still mesh with memory and response, that some fundamental codes of law and rationality still apply—comes as a relief to Micah.

They have hopped off the red carpet and are heading beyond the royal encampment toward the village outskirts in a direction unfamiliar to Micah. Pointing ahead, Mtabi says with some hesitation, "This way lies the *dahtkam.*"

"What's that?" Rose asks.

"Each village has one. Not a graveyard exactly, but a resting place for things that have fallen out of favor. Instruments and items that have overstayed their usefulness. A place of many objects but little wisdom."

"Like a dumping ground," Micah says.

"Yes, sir."

"That's where Izzy's keeping the film?"

"This I do not know."

Flat as Nebraskan badlands, for miles and miles the *dahtkam* stretched. As Mtabi described, the territory is a trash heap, a repository, a junkyard, a world of things made, unmade, an underworld living on the very surface of the village. Scattered across this Whitman's Sampler of things unloved and unnecessary are stacks of tablets with outmoded stories from yesteryear; idols usurped by shinier, more brilliant gods; broken brooms and unraveled mats; punctured water bottles and leaky pots; grubby furnishings, bedding, and birth mats; heaps of smashed and irregularly shaped beads and ornaments; cracked flutes, crushed drums, and busted string instruments that look like undiscovered letters of the alphabet. There are, too, discarded bounties from trading expeditions and missionary visits from bygone times, mechanized wonders grouped haphazardly like river stones. There are heaps of metal paneling given over to orange oxidation and rust. There are nonsensical devices of convenience, electrical whisks and tin openers, an ancient Victrola player with an outstretched arm like an ice skater caught in mid-pirouette, weird pneumatic tubes and twisted Tesla coils, even, if Micah's eyes aren't deceiving him, an ancient cotton gin, its jaws stuffed with yellow discolored fluff, all these devices and mechanical advances rejected as outmoded impositions.

What was it about seeing other people's trash that Micah found so poignant? Why did spotting sidewalk rubbish always trigger in him such profound emotional responses? Was it because a bit of the person who'd possessed it attaches itself to every item? Was it because trash held a special relationship with time and decay, each discarded newspaper page floating down the street a funeral shroud by another name?

Micah picks up what appears to be a perfectly functioning harplike string instrument. "Some of this stuff looks in pretty good working order. Who's to tell the good from the bad?"

"Time makes that judgment," Mtabi answers.

"There he is," Izzy says, breaking free of the others and running ahead, limbs flapping in all directions, earthen shades of brown and green granting him chameleon-like powers of camouflage as he darts in and out of the ever-bending, never-ending slipstream.

Micah bolts after him, gathers force, and overtakes him.

"I'm not trying to get away," Izzy says, loosening his brother's grip on his arm and meeting his eyes. "I'm coming back with you, Micah." He wrestles free and lurches forward again. "But there're things you have to see first."

Ahead of them again, dancing on the perimeter of the horizon line, cast in silhouette, merrily spastic, he might be the Grim Reaper himself leading congregants in a dance of death. "Here we are!" Izzy rings out at last, planting himself before an immense, barren tree from which hangs spectacularly strange fruit. "Here's what I want you to see."

The body's arms and feet have been sawed off, its organs scooped out, the midsection a hollow flap, the skin a tough black leather emerged from a tannery. Every pod and pocket of the body has been peeled away and inverted. The tongue has been excised, the eyes gouged out. In its dimensions, coloration, and exposure of strata, the figure resembles the life-size human-anatomy cutaway model their father kept in his study, the one he'd place on the porch each Halloween. The corpse has been left hanging for weeks, a canvas for the sun to brand, a banquet invitation for hyenas and scavenger birds, a boulevard for field mice and insects to troll. In death the body has become a feasting ground, the cadaver a site of gossipy activity for maggots, worms, and flies. A dark patch of molasses-like dried blood has soaked and stained the grass and sand below the reddish brown of terra-cotta.

Izzy collapses before them on the ground and breaks the silence. "Rose, I'd like you to meet Cri. Cri, meet Rose."

The three of them might not have registered the sight as the remains of a human being were it not for the series of photographs affixed to the tree. There are dozens of them, several for each day Izzy has been back, documenting the prince's physical decomposition, a record of horror and deterioration that bristles each time a breeze stirs. First there is the documentary shock of the stumped and mutilated corpse, its face rotted, sun-stung, and picked at like a Thanksgiving bird, but still recognizably that of the prince. These early photos give way to pictures chronicling a bleary wash of sinew and bone and brittle scarecrow straw. In each of them, Izzy appears standing in the same spot beneath the corpse, posed in the same unnatural position.

"After Cri hung himself, the tribal council decided to chop off his arms and legs to make a lesson of him," Izzy says as dispassionately as a waiter describing the day's blue-plate special. "But the body was remarkably well preserved when I returned."

"Why are you smiling in these?" Micah asks uncertainly.

"Someone points a camera at you, you smile," Izzy says, stating the most obvious thing in the world. "That's what you *do*."

Mtabi faces away from the tree, the photos twittering like leaves, buzzing like insect wings. "This very bad *muntu*."

"Izzy, I want you to listen very carefully to me now," his brother says. "This is no way to honor your friend. We're going to bury the prince properly, and I'd like you to give some thought as to where."

Izzy, who has been pulling fistfuls of dry grass from the earth, slowly begins to nod. "Okay, Micah. I knew you'd know what to do. You always know what to do."

Perhaps ten feet away from them, Izzy's Leica sits on a wooden tripod.

FIVE

The sun begins its descent, and the Malwiki villagers slowly emerge from their huts, like Lazarus awakened from the tomb. They gravitate toward the *dahtkam* like moons pulled into tighter orbit, the tribespeople accompanied by Keneally, his contingent of poker-faced British soldiers, and Talli—the departed king's counselor, now improbably clothed in the dress of empire, as uncomfortable-looking in his buttoned blazer, tie, and jackboots as a child playing a bearded elder in a school play.

Once they are far away from Cri's corpse and deeper into the flatlands, Micah asks about the film. "Have you destroyed it?"

"The footage?" Izzy says. "No, I need it. You know, Micah, legends of King Mishi's patrimony were greatly exaggerated. He had a couple dozen children, sure, but most of them died in childbirth or infancy, as they're likely to do around here. Cri was the eldest son. The others haven't nearly come of age. According to Malwiki law, the line of succession ends with him."

"What does that have to do with anything?"

"You'll see. I'll show you."

Dusk blushes over the sky, and the villagers instinctively mass together and begin forming a line, as orderly a progression as Minnesota housewives waiting to see the latest Valentino picture. As Micah, Rose, and Mtabi watch, Talli stands beside a planted Union Jack collecting the villagers' tickets—the same inscribed strips of bark they'd spotted earlier on the red carpet. An authoritarian figure even when comically outfitted, Talli appears even leaner, his physical bearing more a model of regimental discipline, than Micah remembered. So, too, Micah reads the man's supreme baldness not as a sign of diminished virility so much as a triumph of scalp, muscled bands of forehead razing fields of follicles. During an interval in his ticket taking, Talli marks Micah, Rose, and Mtabi with an expression of recognition that might be called the opposite of kind.

"Ah, Mr. Grand," Keneally says. "I see you made it for the evening's entertainment. You know, there's a movement afoot at present to bring democracy to the Dark Continent. But Blighty's not about to give up her interests on account of a few X's showing up on some ballots, is she? No, your brother seems to've landed on just the right solution," the officer says, eyebrows lifting like drawbridges. "Bread and circuses indeed!"

Those with tickets pass Talli and gain entrance to a great barren field, where they sit Indian style on mats and begin passing around rations of dried lentils and legumes that they eat from wicker sacks and hollowed gourds. Drums are brought out, and music—whirling, sinister, never-ending tribal percussion—begins to fill the valley.

"I wouldn't dignify it by calling it an overture," Keneally offers. "Perhaps what you Yanks might call some pre-show tunes."

Africa, at least what she'd seen of it, had come as an unhappy surprise to Rose. Faced with the bleary, beer-drenched depredations of Belgian Congo and the poverty and illness she witnessed in Malwiki, Rose struggled to preserve the continent's symbolic strength for herself as homeland and cradle. She accomplished this task by putting distance between herself and her surroundings, worryingly there and not there. It troubled her, too, that barring a few individuals she'd encountered so far—the gentle-spirited Mtabi, a Bundini village woman who had braided and plaited her hair, a child of maybe five or six years old who delighted in following her around all day, head permanently cocked at a protractor's forty-five-degree angle—she viewed the Malwiki monolithically; their fantastically black skin, pervasive near nudity, plain starch-filled diet, and strangely singing language, subjects of remotest fascination to her rather than a portal to some deep understanding.

That, and her feet hurt. She'd brought along ruinously wrong shoes for the trip: heels that ground away at her corns and calluses and open-toed sandals with which an ingrown left foot toenail was conducting daily losing negotiations. Since the miscarriage she experienced regular dull stomach pains—she was always hungry but couldn't bring herself to eat—and limp-noodled Micah hadn't touched her with more than brotherly affection in weeks. The sun was doing her no favors either, alarmingly darkening her color from that of light coffee to newly wet sand. In her haste she had brought along neither cocoa butter nor moisturizing lotion, and her skin was suffering from dryness and ash.

She wished she were back in their familiar city, but didn't wish to return. These weeks had been the longest time they'd spent in each other's company, and for all her complaints it had been some kind of idyll. That first morning in the bush with the Bundini, upon waking in the cool hut, Rose created a little routine for herself, the better to normalize the unfamiliar situation. She walked around the perimeter of the village square, careful to respect the men and women bathing in the meager lake. She brushed her teeth with their private stash of clean water. She put a kettle on to make coffee. She wrote a few lines in her journal. She prayed.

These normalizing routines helped keep her pieced together. I live here. I work there. I'm from the other. I'm married to that one. I sleep with him. All factors in the equation that makes her Rose. But were those variables fixed or interchangeable? Were those things heavy cables that bound her or ties that could be severed as easily as snipping a price tag from a blouse? Even her boldest attempts at passing seemed to her now pinched, puny, preordained, the equivalent of an atheist's insistence that there is no God—the very position of being *against* something predicated on a bedrock acknowledgment of something worthy of denial.

More and more, Rose resigned herself to the notion that home isn't something you return to or a place you hold in memory but something you forever build. More and more, Rose was beginning to believe that identity isn't something you're born with or that is ascribed to you but something you make for yourself, something you earn. "You look far away," he says to her. "What're you thinking about?"

"My feet."

"They're swell."

"They're swollen, not swell."

"Stop complaining. My everything's swollen."

"Not everything," she says, eyes drifting crotchward, her chin dimpling like an old lady's. "You think he'll be all right?"

"Izzy? I don't know. I think he's still in shock."

"He'd found his prince."

"Yeah," Micah grumbles, "we should all be so lucky."

"What happens now?" she asks indeterminately, but meaning between the two of them.

"Well, Mtabi's made radio contact with Späten. The boat will be here in three days, and Izzy will be on it if I have to knock him flat."

"What about the Malwiki? Who'll be left in charge after we leave? Talli?"

"Talli? Talli's worse than the Brits." Micah relays to Rose the whole sad story as he'd heard it from Mtabi, how following King Mishi's sacrifice the Iago-like lieutenant convinced the prince to hang himself, how he had encouraged the tribal council to desecrate the prince's corpse, how the man had transformed the king's semi-sacred compound into a trading post, a bartering station for all kinds of Western goods and contrivances, occult objects of no use to the Malwiki. "No, whoever takes the reins needs to be someone close to Mishi, someone they'll trust, someone who can be counted on to rule well."

"Sir," interrupts Mtabi, reaching the pair. He is out of breath, his blue suit smeared with dirt, a small shovel held firm in his hands. "If you concur, I believe I have found a dignified spot for the prince's burial plot."

Overhead, the sky darkens, descending a chandelier of stars. The drumming reaches a crescendo and comes to an end, ushering in a great quiet that sweeps over the flat, the hush of an assembly prior to the beginning of a religious ceremony. At Izzy's signal two able-bodied young men rise from the audience, gather the ends of a couple of coiled cords, and begin working a rope-and-pulley system. A curtain of white, perhaps twelve feet tall and twenty feet across, is raised incrementally, jerkily climbing two wooden poles in spurts. Up the screen goes like a ship's sail, the very definition of white.

"Albeit a bit bent, he's ingenious, your brother," says Keneally, "rigging up all this claptrap."

Micah marvels at the makeshift theater. "How long's he been at it?"

"Ever since he arrived. All those images, reflected back onto themselves. Of course, we've an important official presence, but for all intents and purposes, so long as your brother keeps running that bloody filmstrip each night, his is the real law around here."

A rumble like the sound of a leviathan rising and breaking to the surface calls Micah's attention to a bluff in the distance where Izzy fumbles with a Liberty Motors power generator. Cast in shadow behind the ancient, immense movie projector, winding the filmstrip around the take-up reel, Izzy resembles a child playing train conductor, hands working a dozen valves and knobs at once. The screen bristles in anticipation, gathering animistic force, and Micah is reminded, forever reminded, of the religious function of movies. Sabbath's theater. The secular and vernacular sitting around waiting for revelation. The resurrection of the dead. Signs and wonders by other means.

"Ladies and gentlemen!" Izzy hollers, his strangled voice filling the valley as the carbon arcs of the projector meet, ignite, and the filmstrip flies its loop. "I give you . . . *your king*!"

And there, on-screen, full of lip and noble of brow, appears King Mishi. He is dressed in finest ceremonial robes and stands many meters tall, sealed in silvery monochrome, surveying his subjects. Large as a hut, raised from the crypt, understandably bleached of color, but having gained the wisdom attendant upon time spent in the shadow valley, King Mishi is bigger than any man. Far away but brought close, details of the king's face emerge that his subjects have never noticed before: the irritated skin of his freshly shaven cheeks, the tree-trunk rings circling his eyes, a familiar scar over the right eyebrow transposed by magic to the left. In unison a mass exhalation, a roar of approval that sounds like volumes of water cascading over a great falls, is let up into the heavens. Then people. Trees. Water. Giraffes. Insects. The ingredients of their daily stew elaborated upon and made magnificent, all seen in flashes as they might appear in a nighttime dream pageant. The insistent materialism and heroic amplification of the simplest deeds. The actual instantly supplanted by the gigantic evidence summoned before them. The locket of time sprung, the dead resurrected, the sacred shellacked from the surface of things for some unknown purpose.

Mtabi stares spellbound at his first motion picture. "Is this the product of our earlier cinematic endeavors?"

"Afraid so," Micah moans.

"From their postures and expressions, they take this to be the oracle prophesied from days of yore. They wait daily upon its instruction."

"Fucking hell."

"Looks no different from bondage. Slavery by other means."

"Fucking hell," Rose concurs.

Mtabi turns away, stricken. "The selfsame story of peoples exploited without restraint."

Each night Izzy would play different fragments of the film, reaching deep into the village's imaginative magma for his project of memory retrieval, recutting and rearranging sequences by day so King Mishi could provide fresh instruction by night. Awaiting these visitations from their king, the villagers spent their days in a suspended state of numbness, in the absence of the film falling into grief and inactivity like prisoners tumbling onto cots. Like nocturnal animals, the Malwiki were now capable of functioning only at night, eyes wide and senses peeled. In their collective stupor, each day they bade farewell the reality of lived experience and each night reawakened to have Prometheus's wound freshly ripped away.

Tonight Izzy experiments with running certain sequences in reverse. Accompanied by a live sound track of wild drumming and rattles, the image of the sacrificed bull confronts the audience, the animal's slab butchered and butterflied on the ground, disassembled and scattered, stewing gore. Slowly, a severed leg reattaches itself to the torso's hindquarters, the appendage stitching hair and skin together like a seamstress fixing a child's doll. A broken hoof mends itself. A machete flies away from a chop deep in the animal's midsection, and the carcass instantly heals, eyes opening from eternal sleep to a flash of wild-orbed terror. And there the king appears, a spray of arterial blood whiplashing away from his face and chest, the blade binding the animal's neck together as it withdraws Hebraically from right to left. Cheers go up from the crowd as Mishi resurrects the slaughtered beast, his power made manifest by this visual proof.

Next come a series of abstractions: the jungle canopy as seen from below, its latticework of leaves a lace curtain of whites and grays. Then a close-up of tree bark, as expressive as the lined face of an old, sun-shrunken fisherman. Then shots of water, multitudes of them, from all times of day, puddles and ripples and waves reduced to gray and black and silver bands that look like electricity or thought made visible.

It takes time for Micah to decipher the next sequence. A smattering of matter, like a cloud of engine exhaust preposterously slowed. Then pieces of skin and viscera and skull stuff centripetally winding themselves up like a ball of string, whirlpooling out of the muddle to form a familiar human face.

"Dwarf!" Micah cries, tears pulling from his eyes at the sight of his friend Spiro, alive and standing before them once again. The blast darts back into the muzzle as if on a dare, and there is Cri in his princely handsomeness, shock of confusion reversing itself into the easiest of smiles, the prince delivered to happiness again.

Micah is reminded of the first photographic record of real violence he had ever seen—five or six years before viewing the staged carnage of *Birth of a Nation*. It was an incredible image of the attempted assassination of Mayor William Gaynor, taken moments after the politician had been shot in the throat. The picture had been banned from newspapers when the incident occurred in 1910, but reproductions had circulated among photography enthusiasts, and Micah and Izzy's father had gotten hold of a copy. The picture seemed dangerous to them when the boys first discovered it in their father's desk drawer, and they quickly passed it back and forth between them like a hot potato, not wanting to burn their fingertips by laying hands on the photo for too long. Though it was nearly twenty years ago, Micah could still recall—in ways he could not remember the details of losing his virginity or his wedding day or the births of his sons—the mayor's dark bowler hat, his white beard spackled with blood, and his startled look of arrest, as if caught standing at the entrance of a surprise party. Recalling it even now, Micah believed that photo had everything to say about the medium's aimless aestheticization of horror. But there isn't time to consider these philosophical concerns too deeply, as the picture unfolding before them leaves Spiro standing sturdily in his captain's uniform, securely pinned to the present tense, and moves on to the next sequence.

It is a Dantean vision of flames, lashes of fire bursting from huts and waving like flags, then retreating, burned cinders reconstructing themselves. Villagers that began the scene crawling on all fours before white men in helmets and shiny black boots are restored to upright dignity. Soldiers retreat beyond the frame, beyond the village, beyond the hills, beyond the reach of history, and leave the village in peace.

"Why is he punishing them so?" Mtabi asks.

"I think he's trying to return things to the way they were."

The translator tsk-tsks. "No, sir. This only sows seeds of confusion. The Malwiki are now like a boat without an oar. All this cine-film can do is lead them to ruination."

"He's right, Micah," Rose agrees. "All this watching isn't healthy."

SIX

Since Izzy's return and the commencement of his nightly wielding of wizardly black magic, the Malwiki trod around him as if he were some kind of demiurge. A fearful figure of strangeness, Izzy related to no one, ate his meals in isolation, and spent his days in the king's underground quarters carefully editing and rearranging the trove of footage, burrowing deeper and deeper into the soil and muck of time.

The return of the rooster-haired brother did not bode well. Even absent an interpreter's tongue, one could observe that the siblings' conflict centered on the dream material and their intent to put it to different purposes. That first night in the *dahtkam*, no one knew what to expect until the strange, two-wheeled machine rumbled and a spray of light flew from its tip out over the flatlands to the net across the way. A new kind of vision, it didn't describe, it was. It asked not for interpretation but absorption. The stories we tell each other, the dreams that paid nightly visit, stretched before them all in unanimous agreement. The rest was delirium and soul-sickness. Once they had drunk from the fantastic well of images, the tribespeople were forever thirsty.

Nothing could compare to this blinding world in duplicate. With harvesting work and daily chores and lessons for children the Malwiki grew impatient. The true instruction began when the sun dipped over the horizon and retired for the day. It seemed the very soul of the tribe was being bartered between the brothers, and ultimately the Malwiki longed for the time prior to their visitation, when they were led by the strength of their king, when stories were told by firelight and received by the stars, when the image world would gently beckon and enter the ear and nose and mouth during sleep. When waking life and dream life were not so confused. The last images splash like silver coins across the screen, and all goes black. "They need to be rid of it," Mtabi says.

"Copacetic," Micah says flatly. "We're leaving with the film, for sure."

"No, it needs to be destroyed."

"Can't do it, pal. Too many competing interests back home."

The villagers have begun abandoning the *dahtkam*, abuzz with the messages King Mishi has imparted. "No," Mtabi says with finality. "We need to destroy it. Otherwise this image world threatens to drown them all."

The suggestion that he destroy the work is insupportable to Micah. Apart from his professional pride in what is surely the best work he has ever done, and the footage being a pillar of Marblestone's legacy, there is a Harlem-based queen and her chosen prince awaiting this product half a world away. Stranded in a Gethsemane of his own making, Micah finds himself asking if there isn't some other cup he can take up.

Winded by the time he reaches the projectionist's promontory, Micah finds Izzy leaning against the cool machinery, exuding the triumph of a ballplayer who's just pitched a no-hitter. Seen from the perspective of the villagers down below, pressed against the immense night sky, the brothers appear like giants.

"It's time to go back," Micah says, speaking rapidly as he inhales through a cigarette. "You're not helping things here. You're confusing them, you're infantilizing them."

"We're moviemakers," Izzy says. "This is what we *do*."

"It means something different here. Look, listen to me for a second, will you, Itz? You didn't discover anything new out here. You got *laid*, okay? And you could have done that any night of the week on the Bowery. You *should have* done that on the Bowery."

"Really? And what about you?" Micah's line of attack lighting up Izzy's switchboard of jealousy over his sibling's surfeit of worldly love. "What exactly are you doing out here? Why'd you bring her?"

"It was a gesture of good faith."

"You really haven't figured out that this is the only place you can be with her?"

"That's not true, Itz. Rose and I are fine in New York."

"Where she plays at being white and you play at being married?"

"I didn't come here to talk about my marriage or my sex life."

"And never the twain shall meet."

"*Izzy!* I came here to bring the picture back with us so you don't end up reading about me in the goddamned obituary pages. *They fucking followed me to California. They'll kill us if they don't get what's theirs.*"

"Give me one more night. Leave me be for the day and allow me one last performance. Then, I promise, we're done."

Rose and Micah make love. It isn't the fizzy, happy romping of Micah's boy-wonder days, when the girls were juicy, uncomplicated fun—a young satyr's equivalent of a birthday boy gorging on hamburgers, french fries, cola, ice cream, and cake, astounded at the variety of pleasure that could be yielded from roundness, softness, wetness, sweetness, and coolness. Nor is it for Micah about a solitary absenting of self: his working toward orgasm an expression of the urge to ride oneself like an elevator and burst through one's own roof. Tonight is different. Tonight—their first time together since Rose's miscarriage—is a measure of resolve.

Over the course of the affair, Micah always took for granted that he was the one who provided glamour in Rose's squalid life. It is clear to him now, however, that she is the true source of bedazzlement. She is his spiritual adventure, his exquisite, ecstatic love. It isn't the best they've had together—they've been through too much in recent weeks, blanketed by injury, jangled by shifting time zones, their accommodations too uncomfortable, their bodies suddenly too near to middle-aged for the full acrobatic waterworks—but their reunion is sweet and tender nonetheless. And when it's over, Micah says to her three words he has never said before. At their signal Rose gets up—on thick, womanly thighs, no longer the lithesome legs of a young woman—moves to a corner of the hut, sits down, folds her arms around her knees, and begins rocking back and forth.

"Why are you crying?" he asks.

"Because you had to drag me all the way out here to say it."

SEVEN

t's gone," Izzy says to Micah and Rose the next night once they've regrouped at the outskirts of the *dahtkam*.

"What's gone?" Micah asks, dreading the answer but heartened to find his brother, still emaciated and holy-looking as an El Greco monk, dressed in dungarees and crew-neck T-shirt.

"The film is missing. I spent all night cutting it together, and when I woke up this afternoon, it was gone—the reels, the B-roll, all of it."

They are trotting uphill, Micah holding Rose's hand, Rose holding Izzy's hand, the three of them a gang of lonely children who have just taken a blood oath. Dusk paints rouge across the early-evening sky, and around them the Malwiki are sitting on their mats awaiting the evening's performance, the drummers going full bore. By the time they arrive, the movie screen is already unfurled, bristling with light and pulled tight as a bedsheet, that expanse of childhood wonderment. In the distance, standing firm atop the projectionist's bluff, a familiar figure negotiates the power generator as handily as a suburban dad pulling the chain on a lawn mower.

"Izzy?"

"Yes?"

"Is that Mtabi I see operating our machinery?"

"Yes, I believe it is."

Micah, Izzy, and Rose stop where they are, ready to accept whatever wisdom their guide has in store for them. In the event, the translator has not altered the evening's program at all. It is the longest selection Izzy has edited for the villagers so far, a series of simply presented shots, long takes, in which the entire cast of the departed make appearances in and out of costume. Mtabi did not tamper either with the meaning that Izzy had spent the night assembling from the footage, a simple message that resounded in sequence after sequence: good-bye. Every shot ends with figures turning away from the camera, or walking out of frame, or waving farewell, or fading to black. Izzy had decided this on his own: If he could not mount a challenge against the medium's compulsory present tense, he could at least use it to say farewell.

After an hour or more of this, during a moment that finds King Mishi looking directly out over the crowd, his face at its most serene and benevolent, Mtabi lights a match and sets it to the jumping filmstrip. At first the tear in the film appears like a blotch of shaving foam on the king's left cheek. Then the bubbling hole bursts open—changeable, amorphous forms overtaking the center of the screen, an implacable whiteness that rips through and dissolves the image of the king's face as it spreads to each of the screen's four corners. The rupture is over in an instant, and it leaves behind a blinding blank radiance.

"Let him do it." Izzy raises an arm of restraint against Micah's torso, but the limb meets with no resistance. Instead Micah collapses backward on his rump, raising cartoon clouds of dust.

"It's the best thing we've done," Micah says in a voice void of protest or self-pity. "The best I've got in me."

"I know. Me, too."

"Without it Imperial's going to go bust. I'm dead broke, too."

"Transporting a movie projector to the interior of Africa isn't cheap either, you know."

In the distance Mtabi can be seen liberally watering the industrial equipment with the contents of a gasoline can. The projector catches fire, spraying flames into the sky, reels continuing to spin like wheels on an overturned bicycle, sending licks and crackles sparking in all directions.

"I'm finished," Micah says, thinking of Bumpy and St. Clair awaiting him back in New York.

"We'll shoot around it." Izzy laughs, craning his neck up to follow
the tendrils of smoke and flame that spiral upward and diffuse into the
heavens.

Then, very quietly, Mtabi leaves his station beside the molten projector, turns off the power generator, and makes his way down from the
bluff through the silent seatscape. Single-handedly, he uncoils the rope
that anchors the screen on the left side, then the one on the right, allowing the scrim to cascade down its length and fold in on itself like a deck
chair. Standing before the assembly where the screen once billowed,
Mtabi speaks in the villagers' tongue very simply. Though the brothers cannot decipher the language, they instantly recognize its message.
Mtabi explains that King Mishi is bidding his kingdom and subjects
farewell, that he loves them all and wishes them well, and that his last
gift to his people is a promise to leave them in peace. For the benefit of
the travelers, he speaks in English: "This ocean of hours we are all the
time drinking—it, too, must end at the shore."

Something happens. In unison the hundreds of villagers kneel on
their mats and bow their heads before the translator, a pose of supplication that can mean only one thing: that gentle Mtabi, prudent Mtabi,
watchful Mtabi, wise Mtabi, is now, in fact, King Mtabi.

"Looks like you're the big boss now," Micah says once Mtabi reaches
the three of them, his head hanging in shame and embarrassment for
having destroyed the brothers' work.

"King?" Mtabi asks in wonderment.

"Yes." Micah nods. "It's what Mishi would have wanted."

"I did not do this thing to wrest the mantle of power."

"We know. All the more reason you're the man for the job."

"And what might be your first royal decree?" asks Keneally, lifelong
habits of sycophancy propelling him toward the newly installed monarch. "Your Excellency, King Mtabi?"

"Arrest this man," Mtabi says, pointing to Talli, whose stature has shrunk over the events of the past several minutes, "for the crime of high treason and his role in the untimely death and desecration of Prince Cri."

"Very good, Your Highness," says Keneally, signaling with a whistle to his men, who scoop up Talli and march him off, the traitor's bright red tie fluttering behind his shoulder like a hand waving from the deck of a ship.

"I've got a question for you," Micah asks Mtabi after the commotion settles down. "How'd you figure out how to work the projector?"

"There is in the West"—says Mtabi demurely—"what you call 'a quick study'?"

"Indeed. Eh, King Mtabi," Micah says, trying out the appellation, "you know, there was also a good deal of footage apart from what was screened just now."

"Oh, I made certain to destroy all of the film through various and sundry means, by fire and water and trampling it into the ground."

"Uh-huh, uh-huh. And you're aware that what Izzy's been showing each night is a kind of duplicate, what we call a 'work print,' right?"

"Yes."

"So you're saying you located the negative?"

"This is the inverted image?"

"Yeah, that's right."

"Oh, yes. This was fed to the hippopotamus, the angriest of all the animals."

"Well, you really thought of everything, then."

"Yes, sir."

Micah smiles. "You're the king; don't call me sir."

It is then that Micah's ears tune in to a different, higher frequency, recognizing sounds he has not heard since childhood religious training nearly sixteen years before. His brother, who has slipped away, now leads the African tribespeople in an ancient form of call-and-response, the essence of his plea too singular for misunderstanding. Good-bye. Good-bye, King Mishi. Good-bye, Prince Cri. Good-bye, Arthur and

Spiro. Good-bye. Good-bye. Good-bye. Izzy's farewell, his final gift, a shared shibboleth of mourning:

יִתְגַּדַּל וְיִתְקַדַּשׁ שְׁמֵהּ רַבָּא בְּעָלְמָא דִּי-בְרָא

כִרְעוּתֵהּ, וְיַמְלִיךְ מַלְכוּתֵהּ בְּחַיֵּיכוֹן וּבְיוֹמֵיכוֹן וּבְחַיֵּי

דְכָל בֵּית יִשְׂרָאֵל, בַּעֲגָלָא וּבִזְמַן קָרִיב, וְאִמְרוּ: אָמֵן.

יְהֵא שְׁמֵהּ רַבָּא מְבָרַךְ לְעָלַם וּלְעָלְמֵי עָלְמַיָּא.

יִתְבָּרַךְ וְיִשְׁתַּבַּח, וְיִתְפָּאַר וְיִתְרוֹמַם וְיִתְנַשֵּׂא,

וְיִתְהַדָּר וְיִתְעַלֶּה וְיִתְהַלָּל שְׁמֵהּ דְּקוּדְשָׁא, בְּרִיךְ

הוּא, לְעֵלָּא מִן-כָּל-בִּרְכָתָא וְשִׁירָתָא, תֻּשְׁבְּחָתָא

וְנֶחֱמָתָא דַּאֲמִירָן בְּעָלְמָא, וְאִמְרוּ: אָמֵן.

יְהֵא שְׁלָמָא רַבָּא מִן-שְׁמַיָּא וְחַיִּים עָלֵינוּ וְעַל-כָּל-

יִשְׂרָאֵל, וְאִמְרוּ: אָמֵן.

עֹשֶׂה שָׁלוֹם בִּמְרוֹמָיו, הוּא יַעֲשֶׂה שָׁלוֹם עָלֵינוּ וְעַל

כָּל-יִשְׂרָאֵל, וְאִמְרוּ: אָמֵן.

"What wonderful tongue is this?" asks King Mtabi. "What is the meaning of this beautiful chanting?"

"It's a prayer," Micah answers, his face agleam. "A prayer for the dead."

5

HOME

ONE

Izzy slept little aboard Captain Späten's boat, rising like Caligari's somnambulist from his hammock to wander around the decks in darkest night. It was only when Micah thought to nestle his brother in a crib—a giant equipment crate packed with straw—that sleep came deep and dreamless. Izzy was slowly returning to his brother. He was dressing like a modern-day New Yorker, was taking food regularly, had asked about details of Marblestone's funeral and the Academy Awards dinner, and had even begun hatching plans as to how they might find ways to appease their Harlem benefactors now that their investment had turned to dust.

Other things went unspoken between the brothers. In order to enter into this tentative reunion with himself, Izzy first needed to say goodbye to others. The fact of Cri's death—that is, the status of his being no longer alive—meaning that he was forever, irrevocably, dead. That work—the work of loss, the work of cessation, the work of oceanic grief, the work of things irretrievable, the work of never again—occurred alone, in private, in the darkness of the crate.

While Izzy worked on this fragile project of reclamation, Rose grew more anxious the closer to home they approached, pushing against each of the various modes of locomotion that propelled them forward. She wished the ship would split to splinters, that the train would fly free of its rails, that the airplane would drop from the sky. She longed to be delivered to any fate, any dramatic disruption, that might delay the inevitable moment when she returned uptown and took up residence in her apartment with her barber and Micah was reunited with his family—the moment when, separately, they conformed to the contours of their normal lives.

Home: that warmest, most sentimental, most commodious of words, but one not without its broken windows, damp cellars, busted boilers, creepy attics, and dead cats. As she had hoped it would, travel had neutered hypotheticals about home. The question of who she was had at last become personal. But the trip also produced unexpected reactions in her. She disliked what she'd glimpsed of Old Europe; Britain seemed to her a hunched and haunted place, an aquarium country whose citizenry moved at half speed. Africa she found poignant, but if she was honest with herself, likely of no more personal significance because of the color of her skin than it might be to Micah or Izzy. Beautiful, blasted, and medieval, Africa as she'd experienced it was many, many lives removed from the ruptured reality of her daily urban life.

No, if anything the trip confirmed to Rose that she was undeniably, indisputably American, from the food she ate to the clothes she wore to the words she spoke to the thoughts she thunk. America was home. The place also told her daily, in infinite ways, that she held no purchase on its dream. How she loved her country and how she hated it! How open to possibility and wretchedly preordained it was. How the tall buildings sang to a person's mightiest aspirations while concretizing her insignificance. Only in America might she have *found* a character like Micah; only in America might they be asked to hide from others. Home. The word rang like a prayer and a curse.

They aren't seated together on the plane, and the last leg of the return trip, aboard a fifteen-passenger Ford Tri-Motor 5-AT, is lousy with turbulence. Micah makes a point of leaving his seat every so often and working his way down the narrow aisle to check on her, but as the plane pinballs across the sky, its alternating jolts and gliding gusts provide commentary on Rose's rising and falling fears.

"I'm scared."

"It's just an updraft," Micah says, referring to a particularly rough spell.

"That's not what I mean." Squeezing his hand during a steep drop in altitude.

"Excuse me," Micah says, turning to the fiftyish woman sitting across the aisle from Rose, the cardboard-stiff expression of the passenger's dark sable stole matching her surprise at Micah's request. "We know each other—would you mind swapping seats with me up front for a minute?"

Looking at Rose, at her beautiful, imperfect face, Micah recalls some of their greatest hits: Honeypot cloakroom. Under the boardwalk. The Ambassador in Hollywood. By the train tracks. And simpler things. Water pistols. Shadow puppets on the wall. Finger gougings from peanut-butter jars, their shared attempt to eat the whole rotten world by the gobful. Her face. Her need.

"Listen, Rose, let's agree not to do this. Let's not have the talk like the one that's happening right now between a thousand husbands and wives. Let's agree that's not how we got this far together."

"You're right, Micah. Talking was never our strong suit."

"Y'know, I had that same dream again the other night."

"About the overcoat?"

"Yeah, only this time, after the man left the theater with it, I followed him and chased after the guy and finally caught up to him."

"Did you see who it was?"

"I don't know. He looked familiar, like someone I know, but I couldn't recognize him."

"So what'd you do? Did you tell him he'd taken the wrong one? Did you get into a fight?"

"No, I let him keep the fucking coat."

"Hey, look," Rose says. "There's home."

"It looks different from up here."

"It does. You know what happens now, right?"

"Yeah, hon, I do."

They remain seated together for the last leg of the return, science and ingenuity and will catapulting them toward New York, the city looking crystalline and vulnerable from this vantage. As they make their final descent, towers rise into focus like slices of many-layered cake overloading a platter. The yawning metropolis—curving, arcing, bending—from this perspective confident in its assurance at being the greatest thing ever built or imagined by human hands.

TWO

It is the dead of night when Micah enters the apartment. His plan is, as silently as possible, to have a bath and a shave (these ablutions always being the first things he does upon returning), sort through the mail, have a cheese-and-salami sandwich and a glass of milk at the kitchen table, then fix himself a scotch. He'd carry the drink with him from room to room as he made a quick, Cro-Magnon survey of the place, marking his territory and checking in on his things and his boys, before planting himself with his drink in front of the sitting-room window to take in the twinkling cityscape. Mine, mine, mine. All of it.

He is surprised to find Margaret not only awake and waiting up for him but sitting in the living room, a fire licking at her outline, as alive and alert in her white slippers and nightgown as a wintry bird circling a cornfield. Her posture is that of a prize student poised to challenge an inexperienced teacher, and Micah is exhausted and unprepared at this late hour to entertain the performative function of marriage. He doesn't feel like ramping himself up for conversation or confession.

She came from one of New York's most established Protestant families, and though their backgrounds were dissimilar, they matched up well physically. Her tendrils of auburn, copper, and orange resembled a Hudson Valley landscape in October, and her handsome face—thin lips and aquiline nose set within square and rectangular planes—might have pleased an abstract painter. She was taller than Micah, and strong, with anomalously biggish hands. Even her name, which shared with his a first initial, spoke of a kind of grim determination, dutifully climbing a staircase of syllables compared with Micah's syncopated, fleet-footed two-step.

"You're awake," Micah says, laying down his bags, flipping through his mental manual of marital feints and dodges. "I wasn't expecting to find you up so late."

"I thought I'd wait up." Then, more formally, "How are you, Micah?"

"Good, though my nose is so sunburned I can't touch it. I brought this for the boys!" Holding by its neck a two-foot-tall wood-carved giraffe. "How are they?"

"I put Ben and David to bed hours ago. They were desperate to see you, but tomorrow's school."

He welcomed the news, welcomed hearing his sons' names. Since the burning of the film, he longed to return to his boys, to put his arms around their bony shoulders and smell their hair, to inhale the fantastic fragrance of youth. He wished again to take up the mantle of the heroic father of their infancy, the spinner of stories, wizard of wall shadows, virtuoso of voices, wearer of blanket capes. "Tell us a story," they'd beg him the nights he was home, the boys in duplicate a reminder of the enchanted cave of intimacy he'd shared with Izzy in childhood. "Tell us a story," they would plead, and it pleased him that his boys' fondest wish corresponded with his life's work.

"I thought I'd telegrammed. You know I didn't want to disturb you."

"I received the telegram yesterday but was hoping I could stay up," she says in a voice better suited for a nurse than a wife. "Was the trip a success?"

"We managed to persuade Izzy to return with us, if that's what you're asking."

"*We?*"

"Yes," Micah says, remembering that a good liar always uses the truth. "Me and our guide, Mtabi."

"And what of your other friend?"

Micah strides across the length of the room and kisses her atop the forehead. "You'll have to be more specific, dear. Incredible as it may sound, I have lots of friends in Africa these days." He loosens the knot of his tie and rubs the back of his neck in a single sweeping motion, decides to skip the midnight meal altogether and heads straight for the bar cabinet.

"You know exactly who I mean." Sitting on the love seat, waves of hair fanning out over her shoulders, Margaret appears as regal and full of threat as an empress. "I've always been a good wife to you, and I've always turned away and allowed you to have your adventures so long as you've returned to me and the boys. But this latest involvement cannot continue."

Micah steadies himself with his scotch. He's believed that the true secret of alcohol rests not in its bringing on a sense of abandonment but the opposite: the application of a ruthless precision of focus. He's held that drink didn't slow down one's perceptions but sped them on, serving as an electrical current for the filtering out of the inconsequential, nonsense meaning, and social miscues. He wishes he were drunk now and does his best to hasten that process along.

A full-length mirror hangs in the sitting room across from where he's situated. In it he sees a fattish man, the middle button of his vest straining beneath his suit jacket, the space between his chin and neck alarmingly pink and shapeless, a foppish red handkerchief leering from his pocket, a boyish man with a boy's smooth face careering toward middle age, a balding lothario, chaser of easy marks, maker of contrivances. The pitiable, fatuous fellow nodding back at him in the mirror attempts a stern, resolute expression, the false face of an adolescent making a show of manliness. He reaches a hand out to confirm that, yes, the comic figure waving back is himself.

And in a rush this shadowy creature is planted curbside at a parade of regret, a carnival of missed opportunities and fates never made. They stream by: thoughts of the women he'd never love and the good work he'd never do and the children he'd never raise and the understanding he'd never attain and the qualities he'd never foster and the challenges he'd never dare and the greatness he'd never will himself into achieving, a future of self-recriminations stacking up like newspapers in the hall. These are the people you've loved. These are the people you've been given and chosen to love in your one spin around. These are the people you've failed. You envisioned yourself a romantic hero, but you can't even best your wife in a lousy late-night conversation. You told yourself you'd walk through fire for her, drink vinegar, eat a crocodile, but, no, you really wouldn't. You're not willing to give up anything for her. He hates himself, but he doesn't hate her. He'd sooner end it than renounce her.

"I won't insult you by suggesting I don't know who you're talking about," he says, using a tone that's unfamiliar in their marriage and taking a seat on the couch across from her.

"Good."

"Or that I believe you've been unaware of some of my other affiliations."

"I'm not asking for a confession, Micah."

"Thank you for that."

"But I am asking for it to stop."

"I want you to know, Margaret," he says, too pleased with this formulation, "I never meant to embarrass you."

"Oh, Micah," she sighs. "Let me be very clear about this. It's not *my* embarrassment we're talking about. This isn't about the humiliation *I* feel or that *the boys* will feel. I'm talking about how others see you. Have no illusions about this, dear. I'm not the one preventing you from continuing this association. Running around with colored girls— really? It's just not the way things are done."

A bauble on the coffee table draws his attention. He picks it up. A paperweight, a snow globe, slippery in his hand. Embedded deep in its base, beyond the blizzarding clouds of confetti, an imperfection, a tiny bubble, no larger than one that might be found resting on a baby's lip. In it Micah is certain he can catch the reflection of Rose's room eighty blocks uptown, the amber dream of happiness, his phantom limb hidden four miles away. In the object the fireplace crackles in miniature, drawing him in. Reaching to place it back on the table, he falls off the couch and ends up on the floor. More comfortable there than in a hard-backed chair or on the overly formal sitting-room furniture she's chosen, he stays put.

"This is difficult to say"—holding the paperweight, not looking at his wife—"but I don't know if I'm a good man. What I mean to say is, I don't know if I haven't spent my life dedicated to entirely the wrong things. Does that make sense? Do you understand what it is I'm trying to say? I don't know if I've ever *tried* to be a good man. If I'm equipped for it."

"That has little to do with how you're meant to handle things," she says, radiating energy, red hair and white robe like fire on snow.

From the floor Micah looks up at his wife. "What would you have me do?"

"I want to hear you say it. I want you to say you'll end it."

"Okay, I'll end it."

"And I want you to tell me you never cared for that colored whore of yours."

"I don't know what I was doing, Margaret."

"And?"

"It didn't mean anything to me."

"Tell me her name. Say everything again—only call her by name so I believe it—and then you can sleep in your bed."

"Rose. Her name is Rose. Rose Letty." He places the paperweight back on the table, in scalloped shadow revealed to be a cheap trinket. "No, that's not right. . . . She's married now. So I suppose her name is Rose Dobie. And she never meant anything to me."

"Oh, what am I to do with you?" she answers as she might an exasperating toddler. "You've acted like a child, Micah. Now it's time to put away childish things."

"I will," he says, crawling across the floor to her. "I will," he pledges again and again and again, reaching her slippered feet and beginning to stroke her bare ankles in an ecstasy of supplication and instruction until her white arms reach down, take him up, and fold him into her like a snowdrift.

THREE

The brothers had come home to New York City to the welcome news that Bumpy Johnson was in prison awaiting trial on bootlegging and racketeering charges, his seventh arrest in twenty-four years. Upon a return visit to her Harlem town house, Micah found Stephanie St. Clair to be keenly interested in the outcome of his second African adventure. Relaxing into the couch cushions while Troy looked on, Micah regaled the great lady with tales from the most recent trip, drinking deep from a perspiring glass of lemonade. And he did not flinch when it came time to inform her how Mtabi had destroyed the film in which the queen held so valuable a stake.

"Certainly, Mr. Grand," St. Clair said, passing a plate of gingerbread cookies to Micah with spidery hands festooned with gemstones that were visibly old, beautiful, and deep of the earth, "a businessperson as sophisticated as yourself wouldn't have thought to see me without first having considered some other arrangement."

Well, there was ninety minutes of movie to make, Micah explained, and he had the muscle to fill it. Appealing to the hardworking woman's sense of commerce, Micah presented the brothers' plan. They would abandon the unlikely historical project and offer St. Clair instead a greater percentage of the new Henry Till picture.

"You're proposing to exchange a tragic story for a comedic one?"

"Yes, that's right."

"That isn't the picture we agreed to make."

"No, it's not."

"It sounds like this other picture promises to be just more mockery and monkey business."

"That's correct. The Grand brothers are back in the blackface-and-custard-pie business. Well, Madam Queen, what's your ruling?"

Micah didn't flinch when the great lady leaned back in her love seat, weighed her deliberation, and offered a response that might provide for the filmmaker a worthy tombstone inscription. "When audiences laugh," St. Clair said, "it's never wrong."

They shot fast and cheap in the Brooklyn Armory and the Biograph Studio in the Bronx in ways that would have made their mentor proud. This would be the last film to wave the Imperial Pictures banner. Marblestone's burial had uncovered entire mountain ranges of debt, and with it the yard work of dismantling the company, divvying up the assets and the swatch of studio lot among disgruntled producers, California real-estate investors, European backers, and a gang of nickname-wielding disreputables (Sammy the Schvitz, Paulie Knuckles, Jimmy the Spritz). The butter-and-egg business of measuring, assessing, parsing, and dividing that Micah hoped would have Marblestone cackling through eternity.

Once they completed a rough cut of the picture—the brothers' worst, crassest effort, they all cheerfully agreed—Micah journeyed back to Los Angeles to work on poster treatments, discuss print and advertising budgets, and help clean out the Augean stable of Marblestone's studio. It was September 1929, and despite some rumblings—rising unemployment, farm failures across the South and West—the country's dream of itself shone undimmed.

Wandering around the Imperial Pictures lot as burly movers pick apart the remaining pieces of the soundstage, Micah comes across a freestanding staircase, blazoned with glitter and flags, a prop from the recently wrapped backstage musical *The Brooms of Broadway*. Laid on its side like a wounded horse, the stairwell is being wheeled on a flatbed toward a moving truck, its top and bottom steps connecting nothing to nothing, floating freely under California's marmalade sky. It is an image full of portent and mystery. Were he a writer, Micah thinks, he might attempt a poem around it.

"When can we see the trailer?" Micah asks Sherman Penderson, the northwestern furniture magnate and efficiency expert who'd been brought in to reallocate the company's resources. It grieved Micah to think of Marblestone's life work reduced to some papers and balance sheets carried around in a red briefcase by this officious prick, someone with no sense of stories, no feel for faces as food for the soul.

"I assure you, Mr. Grand," Mr. Penderson tells Micah in the neutral tones of a tax auditor, "we've got some top cutters working on it."

"I'm sure you do, but Izzy and I had a verbal agreement with Arthur—we always cut our own trailers."

"Audiences are changing, Mr. Grand." Mr. Penderson's eyes lift from the ledger and rise over the rims of his glasses like a pole vaulter just clearing the bar. "As I said, we've got top men working on the footage."

"Who?"

"Top men."

Tradition dictated that on premiere days in New York, Micah would trek out to Coney Island to walk along the boardwalk, eat a hot dog, play some Skee-Ball, and be reminded once again that his fledgling industrial art was born from cotton-candy amusements. Micah also liked treating himself to a shoeshine, even if these weren't the shoes he'd be wearing with his tuxedo later that evening.

New York was experiencing an Indian summer in mid-October, and walking through Luna Park on this unusually crowded fall day, Micah was reminded of the last time he'd been here, filming *Quicktime* with Babe Ruth on that glorious June day the summer before. Through the weave of happy cries and wave sounds, Micah makes out a familiar jingle:

Just twenty cents a shine,
Come rain or come shine,
Not a quarter, nickel, or dime,
Just twenty cents a shine!

Recognizing the shoeshine boy from the previous summer, Micah notes that the kid has shot up several inches since the filmmaker saw him last. The youth's face is now stripped of baby fat, round-cheeked insouciance beginning to be replaced with the hardening clay of adolescent features. Micah has marked the stirrings of similar transformations in the faces of his boys, a development that fills him with wistfulness and pride.

The boy unties the laces of Micah's shoes, spreads wide the uppers, lifts the tongue up and out, and begins working dark wax polish into the leather with a worn piece of ladies' hose. "Nice shoes."

"Thanks."

"Take good care of your shoes, they'll take good care of you."

"Sound advice."

"Y'see much of Babe these days?" the boy nonchalants, clockwising the polish into the leather.

"No, just that one time," Micah says, delighted that the kid remembers the production company's triumph.

"Wanna hear something?" Working the rag now with real vigor.

"Sure."

"I work here in Coney couple days a week but *downtown* the others," the boy says, conspiratorially swathing the financial district in italics.

"Well, you seem to be an industrious young man."

"And the fellas down there—talking 'mongst themselves—they chattering 'bout how they taking it out, taking all that money out and putting it under a mattress for safekeeping. How Wall Street's the one place in the world where something goes on sale and no one wants to buy it."

"The market's been up all summer, kid," Micah says, searching the boy's face, looking intently into eyes that signal the impression of having already seen too much. "Still, I'm inclined to take your advice. Besides, what goes up must come down, right?" Micah says, pointing to a coaster across the way that cradles in its last carriage a pretty girl who improbably holds a small parasol. "That's not just the nature of things, it's *entertainment*."

"That's how I'm thinking, too, mister." He spits a gob onto the film-maker's shoe and begins attacking it with a horsehair brush as, in the distance, the Cyclone veers up again, roaring like a mechanical dragon in search of its next meal.

"Well," says Micah, tossing the boy a quarter in exchange for saving his wife's family fortune, "thanks for the tip, kid."

FOUR

It promised to be a good night. Till was in town with Emily for the premiere, as was Lili Damita, the new heart-shape-faced French starlet who had taken New York by storm and whom Micah was eager to meet. Johnny Beaujolais promised to cover the event for both *Moving Picture World* and his weekly radio broadcast, and advance word on the picture was good, suggesting that Till might be one of the select group of comic actors whom audiences might still accept in silent films.

It was no accident that they had planned the premiere for the day the spike was finally affixed to the top of the Chrysler Building, making the approximately thousand-foot tower the tallest building in the world. The crowds could see the skyscraper from the Rivoli Theatre across town, its terraced Art Deco crown resembling a religious headdress.

Premieres felt different in Times Square than in Los Angeles. It was the essential contradiction of New York: Since the place was forever grabbing you by the lapels to impress upon you that it was the epicenter of the whole whirligigging world, here you could relax in the certitude that you were never the biggest show in town. Even so, the blinking marquees, klieg lights, and rows of dark, square-backed cars, shiny as stoves, always gave Micah a thrill, even if premieres made just small-kilowatt contributions to busy Broadway boulevards already bustling with offerings from the Rialto and the Criterion and the Paramount and a hundred other theaters.

"Entertainment is a big industry but a small business," Micah assured Stephanie St. Clair the afternoon they signed a formal contract giving her a 20 percent stake in *Pot of Trouble*, and he is reminded of those words as he steps from the limousine. Sleek and shiny as a hood ornament, freshly shaved and peppermint scented, all brightness and gloss, Micah dives into a pool awash in exposed female limbs and watery illuminated streaks, blinking across waves of familiar faces that cling to red-carpet stanchions like buoys.

Camera bulbs pop, and here comes everybody. There are the gag writers Shecky Sugarman, Wendell Wilkins, and Amsterdam McSweeney. There is Benny Castor and Trudy, whom Micah is scheduled to entertain with Margaret while the couple is in town. There is Izzy's friend Howard Mansfield, looking bald and dapper and, for the first time Micah can recall, near to happiness. Wisping along strobiscopically, he is certain of it, he sees Rose, three or four persons deep in the crowd, wearing a bonnet and a plain brown dress, her beautiful frowning face viewed in a flash as welcome to him as water to a man lost in a desert. It is not until he feels a prick of dampness, and looks down at the spot asterisking on his white tuxedo shirt, that he realizes she's shot him with a water pistol. He looks up again, hoping to spot her, fingers clutching the incriminating novelty item's trigger, but she is nowhere. Absorbed by the crowd.

"And we're here with the picture's director, Mr. Micah Grand," says Johnny Beaujolais, corralling the filmmaker and pressing an ice-cream-cone-shaped microphone into his face. In his hand Beaujolais holds an index card listing several capitalized items ("AFRICA," "HENRY TILL," "SILENT PICTURE") committed in a child's penmanship that Micah finds oddly poignant. In the photograph that accompanies Beaujolais's syndicated newspaper column, the reporter is always shot in rakish profile, and speaking with the man up close, Micah understands why. Of the facial disfigurement earned as a war correspondent at the Battle of the Marne, the radio announcer displays no signs of embarrassment, leading the interview with an aggressive chin and enjoyably rat-a-tat-tat delivery.

"Mr. Grand, lions, tigers, Pygmies—*Pot of Trouble* promises to be Henry Till's greatest adventure yet, does it not?"

"Indeed."

"And for the listeners at home, how might this picture be different from previous Henry Till comedies?"

"Well, the laughs are bigger, the stunts are more dangerous, and Till is dressed in a safari suit."

"I think it's fair to say he really lands in the thick of it in this one?"

"It is."

"Mr. Grand, are the rumors true that some of the picture was actually shot *on location* in Deepest Darkest?" Beaujolais asks, vocally goosing his listeners.

"We did do some filming in Africa, that's correct, but it was for a different project."

"And what, might I ask, made you travel to the other end of the world just to snap some pictures?"

Micah looks around, taking it all in, the night a jigsaw puzzle of his making, everything slotting into place. "I enjoy the work."

"I understand that this latest comedic effort is a silent picture. With talkies the cat's pajamas, does Henry Till have any plans to make synchronized-sound pictures?"

Micah is surprised by the directness of the man's question. He hesitates, drawn to the demolished portion of the radio announcer's jaw. Illuminated in the photographers' gun-popping salute, the stratum of scar tissue reveals hidden depths and colors, strains of yellow and blue like veins in an exotic vegetable or a fine smelly cheese. "When you're being chased by a lion," he submits, "there's not much room for dialogue."

"And that's Micah Grand, director of the new Henry Till picture *Pot of Trouble*. This is Johnny Beaujolais, reporting live from the red carpet at tonight's premiere in New York City for *Moving Picture World News*."

An arm crooks into Micah's as the interview ends, swiftly navigating him past the theater entrance and into the lobby. Sidney Bloat is a man for whom movie premieres might have been invented. Everything about him is polished, everything about him glows: brilliantined hair, mustache, tuxedo, shoes with a reflection you could read by, teeth uniform and white as a Christmas nutcracker's.

"Ah, the great *sadness* of the cinema! Much like a wedding, or a funeral, these premiere occurrences," Bloat says. He acknowledges a nearby light box that frames a *Pot of Trouble* one-sheet, an illustration of Till in his safari duds surrounded by spear-waving Zulus. "I suspect what happens with every technology will in time be proven true of your motion pictures: What arrive as signs and wonders come to pave paths of boredom. I have to say, though, Mr. Grand, I'm impressed that you were able to salvage the picture. Much like a pastry chef frosting over his mistakes."

"More like why use a brush when you have a club?"

"And how is Izzy reacclimating?"

"He's back to making pictures."

"Then all's well that ends well." Bloat removes from his vest a white-haired Moses *Pfefferminz* dispenser and pops a rectilinear mint into his mouth as the lobby house lights dim and rise, alerting the audience to take their seats. "You know, I wouldn't dare say this to your brother," Bloat whispers, tongue encircling the sweet, "but as far as Malwiki is concerned, the misery continues there unabated. I'm afraid symbolic gestures on the part of entertainment people are little cure for that continent's woes. But then, you're the brothers Grand, not the Brothers Grimm." He spreads his arms wide, like a reverend embracing the congregation. "Without a killing there can be no feast. Good luck with the picture!"

FIVE

Izzy didn't stay for the movie. Though he promised Howard he'd meet up with him afterward, Izzy could never bear watching one of their pictures with an audience, let alone while outfitted in formal wear and feeling like a creature escaped from Barnum's museum of wonders. Instead he had agreed to meet one of his former crewmates for coffee at a spot nearby.

Baxter's Diner, on the corner of Forty-Third and Seventh, looks to be an average and inviting enough setting, but it isn't until he enters and sees Early emerge from the kitchen, drying his hands on a grease-stained apron, that Izzy understands why his former colleague asked that they meet there. Settling into a corner booth, Izzy experiences the pang of pleasure that comes from visiting a place that is also an archetype of itself: on the table, a glass of fountain drink straws like miniature striped barber poles and a pair of laminated red menus; beyond it a great, smooth, lime-green apothecary counter; in the air pleasing smells of fried onions, cooked chicken fat, chocolate syrup, cola, and ammonia.

"You're late," Early says after they've ordered.

"These things never start on time." Izzy hasn't seen Rose's brother since the first trip to Africa, and Early looks thinner than before, more drawn, his complexion more matte and muted. The muscles in his sleeveless T-shirt are better defined yet also show the atrophy and indifference of having settled into repetitive, dull work, of belonging to a body that's prematurely resigned itself to failure.

"Well, I've only got about ten minutes left to my break," Early says, making fork tracks in his rice pudding, a maraschino cherry bleeding syrup into a pompadour of whipped cream.

Izzy takes up the sugar dispenser, tilts it over his cup, and begins counting backward from ten . . .

"Want some coffee with that?"

"You should've come tonight," Izzy says. "You were an important part of that picture."

"Nah, have to work. Gotta get paid. Besides, that wasn't the movie we made. I'll be sure to catch it, though."

"Skip it."

From the kitchen appears a crumpled, heavyset man with a ropy black handlebar mustache, Greek or Russian or Romanian. He parts forearm forestry, consults his wristwatch, and announces "Ten minutes" in Early's general direction.

"Got it, boss," Early responds, loud enough to pull the man's attention toward the table. And it occurs to Izzy as his gaze meets the restaurant owner's that Early is showing off the cameraman, that he looks upon his association with the tuxedo-clad filmmaker as a source of pride.

"You know, there's always a spot for you on our crew, whenever we decide to shoot our next picture," Izzy suggests, uncertain as he says it if he means it. "We could even look into sponsoring you for one of the unions. It's not unheard of."

"Thanks, Mr. Grand. I appreciate it, but I think I'm done with pictures. Same with numbers, really. I'm thinking I might try going back to school, learn a trade. Plumbing. Electrics." And here he presses the fire-hydrant-shaped salt and pepper shakers together and slides them across the table, lining them neatly against the sugar dispenser and the ketchup bottle. Black, white, and red. It is night now, and through the window colors come and go at intervals, like beams from a lighthouse. "In the meantime there's dignity in all kinds of work."

"You're right about that, but you're good at something," Izzy says, his voice rising. "It's not every day a person's good at something. It's unusual."

Early works at picking from the lip of his coffee cup a dried potato peel or a fleck of oatmeal. "You hear Bumpy got eighteen months?"

"Yeah, but Micah's squared everything away with Madam Queen. We don't have to worry about him anymore."

"Oh, I never sweated it much with Bumpy anyway. All he asked for before he got sent up were some history books and guides on how to play chess."

"Chess, huh. How's Rose?"

"You didn't see her tonight? Told me she won a pair of tickets from one of the movie magazines, said she was planning on making it."

"No, I haven't seen her in months."

"Not many women friends?"

"Suppose not."

"You're a nice-looking man, Mr. Grand. Why don't you leave that monkey business behind, find yourself a wife?"

"Maybe not for me."

"Yeah, I hear you. A wife, kids, babies, all the trouble they bring . . ." Early sounds suddenly older, wearier, than his twenty years, looking into his steaming cup of coffee as if hoping to find there the answer to some impregnable question about how to manage a life. "You know, Rose really wanted something that was part of Micah."

"You mean the baby?"

"Yeah."

"The one she lost?"

"Rose lost a baby in Los Angeles, but only one."

The symmetry dawning on Izzy. "Twins?"

"They should take that quack doctor of Mr. Till's out back and shoot him, but, yeah, she managed to hold on to one of them."

"Micah doesn't know that."

"She didn't want to trouble him with all that after they split. It's for her, you understand? It's something for her. I wish Rose could have seen him working out there, though. He's a better man than he pretends to be."

"Yeah, okay, but the baby belongs to her husband, right? That's what Micah always believed."

"Dobie, that old fool?" Early pshaws. "He's fifty-three! Got his dick halfway blown off in the war. Dobie's not making any babies with Rose. No, Mr. Grand, it's Micah's. Rose is sure of it. The baby is Micah's."

Returning to the theater, Izzy finds Micah sitting alone on the lobby stairs, his face cupped in one hand, looking hollowed out, all husk. Micah sits with his lips pursed, as if readying to kiss someone. Though no notes come out, he attempts to whistle, this being an activity that in Izzy's experience usually indicates a kind of absentminded loneliness, a desire to fill empty spaces with human sound. Crossing the lobby and reaching the staircase, Izzy steps over Micah and sits one rung higher, establishing a couple of inches of superiority over his brother.

"Why are these stairs so cold?" asks Izzy on shifting buttocks.

"Marble," Micah answers, "stone."

"Of course. Our frozen asses a fitting tribute. How's it look inside?"

"I've seen worse. How about you?"

"Couldn't face it. I slipped out soon as the picture got going. Just came from seeing Early."

"Early?" Perking up at the name. "What kind of trouble has he been getting into these days?"

"Working at a diner." Izzy passes Micah a book of matches from Baxter's. "I think he's finished with movies."

Micah peels from the stair in front of him a discarded event program and begins shredding its glossy pages into long strips. "Think you'll ever go back?"

"Where to, Africa? No. You?"

"Can't see why I would."

"Here," Izzy says, leaning over and fixing it, "your tie is crooked."

"Thanks. Hey, I spotted Howard earlier. He's looking well. How's your friendship going?"

"What can I say, Micah, the man makes a mean Tom Collins. How about you? How've your friendships been these days?"

"I don't keep any friends, Izzy, you know that." Waving the program's paper legs between them like a hula skirt. "I've got collaborators, business associates, admirers, detractors, rivals, dependents, conquests, but I've always traveled light in the friends department."

"You'd like to believe that, but I don't think it's true. And I suspect she feels the same." Izzy nods across the lobby expanse to Rose, who has just emerged from the theater on her way to the ladies' room. Six or seven months pregnant, Rose looks like herself, only more so. The plain patterned brown maternity dress she's wearing looks more like a blanket, some shelter safe and warm where you want to take up residence and never leave.

"I have to pee, boys," she says, thawing an awkward moment. "But if you'll be around, Micah, it'd be nice to talk to you. Izzy, would you mind making yourself scarce for a minute?"

"Yes, ma'am."

"Thanks." Rose's face a mural of confusion, happiness, and sheer biological relief as she pushes through the restroom doors.

"Izzy?"

"Yes, sir."

"Admitting that there exist large gaps when it comes to my understanding of women, would it be fair to say Rose looks to be in a family way?"

"Yes, that's correct."

"Mm-hm, mm-hm. And how might this development be possible?"

"She lost a baby in California, but just one."

"Twins?"

"Yeah."

"Figures," Micah says, tearing the program completely through and allowing the strips to fall across the stairs like ticker tape. "Do me a favor, Itz, go outside and play in traffic for a while, will you?"

"With pleasure."

Izzy has always made a living with his eyes. For as long as they've made movies together, his brother's nickname for him has been "Eyes." And for a long time, Izzy's own eyes—Mediterranean blue, raccoon-rimmed, with a pleasing proportion of white to iris—were the sole physical feature of his person he deemed attractive. Izzy prided himself on being especially attuned to the eyes of actors, on being able to discern in them flickers of feeling that others couldn't intuit until material proof was amplified and projected before them. All of which is a way of saying that Izzy has never before seen his brother look at another person the way he looked at Rose then, and he knew she was his life.

After the brothers learned of her death—in a grocery-store robbery uptown, two years after they had last seen her—Izzy watched Micah try to transform his sense of shame and heartbreak into something else: some dignified and tragic project, an insupportable position that only left him feeling smaller, more diminished.

Long before they'd stopped making movies, decades before they'd grown old, both brothers knew that their legacy would never take the form of a catalog of films, a record of talent. They recognized that the true, impossible inheritance was one's secret history: a tangle of relationships, a latticework of touches, missed signals, parting glances. More honest and mysterious than the official docket of biographical data and accomplishment, these were the things, simple things, that made a life. Exchanges, looks, a child's candy-apple smile, a trinket won at a fair, your lover's hair shining in the sunlight.

In later years, when Micah would gather around him a gallery of ghosts and reminiscences and regrets, it was with the knowledge that Rose would forever occupy for him a place first, last, always, and alone. That she was the best person he had known: the toughest, the most honest, the best and most loved. That the girl with the water pistol had held truest aim. And he had let her go. Though the remaining decades were rich and full with good, exciting work in movies and the early days of television—satisfying years filled with travel and material possessions and, later, delight in knowing his sons as adults and the joys of

being a grandfather—this chorus of self-recrimination was the uninterrupted song of Micah's private thoughts.

Those were different times, Izzy would tell Micah over coffee and
cake in the various bachelor apartments he kept through the years in
New York and Los Angeles. Those were different times, Izzy would say,
and Micah would repeat those meaningless, forgiving words to himself
when she would visit him during the night. It was better to forget. He
had held briefly the bright balloon of happiness and should be grateful.
One had to forget.

Forward and back across the decades from that night, she smiles at
him with her pomegranate mouth, slowly lowering herself onto a shared
step like a crane moving a container off a ship. Looking at her, even
entrancingly happy to see her, he knows she is already a ghost.

"Truce?" she says, pressing the plastic water pistol into his hand.

"Okay, we'll hold fire," Micah says, brandishing the toy like a baby
rattle. "You look like a lightbulb."

"Gee, thanks, Micah. You always knew what to say to a girl." Uncon-
sciously twirling her pointer finger around thick coils of hair that had
exploded Rapunzel-like during her pregnancy. "Thanks for pointing out
that I'm waddling around like a duck."

"I don't mean your shape. Your color, your skin: You look all lit up."

"Well, I try to make an effort for special occasions."

"Doesn't go unnoticed, miss. . . . How've you been, Rose? How's
your time been?"

"I've been okay. Still able to work. Haven't been too uncomfortable
so far. Eating a lot of peanut-butter-and-jelly sandwiches and hard-
boiled eggs."

"Christ, can I give you something?" His unarmed hand rummaging
around in his jacket pocket. "Some money?"

"You can take that up with my husband."

"Fair enough." Stilling himself. "And how's Jacob doing these
days?"

"He's a barber. The baby will just mean more bibs for him."

A high pop of laughter reaches them from inside the theater, a quick, sharp sound like a baseball player hitting a foul. Then echoey silence. After a while Micah breaks it.

"How'd we do, you and I?"

"Depends who's asking, who's doing the telling."

Micah fiddles with the toy gun and finds himself pointing it at his chest halfheartedly, wishing it were real. "It's like cards," he says finally. "The loss has to hurt if it's to mean anything. I didn't know that before."

Rose sighs, relieves him of the water pistol, and places it in her handbag. "We did all right. I think we did as well as anyone might have done given the circumstances. But you know, Micah, you promised me something once."

"I know." Holding her hands now.

"That if you went, you'd bring back something good."

"You're right."

"And the picture's terrible, Micah."

"I know."

"I mean really, really terrible."

"Thanks, Rose, I get it. I know. I'm sorry I couldn't keep my promise to you."

"Well," she says, withdrawing her hands and placing them across her stomach, "I think your best work might still be ahead of you. Come on, Em, let's go in. I want to show you something."

She rises with some difficulty. Micah follows, supporting her in sequence by the wrist, upper arm, back. Standing firm now, she leads him by the hand, waltzing along a sea of red carpet until the theater doors silently swing open and their silhouettes find themselves joined in the back of the auditorium by Izzy, who greets the couple with a shrug.

The three of them stand and watch the projector booth's beam cleave the dark, light baptizing the audience, whirring machinery music the sound of memory itself. Before them the screen stretches wide as a ship's sail, as open to possibility as a parchment across which any history might be written. They would never grow tired of this procession of enchantment: a lightstorm of imagery flooding from behind that unearths the hidden and unimagined as from an archaeological dig. The Grand brothers stand in the back of the theater and watch their work, able to appreciate that their efforts—their good and brave efforts, their historic efforts in a youthful and brazen art form—were neither good enough nor brave enough. They watch, knowing that for now it would have to do for the audience and the nation that birthed it to be briefly, magically united in the pitch of its wild collective dream. Lit from without and within, the Grand brothers watch their work and try to forgive themselves at last for being in concord with their era and conversant with time, that most rarefied and ineffable thing. Time.

THE END

Acknowledgments

Significant portions of this novel were written at Ledig House International Writers Residency and Yaddo, special places to which I offer the deepest thanks.

I owe a great debt to my agent, Bonnie Nadell, for her tenacity and tough love and for being the M.F.A. program I never had. Likewise, enormous thanks are due to my editor at Hogarth, Alexis Washam, for her superb instincts and brilliant editorial guidance.

Special gratitude to the early readers of this book, each of whom provided invaluable support and criticism: Andrea Berloff, Drew Filus, Ray Forsythe, Michael Gurton, Nova Halliwell, Philip Kang, Nic Kelman, Paul LaFarge, Jason Lee, Richard Nash, Benjamin Strong, and Luke Wilcox.

The real Arthur Marblestone for generously allowing me to use his wonderful and fiction-worthy name.

Robert Sawyer for deepest friendship, insight, and "there are exits, but there are no escapes."

All of my love to Marcia, Robert, and Jennifer Conn.

To Kay Suzanne Conn, the light that illuminated the writing of this book.

And to Alyth Darby Conn, who lights the way forward.